ANGORA NAPKIN™

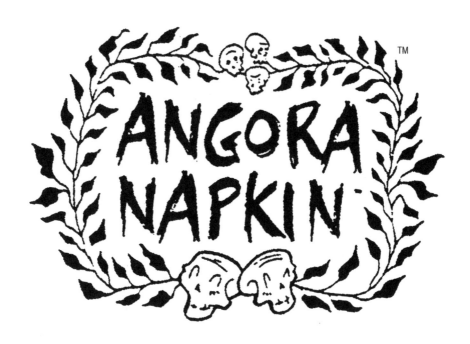

For Brenda,
Thank you for everything!

IDW founded by Ted Adams, Alex Garner, Kris Oprisko, and Robbie Robbins |

ISBN: 978-1-61377-528-8

15 14 13 12   1 2 3 4

Ted Adams, CEO & Publisher
Greg Goldstein, President & COO
Robbie Robbins, EVP/Sr. Graphic Artist
Chris Ryall, Chief Creative Officer/Editor-in-Chief
Matthew Ruzicka, CPA, Chief Financial Officer
Alan Payne, VP of Sales
Dirk Wood, VP of Marketing
Lorelei Bunjes, VP of Digital Services

Become our fan on Facebook **facebook.com/idwpublishing**
Follow us on Twitter **@idwpublishing**
Check us out on YouTube **youtube.com/idwpublishing**
www.IDWPUBLISHING.com

HARVEST OF REVENGE

by

TROY LITTLE

Angora Napkin created by

TROY LITTLE & NICK CROSS

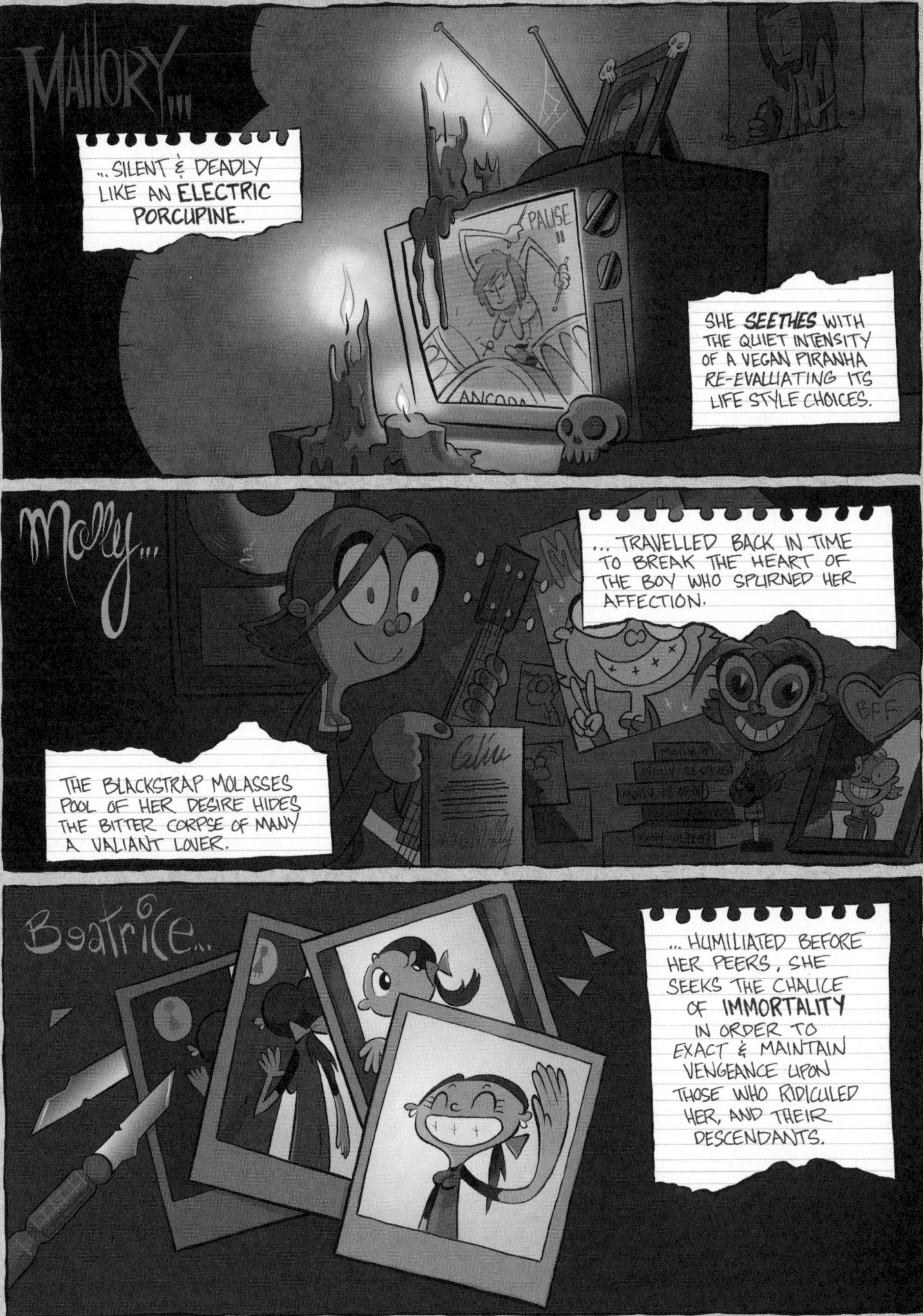
MALLORY...
...SILENT & DEADLY LIKE AN ELECTRIC PORCUPINE.
PAUSE
SHE SEETHES WITH THE QUIET INTENSITY OF A VEGAN PIRANHA RE-EVALUATING ITS LIFE STYLE CHOICES.
Molly...
...TRAVELLED BACK IN TIME TO BREAK THE HEART OF THE BOY WHO SPURNED HER AFFECTION.
BFF
THE BLACKSTRAP MOLASSES POOL OF HER DESIRE HIDES THE BITTER CORPSE OF MANY A VALIANT LOVER.
Beatrice...
...HUMILIATED BEFORE HER PEERS, SHE SEEKS THE CHALICE OF IMMORTALITY IN ORDER TO EXACT & MAINTAIN VENGEANCE UPON THOSE WHO RIDICULED HER, AND THEIR DESCENDANTS.

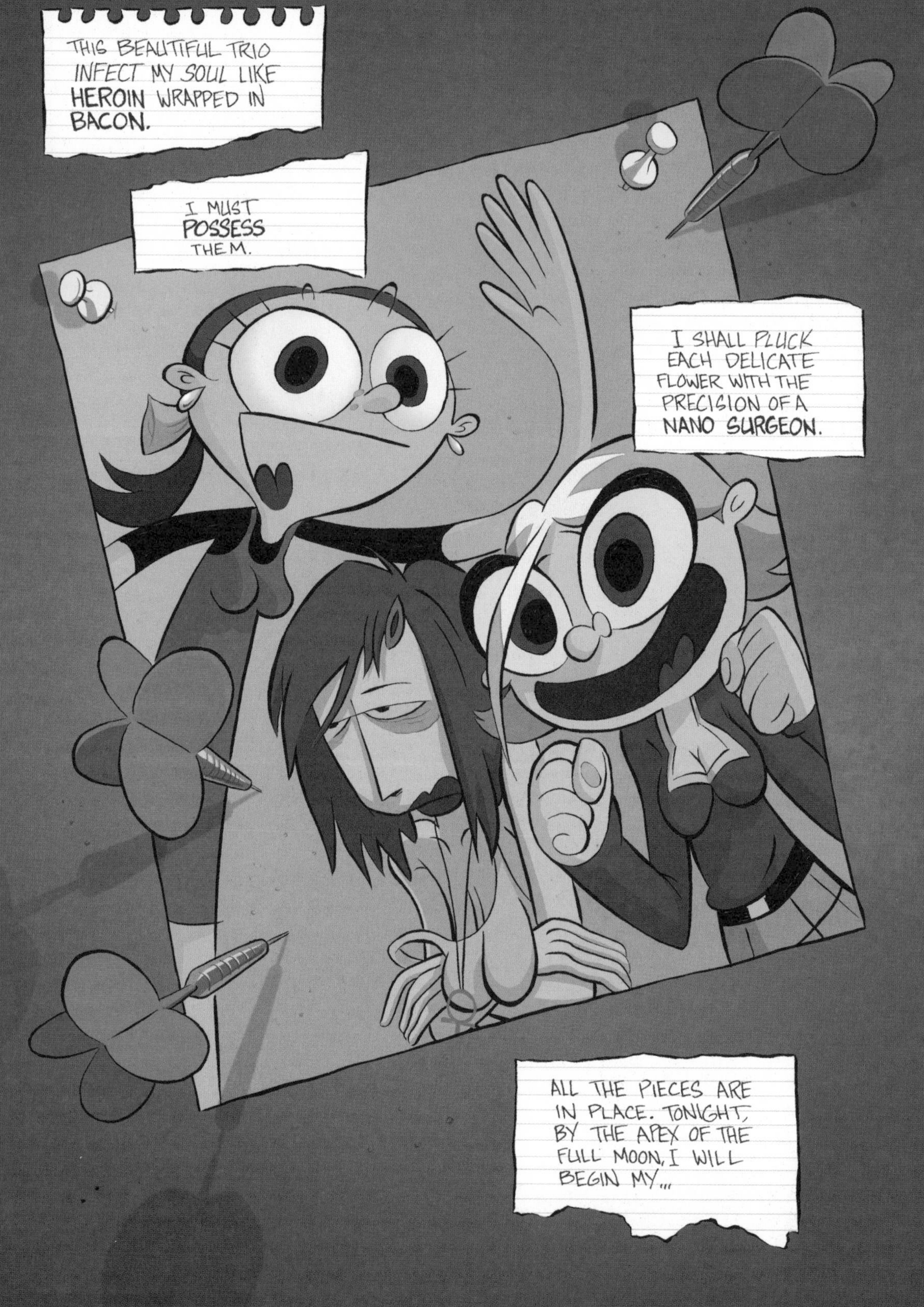

THIS BEAUTIFUL TRIO INFECT MY SOUL LIKE HEROIN WRAPPED IN BACON.
I MUST POSSESS THEM.
I SHALL PLUCK EACH DELICATE FLOWER WITH THE PRECISION OF A NANO SURGEON.
ALL THE PIECES ARE IN PLACE. TONIGHT, BY THE APEX OF THE FULL MOON, I WILL BEGIN MY...

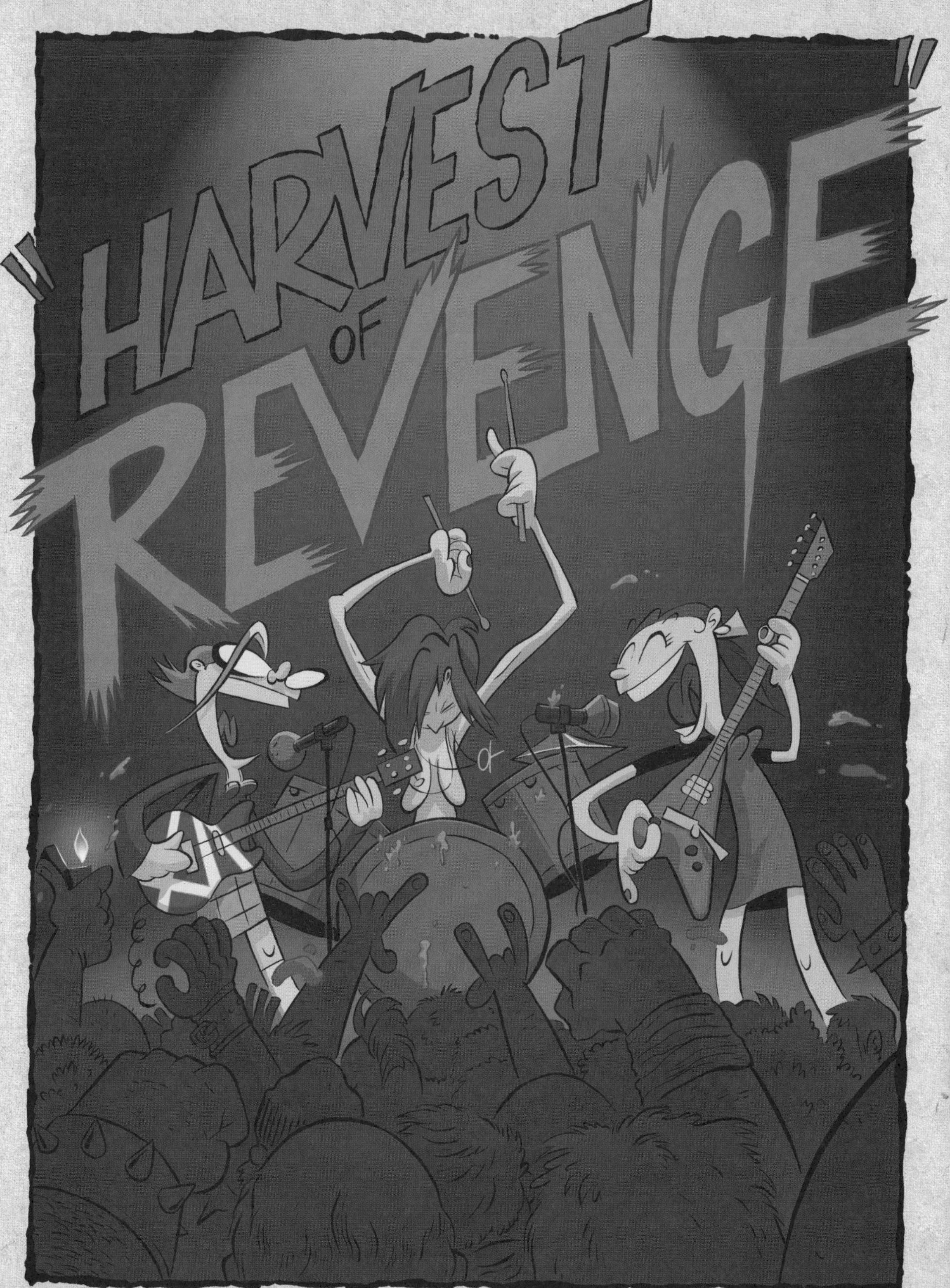
"HARVEST OF REVENGE"

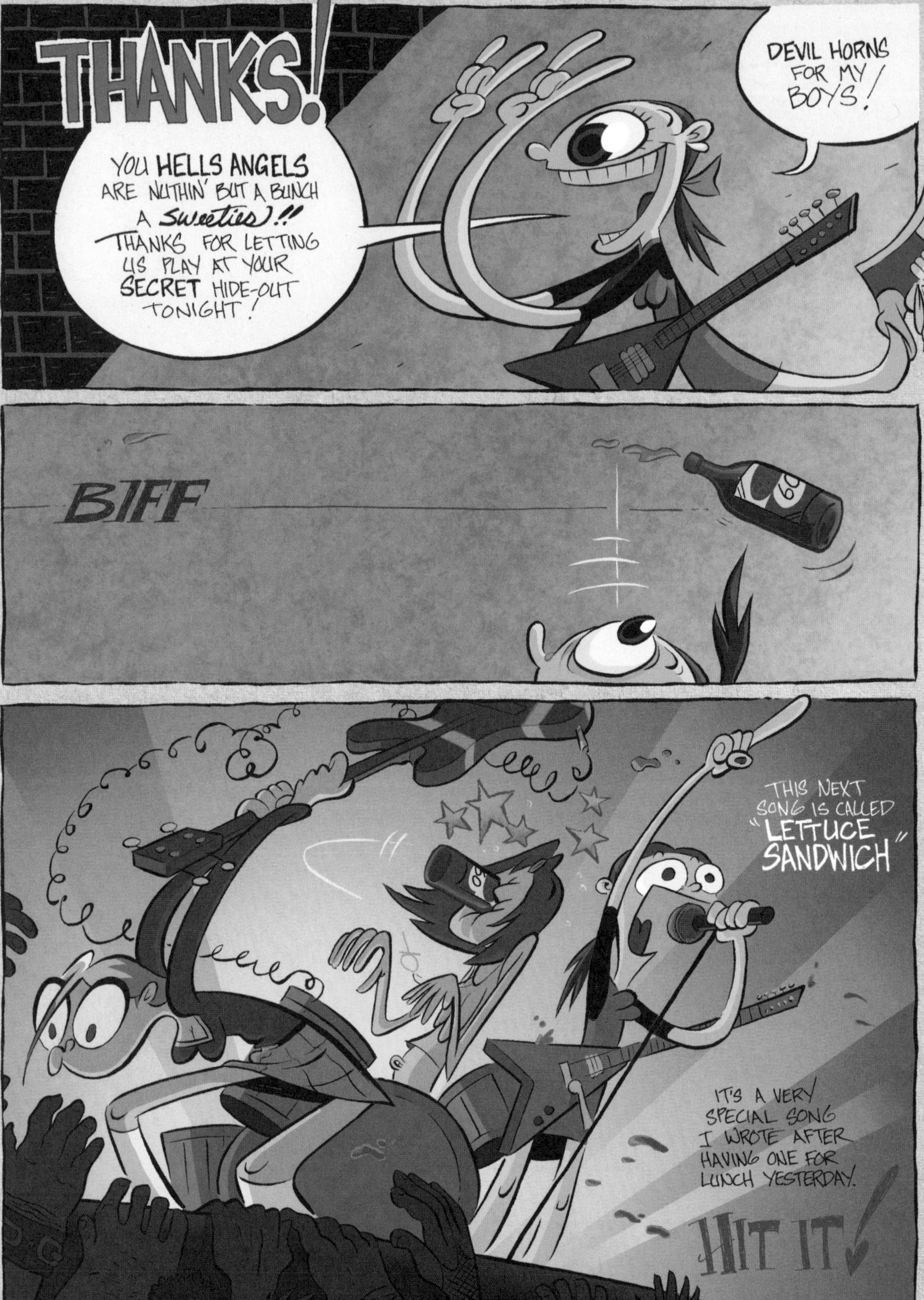
THANKS!
YOU HELLS ANGELS ARE NUTHIN' BUT A BUNCH A Sweeties!!! THANKS FOR LETTING US PLAY AT YOUR SECRET HIDE-OUT TONIGHT!
DEVIL HORNS FOR MY BOYS!
BIFF
THIS NEXT SONG IS CALLED "LETTUCE SANDWICH"
IT'S A VERY SPECIAL SONG I WROTE AFTER HAVING ONE FOR LUNCH YESTERDAY.
HIT IT!

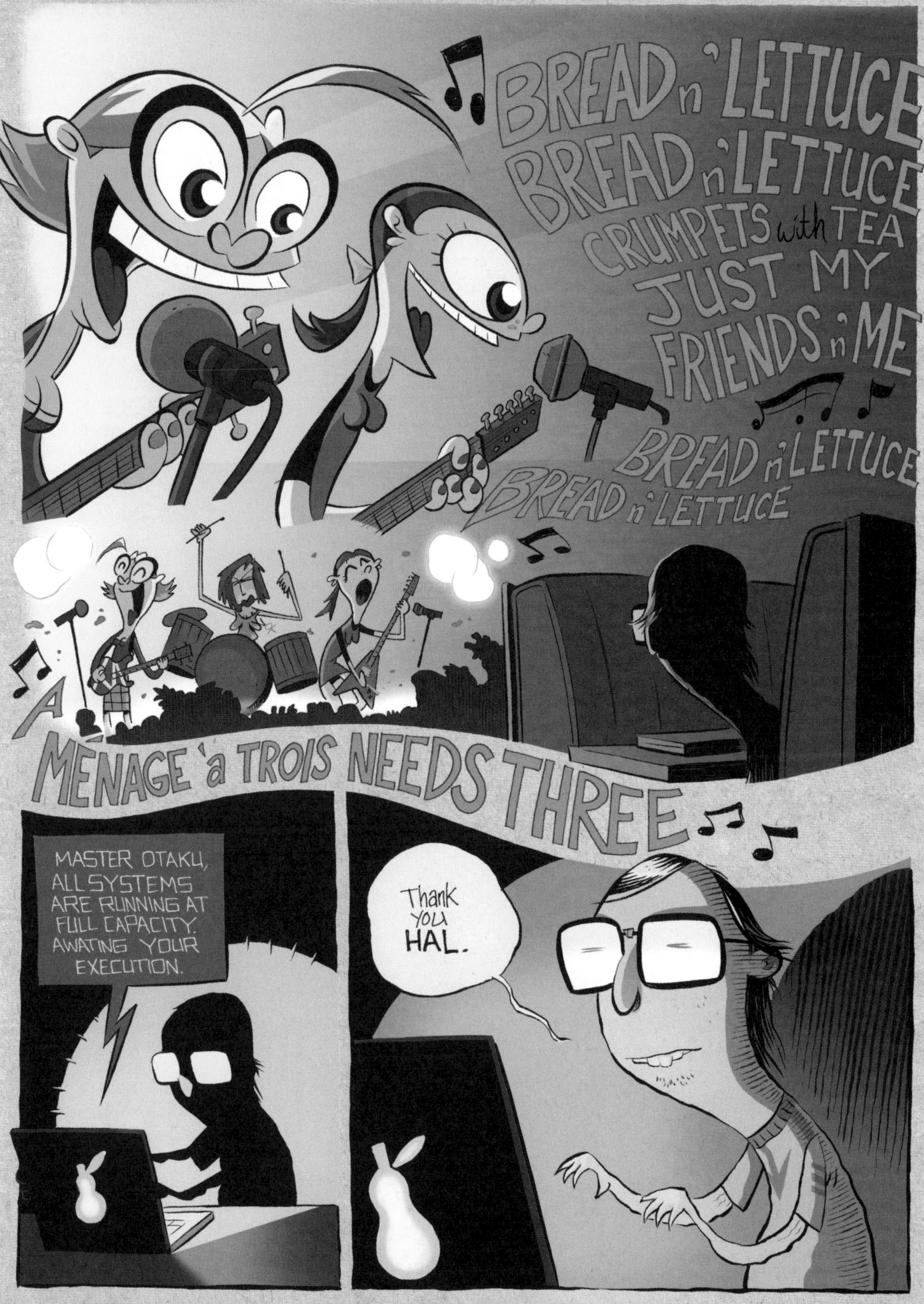

BREAD n' LETTUCE
BREAD n' LETTUCE
CRUMPETS with TEA
JUST MY
FRIENDS n' ME
BREAD n' LETTUCE
BREAD n' LETTUCE
A MÉNAGE 'a TROIS NEEDS THREE
MASTER OTAKU, ALL SYSTEMS ARE RUNNING AT FULL CAPACITY. AWATING YOUR EXECUTION.
Thank you HAL.

LOOK AT THEM... PRANCING AROUND LIKE A **DELICATE** PACK OF GAZELLES, UNAWARE OF THE **JACKAL** IN THEIR MIDST.

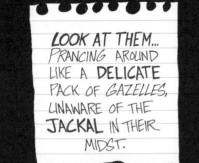

MOLLY, SLAPPING THE BASS LIKE A **PLAYFUL** LES CLAYPOOL WHILE INVOKING THE *RUTHLESS* ENERGY OF SID VICIOUS.

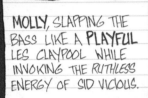

BUDDA BUDDA BUD BUD

I WOULD CRY OUT; "**LET ME BE YOUR NANCY!**" IN ORDER TO WIN HER HEART, BUT THANKFULLY I CONTROL THIS **URGE**.

BEATRICE RIFFS AS YNGWIE MALMSTEEN WOULD IF HE PLAYED IN THE **RAMONES**. IT'S MADNESS **INCARNATE**.

DETH HEAD

HER **SULTRY**, SIREN-LIKE VOICE HAS BEEN SAID TO CAUSE A **CHEMICAL REACTION** THAT CURES SCURVY IN LAB RATS.

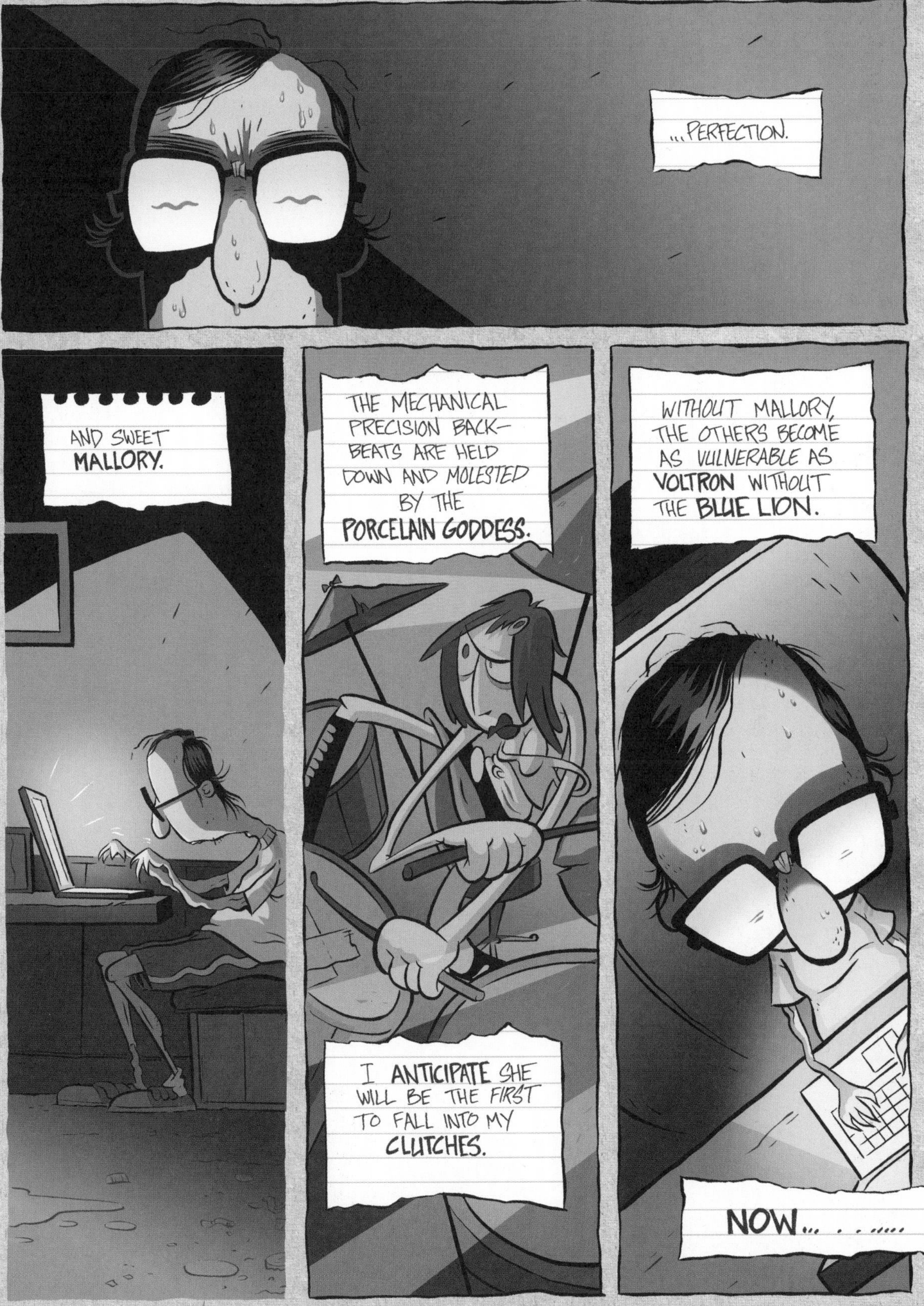

...PERFECTION.
AND SWEET MALLORY.
THE MECHANICAL PRECISION BACK-BEATS ARE HELD DOWN AND MOLESTED BY THE PORCELAIN GODDESS.
I ANTICIPATE SHE WILL BE THE FIRST TO FALL INTO MY CLUTCHES.
WITHOUT MALLORY, THE OTHERS BECOME AS VULNERABLE AS VOLTRON WITHOUT THE BLUE LION.
NOW... . . ..

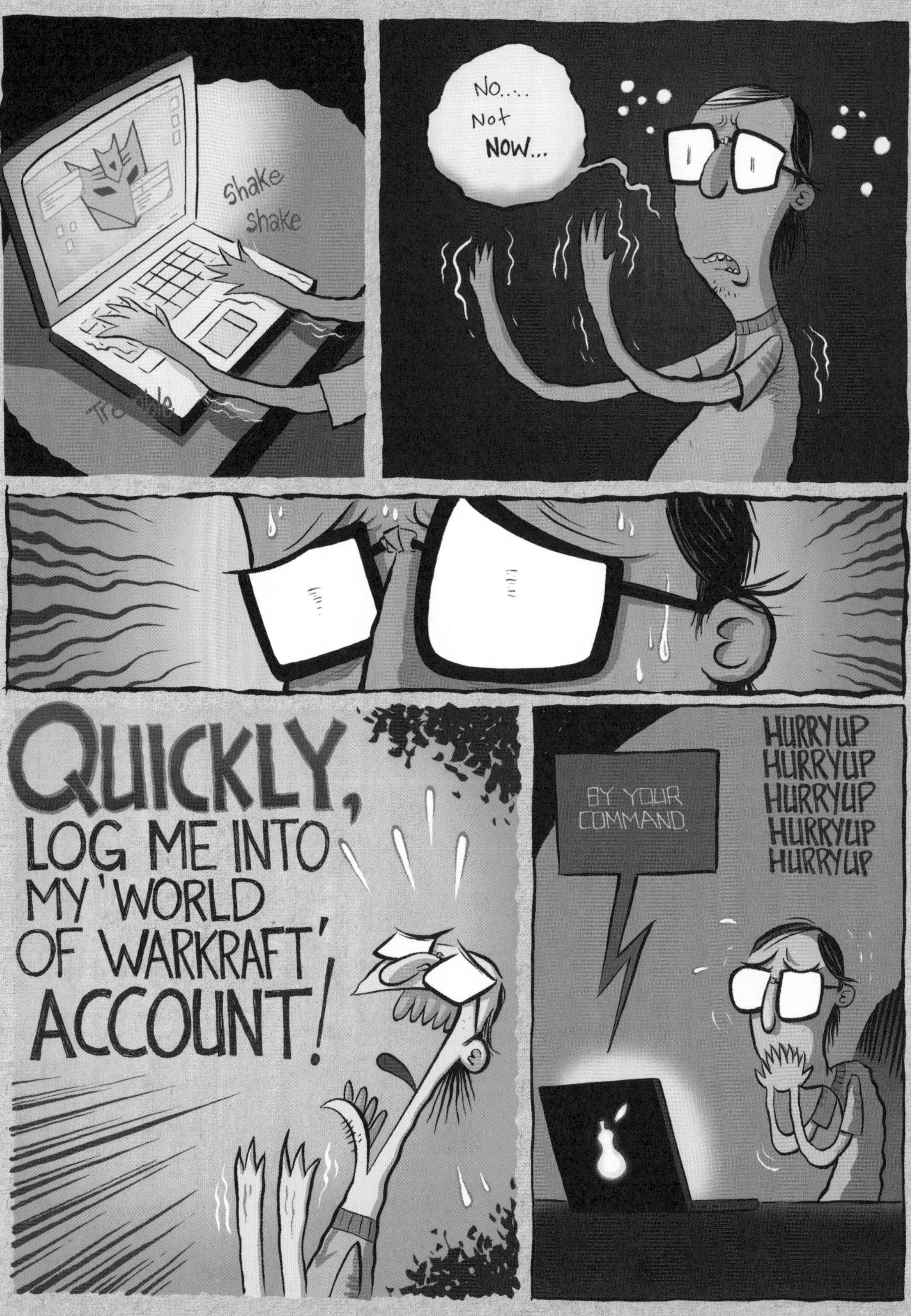
shake
shake
Tremble
No....
Not
NOW...
QUICKLY,
LOG ME INTO
MY 'WORLD
OF WARKRAFT'
ACCOUNT!
BY YOUR
COMMAND.
HURRYUP
HURRYUP
HURRYUP
HURRYUP
HURRYUP

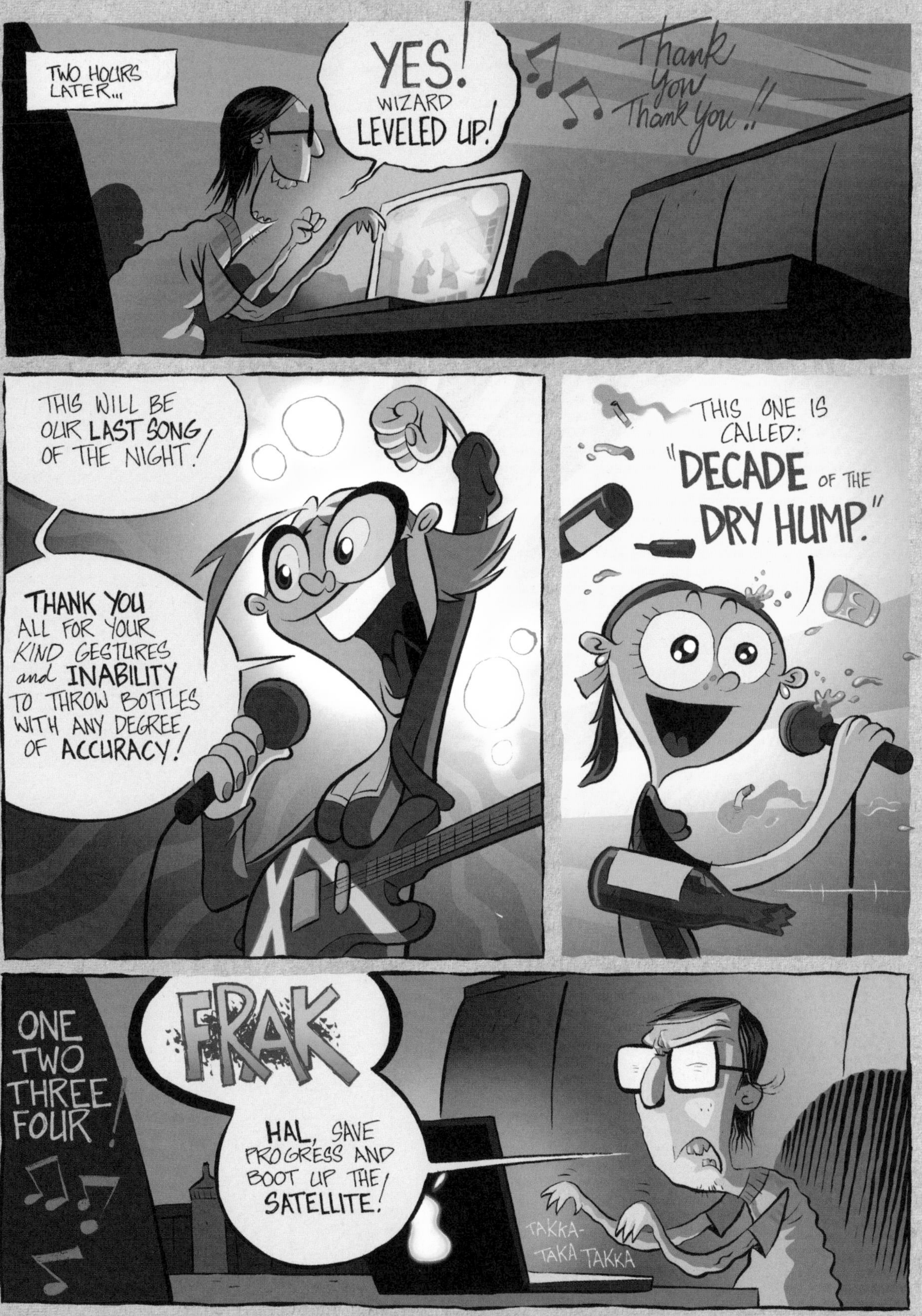
TWO HOURS LATER...
YES! WIZARD LEVELED UP!
Thank you Thank you!!
THIS WILL BE OUR LAST SONG OF THE NIGHT!
THANK YOU ALL FOR YOUR KIND GESTURES and INABILITY TO THROW BOTTLES WITH ANY DEGREE OF ACCURACY!
THIS ONE IS CALLED: "DECADE OF THE DRY HUMP."
ONE TWO THREE FOUR!
FRAK
HAL, SAVE PROGRESS AND BOOT UP THE SATELLITE!
TAKKA-TAKA TAKKA

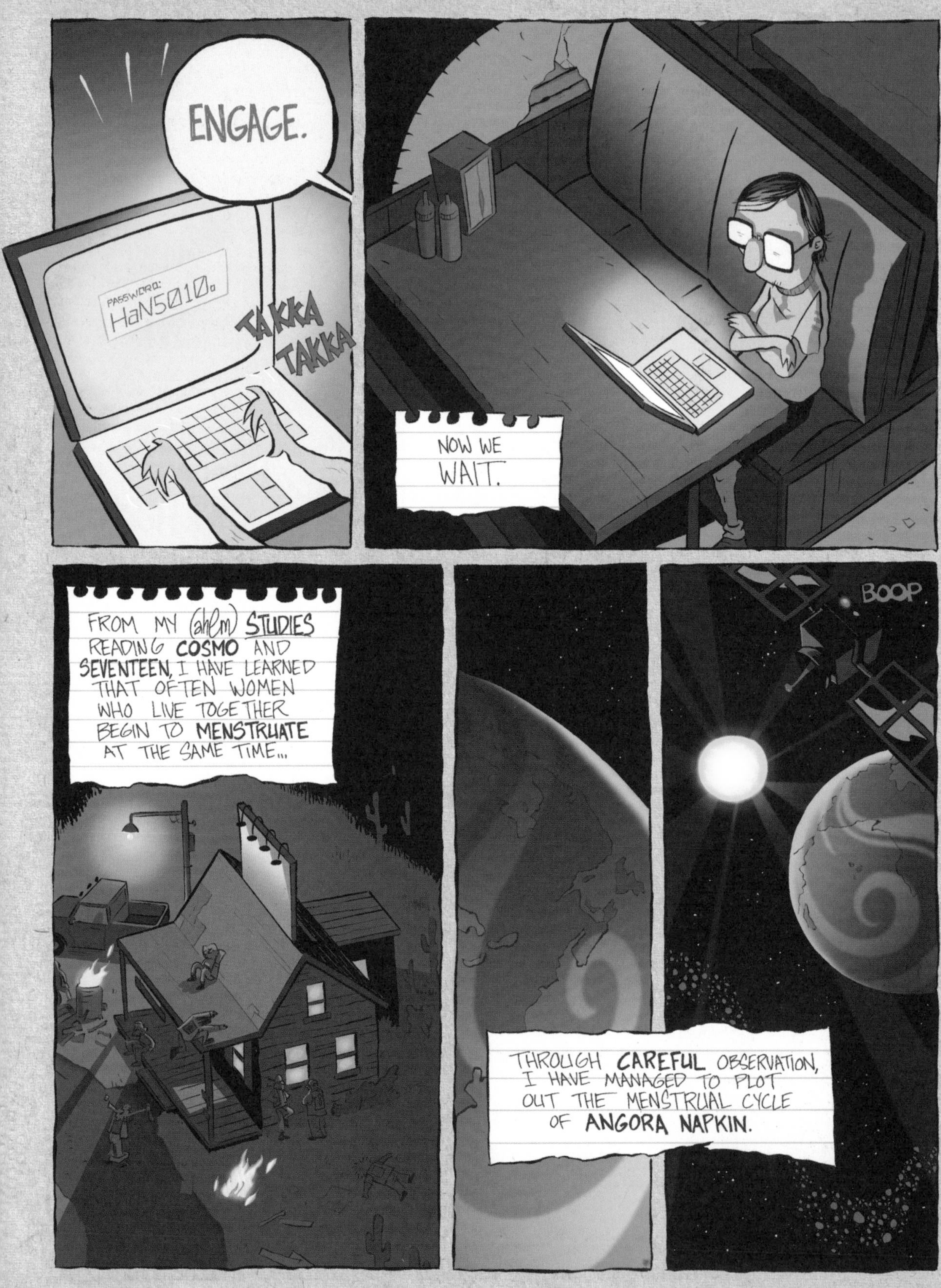
ENGAGE.
PASSWORD: HaN5010.
TAKKA TAKKA
NOW WE WAIT.
FROM MY (ahem) STUDIES READING COSMO AND SEVENTEEN, I HAVE LEARNED THAT OFTEN WOMEN WHO LIVE TOGETHER BEGIN TO MENSTRUATE AT THE SAME TIME...
BOOP
THROUGH CAREFUL OBSERVATION, I HAVE MANAGED TO PLOT OUT THE MENSTRUAL CYCLE OF ANGORA NAPKIN.

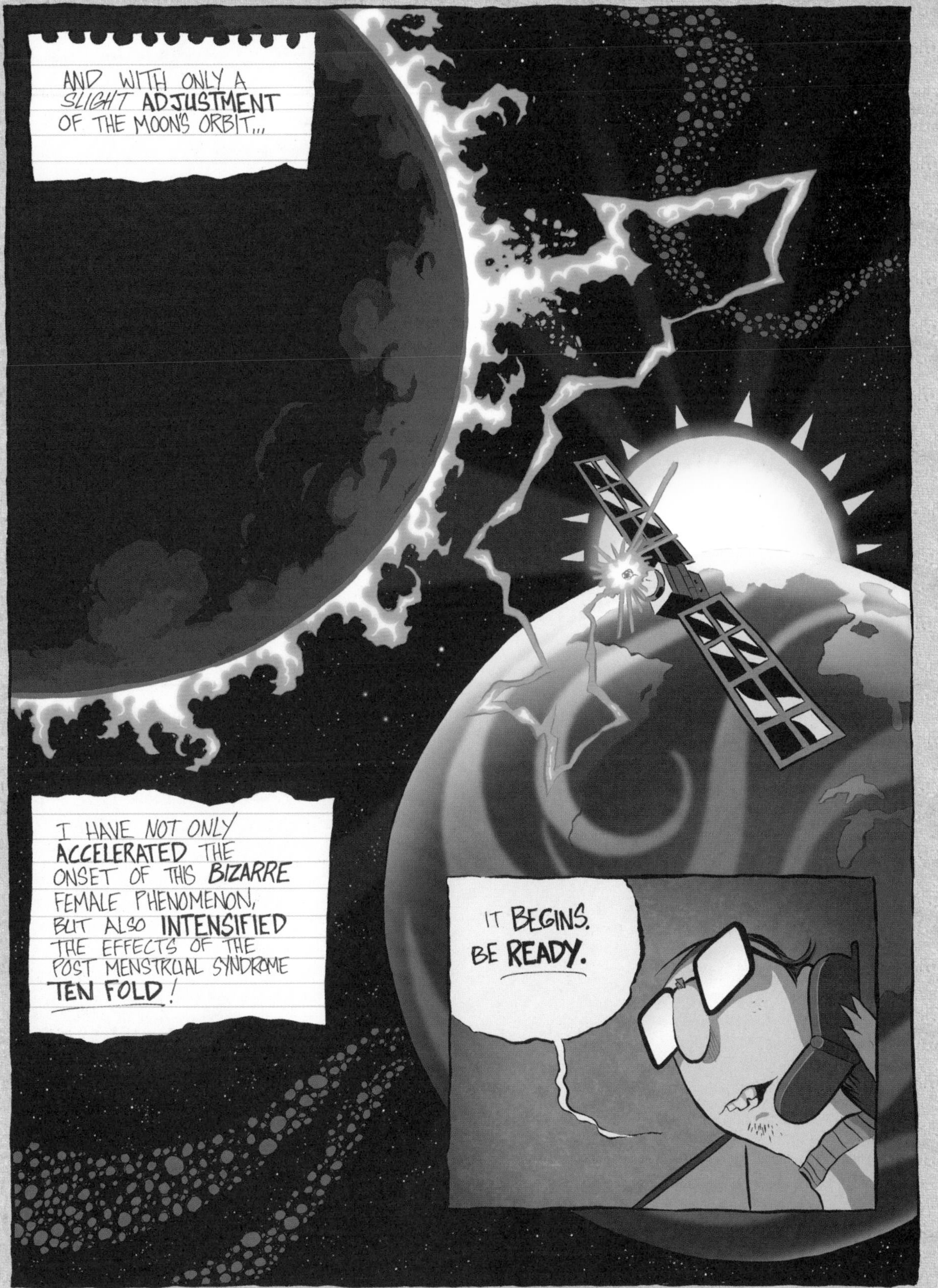

AND WITH ONLY A SLIGHT ADJUSTMENT OF THE MOON'S ORBIT...
I HAVE NOT ONLY ACCELERATED THE ONSET OF THIS BIZARRE FEMALE PHENOMENON, BUT ALSO INTENSIFIED THE EFFECTS OF THE POST MENSTRUAL SYNDROME TEN FOLD!
IT BEGINS. BE READY.

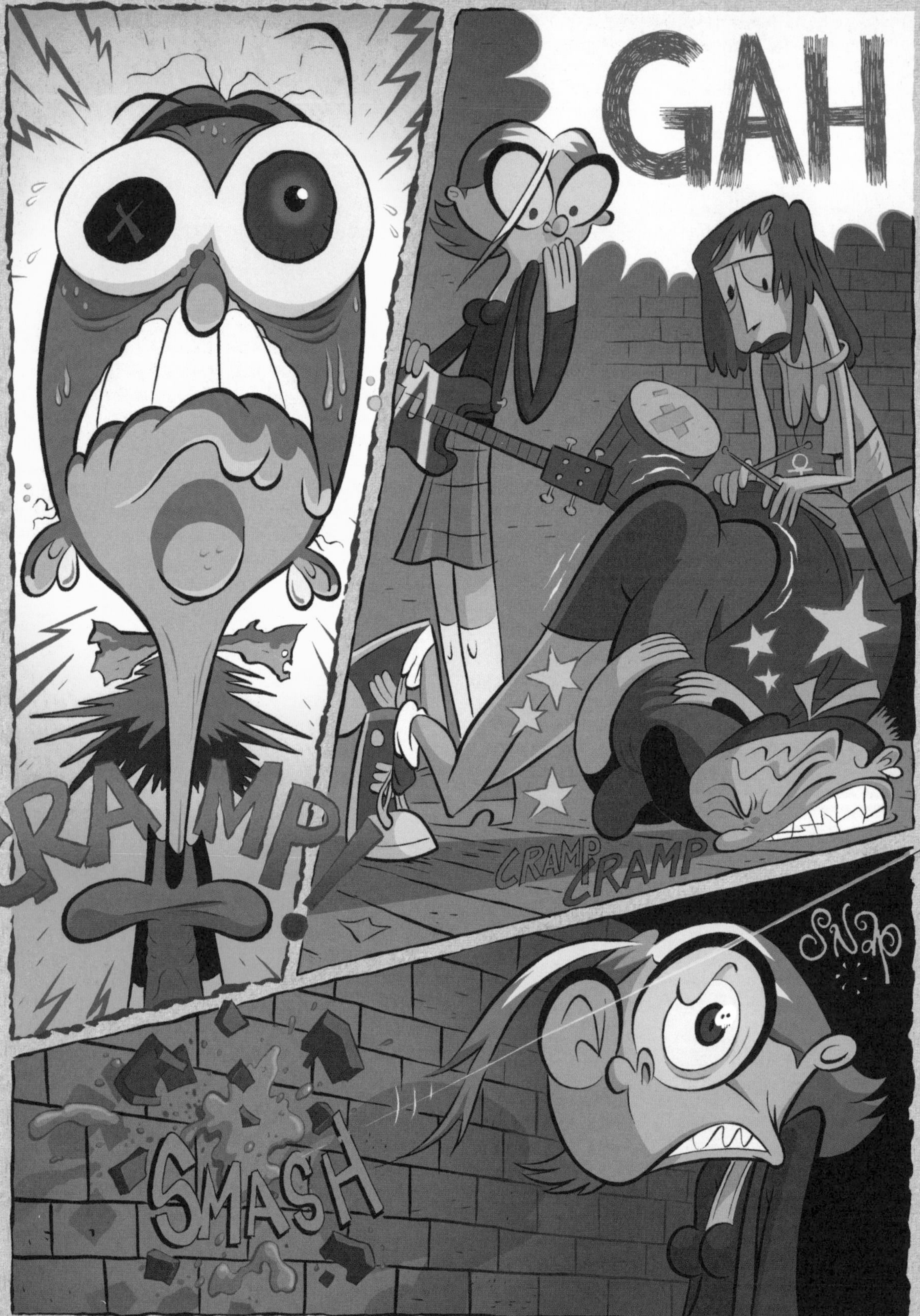
GAH
CRAMP!
CRAMP CRAMP
SNAP
SMASH

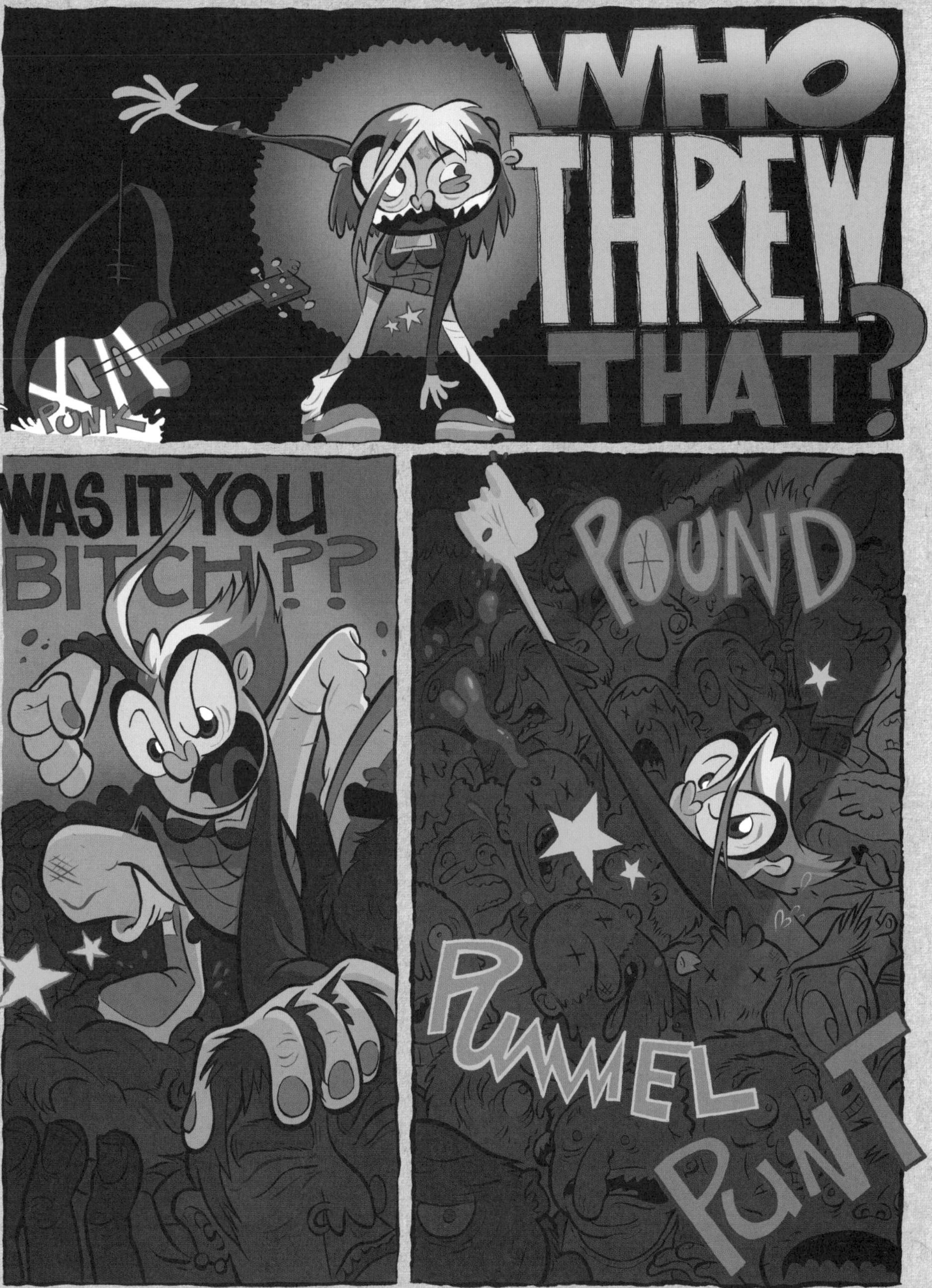
PUNK
WHO THREW THAT?
WAS IT YOU BITCH??
POUND
PUMMEL
PUNT

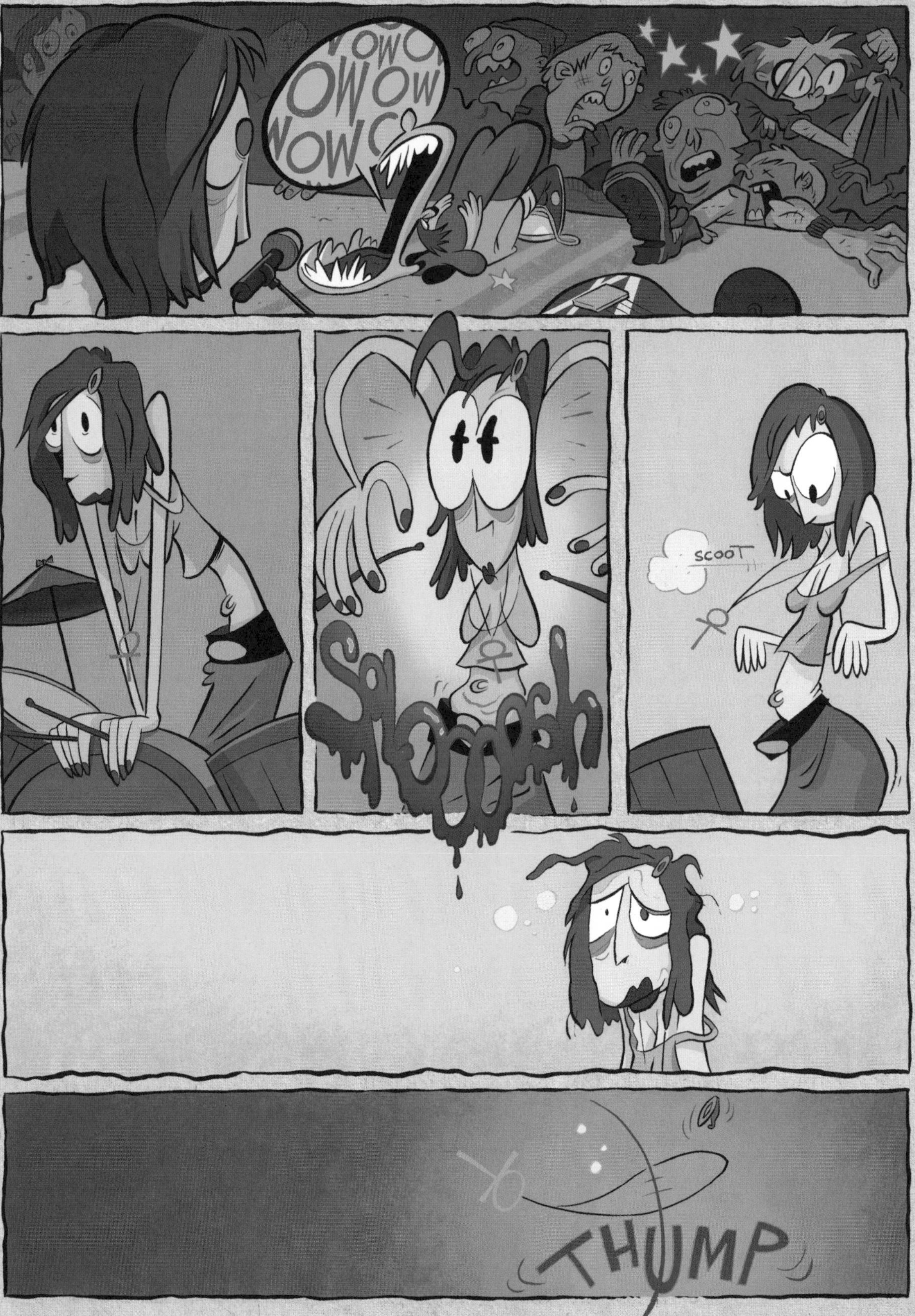
WOWO
OWOW
WOWO
SCOOT
Sploosh
THUMP

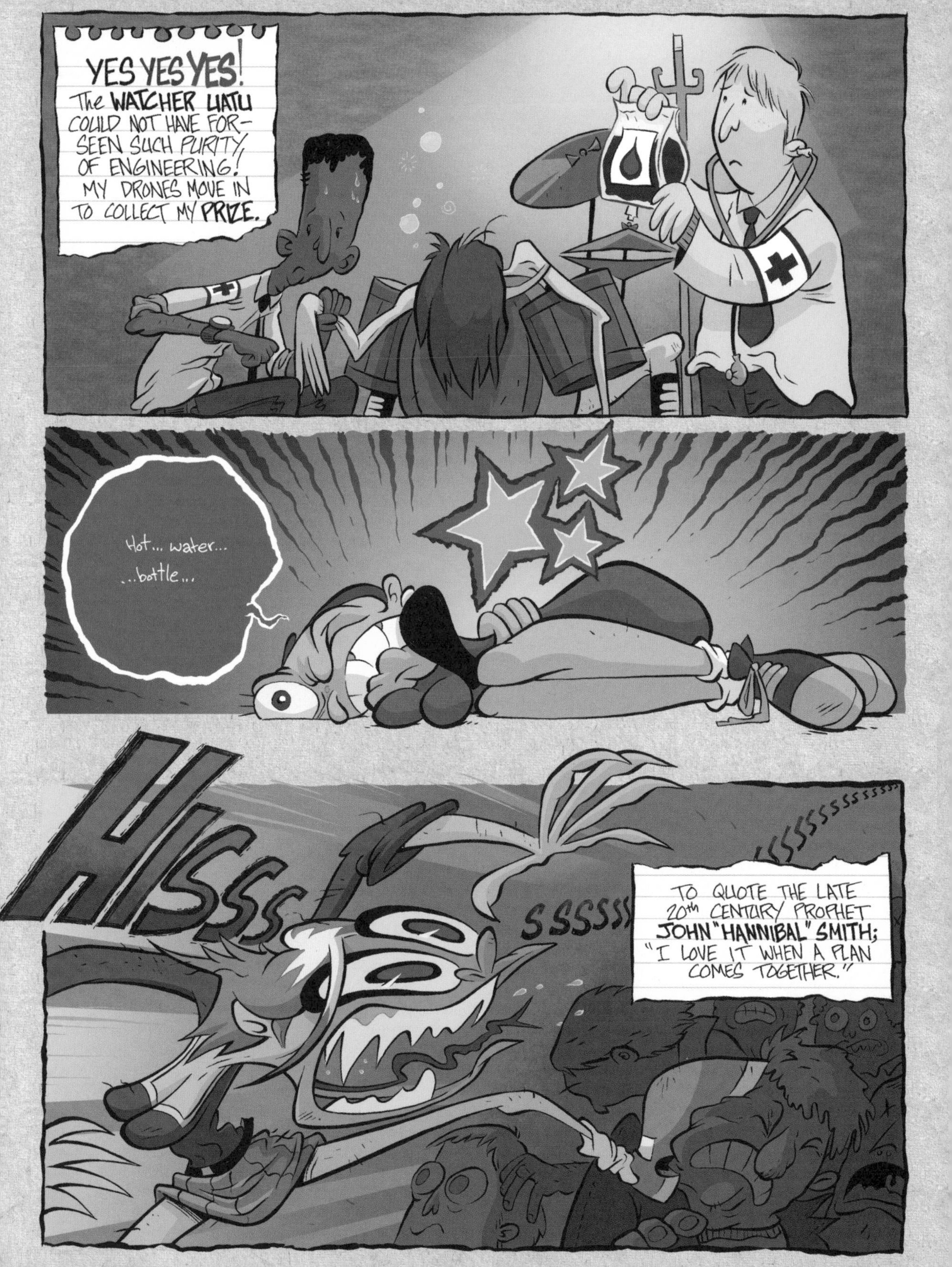

YES YES YES! The WATCHER UATU COULD NOT HAVE FORSEEN SUCH PURITY, OF ENGINEERING! MY DRONES MOVE IN TO COLLECT MY PRIZE.
Hot... water... ...bottle...
HISSSS
SSSSSS
TO QUOTE THE LATE 20th CENTURY PROPHET JOHN "HANNIBAL" SMITH; "I LOVE IT WHEN A PLAN COMES TOGETHER."

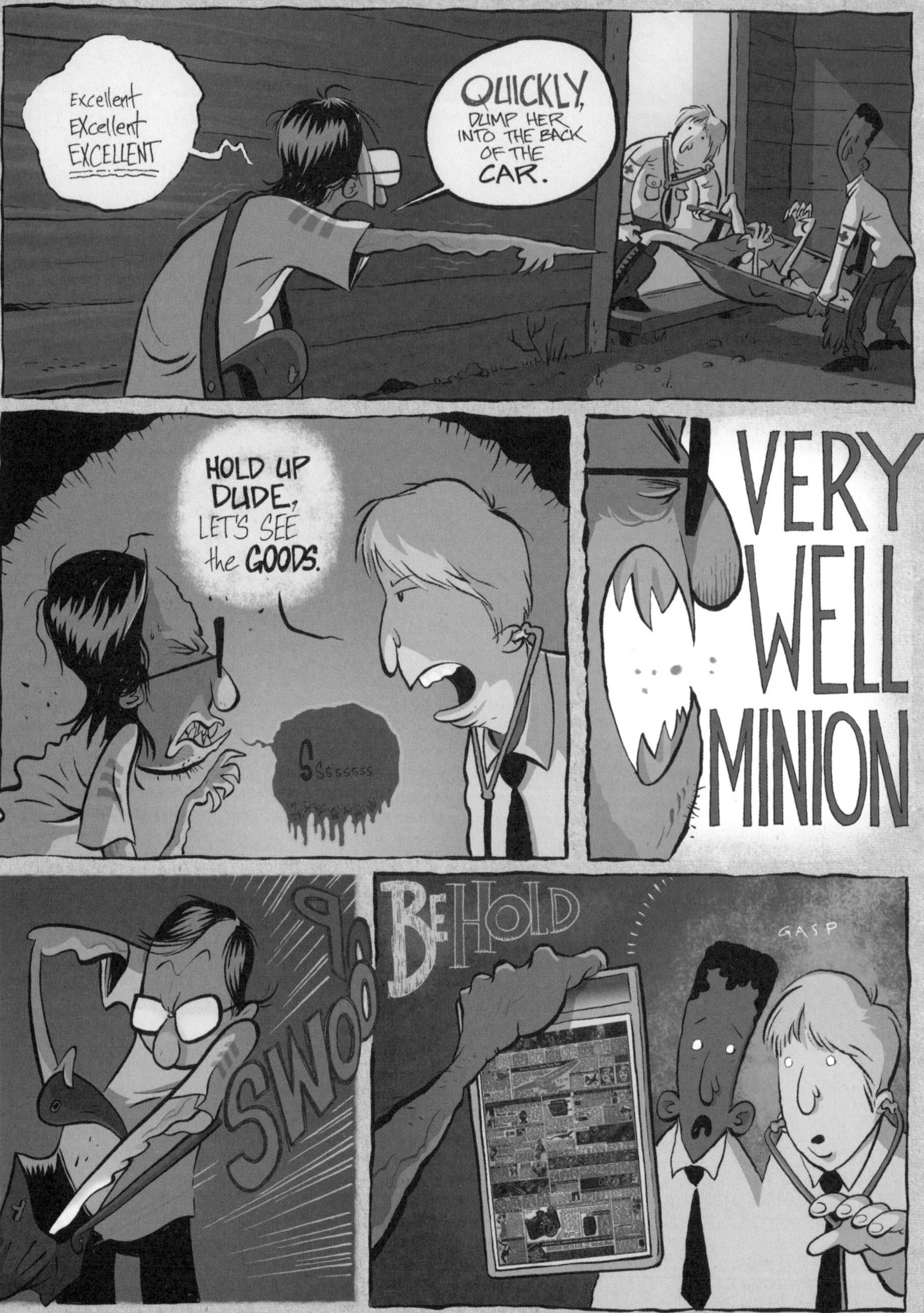
Excellent
EXcellent
EXCELLENT
QUICKLY, DUMP HER INTO THE BACK OF THE CAR.
HOLD UP DUDE, LET'S SEE the GOODS.
Sssssss
VERY WELL MINION
SWOOP
BEHOLD
GASP

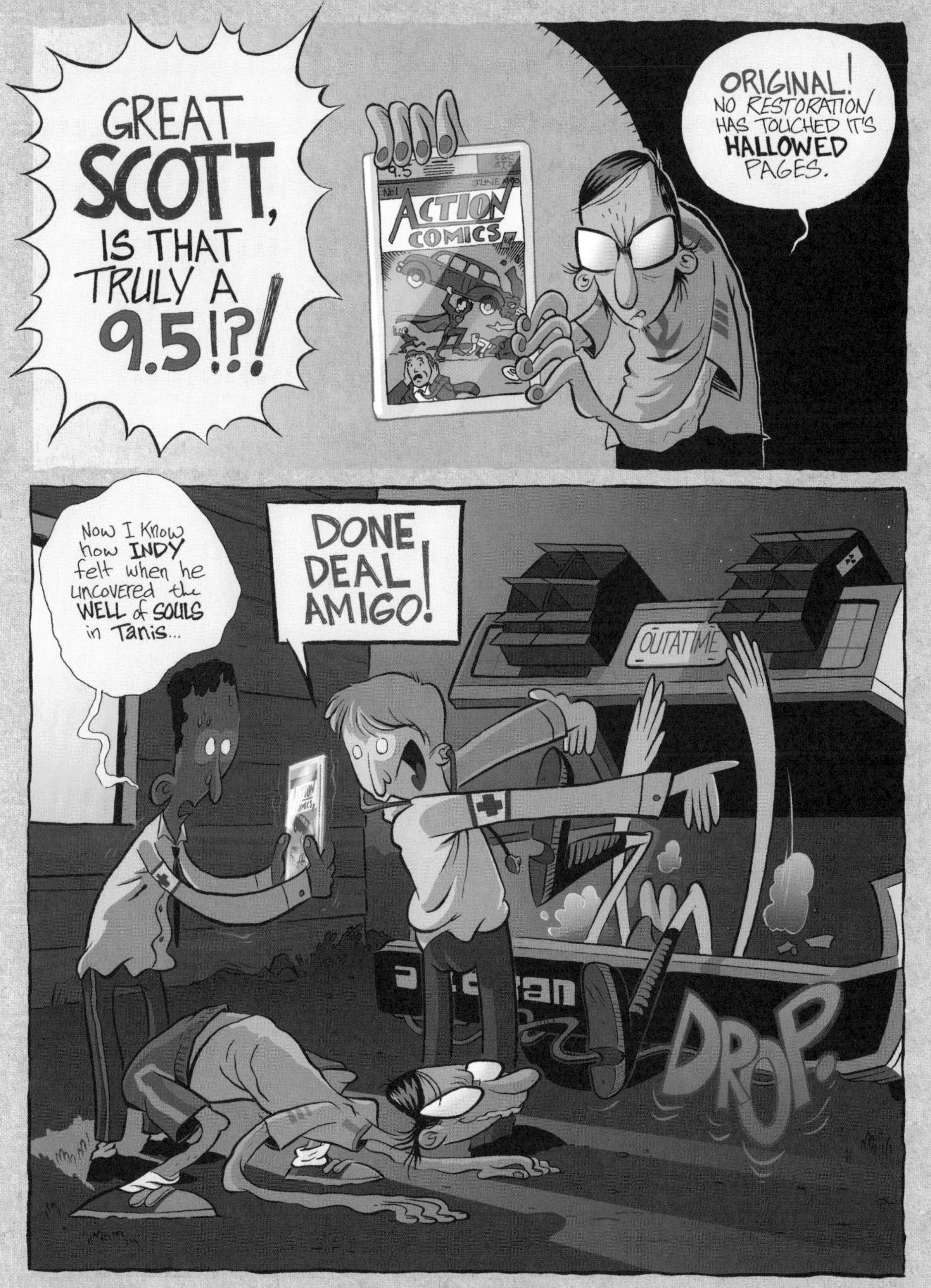

GREAT SCOTT, IS THAT TRULY A 9.5!?!
ORIGINAL! NO RESTORATION HAS TOUCHED IT'S HALLOWED PAGES.
ACTION COMICS
Now I Know how INDY felt when he uncovered the WELL of SOULS in Tanis...
DONE DEAL AMIGO!
OUTATIME
DROP.

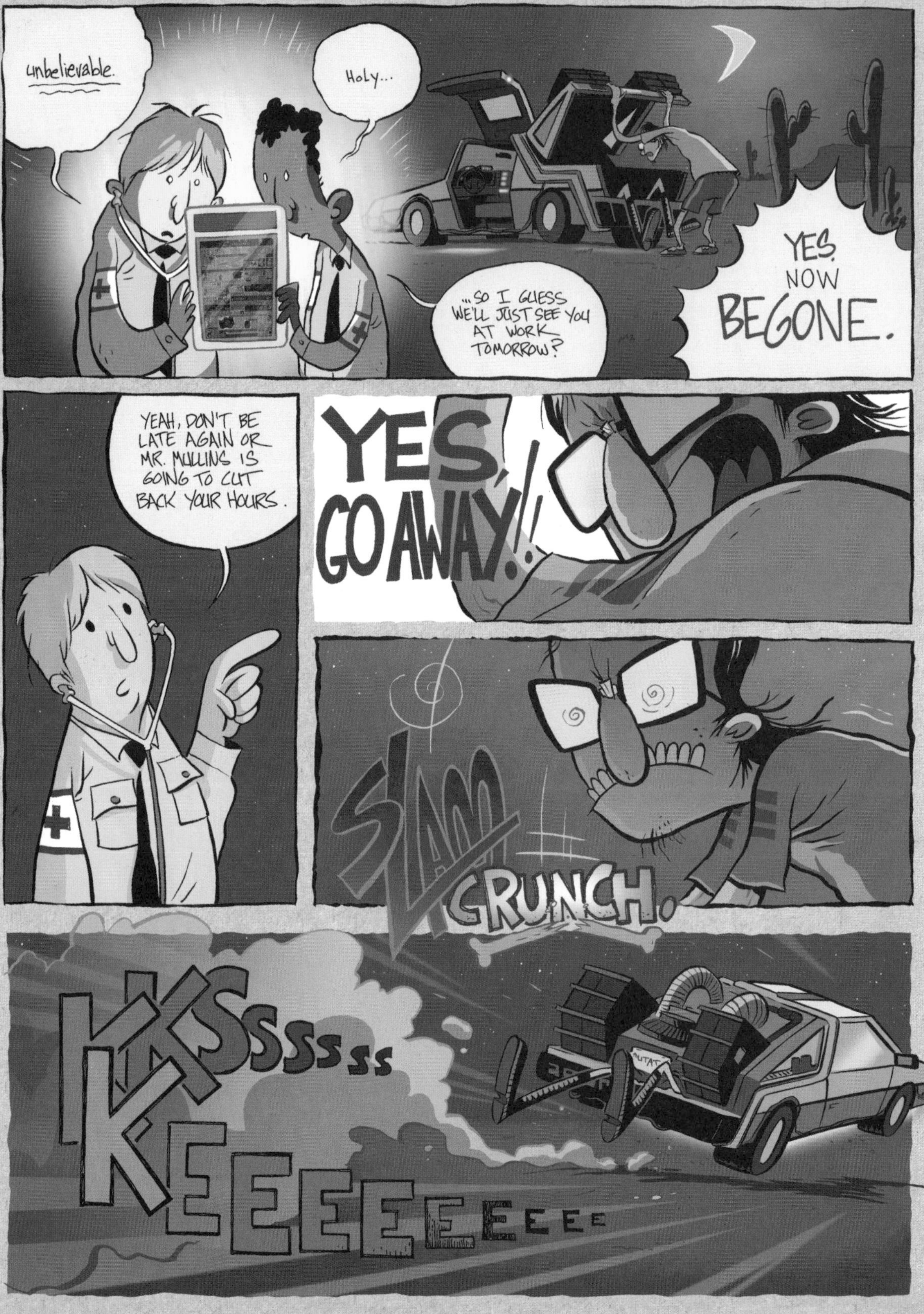
unbelievable.
Holy...
...SO I GUESS WE'LL JUST SEE YOU AT WORK TOMORROW?
YES. NOW BEGONE.
YEAH, DON'T BE LATE AGAIN OR MR. MULLINS IS GOING TO CUT BACK YOUR HOURS.
YES, GO AWAY!!
SLAM
CRUNCH.
KKSSSSSSS
KEEEEEEEEEE

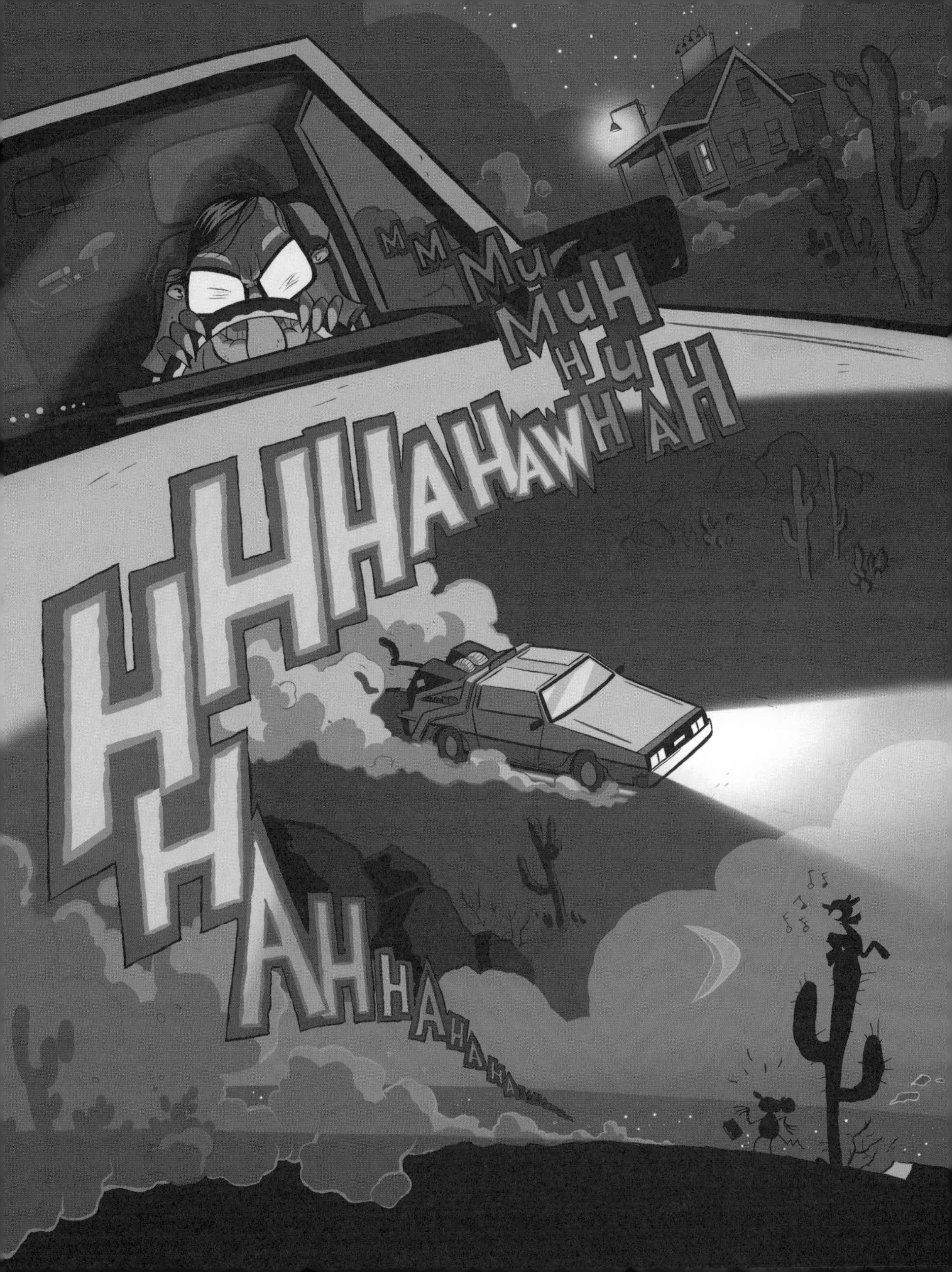
MMMUH MUH MHUH
HHHAHAHAWHAH
HAHHAHAHAHA

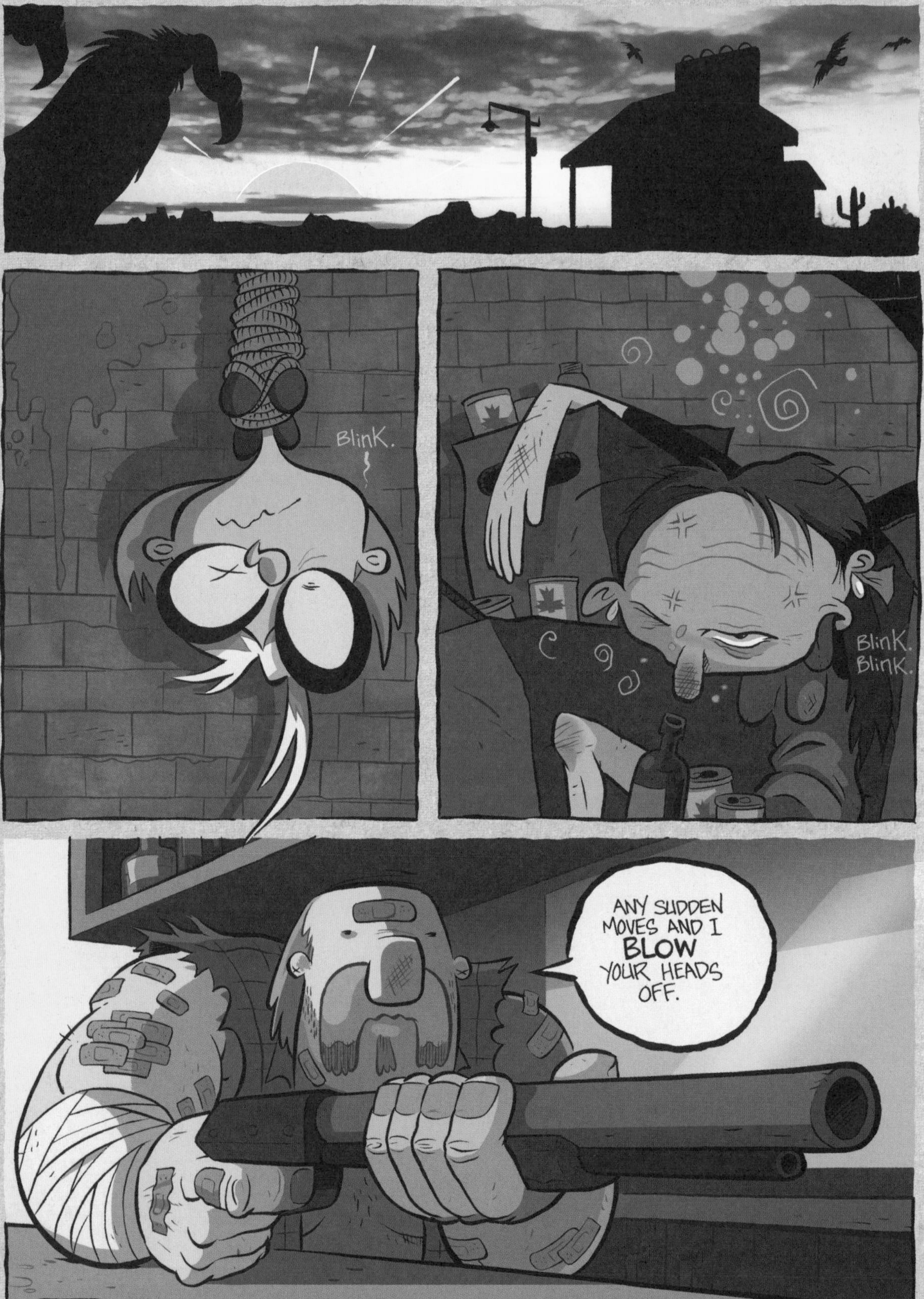
BlinK.
BlinK.
BlinK.
ANY SUDDEN MOVES AND I **BLOW** YOUR HEADS OFF.

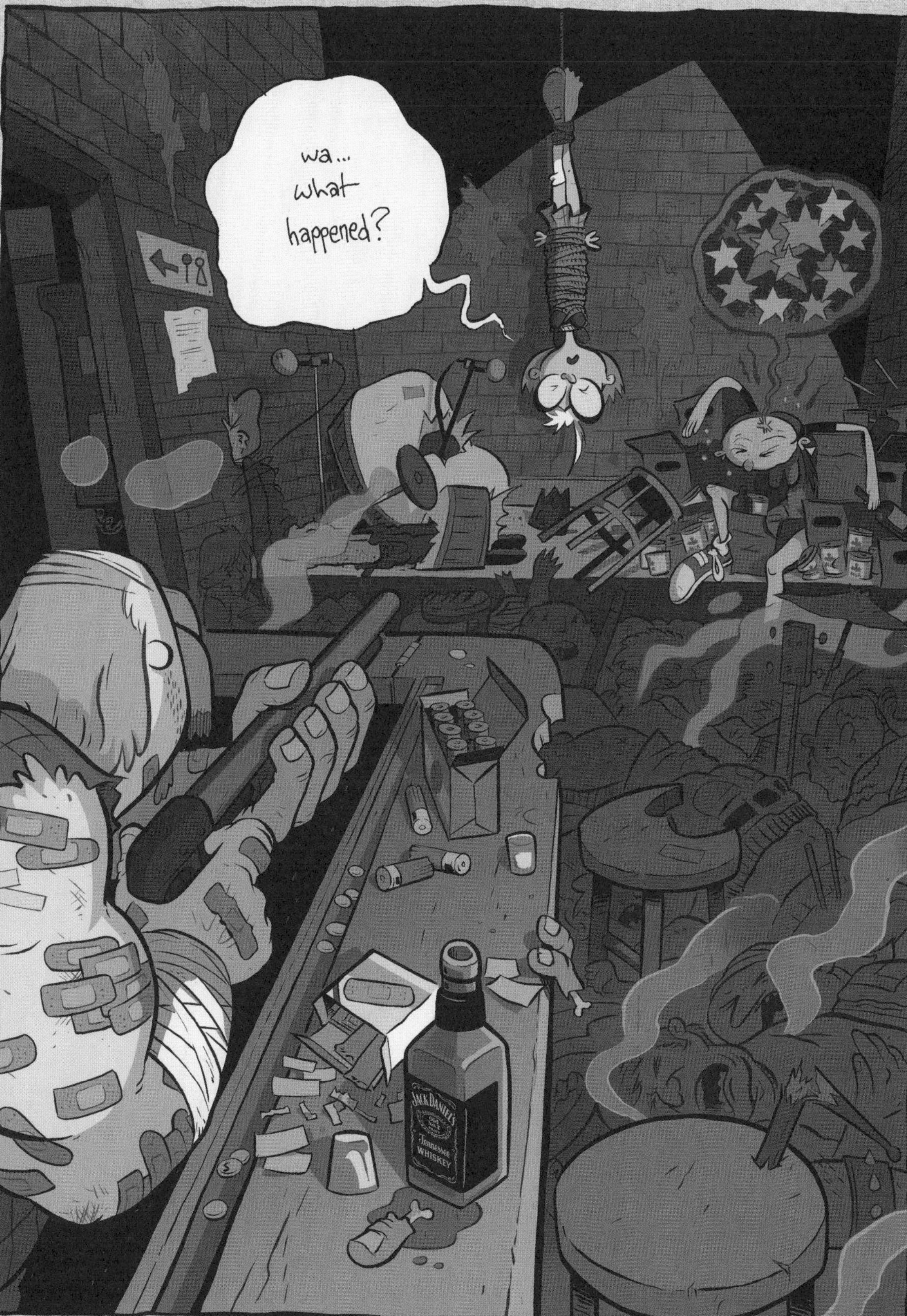
wa... what happened?
JACK DANIEL'S
Tennessee WHISKEY

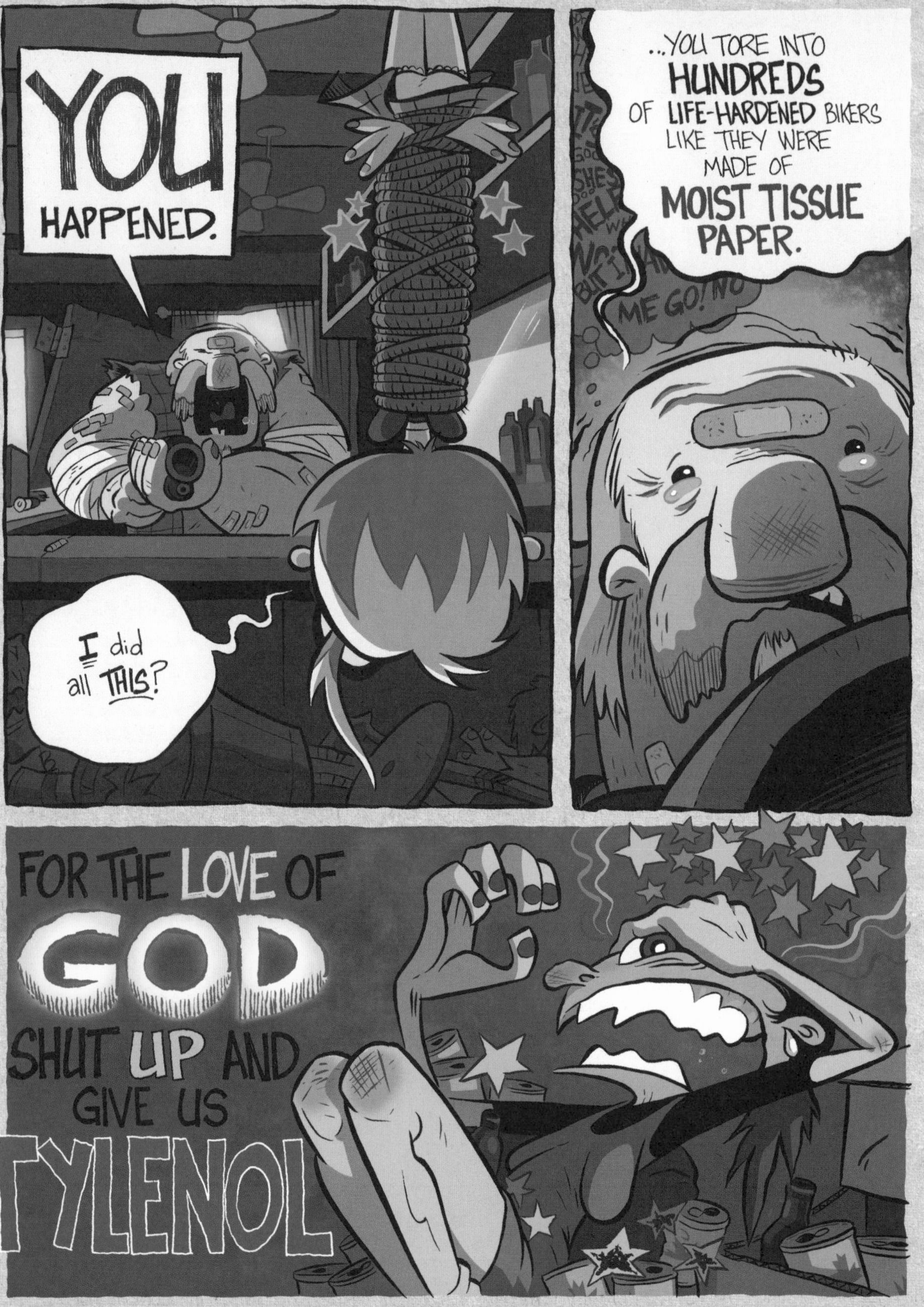

YOU HAPPENED.
I did all THIS?
...YOU TORE INTO HUNDREDS OF LIFE-HARDENED BIKERS LIKE THEY WERE MADE OF MOIST TISSUE PAPER.
ME GO! NO
FOR THE LOVE OF GOD SHUT UP AND GIVE US TYLENOL

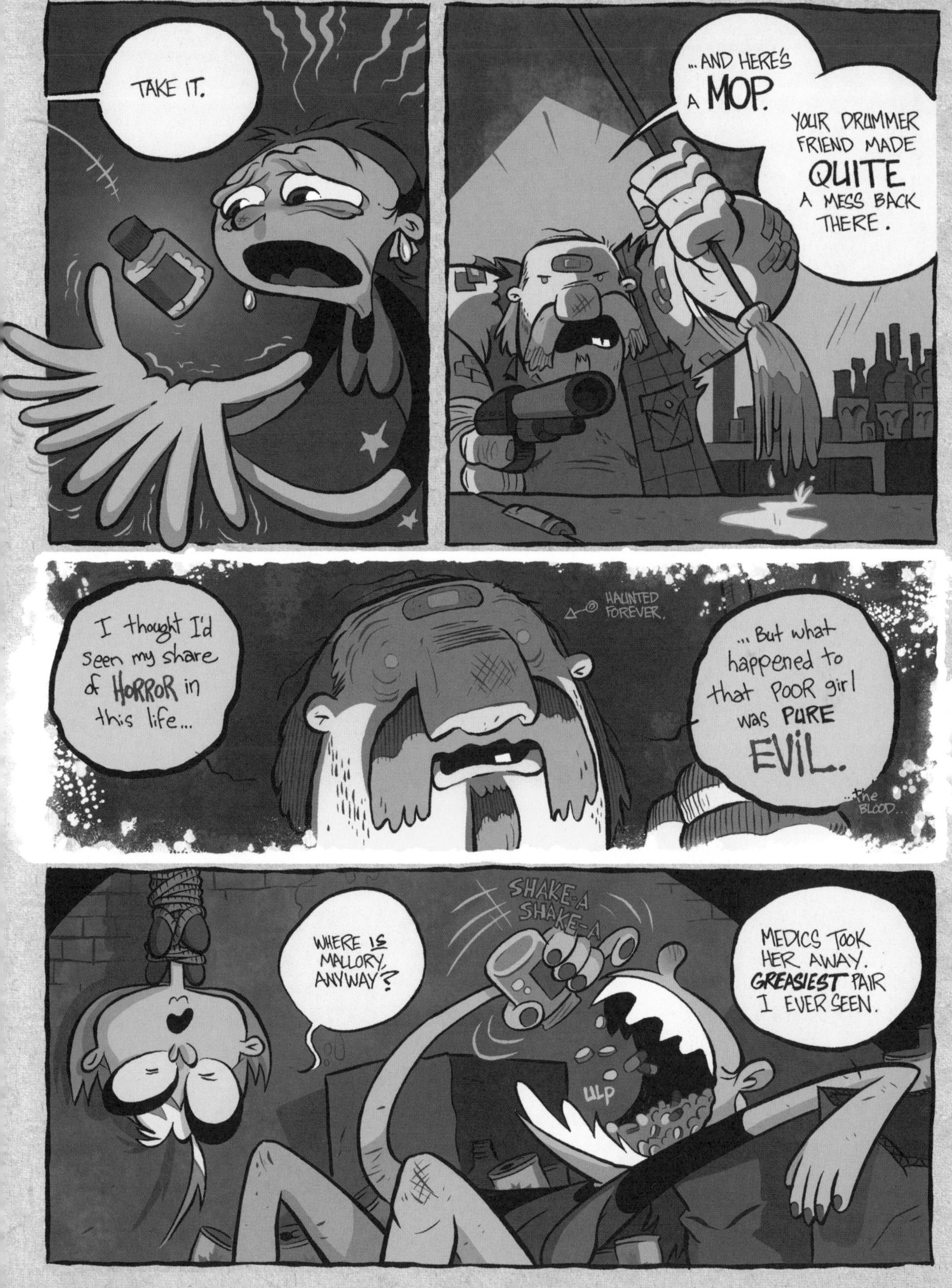
TAKE IT.
...AND HERE'S A MOP.
YOUR DRUMMER FRIEND MADE QUITE A MESS BACK THERE.
I thought I'd seen my share of HORROR in this life...
HAUNTED FOREVER.
...But what happened to that POOR girl was PURE EViL.
...the BLOOD...
SHAKE-A SHAKE-A
WHERE IS MALLORY, ANYWAY?
MEDICS TOOK HER AWAY. GREASIEST PAIR I EVER SEEN.
ULP

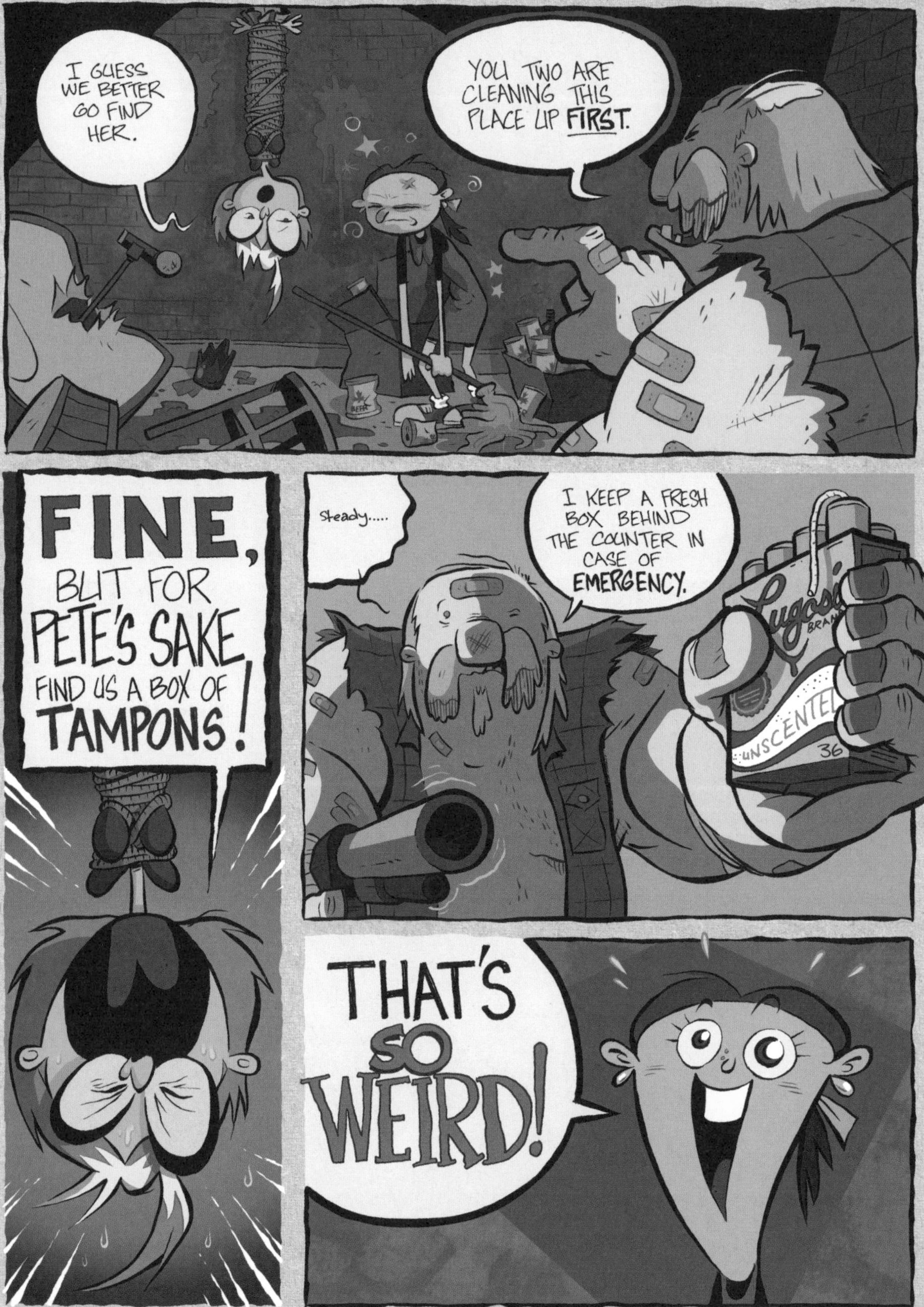
I GUESS WE BETTER GO FIND HER.
YOU TWO ARE CLEANING THIS PLACE UP FIRST.
FINE, BUT FOR PETE'S SAKE FIND US A BOX OF TAMPONS!
Steady.....
I KEEP A FRESH BOX BEHIND THE COUNTER IN CASE OF EMERGENCY.
UNSCENTED
36
THAT'S SO WEIRD!

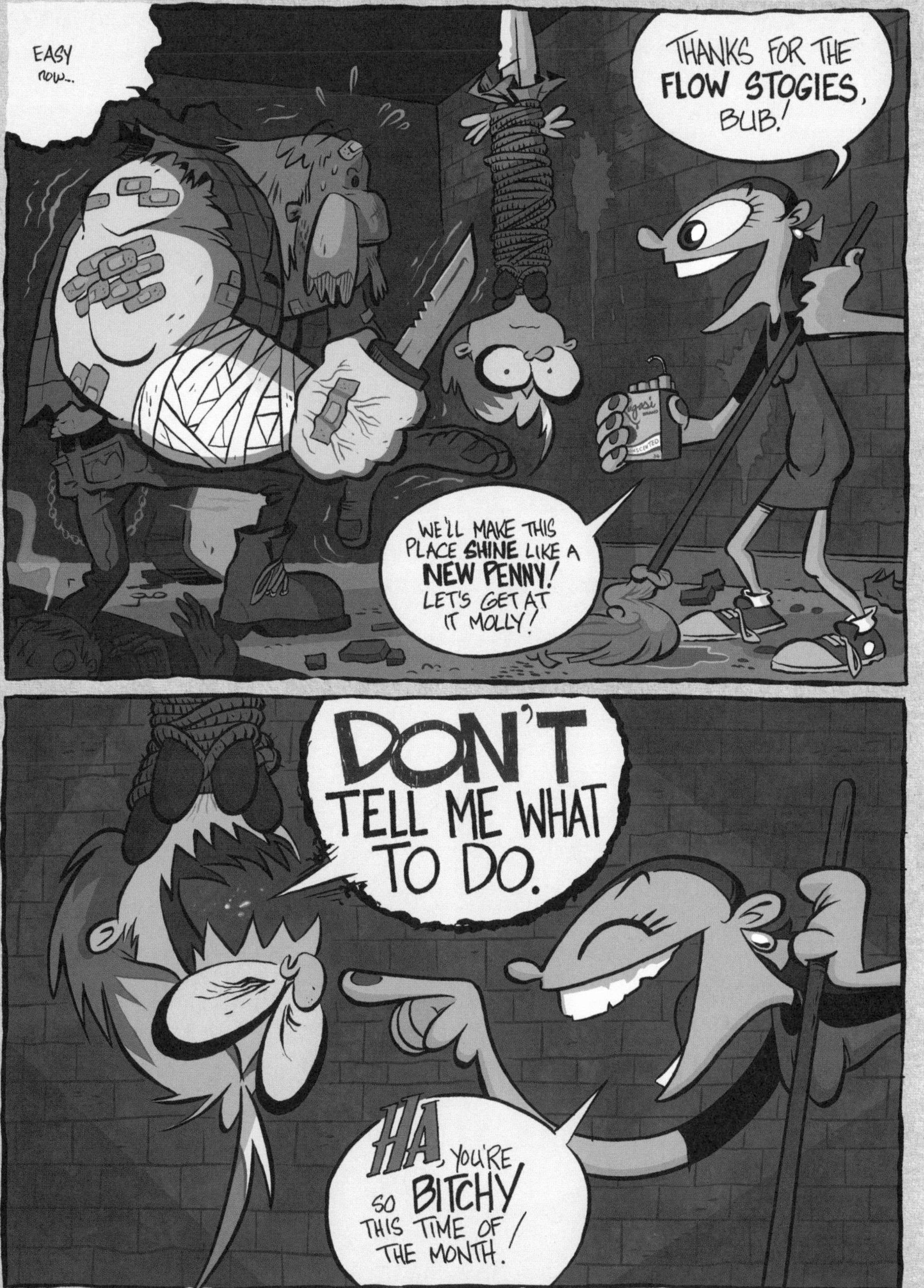
EASY now...
THANKS FOR THE FLOW STOGIES, BUB!
WE'LL MAKE THIS PLACE SHINE LIKE A NEW PENNY! LET'S GET AT IT MOLLY!
DON'T TELL ME WHAT TO DO.
HA, YOU'RE SO BITCHY THIS TIME OF THE MONTH!

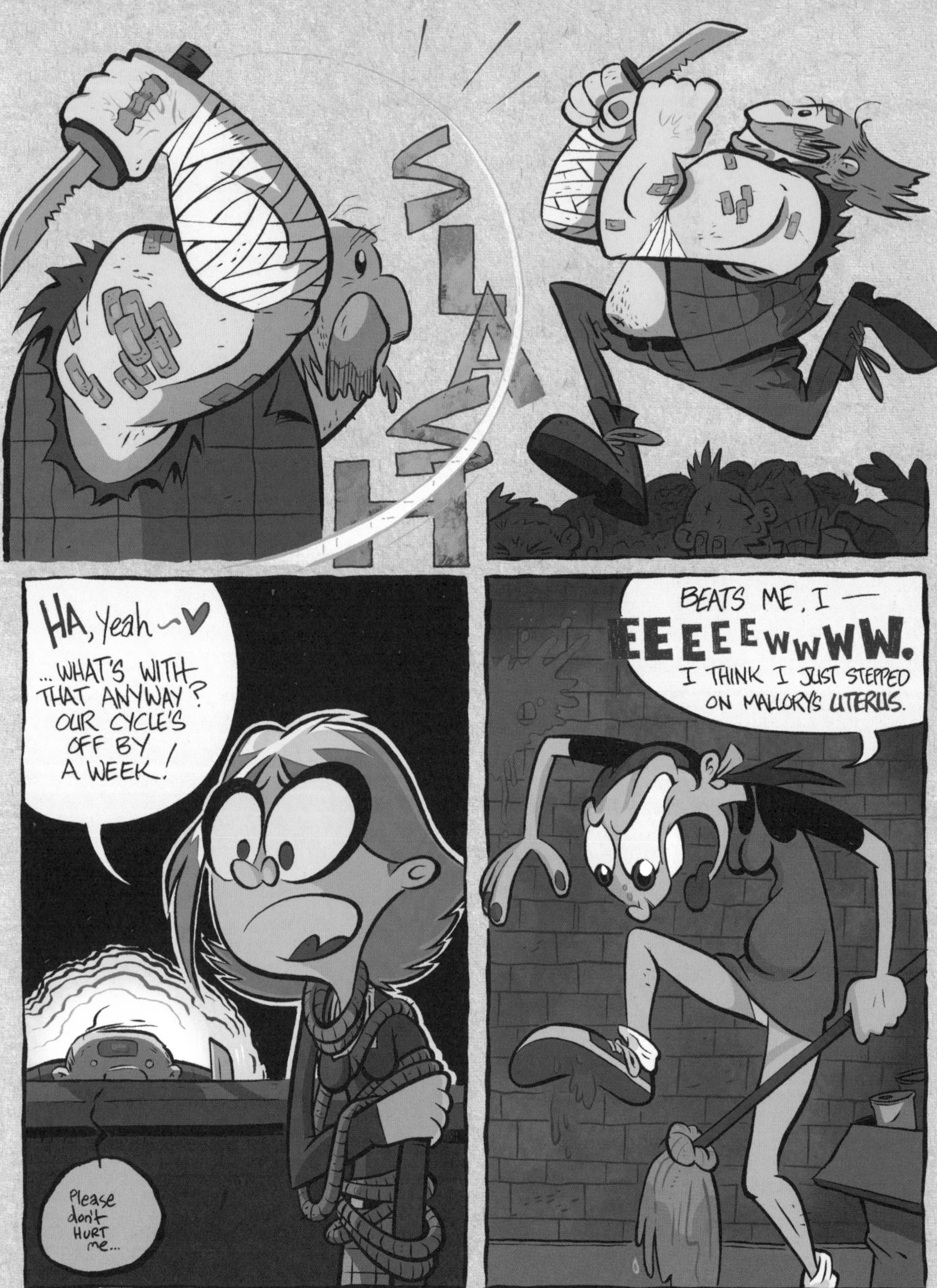
SLASH
HA, Yeah ~♥
...WHAT'S WITH THAT ANYWAY? OUR CYCLE'S OFF BY A WEEK!
Please don't HURT me...
BEATS ME. I —
EEEEEWWWWW.
I THINK I JUST STEPPED ON MALLORY'S UTERUS.

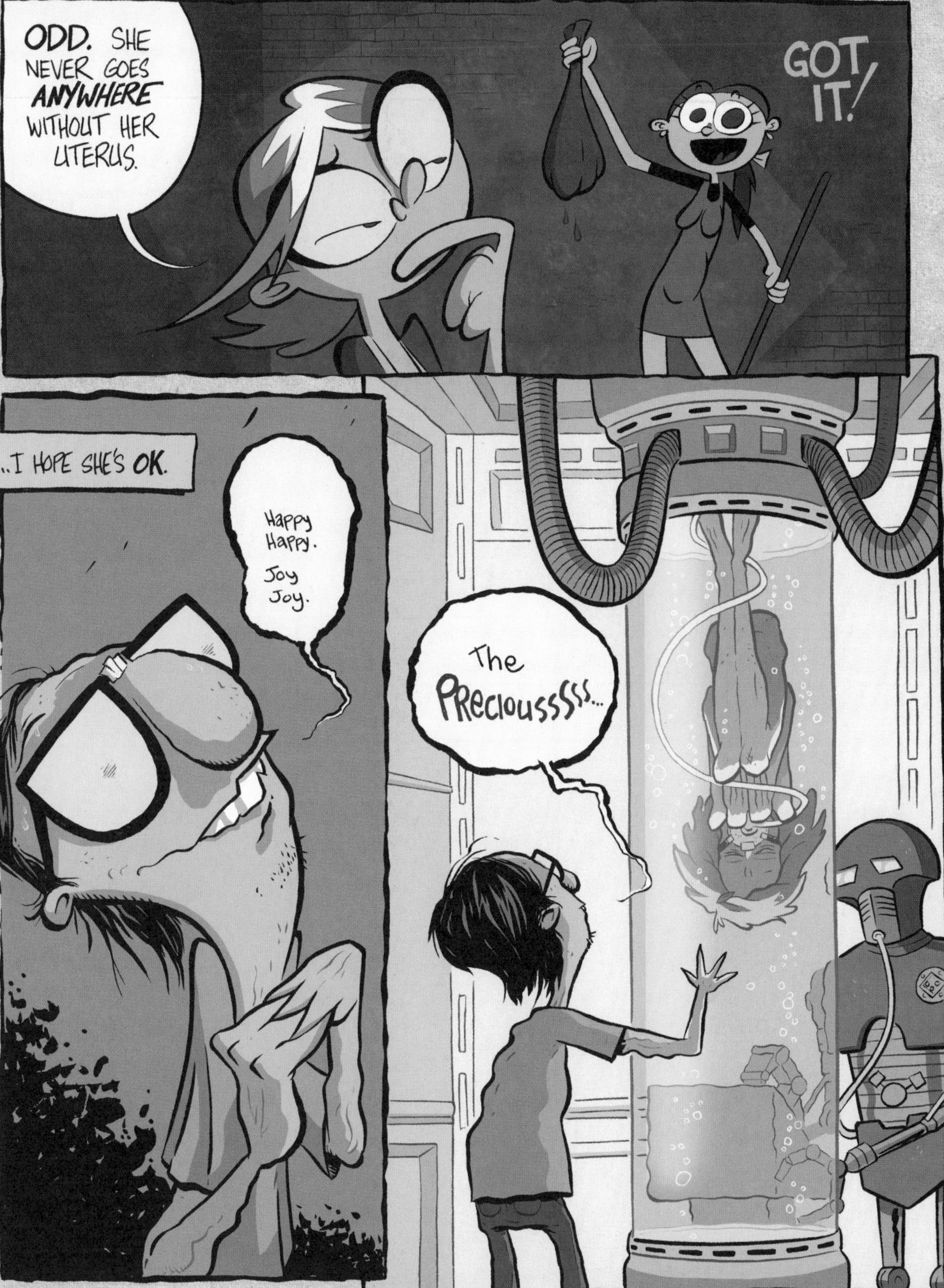
ODD. SHE NEVER GOES ANYWHERE WITHOUT HER UTERUS.
GOT IT!
...I HOPE SHE'S OK.
Happy Happy. Joy Joy.
The PReciousssss...

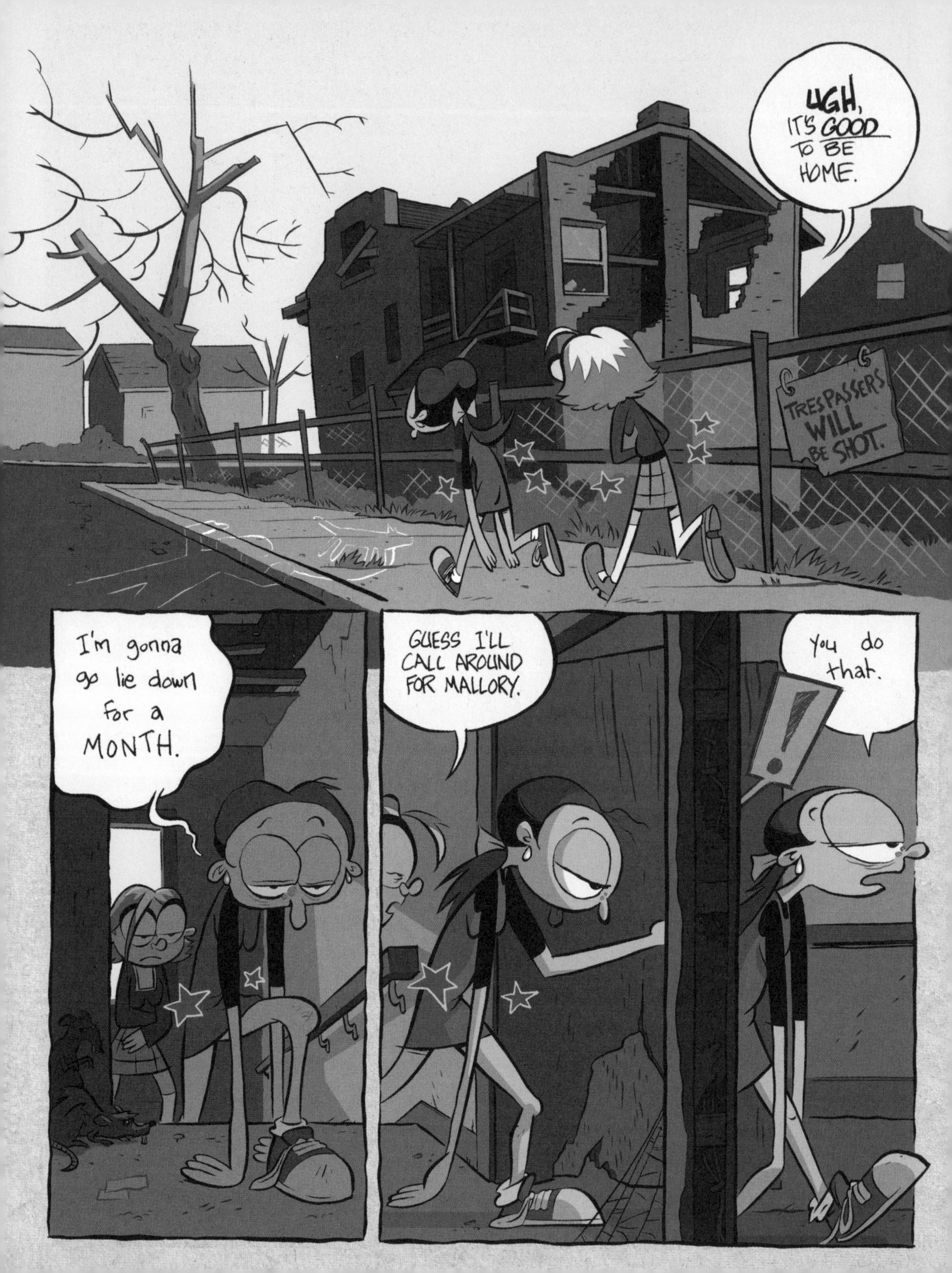
UGH, IT'S GOOD TO BE HOME.
TRESPASSERS WILL BE SHOT.
I'm gonna go lie down for a MONTH.
GUESS I'LL CALL AROUND FOR MALLORY.
!
You do that.

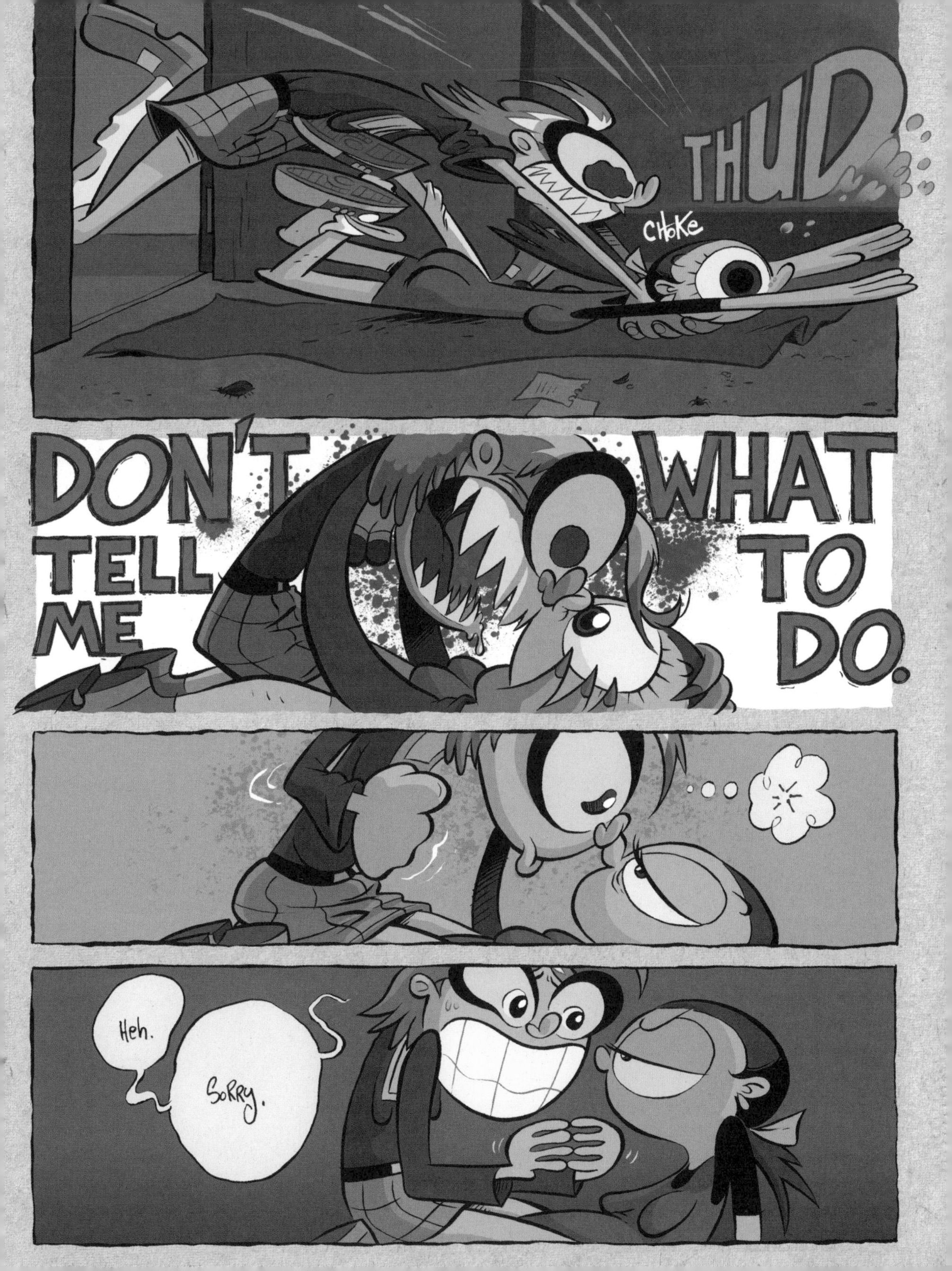
THUD
CHOKE
DON'T TELL ME WHAT TO DO.
Heh.
SORRY.

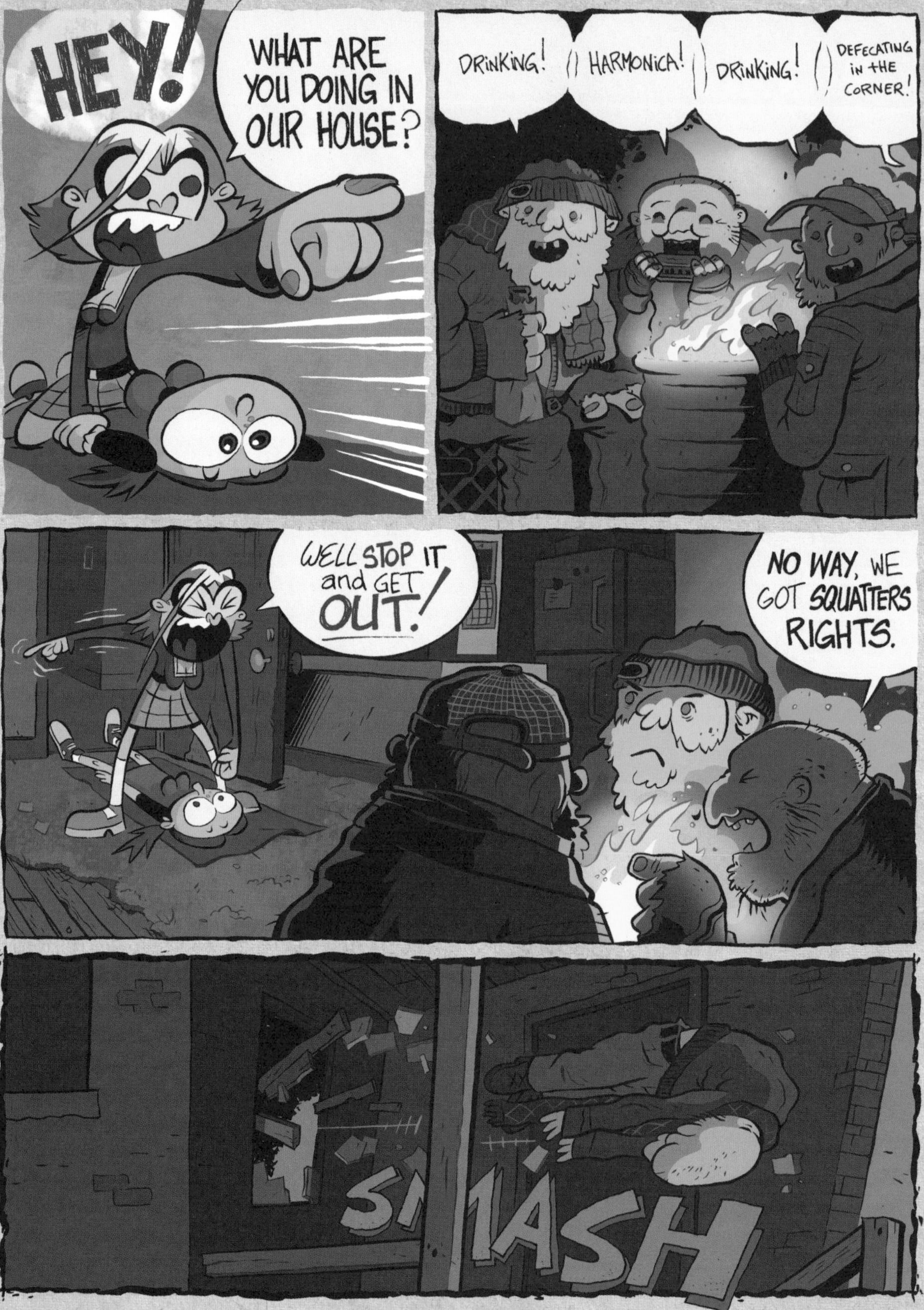
HEY!
WHAT ARE YOU DOING IN OUR HOUSE?
DRINKING!
HARMONICA!
DRINKING!
DEFECATING IN THE CORNER!
WELL STOP IT and GET OUT!
NO WAY, WE GOT SQUATTERS RIGHTS.
SMASH

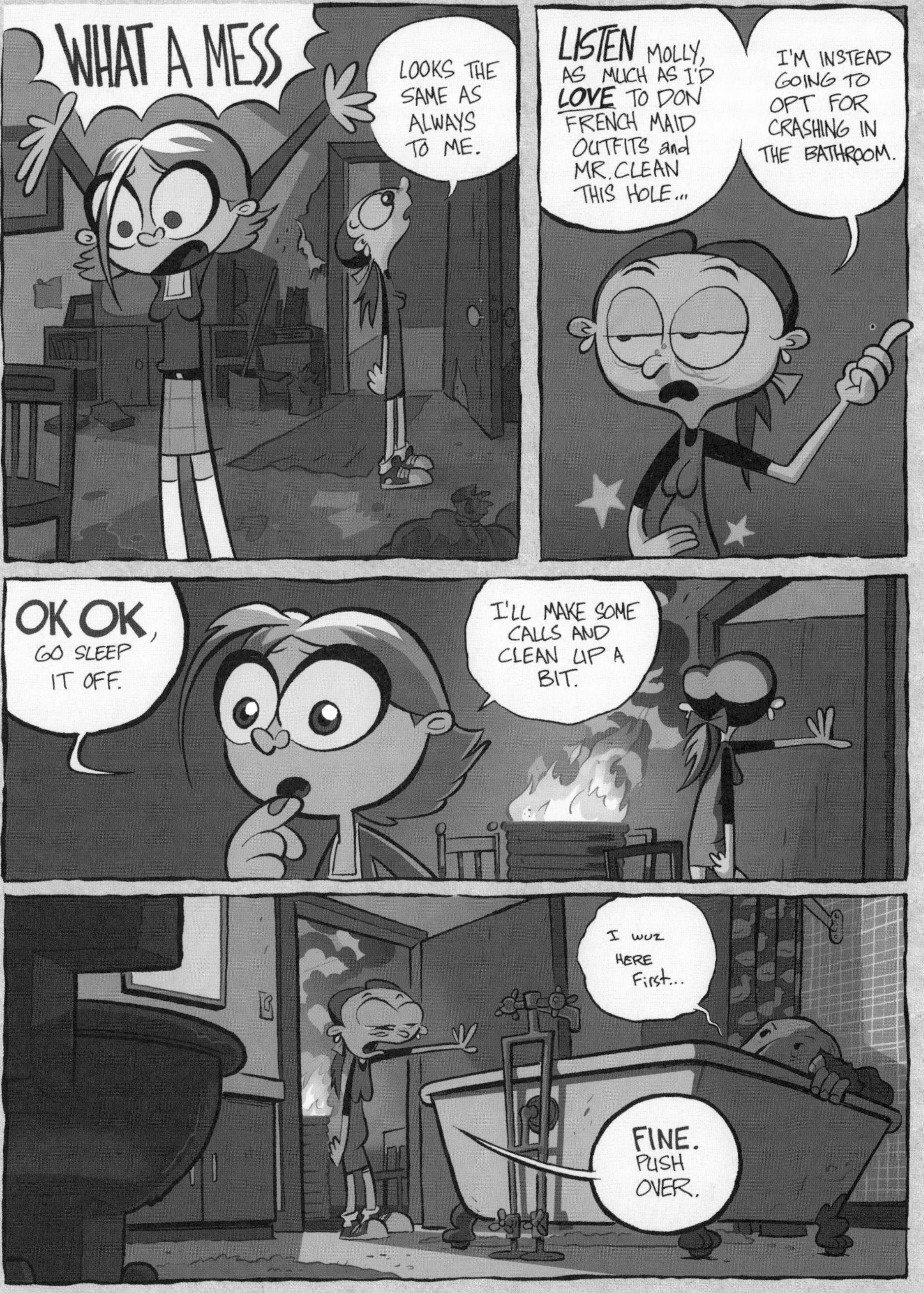
WHAT A MESS
LOOKS THE SAME AS ALWAYS TO ME.
LISTEN MOLLY, AS MUCH AS I'D LOVE TO DON FRENCH MAID OUTFITS and MR. CLEAN THIS HOLE...
I'M INSTEAD GOING TO OPT FOR CRASHING IN THE BATHROOM.
OK OK, GO SLEEP IT OFF.
I'LL MAKE SOME CALLS AND CLEAN UP A BIT.
I WUZ HERE First...
FINE. PUSH OVER.

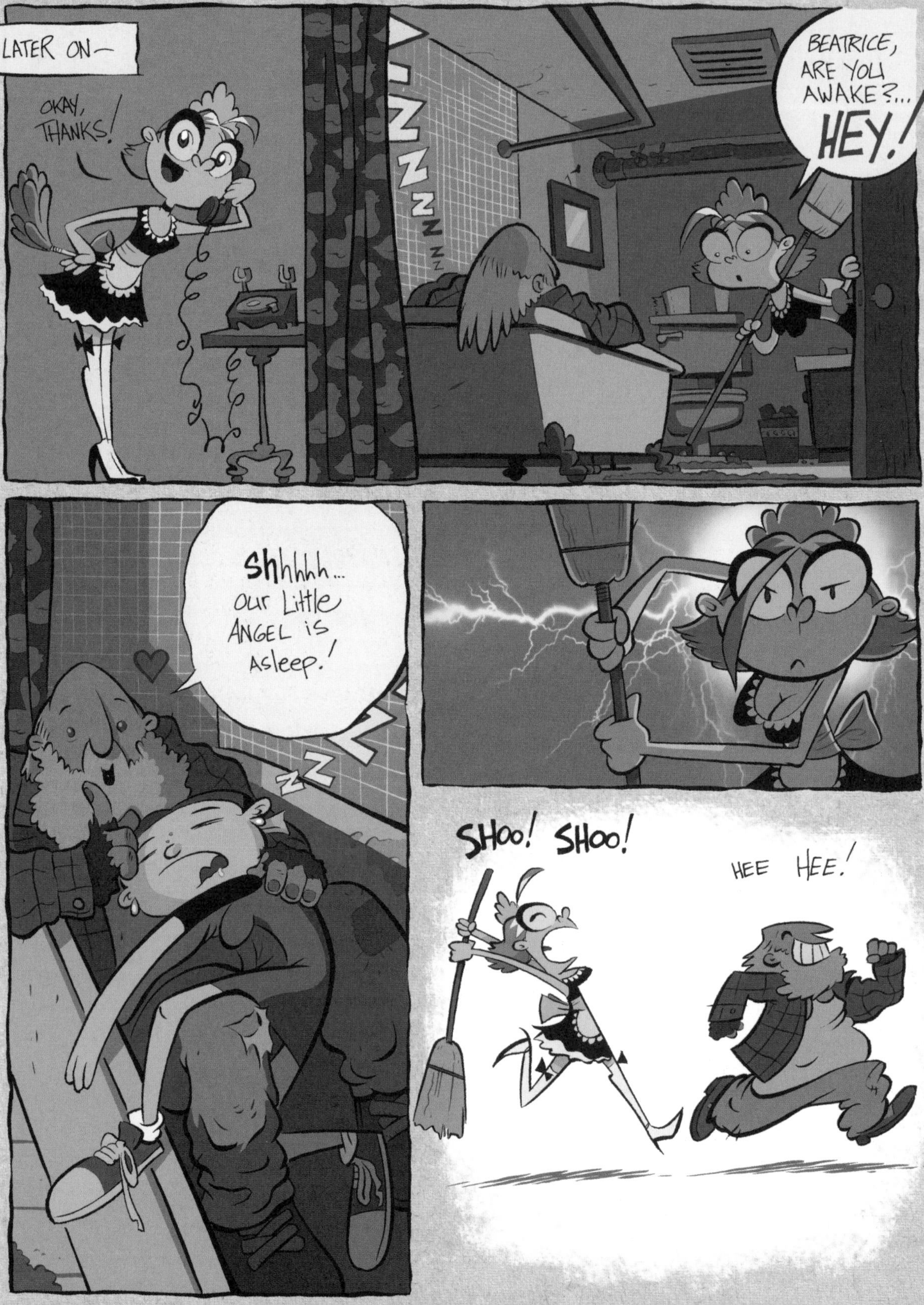
LATER ON—
OKAY, THANKS!
BEATRICE, ARE YOU AWAKE?... HEY!
Shhhhh... our Little ANGEL is Asleep!
SHOO! SHOO!
HEE HEE!

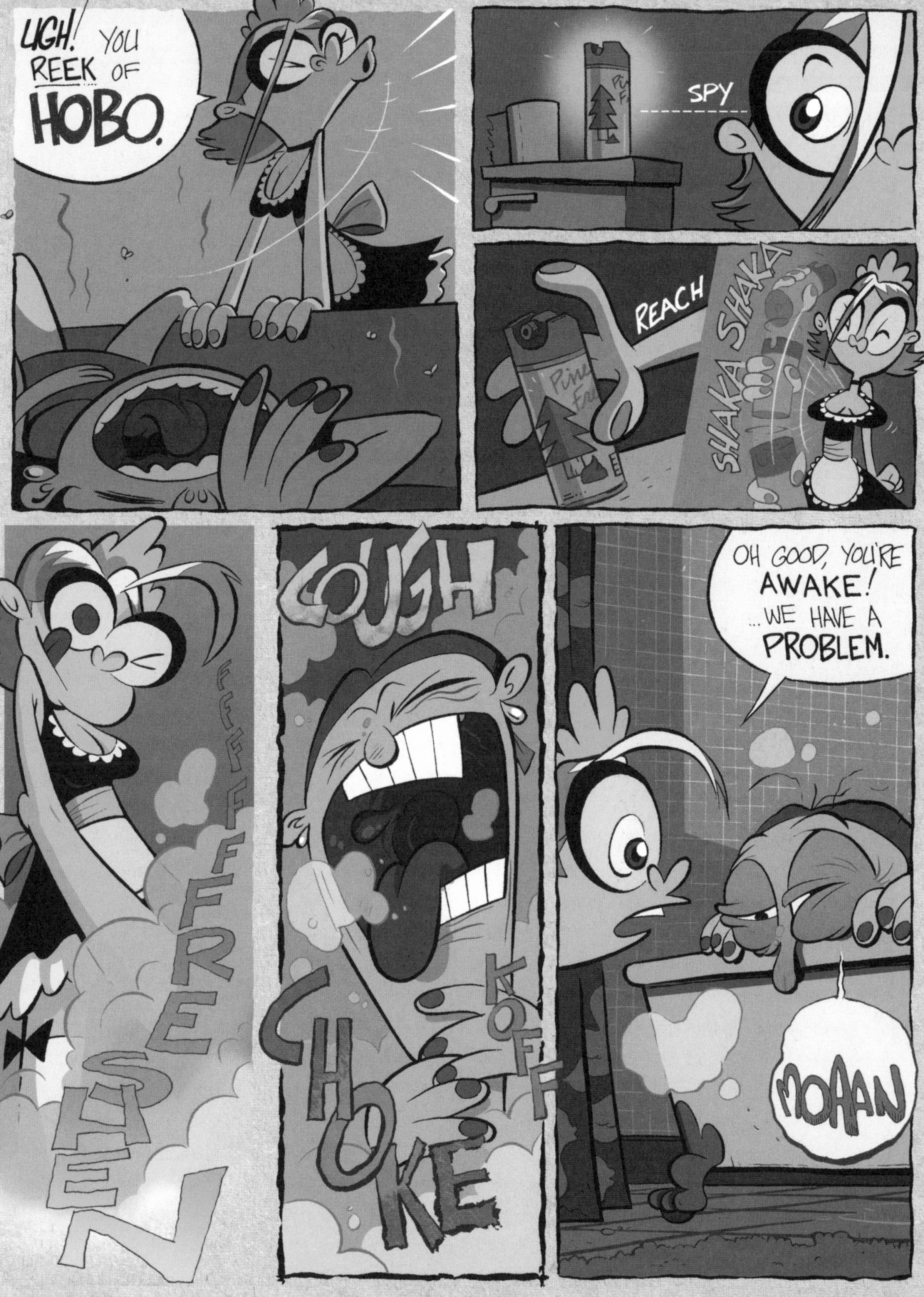
UGH! YOU REEK OF HOBO.
SPY
REACH
SHAKA SHAKA
FFFFFFF
FRESHENEZ
COUGH
CHOKE
KOFF
OH GOOD, YOU'RE AWAKE! ...WE HAVE A PROBLEM.
MOAAN

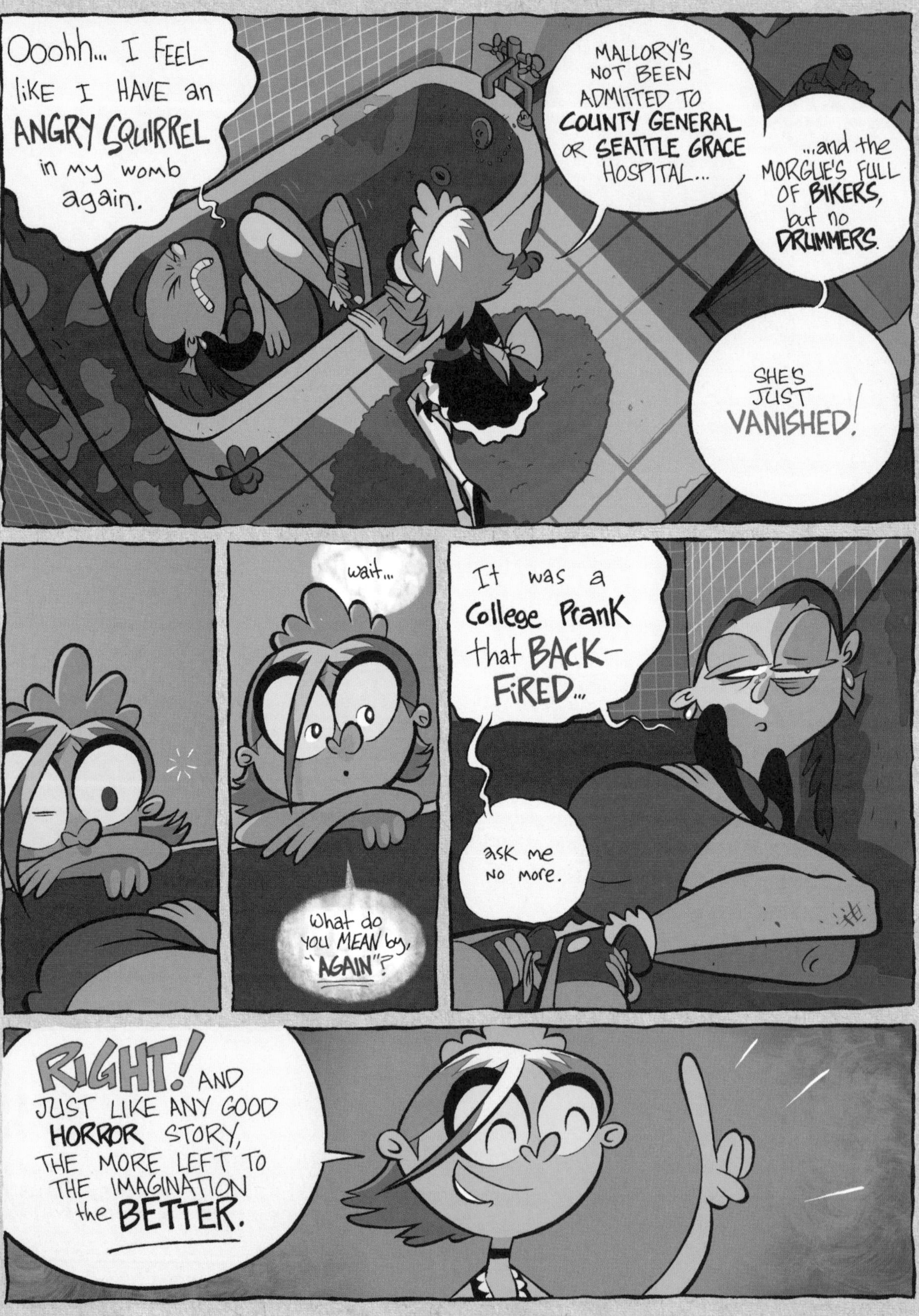

Ooohh... I FEEL like I HAVE an ANGRY SQUIRREL in my womb again.
MALLORY'S NOT BEEN ADMITTED TO COUNTY GENERAL OR SEATTLE GRACE HOSPITAL...
...and the MORGUE'S FULL OF BIKERS, but no DRUMMERS.
SHE'S JUST VANISHED!
wait...
What do you MEAN by, "AGAIN"?
It was a College Prank that BACK-FIRED...
ask me no more.
RIGHT! AND JUST LIKE ANY GOOD HORROR STORY, THE MORE LEFT TO THE IMAGINATION the BETTER.

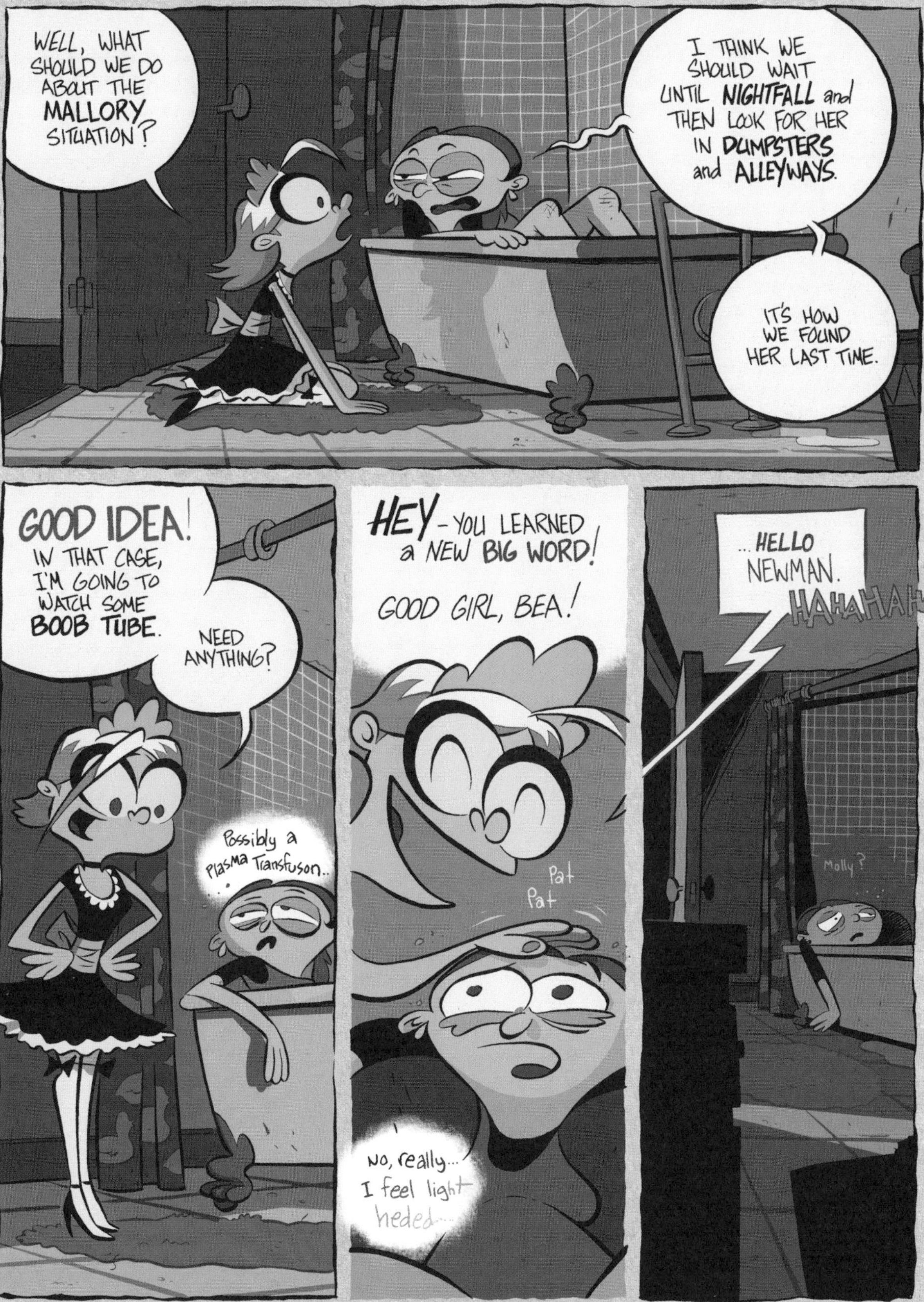
WELL, WHAT SHOULD WE DO ABOUT THE MALLORY SITUATION?
I THINK WE SHOULD WAIT UNTIL NIGHTFALL and THEN LOOK FOR HER IN DUMPSTERS and ALLEYWAYS.
IT'S HOW WE FOUND HER LAST TIME.
GOOD IDEA! IN THAT CASE, I'M GOING TO WATCH SOME BOOB TUBE.
NEED ANYTHING?
Possibly a Plasma Transfuson...
HEY - YOU LEARNED a NEW BIG WORD!
GOOD GIRL, BEA!
Pat Pat
No, really... I feel light heded....
...HELLO NEWMAN.
HAHAHAHA
Molly?

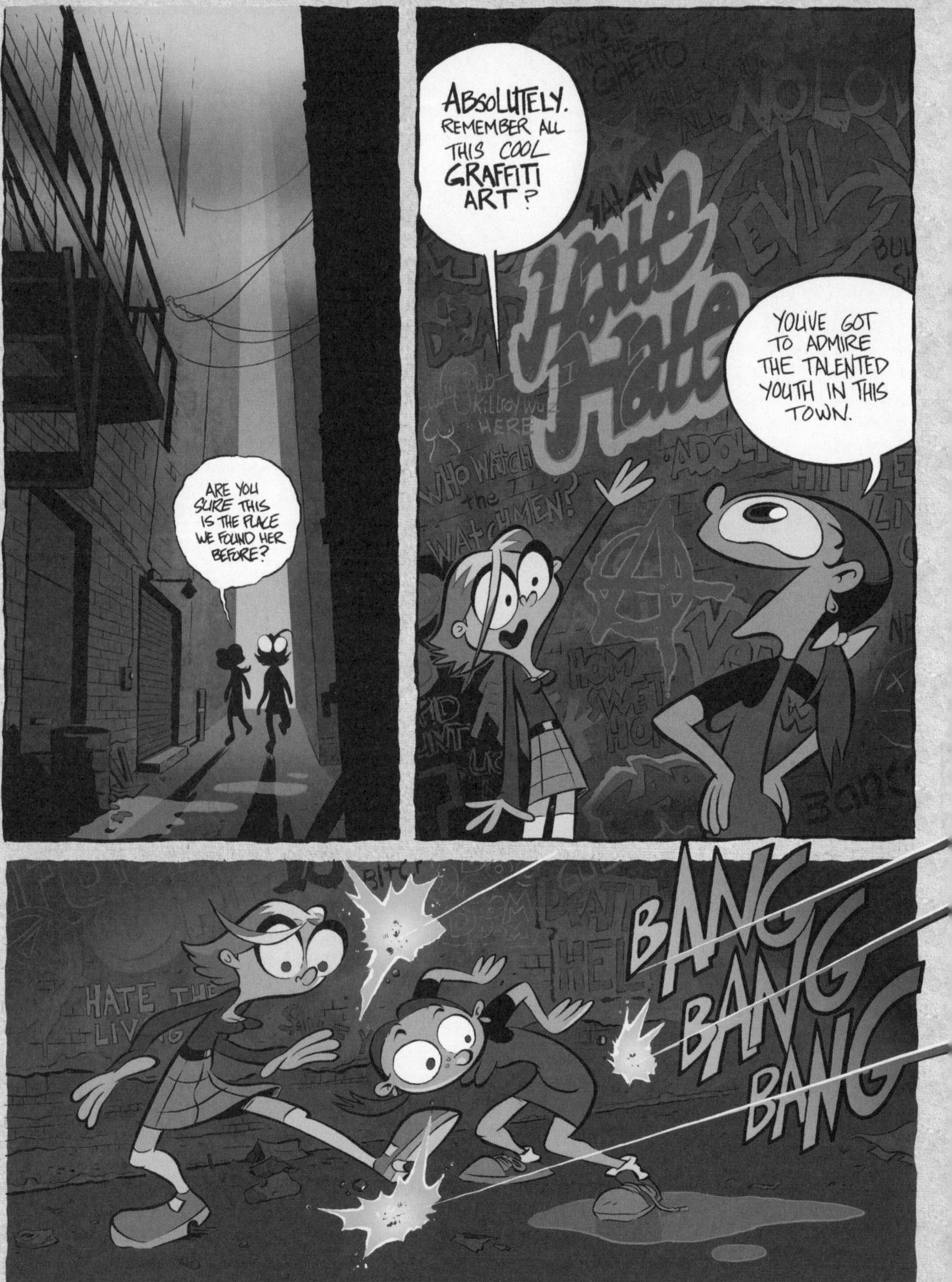
ARE YOU SURE THIS IS THE PLACE WE FOUND HER BEFORE?
ABSOLUTELY. REMEMBER ALL THIS COOL GRAFFITI ART?
YOU'VE GOT TO ADMIRE THE TALENTED YOUTH IN THIS TOWN.
BANG
BANG
BANG

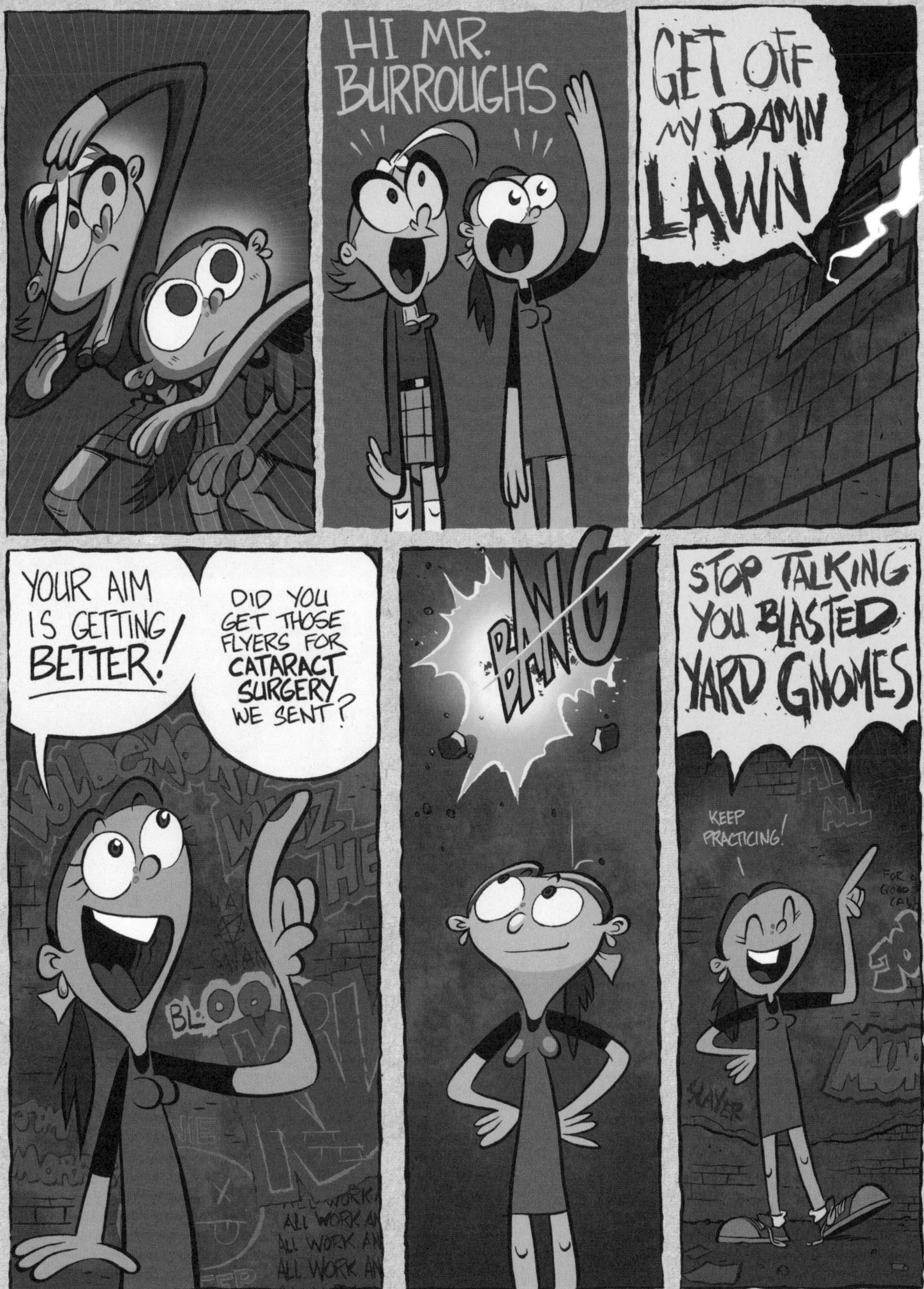
HI MR. BURROUGHS
GET OFF MY DAMN LAWN
YOUR AIM IS GETTING BETTER!
DID YOU GET THOSE FLYERS FOR CATARACT SURGERY WE SENT?
BANG
STOP TALKING YOU BLASTED YARD GNOMES
KEEP PRACTICING!

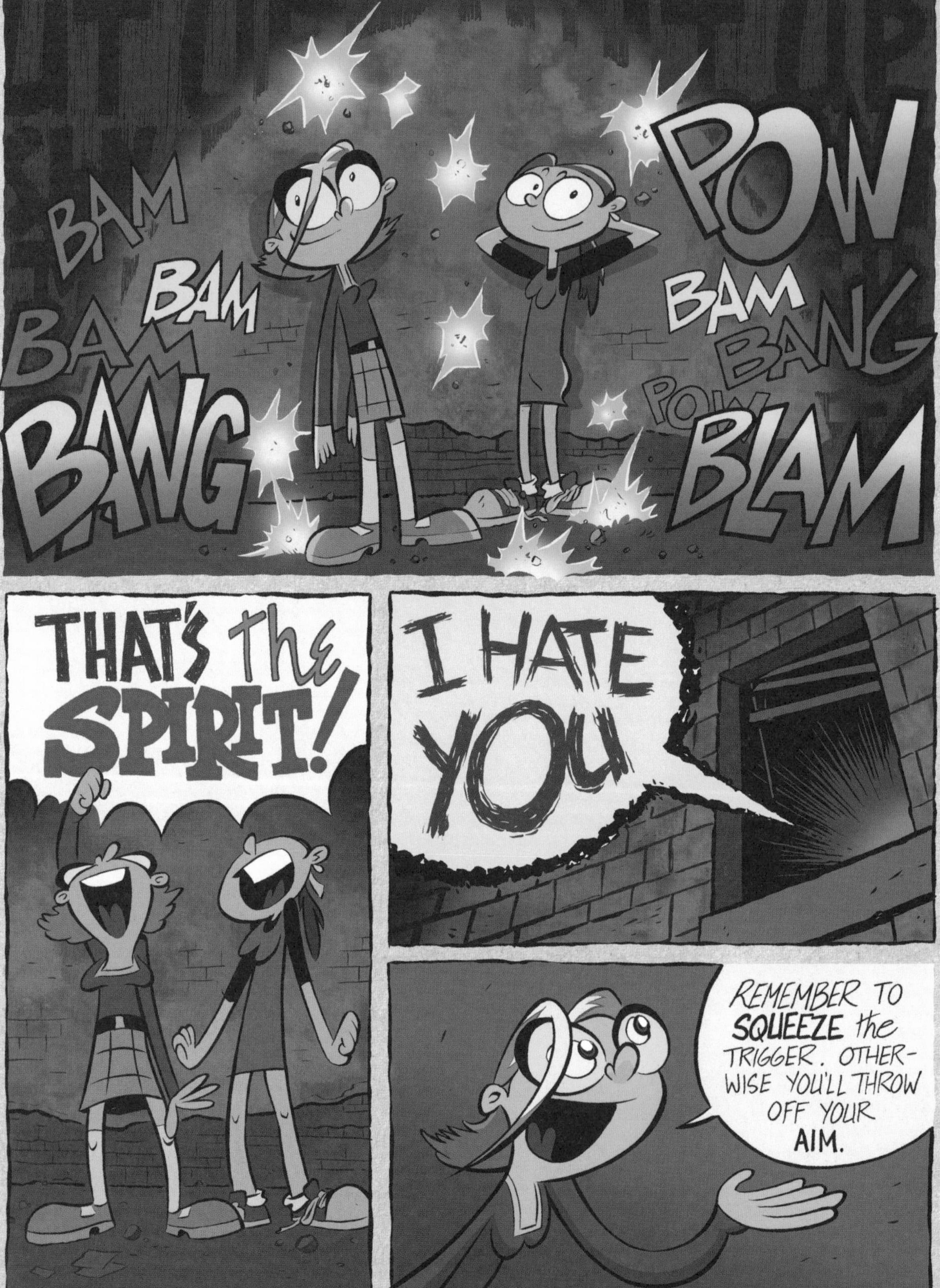
BAM
BAM
BAM
BANG
POW
BAM
BANG
POW
BLAM
THAT'S the SPIRIT!
I HATE YOU
REMEMBER TO SQUEEZE the TRIGGER. OTHER- WISE YOU'LL THROW OFF YOUR AIM.

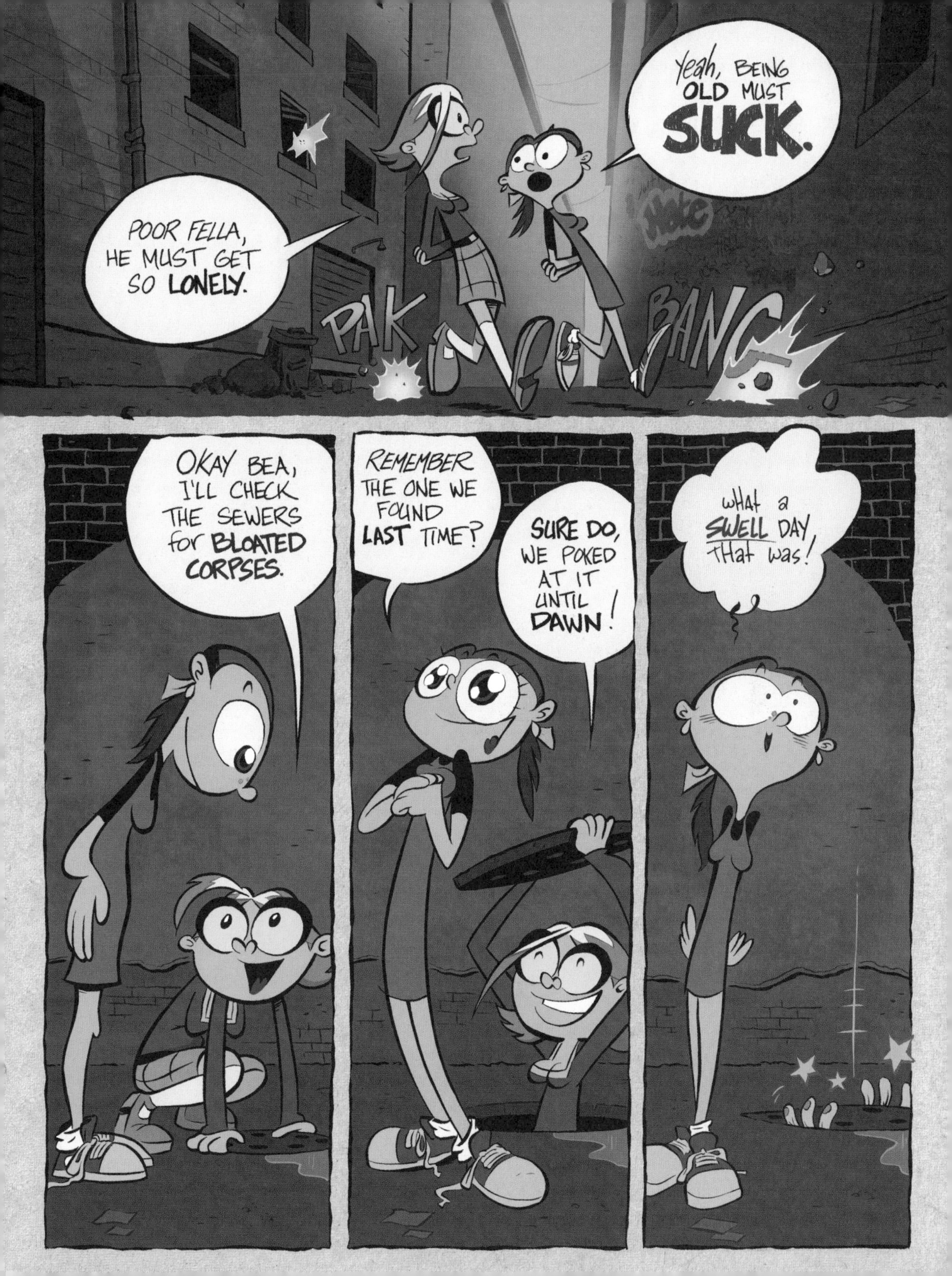
POOR FELLA, HE MUST GET SO LONELY.
Yeah, BEING OLD MUST SUCK.
PAK
BANG
OKAY BEA, I'LL CHECK THE SEWERS for BLOATED CORPSES.
REMEMBER THE ONE WE FOUND LAST TIME?
SURE DO, WE POKED AT IT UNTIL DAWN!
wHat a SWELL DAY That was!

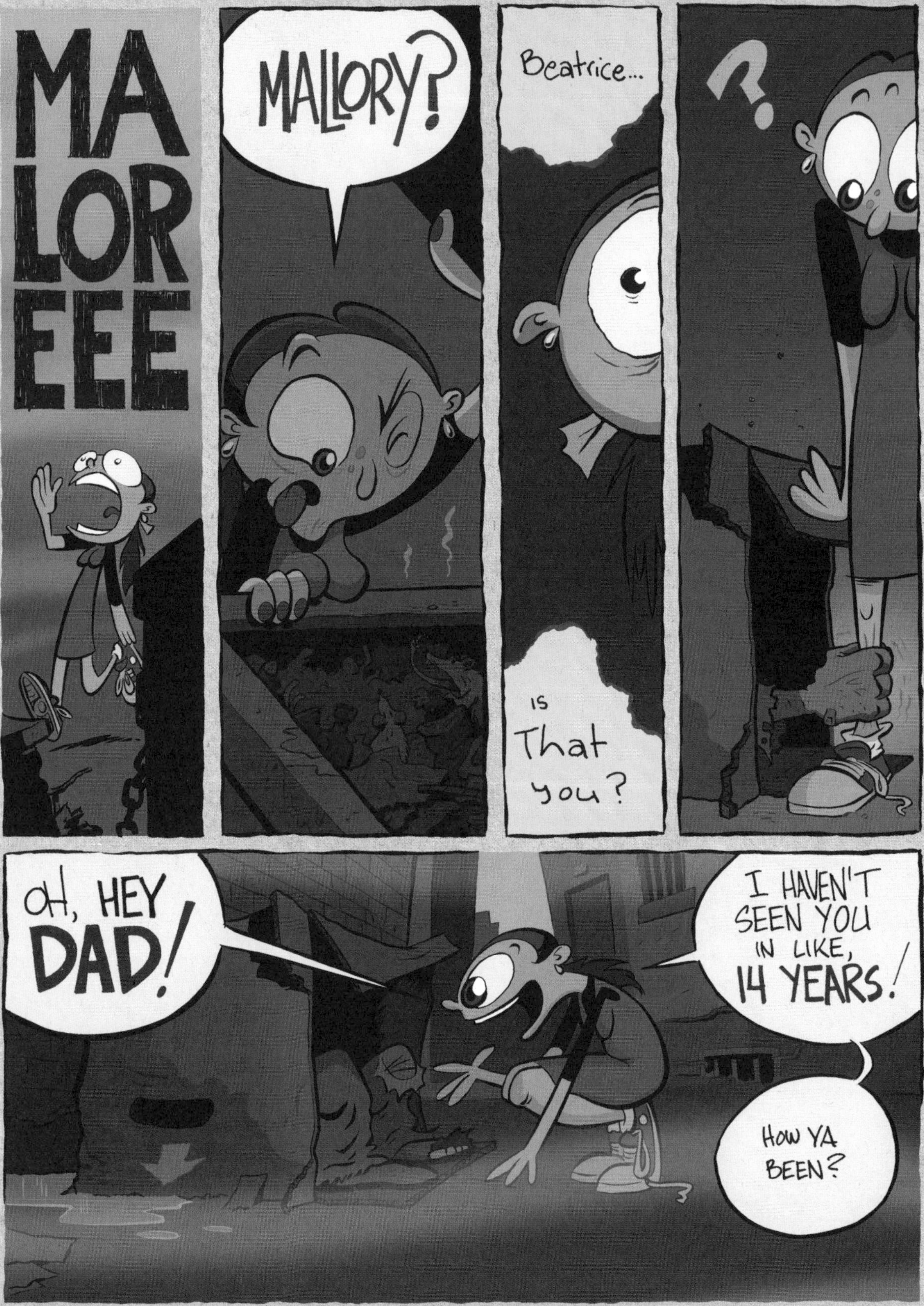

MALOREEE
MALLORY?
Beatrice...
?
IS That you?
OH, HEY DAD!
I HAVEN'T SEEN YOU IN LIKE, 14 YEARS!
HOW YA BEEN?

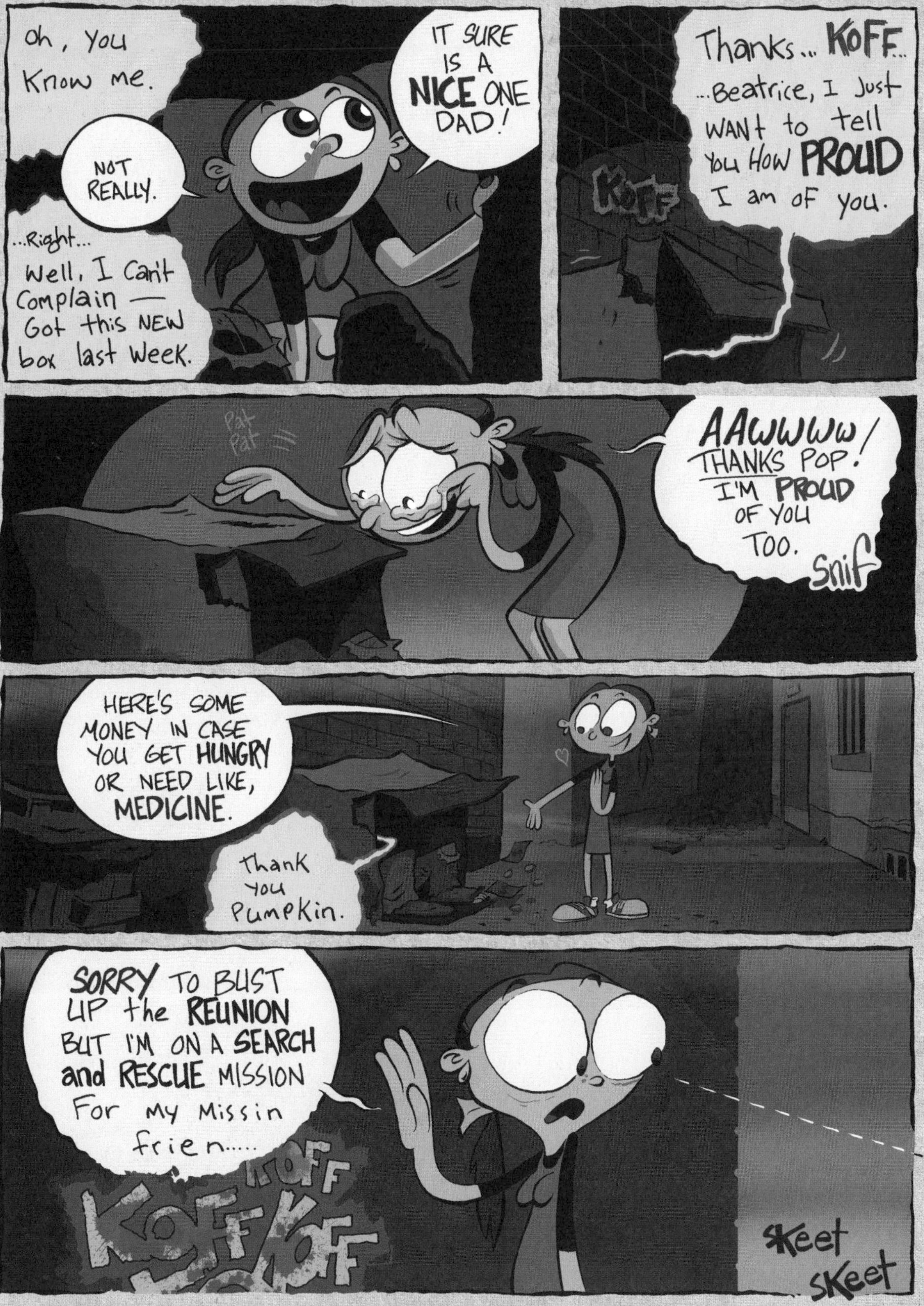
Oh, You Know me.
IT SURE IS A NICE ONE DAD!
NOT REALLY.
...Right... Well, I Can't Complain — Got this NEW box last Week.
Thanks... KOFF... ...Beatrice, I Just WANT to tell You HOW PROUD I am of you.
KOFF
Pat Pat
AAWWWW! THANKS POP! I'M PROUD OF YOU TOO.
Snif
HERE'S SOME MONEY IN CASE YOU GET HUNGRY OR NEED LIKE, MEDICINE.
Thank You Pumpkin.
SORRY TO BUST UP the REUNION BUT I'M ON A SEARCH and RESCUE MISSION For My Missin frien.....
KOFF KOFF KOFF
SKeet SKeet

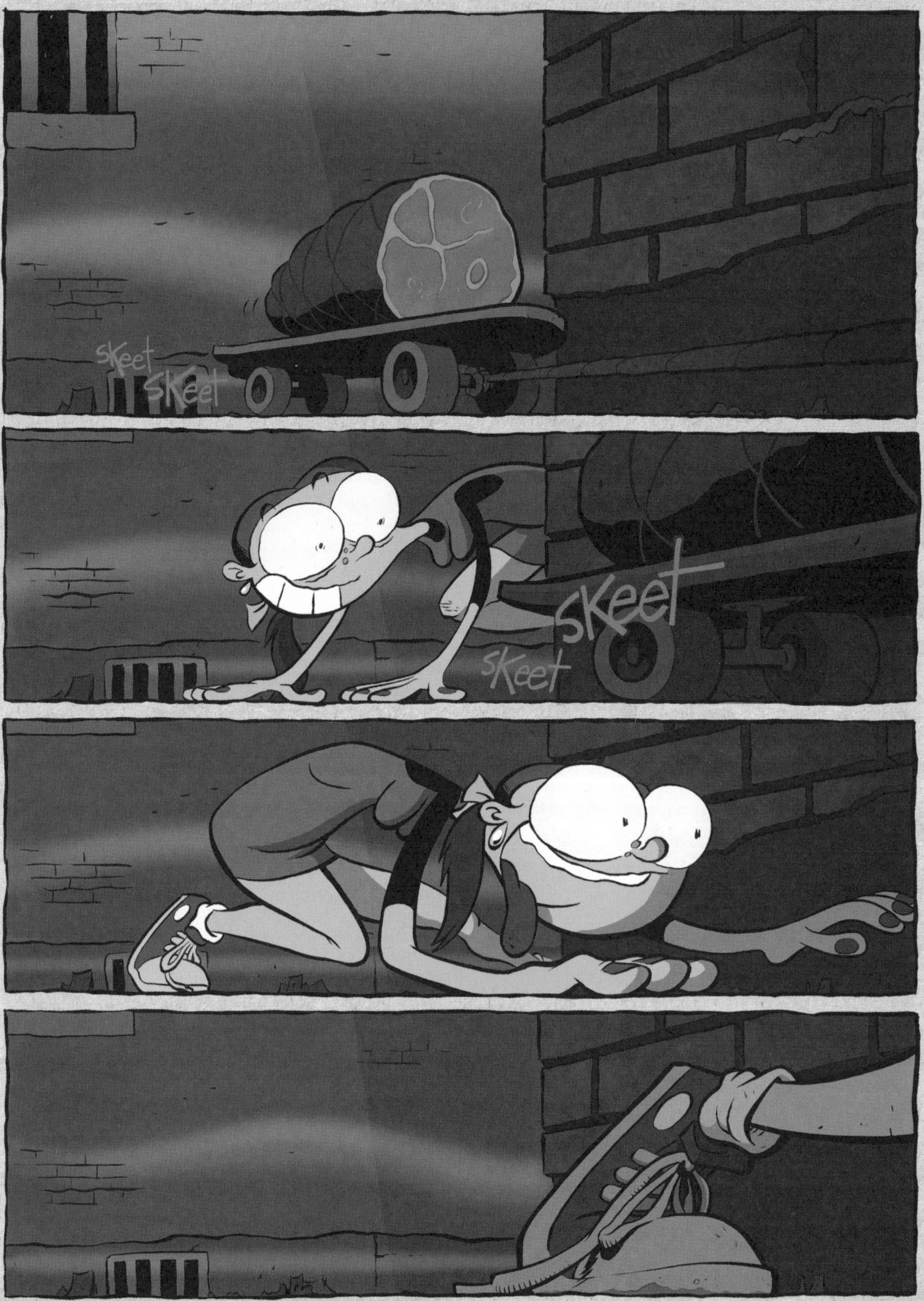
sKeet
sKeet
sKeet
sKeet

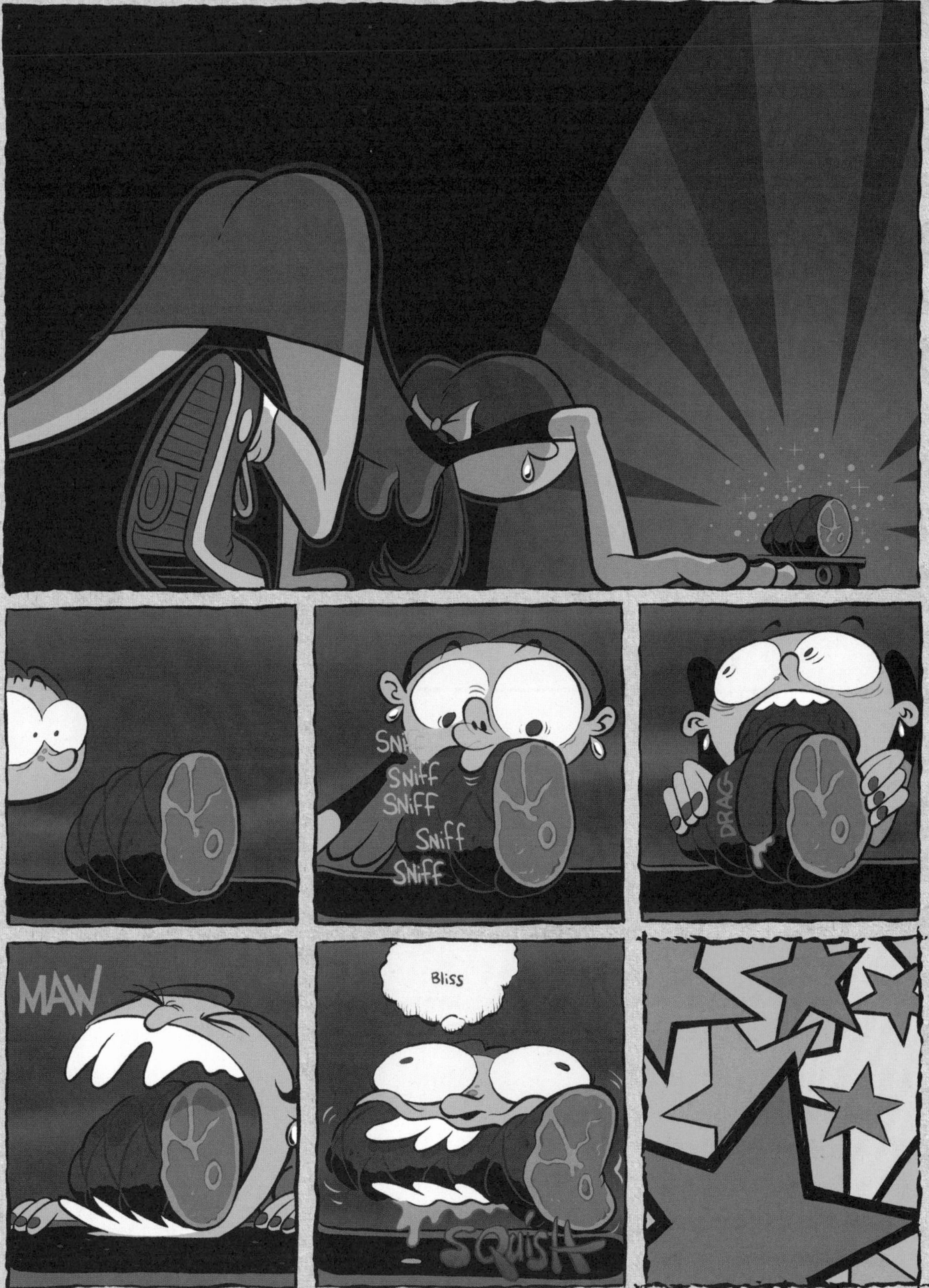
SNIFF
SNIFF
SNIFF
SNIFF
SNIFF
DRAG
MAW
Bliss
SQUISH

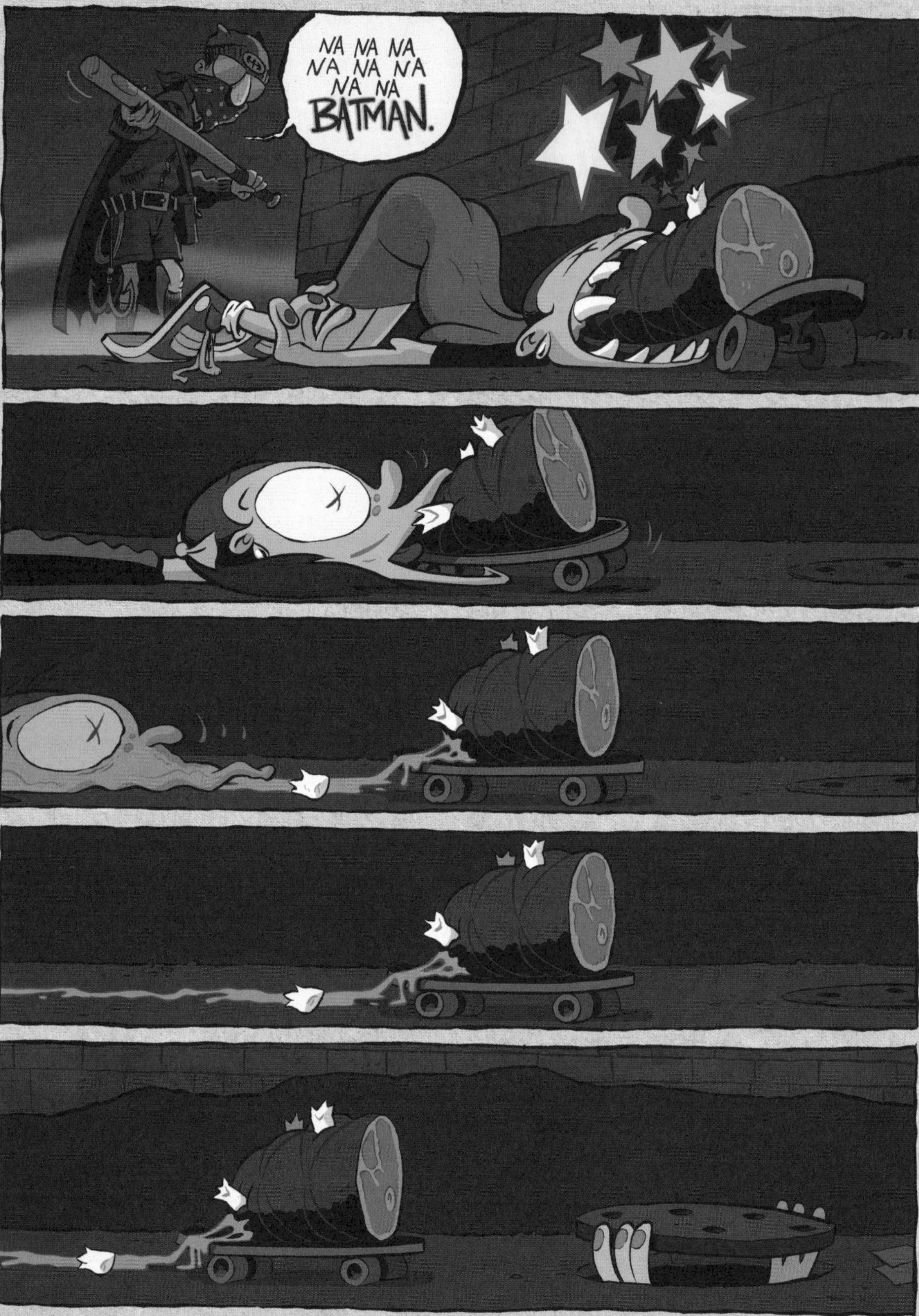
NA NA NA
NA NA NA
NA NA
BATMAN.

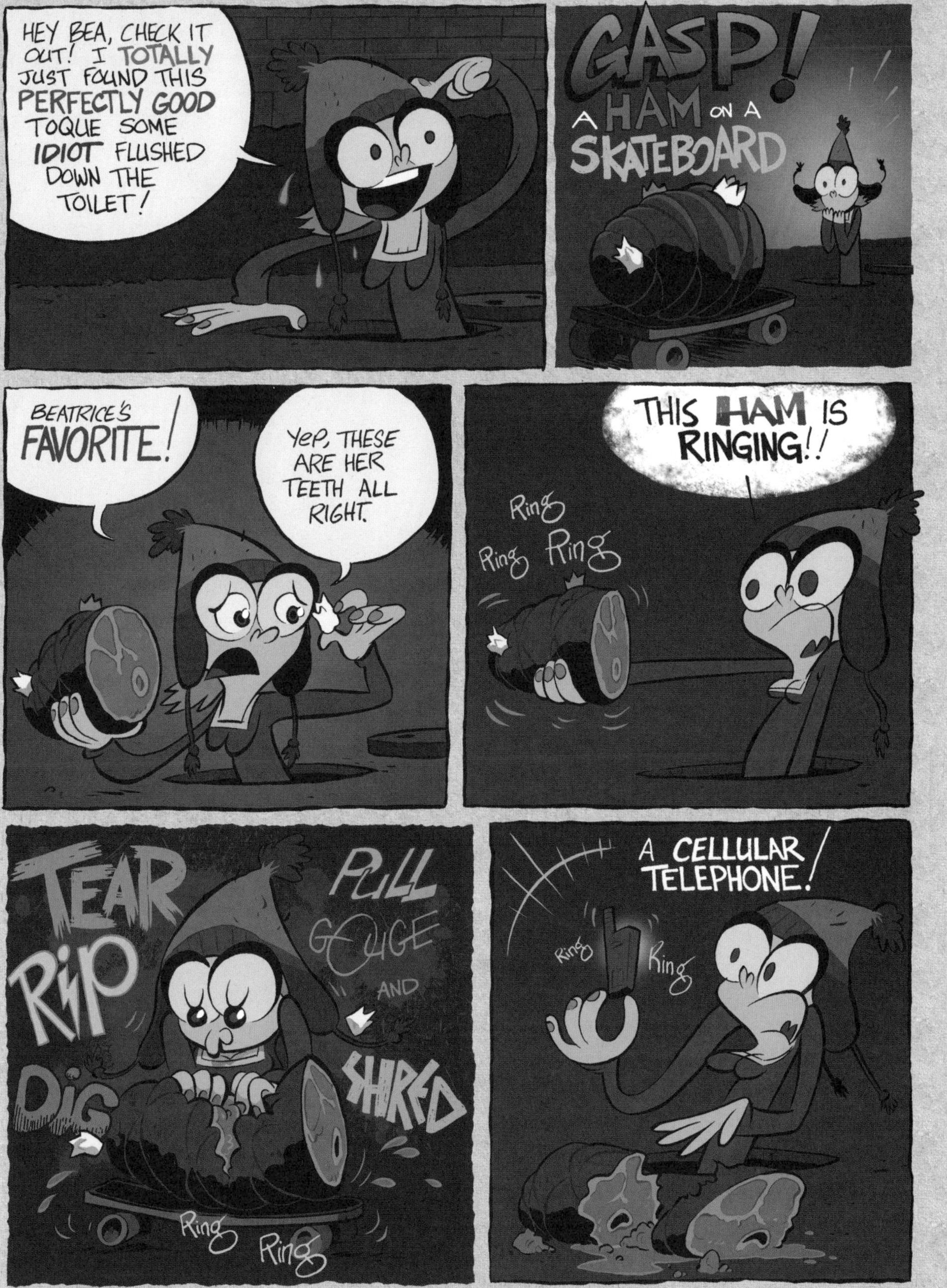

HEY BEA, CHECK IT OUT! I TOTALLY JUST FOUND THIS PERFECTLY GOOD TOQUE SOME IDIOT FLUSHED DOWN THE TOILET!
GASP!
A HAM ON A SKATEBOARD
BEATRICE'S FAVORITE!
YEP, THESE ARE HER TEETH ALL RIGHT.
THIS HAM IS RINGING!!
Ring Ring Ring
TEAR
RIP
DIG
PULL
GOUGE
AND
SHRED
Ring Ring
A CELLULAR TELEPHONE!
Ring Ring

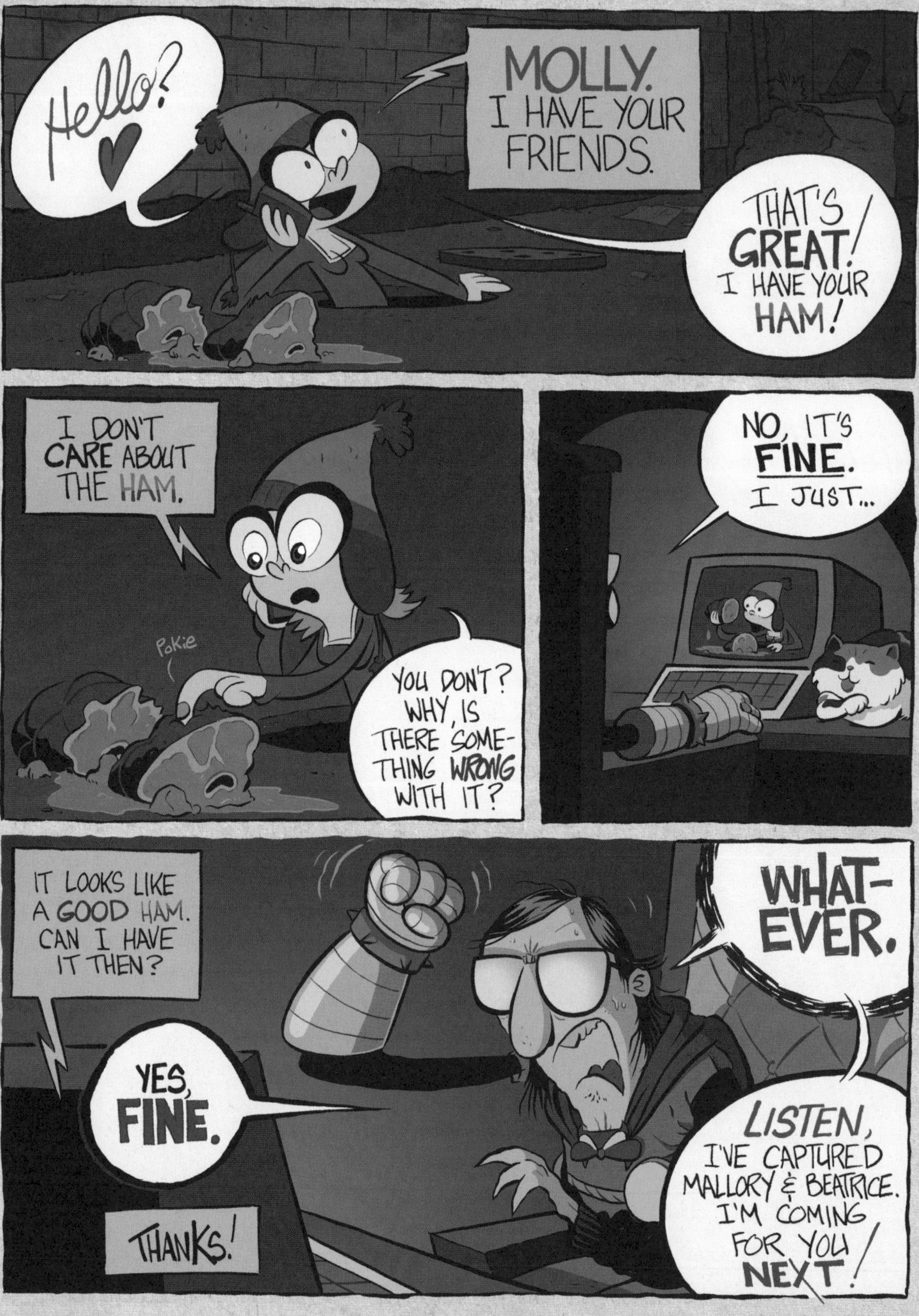
Hello?
MOLLY. I HAVE YOUR FRIENDS.
THAT'S GREAT! I HAVE YOUR HAM!
I DON'T CARE ABOUT THE HAM.
Pokie
YOU DON'T? WHY, IS THERE SOME-THING WRONG WITH IT?
NO, IT'S FINE. I JUST...
IT LOOKS LIKE A GOOD HAM. CAN I HAVE IT THEN?
WHAT-EVER.
YES, FINE.
LISTEN, I'VE CAPTURED MALLORY & BEATRICE. I'M COMING FOR YOU NEXT!
THANKS!

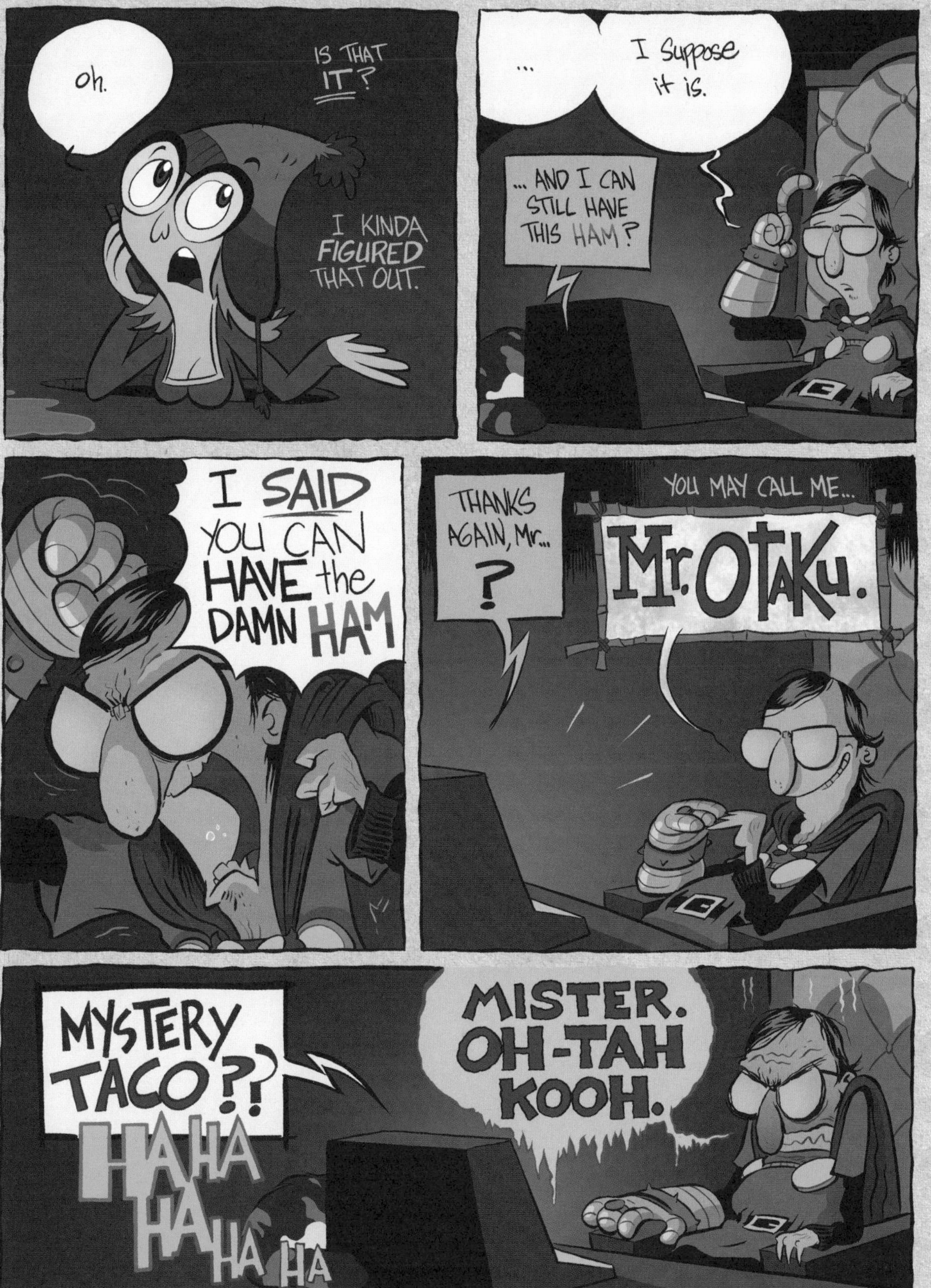
oh.
IS THAT IT?
I KINDA FIGURED THAT OUT.
... I suppose it is.
... AND I CAN STILL HAVE THIS HAM?
I SAID YOU CAN HAVE the DAMN HAM
THANKS AGAIN, Mr... ?
YOU MAY CALL ME...
Mr. OTAKU.
MYSTERY TACO?!
HAHA HA HA HA HA
MISTER. OH-TAH KOOH.

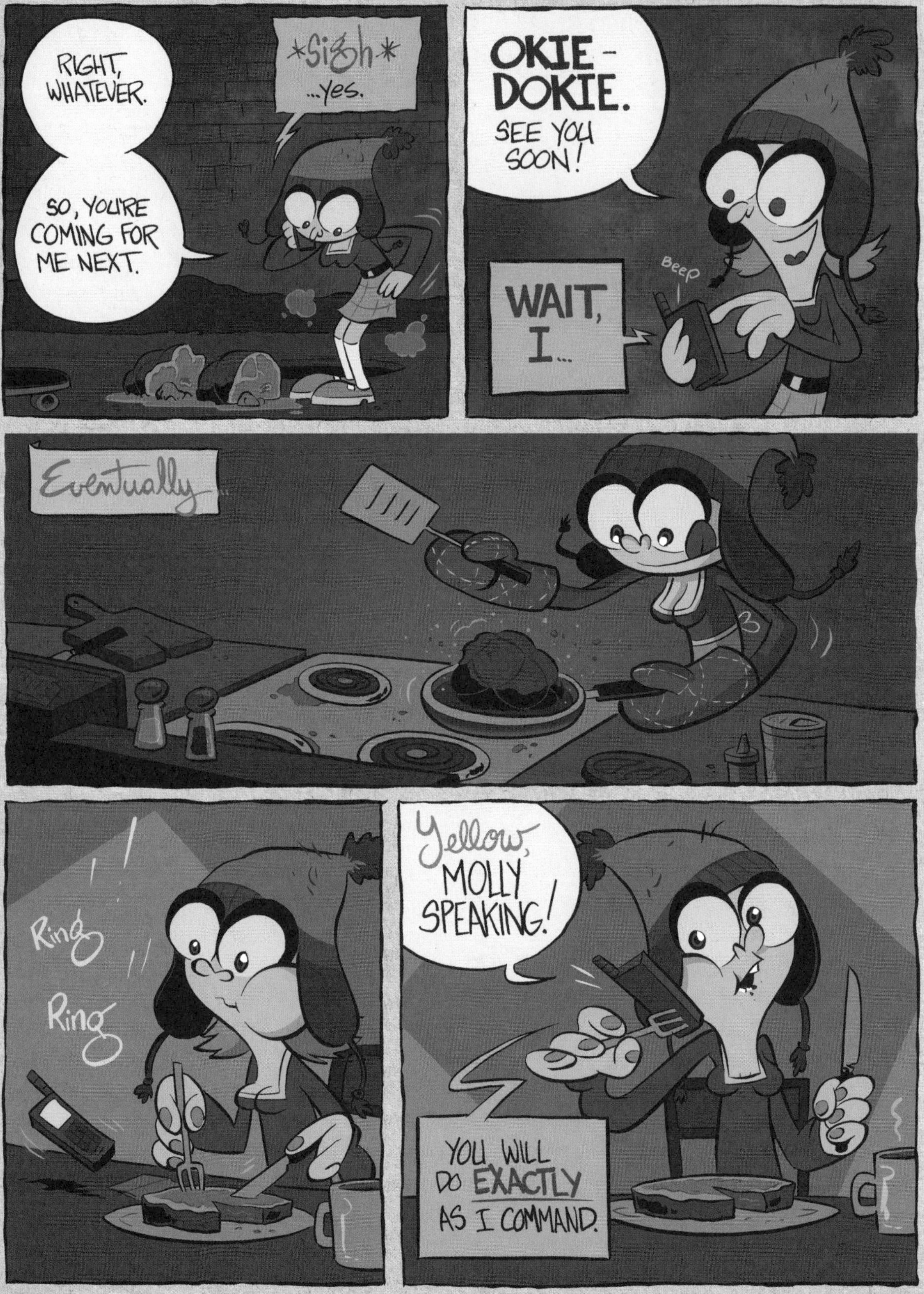
RIGHT, WHATEVER.
Sigh ...yes.
SO, YOU'RE COMING FOR ME NEXT.
OKIE-DOKIE. SEE YOU SOON!
Beep
WAIT, I...
Eventually...
Ring
Ring
Yellow, MOLLY SPEAKING!
YOU WILL DO EXACTLY AS I COMMAND.

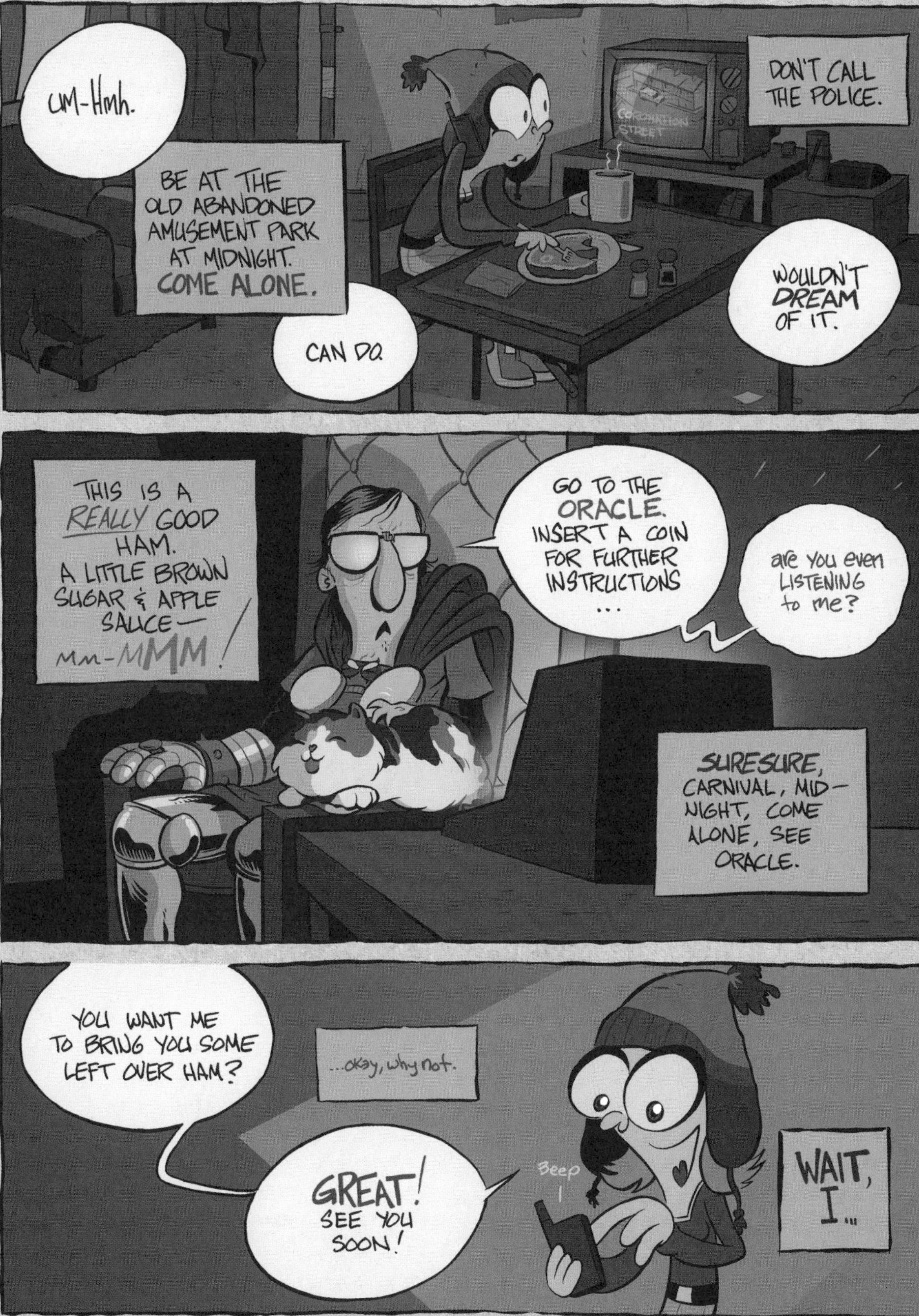
UM-Hmh.
BE AT THE OLD ABANDONED AMUSEMENT PARK AT MIDNIGHT. COME ALONE.
CAN DO.
DON'T CALL THE POLICE.
WOULDN'T DREAM OF IT.
CORONATION STREET
THIS IS A REALLY GOOD HAM. A LITTLE BROWN SUGAR & APPLE SAUCE— Mm-MMM!
GO TO THE ORACLE. INSERT A COIN FOR FURTHER INSTRUCTIONS...
are you even LISTENING to me?
SURESURE, CARNIVAL, MID-NIGHT, COME ALONE, SEE ORACLE.
YOU WANT ME TO BRING YOU SOME LEFT OVER HAM?
...okay, why not.
GREAT! SEE YOU SOON!
Beep!
WAIT, I...

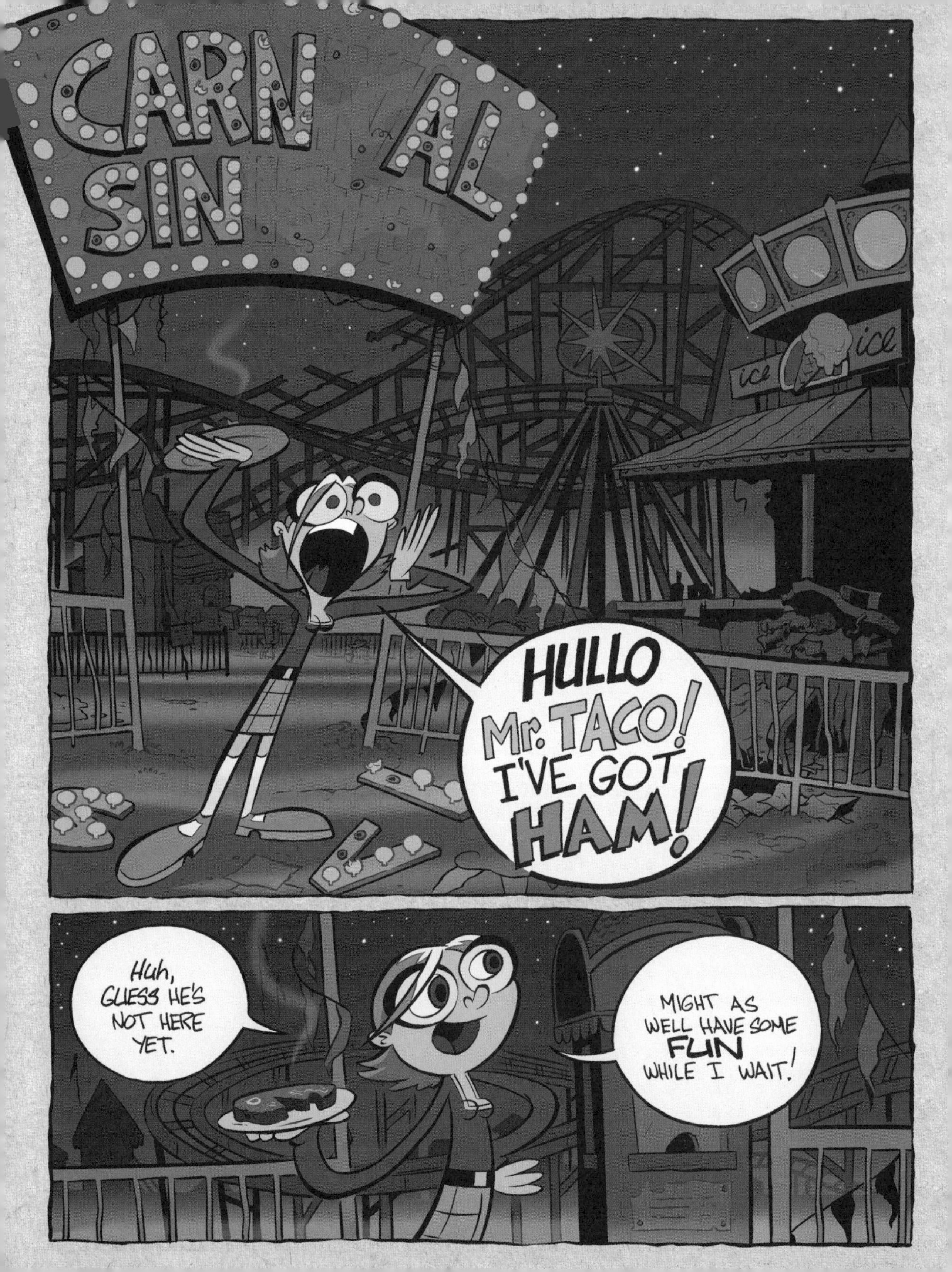
CARN AL SIN
ice
ice
HULLO Mr. TACO! I'VE GOT HAM!
Huh, GUESS HE'S NOT HERE YET.
MIGHT AS WELL HAVE SOME FUN WHILE I WAIT!

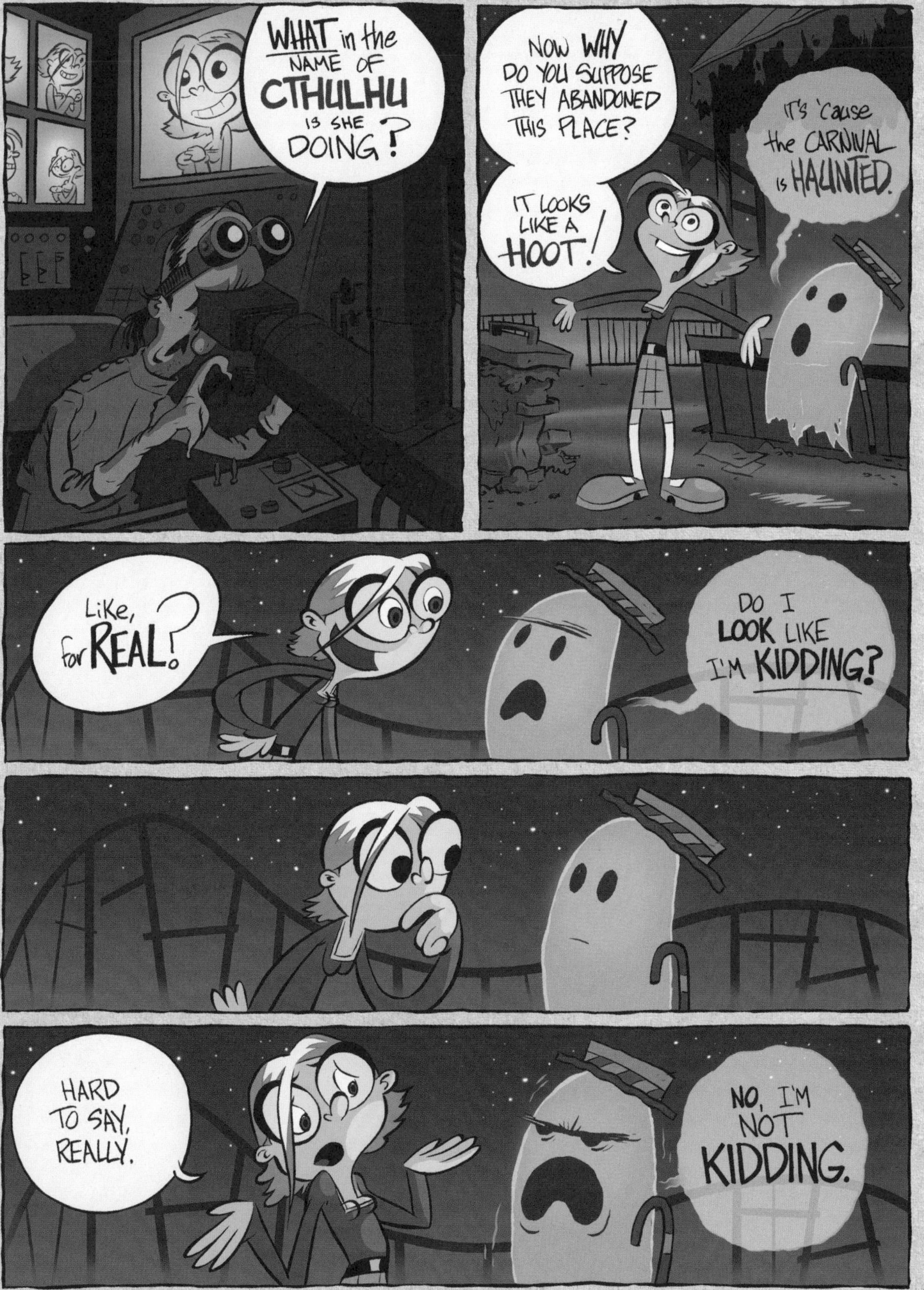

WHAT in the NAME OF CTHULHU IS SHE DOING?
NOW WHY DO YOU SUPPOSE THEY ABANDONED THIS PLACE?
IT LOOKS LIKE A HOOT!
IT'S 'CAUSE the CARNIVAL is HAUNTED.
Like, for REAL?
DO I LOOK LIKE I'M KIDDING?
HARD TO SAY, REALLY.
NO, I'M NOT KIDDING.

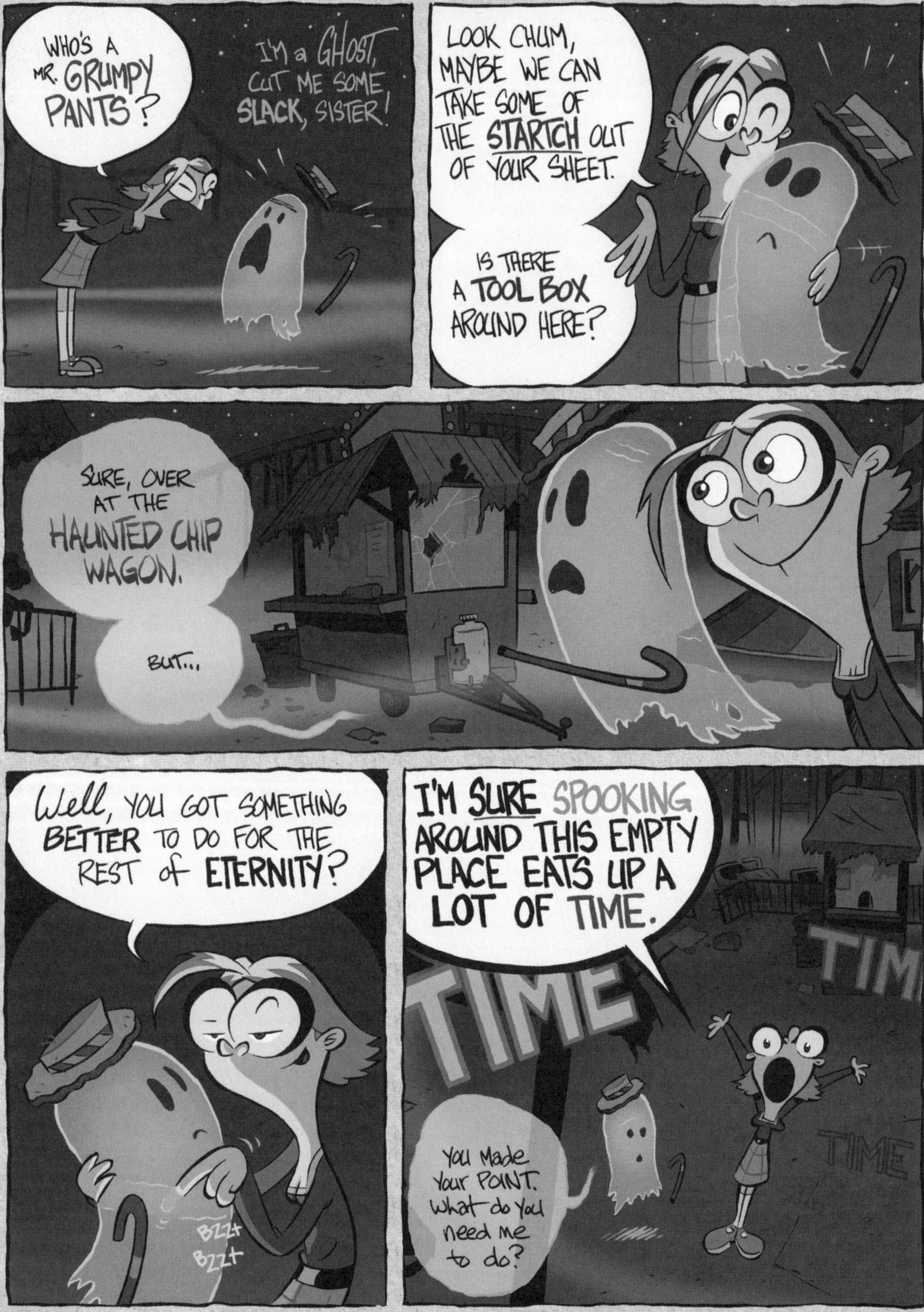

WHO'S A MR. GRUMPY PANTS?
I'M a GHOST, CUT ME SOME SLACK, SISTER!
LOOK CHUM, MAYBE WE CAN TAKE SOME OF THE STARTCH OUT OF YOUR SHEET.
IS THERE A TOOL BOX AROUND HERE?
SURE, OVER AT THE HAUNTED CHIP WAGON.
BUT...
Well, YOU GOT SOMETHING BETTER TO DO FOR THE REST of ETERNITY?
BZZT
BZZT
I'M SURE SPOOKING AROUND THIS EMPTY PLACE EATS UP A LOT OF TIME.
TIME
TIME
TIME
You Made Your POINT. What do You need me to do?

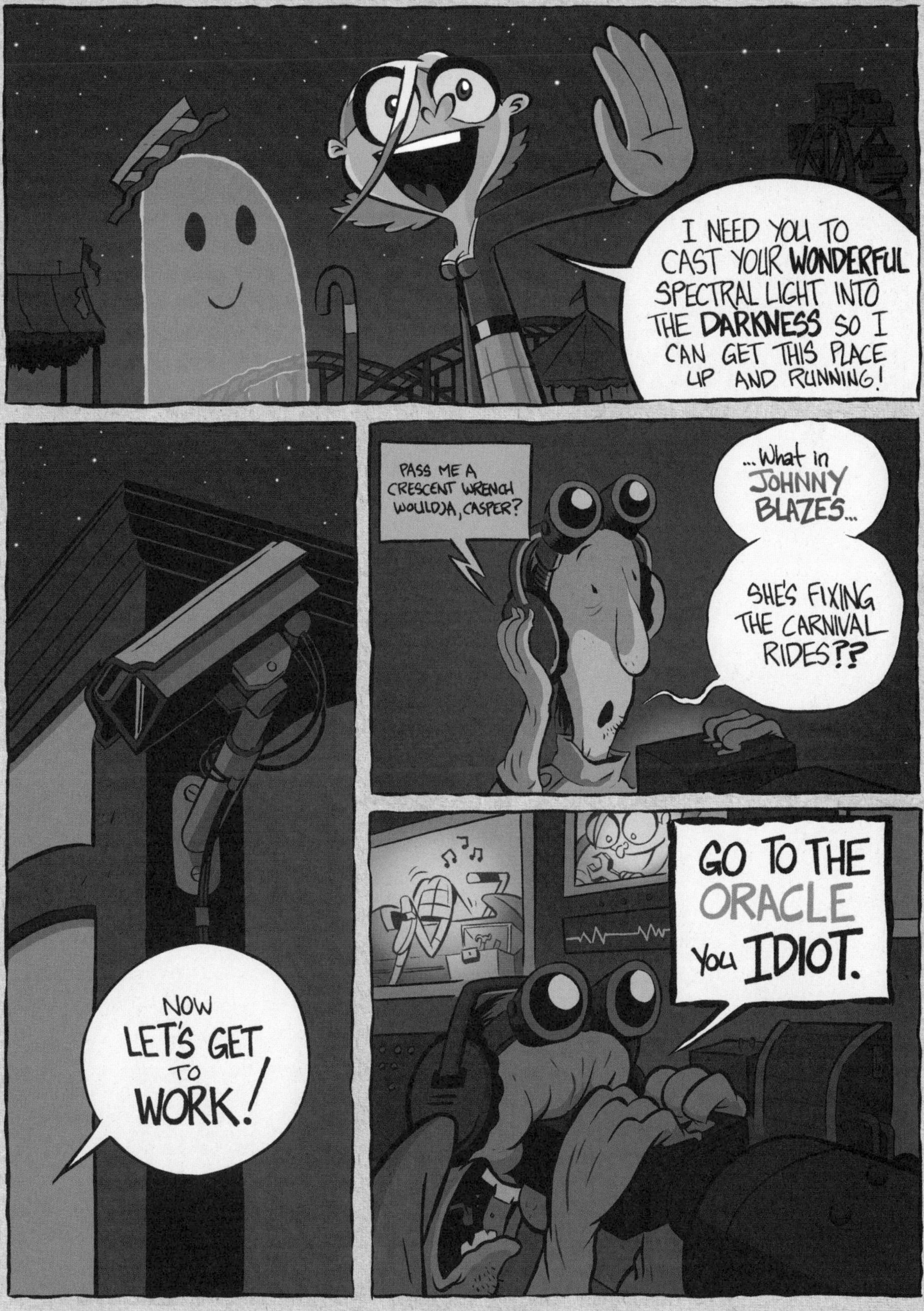
I NEED YOU TO CAST YOUR WONDERFUL SPECTRAL LIGHT INTO THE DARKNESS SO I CAN GET THIS PLACE UP AND RUNNING!
NOW LET'S GET TO WORK!
PASS ME A CRESCENT WRENCH WOULDJA, CASPER?
...What in JOHNNY BLAZES...
SHE'S FIXING THE CARNIVAL RIDES??
GO TO THE ORACLE You IDIOT.

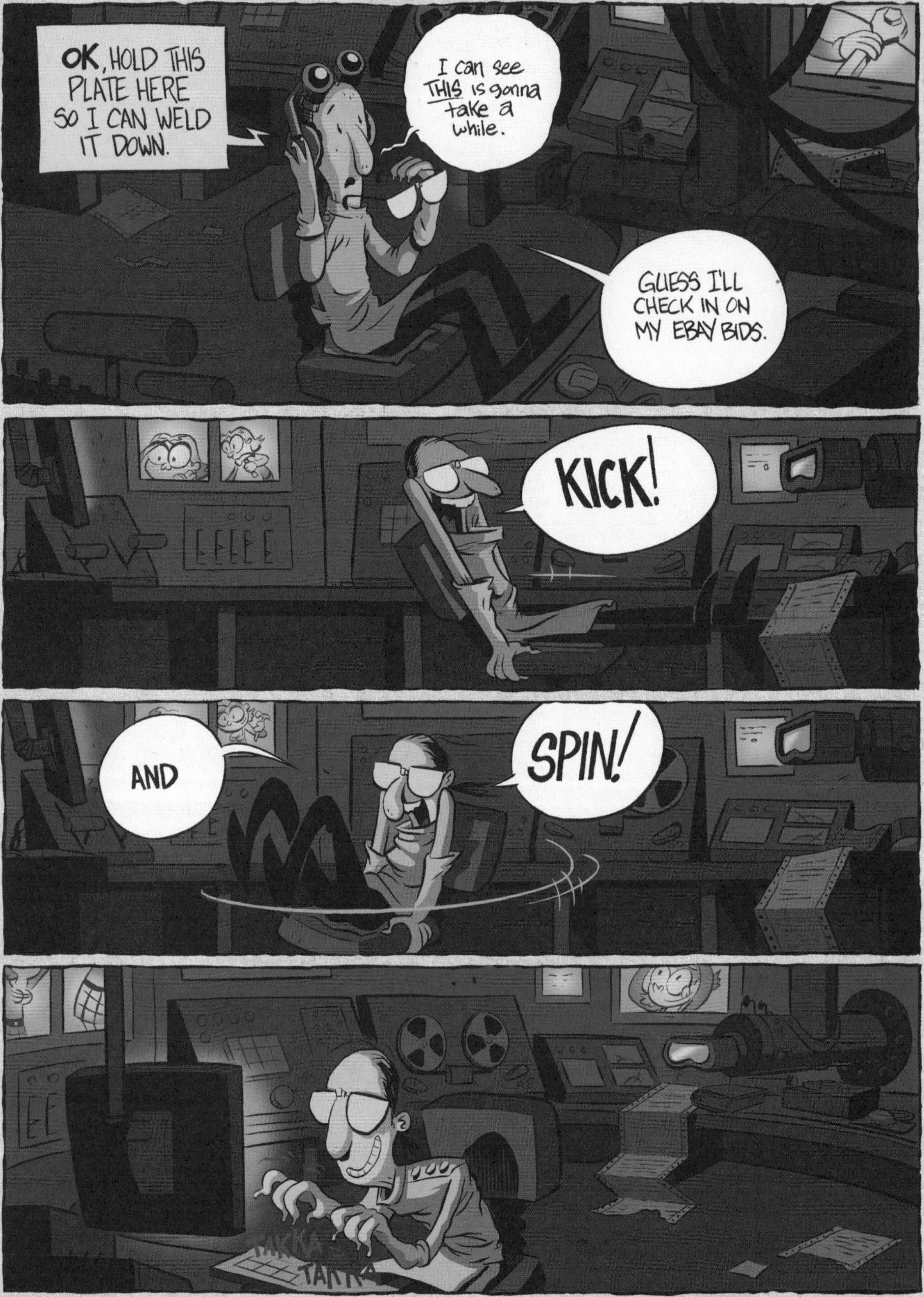
OK, HOLD THIS PLATE HERE SO I CAN WELD IT DOWN.
I can see THIS is gonna take a while.
GUESS I'LL CHECK IN ON MY EBAY BIDS.
KICK!
AND
SPIN!
TAKKA TAKKA

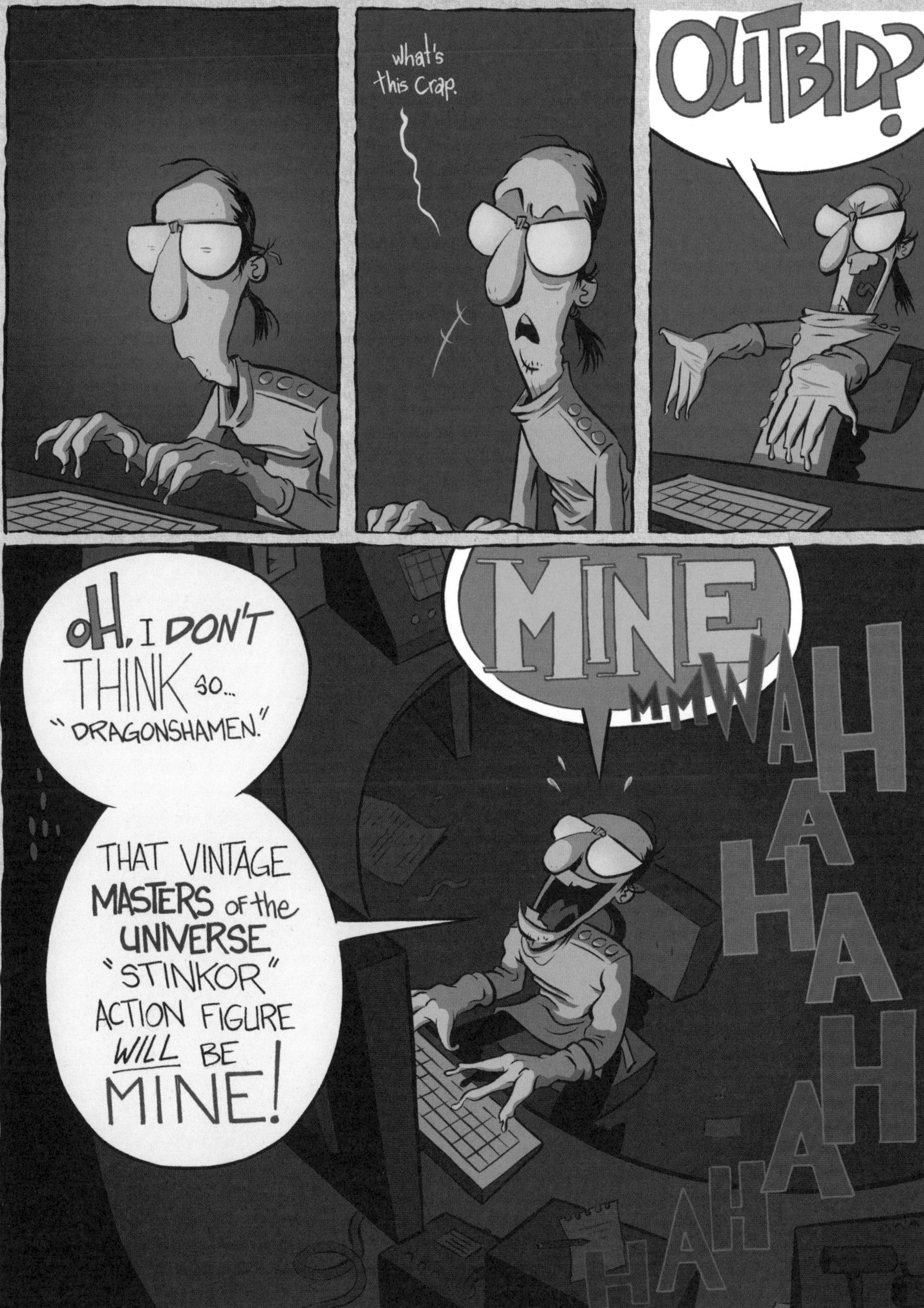

what's this Crap.
OUTBID?
oH, I DON'T THINK so... "DRAGONSHAMEN."
THAT VINTAGE MASTERS of the UNIVERSE "STINKOR" ACTION FIGURE WILL BE MINE!
MINE
MMWAHAHAHAHAHAHAHAHAHAHA

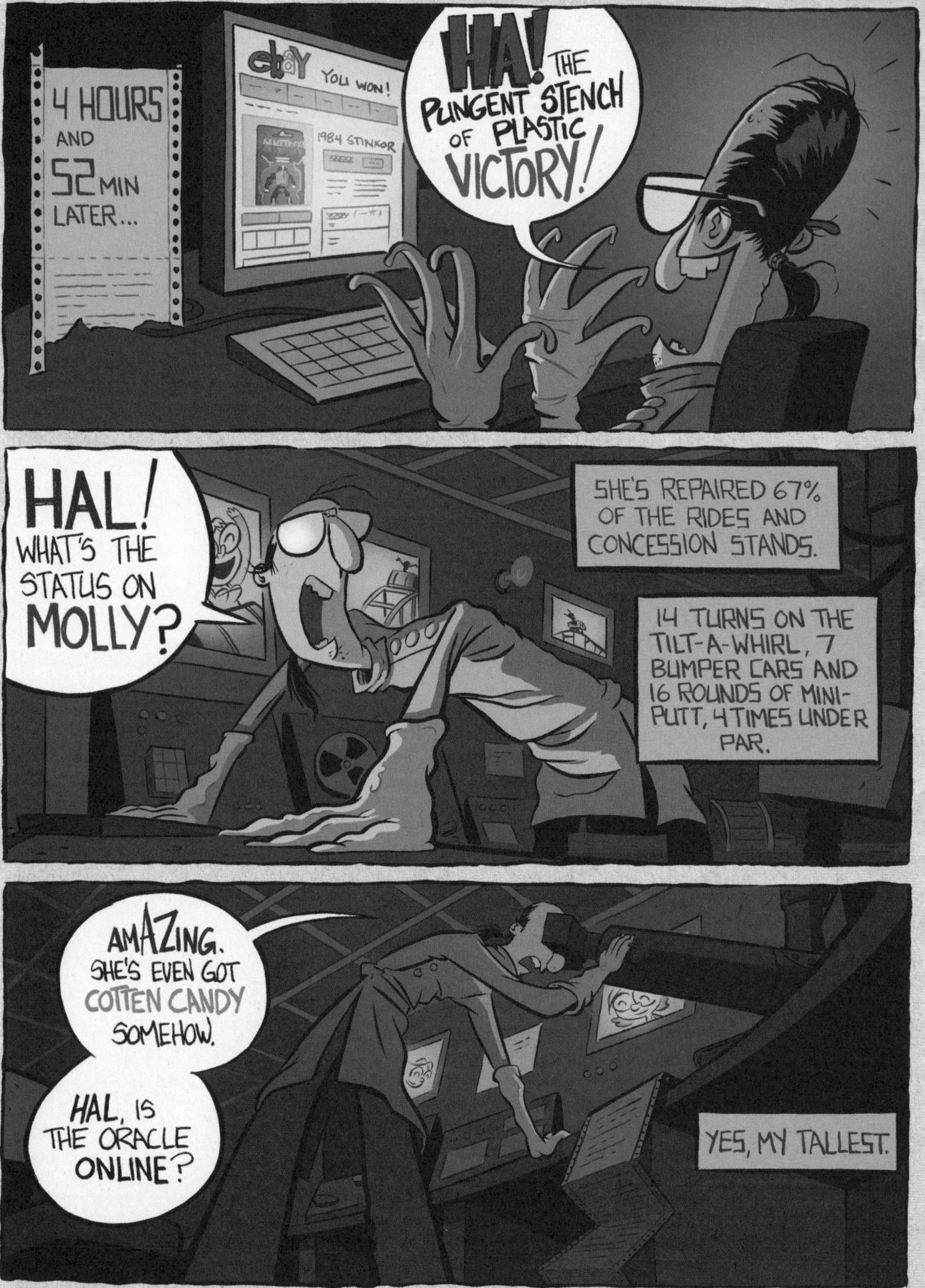
4 HOURS AND 52 MIN LATER...
eBay
YOU WON!
1984 STINKOR
HA! THE PUNGENT STENCH OF PLASTIC VICTORY!
HAL! WHAT'S THE STATUS ON MOLLY?
SHE'S REPAIRED 67% OF THE RIDES AND CONCESSION STANDS.
14 TURNS ON THE TILT-A-WHIRL, 7 BUMPER CARS AND 16 ROUNDS OF MINI-PUTT, 4 TIMES UNDER PAR.
AMAZING. SHE'S EVEN GOT COTTEN CANDY SOMEHOW.
HAL, IS THE ORACLE ONLINE?
YES, MY TALLEST.

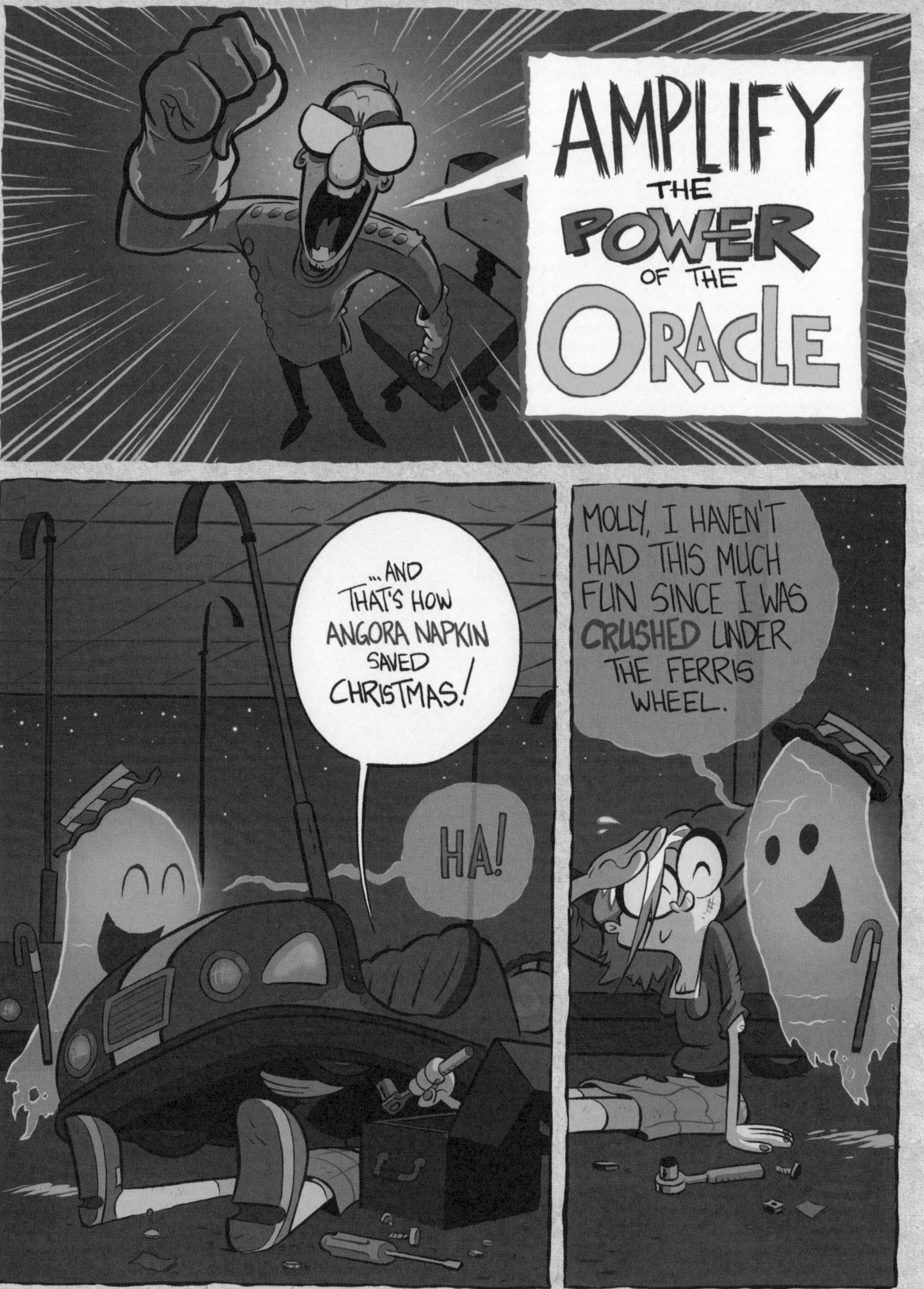
AMPLIFY THE POWER OF THE ORACLE
...AND THAT'S HOW ANGORA NAPKIN SAVED CHRISTMAS!
HA!
MOLLY, I HAVEN'T HAD THIS MUCH FUN SINCE I WAS CRUSHED UNDER THE FERRIS WHEEL.

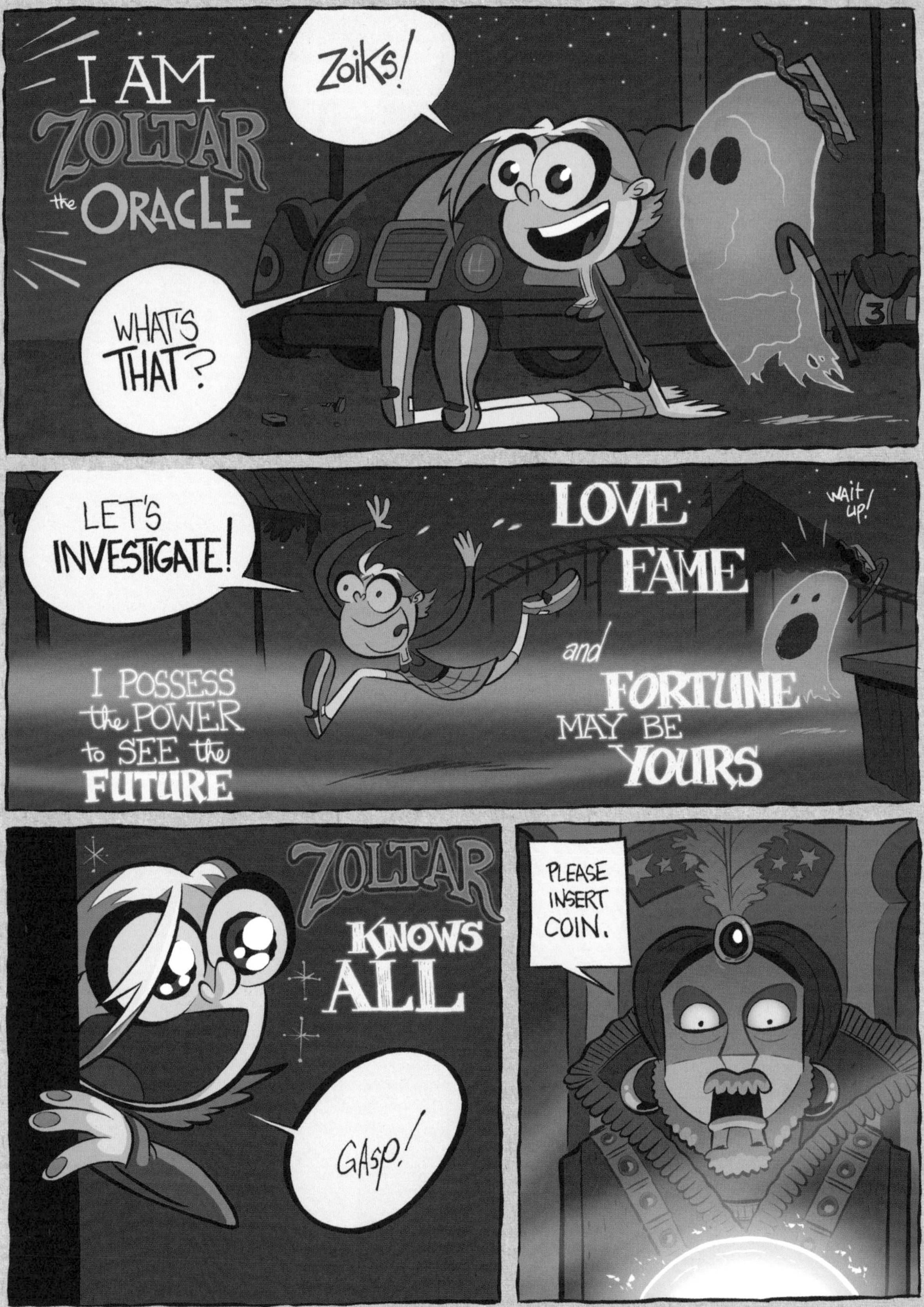
I AM ZOLTAR the ORACLE
ZOIKS!
WHAT'S THAT?
LET'S INVESTIGATE!
I POSSESS the POWER to SEE the FUTURE
LOVE FAME and FORTUNE MAY BE YOURS
WAIT UP!
ZOLTAR KNOWS ALL
GASP!
PLEASE INSERT COIN.

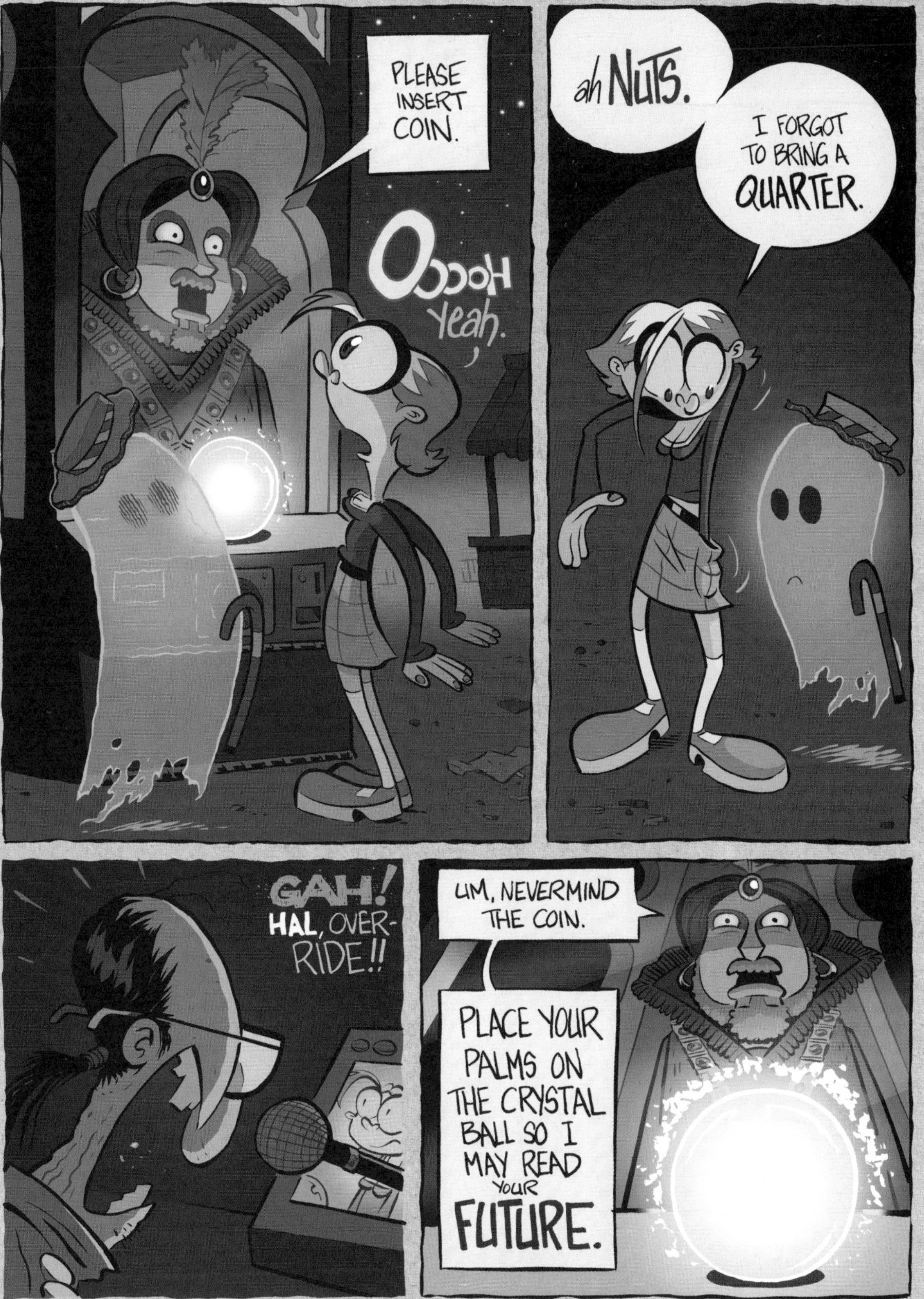
PLEASE INSERT COIN.
OOOOOH yeah.
ah NUTS.
I FORGOT TO BRING A QUARTER.
GAH! HAL, OVER-RIDE!!
UM, NEVERMIND THE COIN.
PLACE YOUR PALMS ON THE CRYSTAL BALL SO I MAY READ YOUR FUTURE.

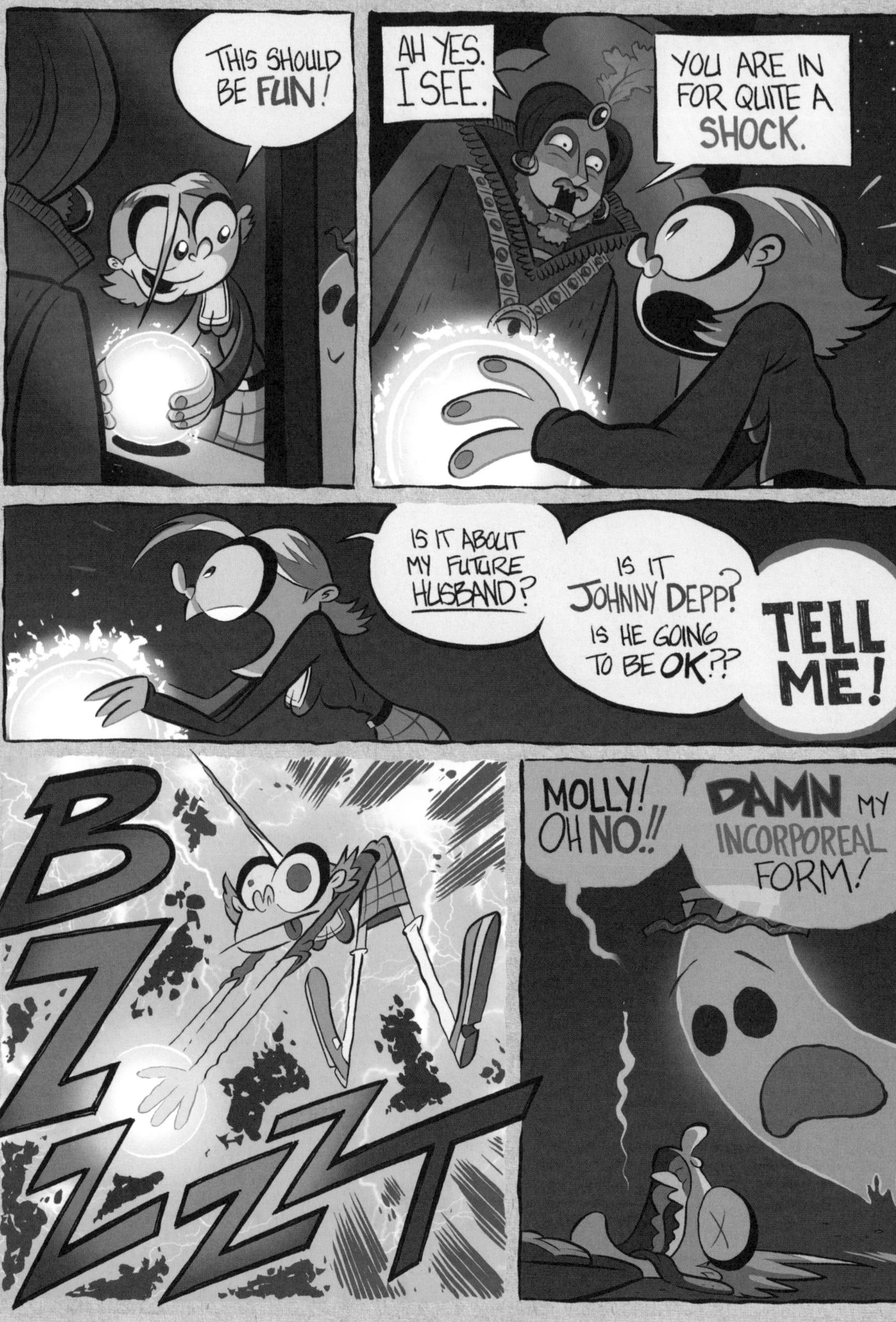
THIS SHOULD BE FUN!
AH YES. I SEE.
YOU ARE IN FOR QUITE A SHOCK.
IS IT ABOUT MY FUTURE HUSBAND?
IS IT JOHNNY DEPP? IS HE GOING TO BE OK??
TELL ME!
BZZZZT
MOLLY! OH NO.!!
DAMN MY INCORPOREAL FORM!

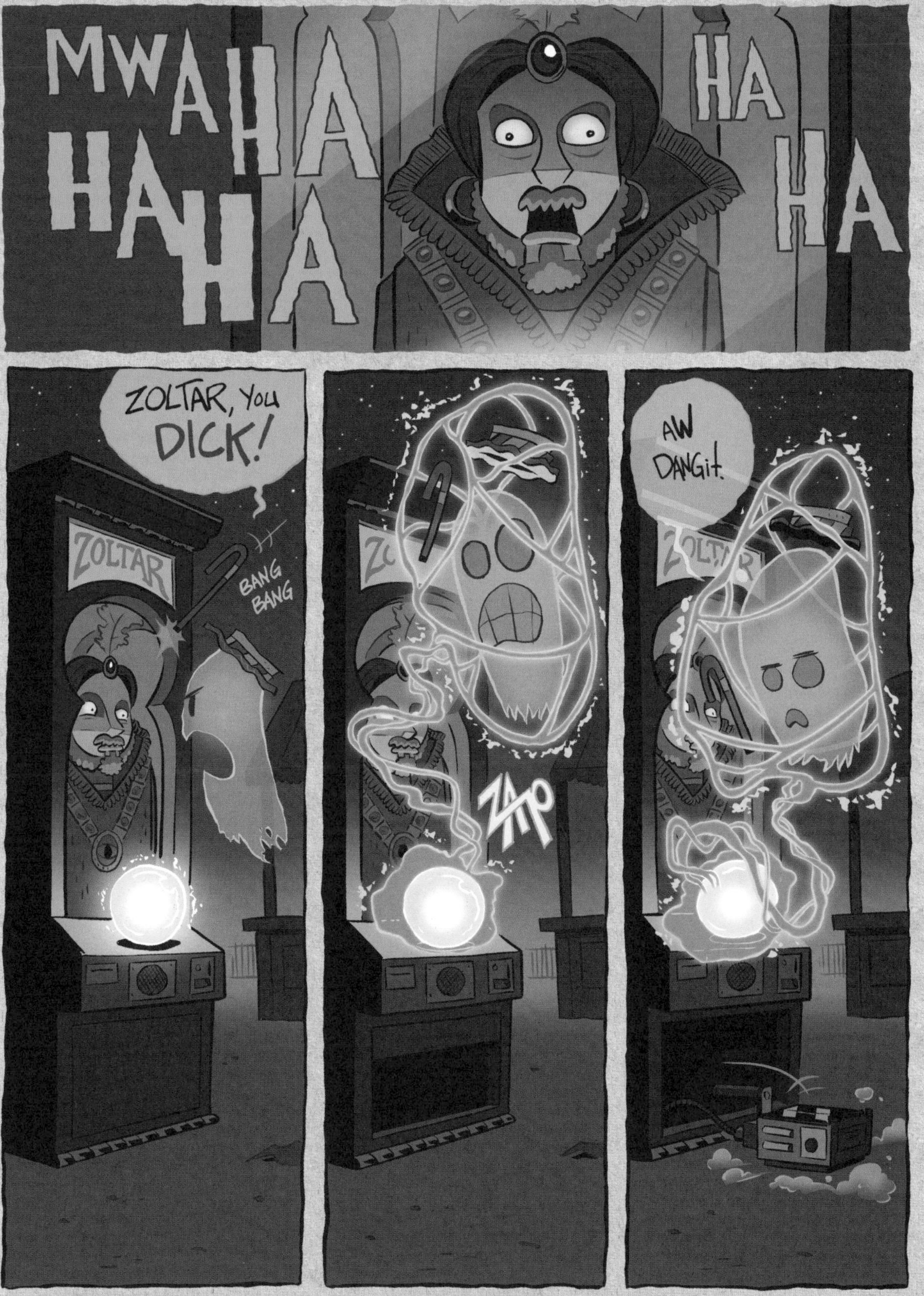
MWAHAHAHAHA
HAHAHA
ZOLTAR, YOU DICK!
ZOLTAR
BANG BANG
ZAP
AW DANGIT.

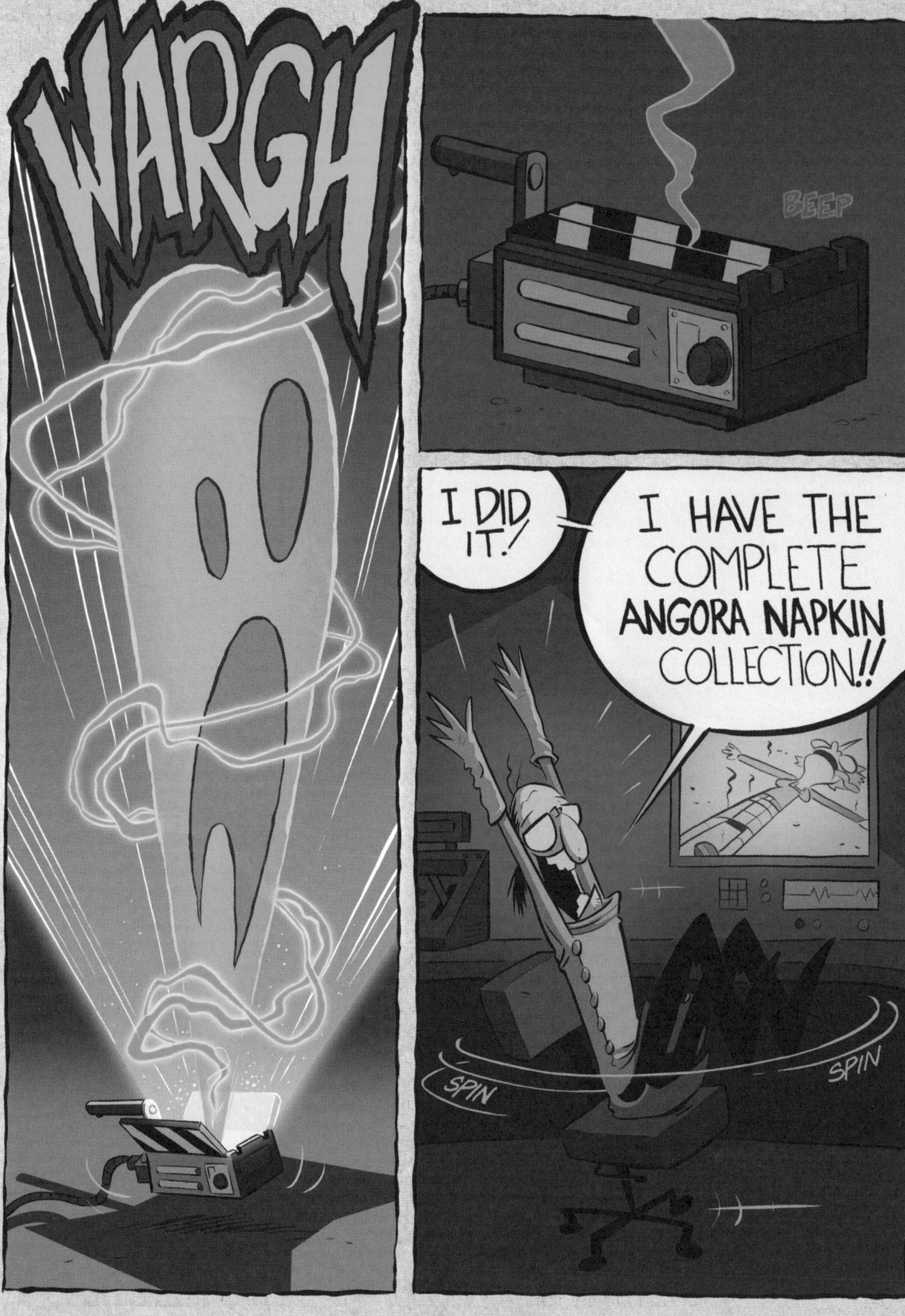
WARGH
BEEP
I DID IT!
I HAVE THE COMPLETE ANGORA NAPKIN COLLECTION!!
SPIN
SPIN

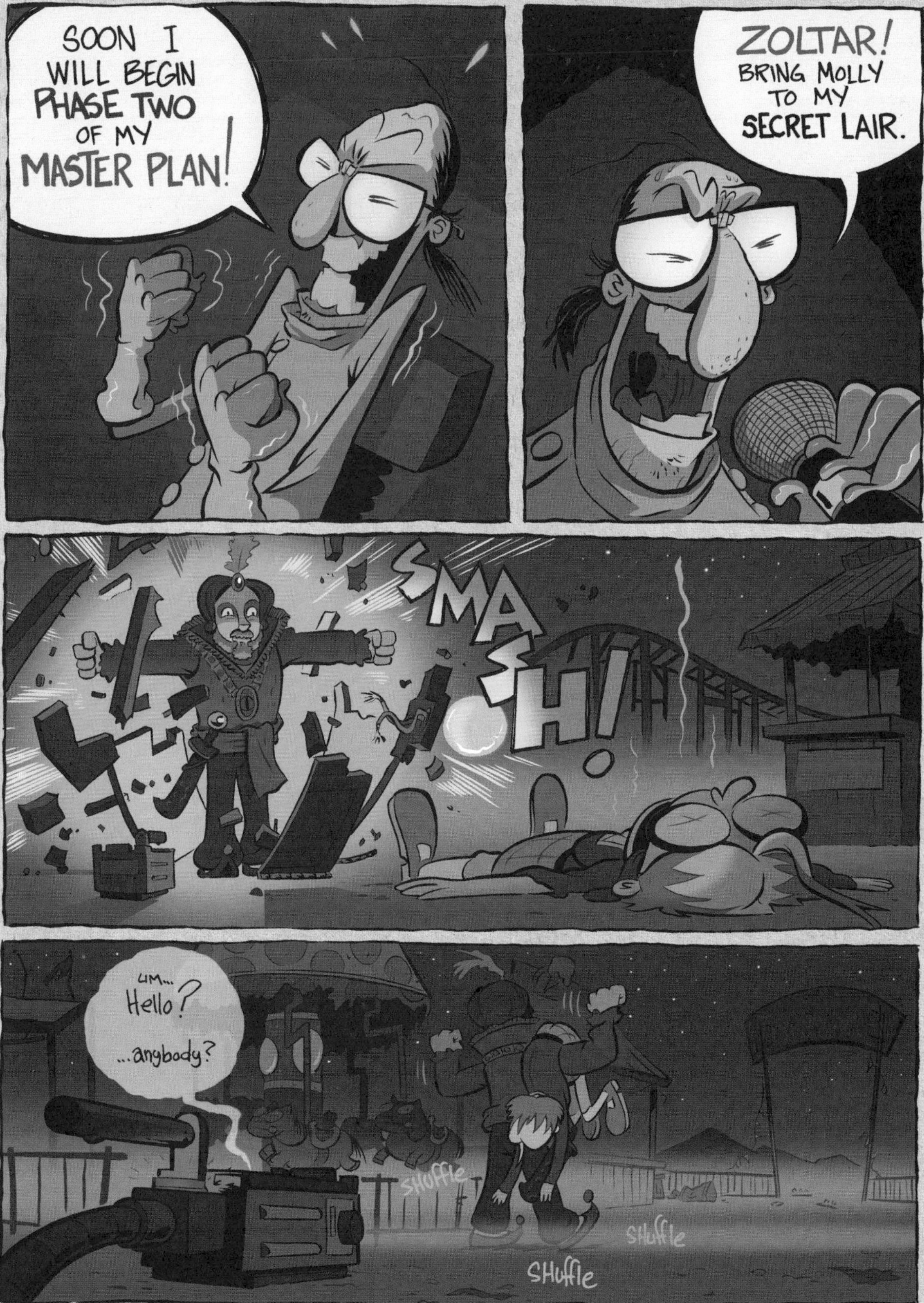
SOON I WILL BEGIN PHASE TWO OF MY MASTER PLAN!
ZOLTAR! BRING MOLLY TO MY SECRET LAIR.
SMASH!
UM... Hello? ...anybody?
SHuffle
SHuffle
SHuffle

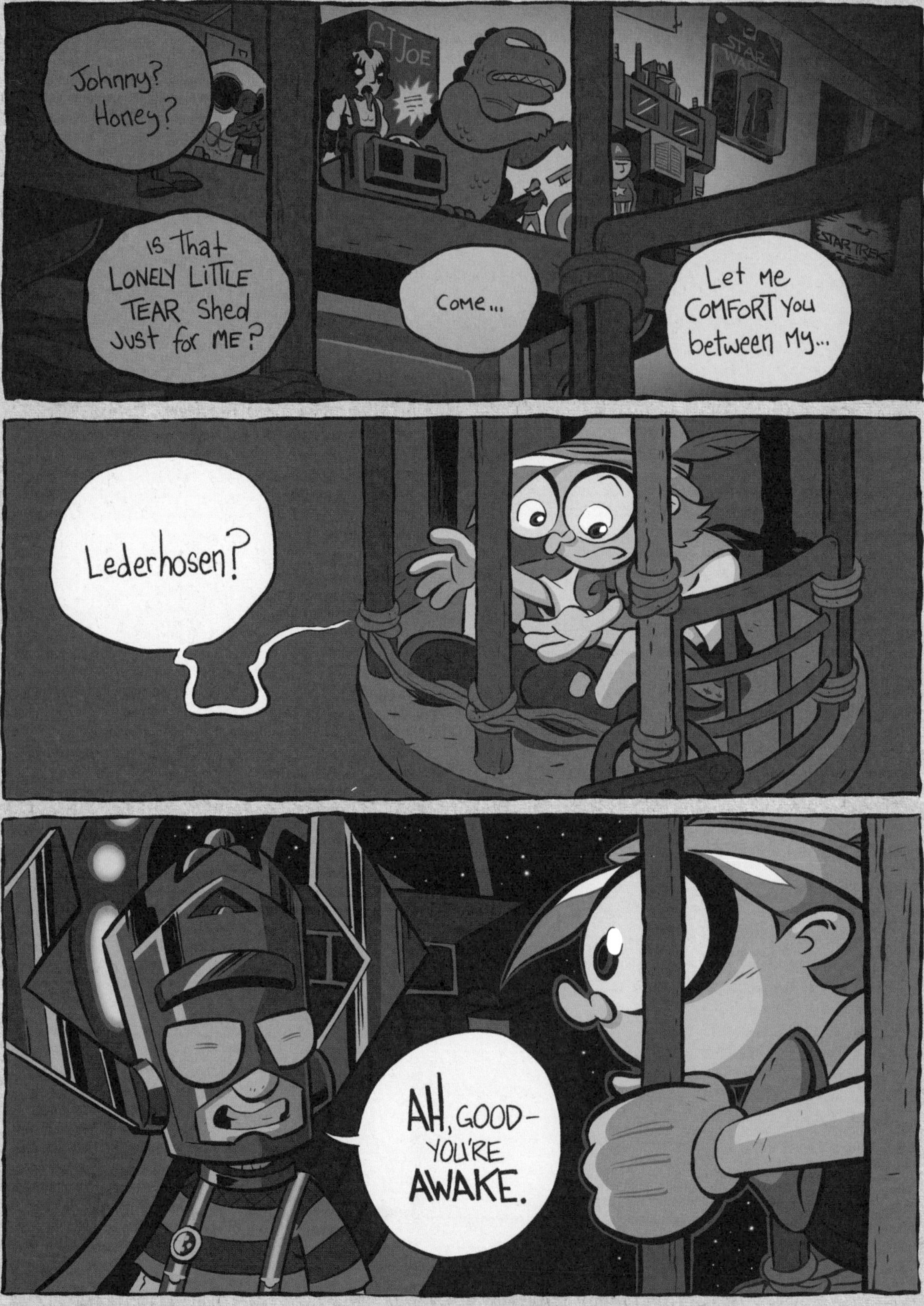
Johnny? Honey?
GI JOE
STAR WARS
STAR TREK
IS That LONELY LITTLE TEAR Shed Just for ME?
Come...
Let me COMFORT you between My...
Lederhosen?
AH, GOOD- YOU'RE AWAKE.

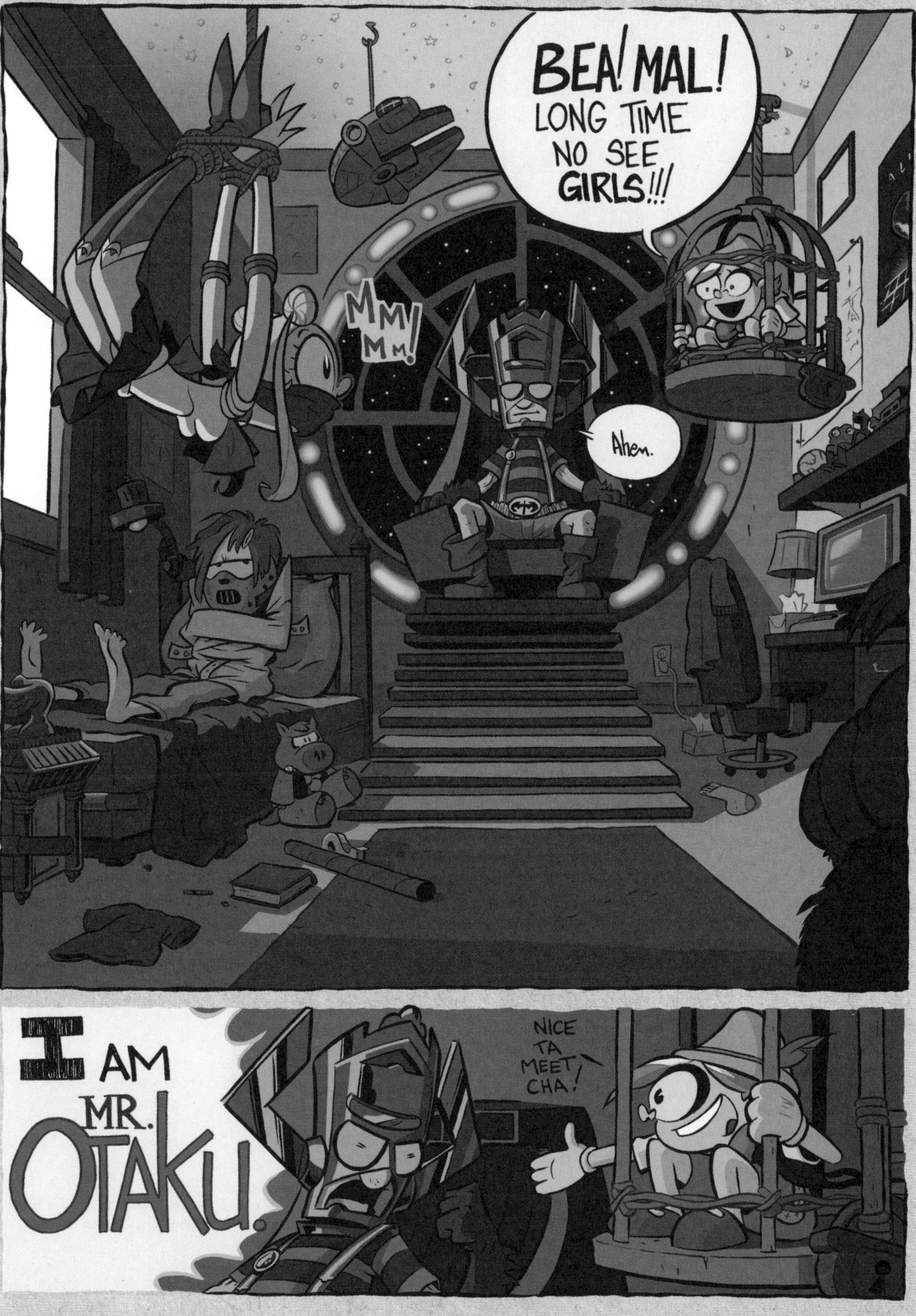
BEA! MAL! LONG TIME NO SEE GIRLS!!!
MMM MM!
Ahem.
I AM MR. OTAKU.
NICE TA MEET CHA!

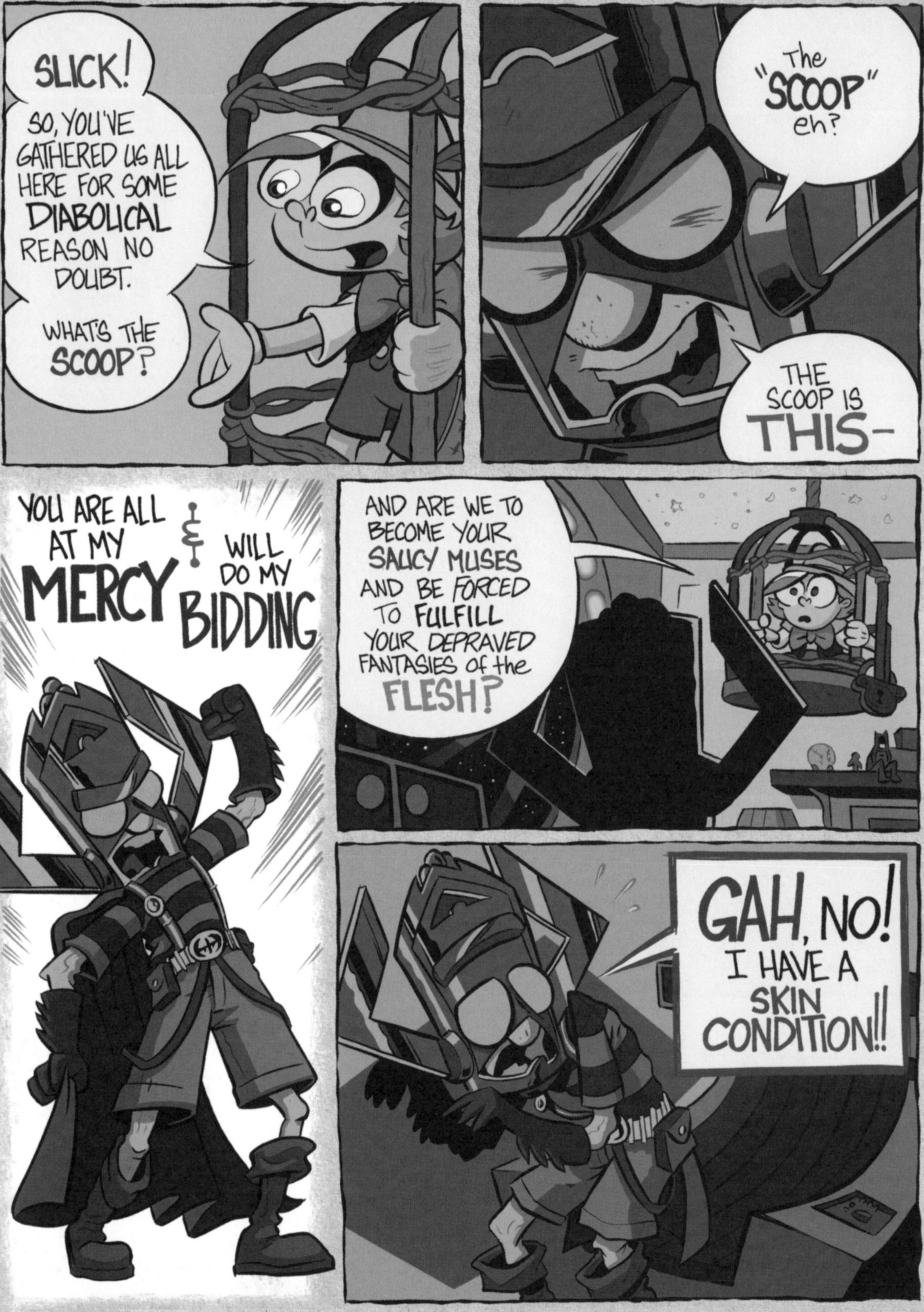
SLICK!
SO, YOU'VE GATHERED US ALL HERE FOR SOME DIABOLICAL REASON NO DOUBT.
WHAT'S THE SCOOP?
The "SCOOP" eh?
THE SCOOP IS THIS-
YOU ARE ALL AT MY MERCY & WILL DO MY BIDDING
AND ARE WE TO BECOME YOUR SAUCY MUSES AND BE FORCED TO FULFILL YOUR DEPRAVED FANTASIES of the FLESH?
GAH, NO! I HAVE A SKIN CONDITION!!

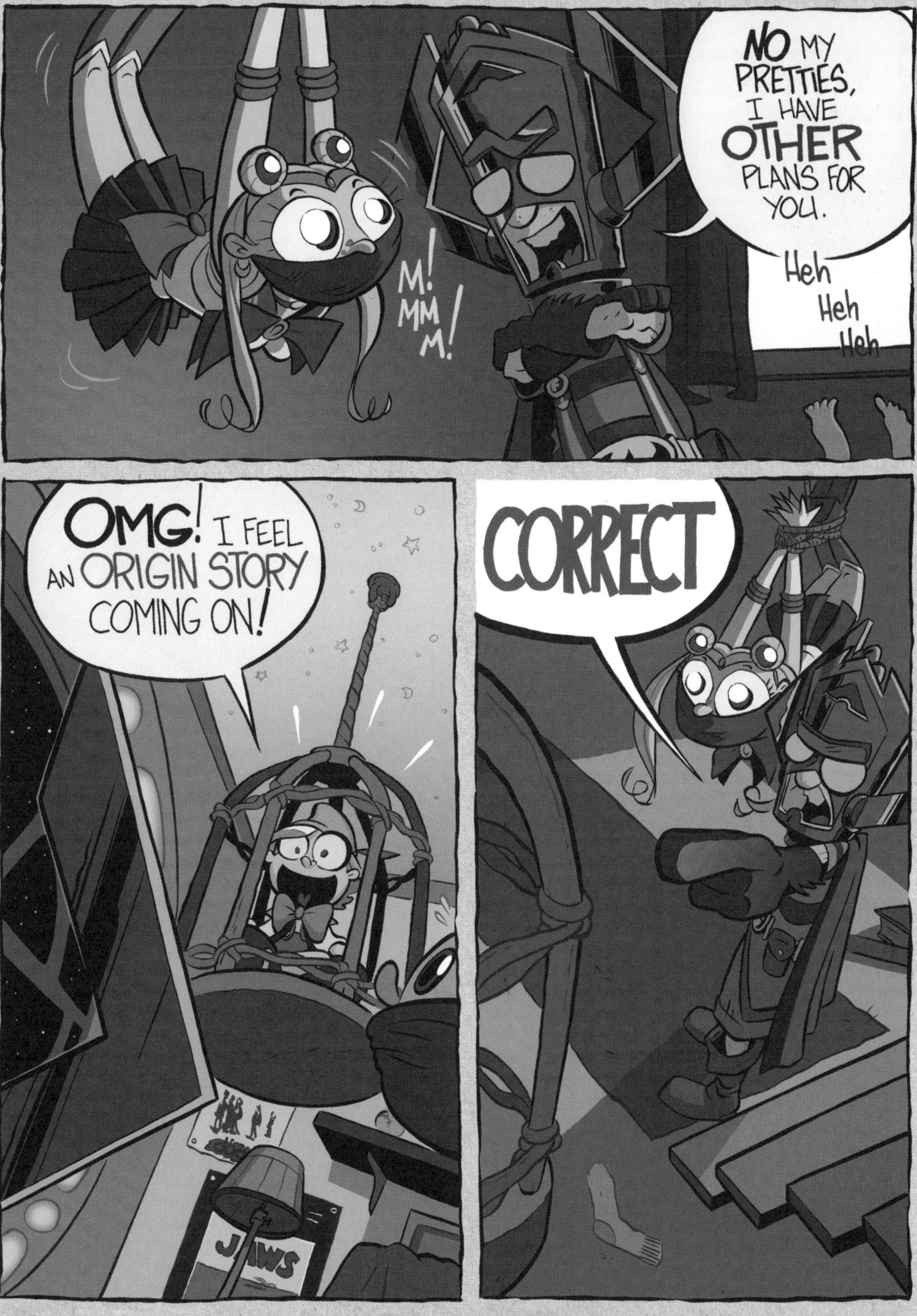
NO MY PRETTIES, I HAVE OTHER PLANS FOR YOU.
Heh Heh Heh
M! MM M!
OMG! I FEEL AN ORIGIN STORY COMING ON!
CORRECT
JAWS

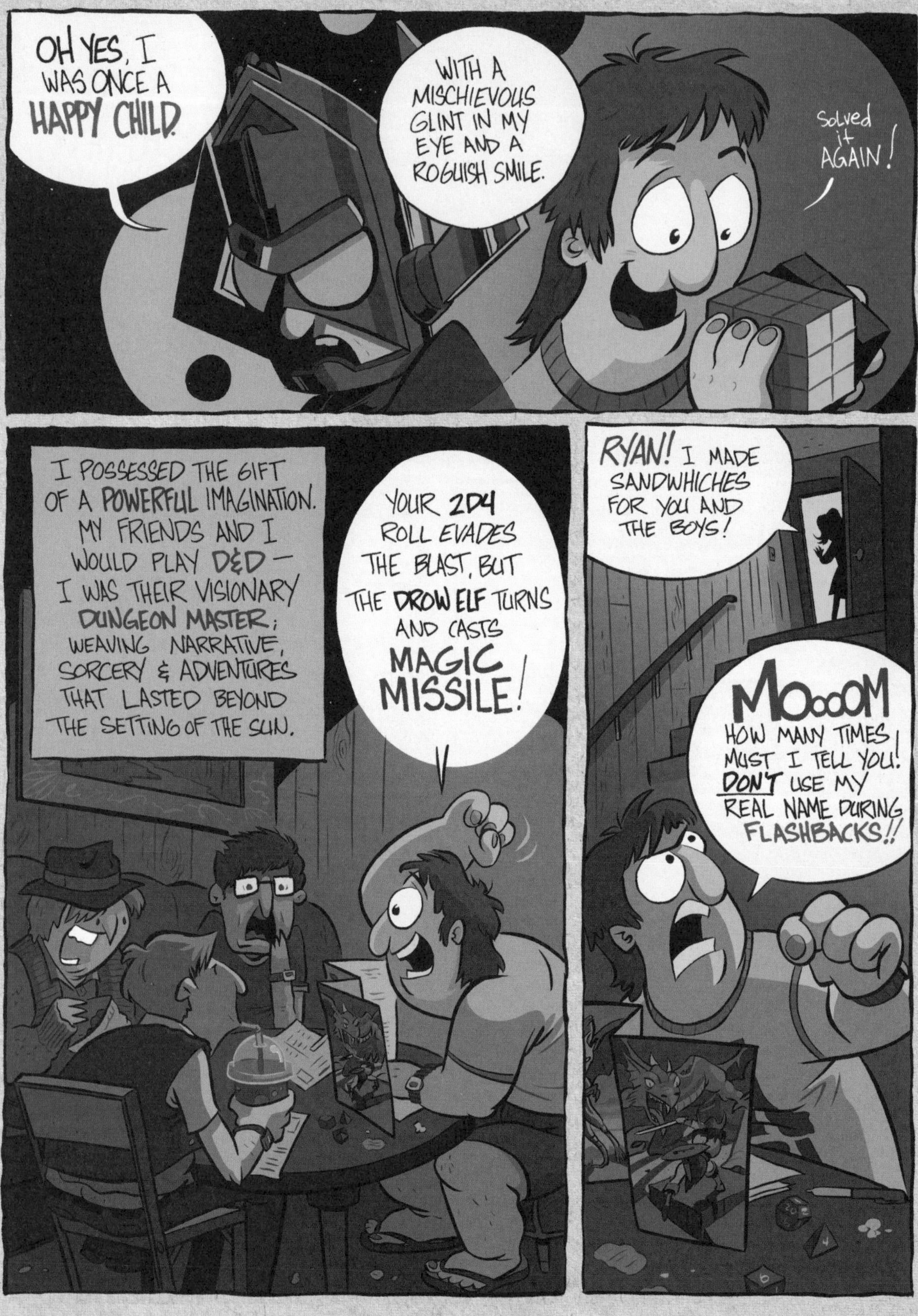
OH YES, I WAS ONCE A HAPPY CHILD.
WITH A MISCHIEVOUS GLINT IN MY EYE AND A ROGUISH SMILE.
Solved it AGAIN!
I POSSESSED THE GIFT OF A POWERFUL IMAGINATION. MY FRIENDS AND I WOULD PLAY D&D — I WAS THEIR VISIONARY DUNGEON MASTER; WEAVING NARRATIVE, SORCERY & ADVENTURES THAT LASTED BEYOND THE SETTING OF THE SUN.
YOUR 2D4 ROLL EVADES THE BLAST, BUT THE DROW ELF TURNS AND CASTS MAGIC MISSILE!
RYAN! I MADE SANDWHICHES FOR YOU AND THE BOYS!
MOoooOM HOW MANY TIMES MUST I TELL YOU! DON'T USE MY REAL NAME DURING FLASHBACKS!!

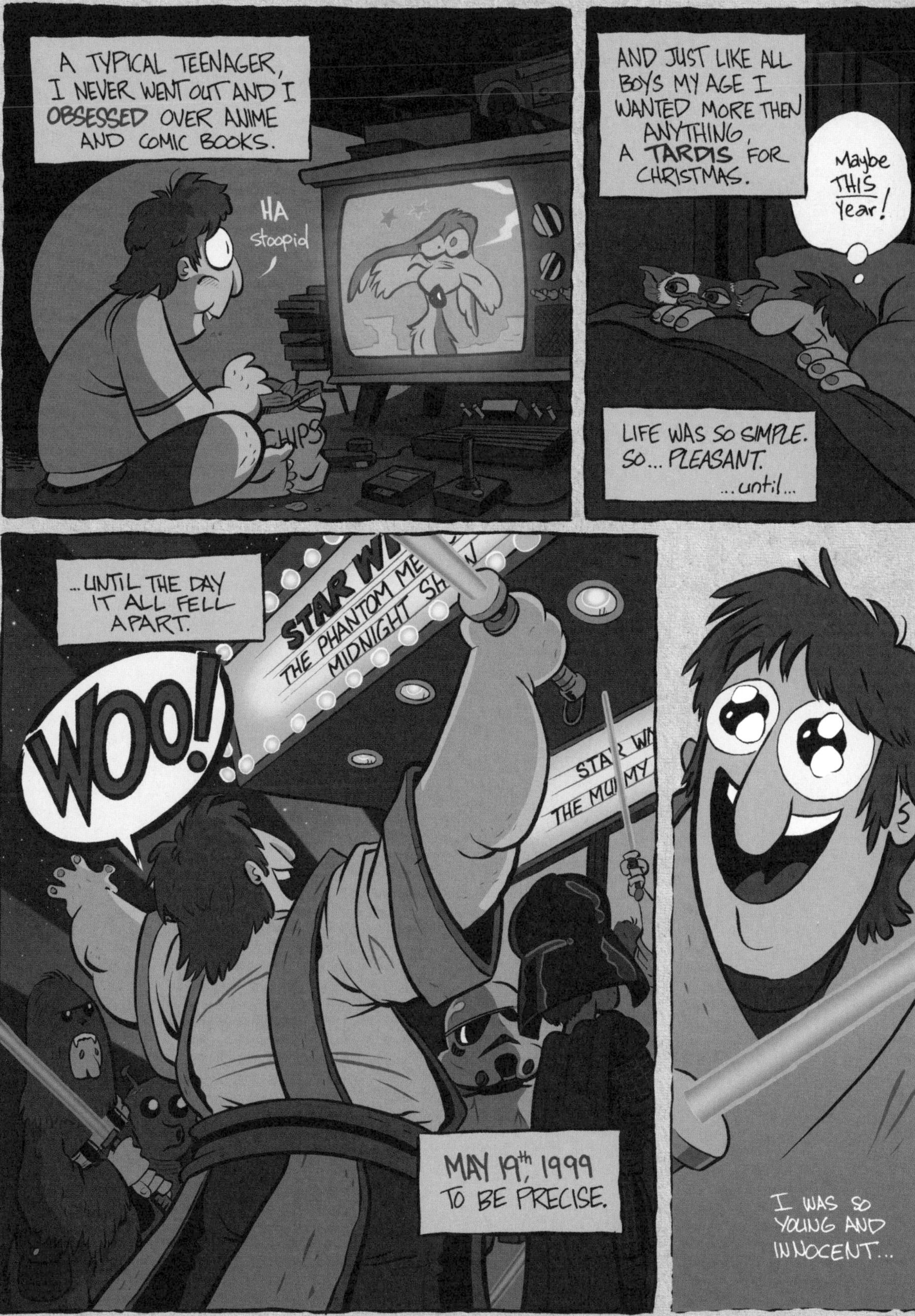
A TYPICAL TEENAGER, I NEVER WENT OUT AND I OBSESSED OVER ANIME AND COMIC BOOKS.
HA stoopid
CHIPS
AND JUST LIKE ALL BOYS MY AGE I WANTED MORE THEN ANYTHING, A TARDIS FOR CHRISTMAS.
Maybe THIS Year!
LIFE WAS SO SIMPLE. SO... PLEASANT.
...until...
...UNTIL THE DAY IT ALL FELL APART.
STAR W
THE PHANTOM ME
MIDNIGHT SH
WOO!
STAR W
THE MU MY
MAY 19th, 1999 TO BE PRECISE.
I WAS SO YOUNG AND INNOCENT...

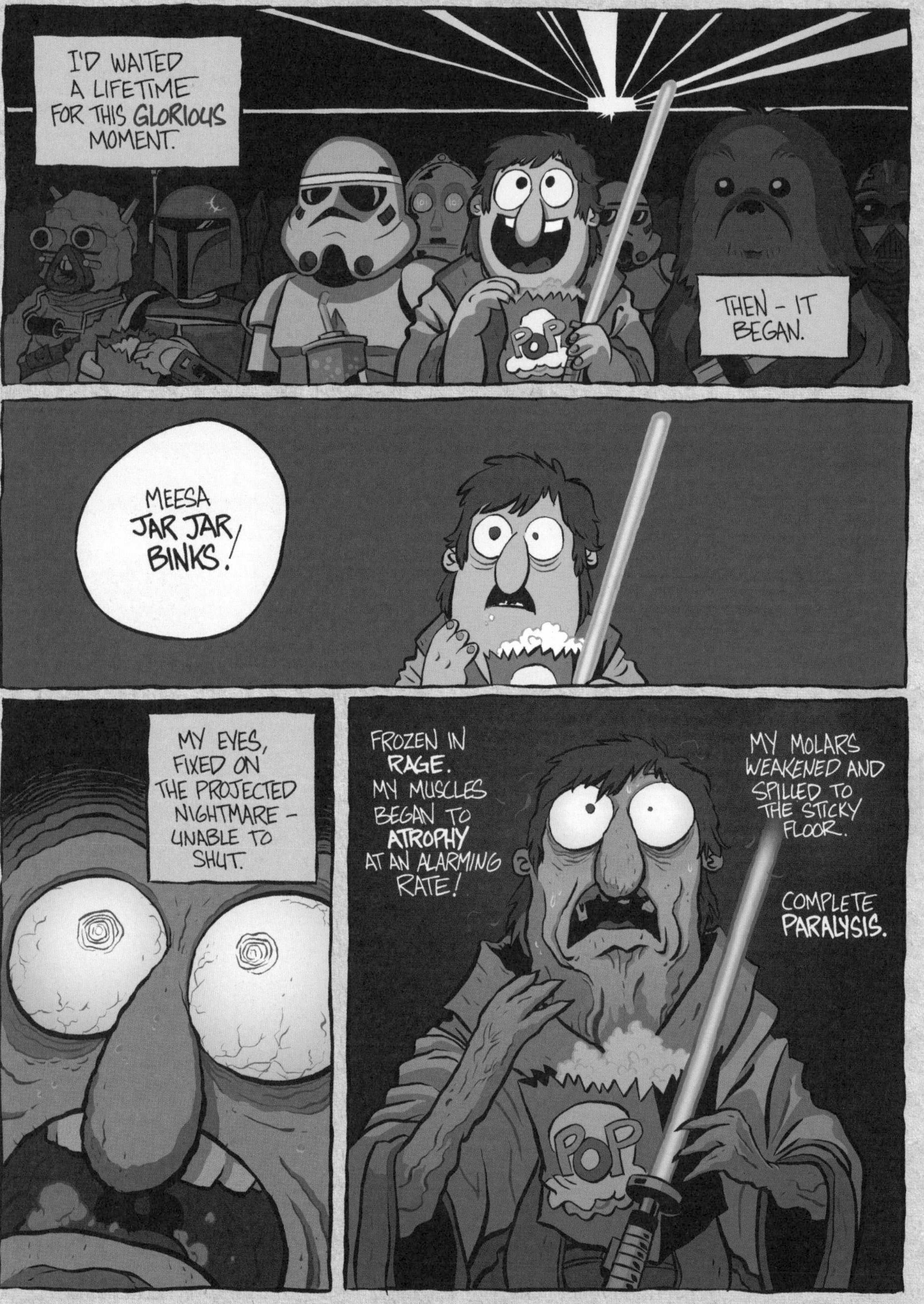

I'D WAITED A LIFETIME FOR THIS GLORIOUS MOMENT.
POP
THEN - IT BEGAN.
MEESA JAR JAR BINKS!
MY EYES, FIXED ON THE PROJECTED NIGHTMARE - UNABLE TO SHUT.
FROZEN IN RAGE. MY MUSCLES BEGAN TO ATROPHY AT AN ALARMING RATE!
MY MOLARS WEAKENED AND SPILLED TO THE STICKY FLOOR.
COMPLETE PARALYSIS.
POP

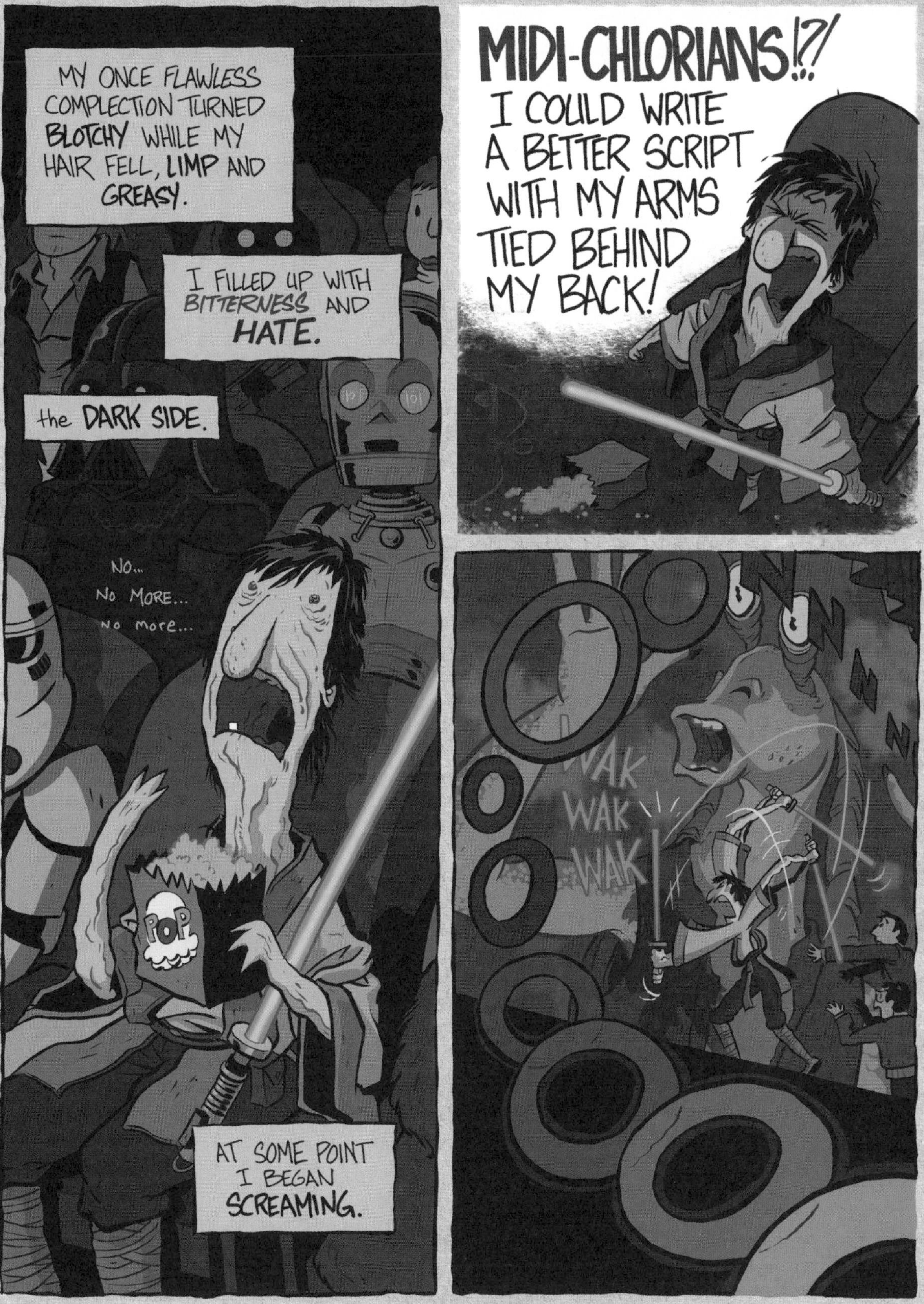

MY ONCE FLAWLESS COMPLECTION TURNED BLOTCHY WHILE MY HAIR FELL, LIMP AND GREASY.
I FILLED UP WITH BITTERNESS AND HATE.
the DARK SIDE.
No...
No MORE...
no more...
POP
AT SOME POINT I BEGAN SCREAMING.
MIDI-CHLORIANS!?!
I COULD WRITE A BETTER SCRIPT WITH MY ARMS TIED BEHIND MY BACK!
WAK
WAK
WAK

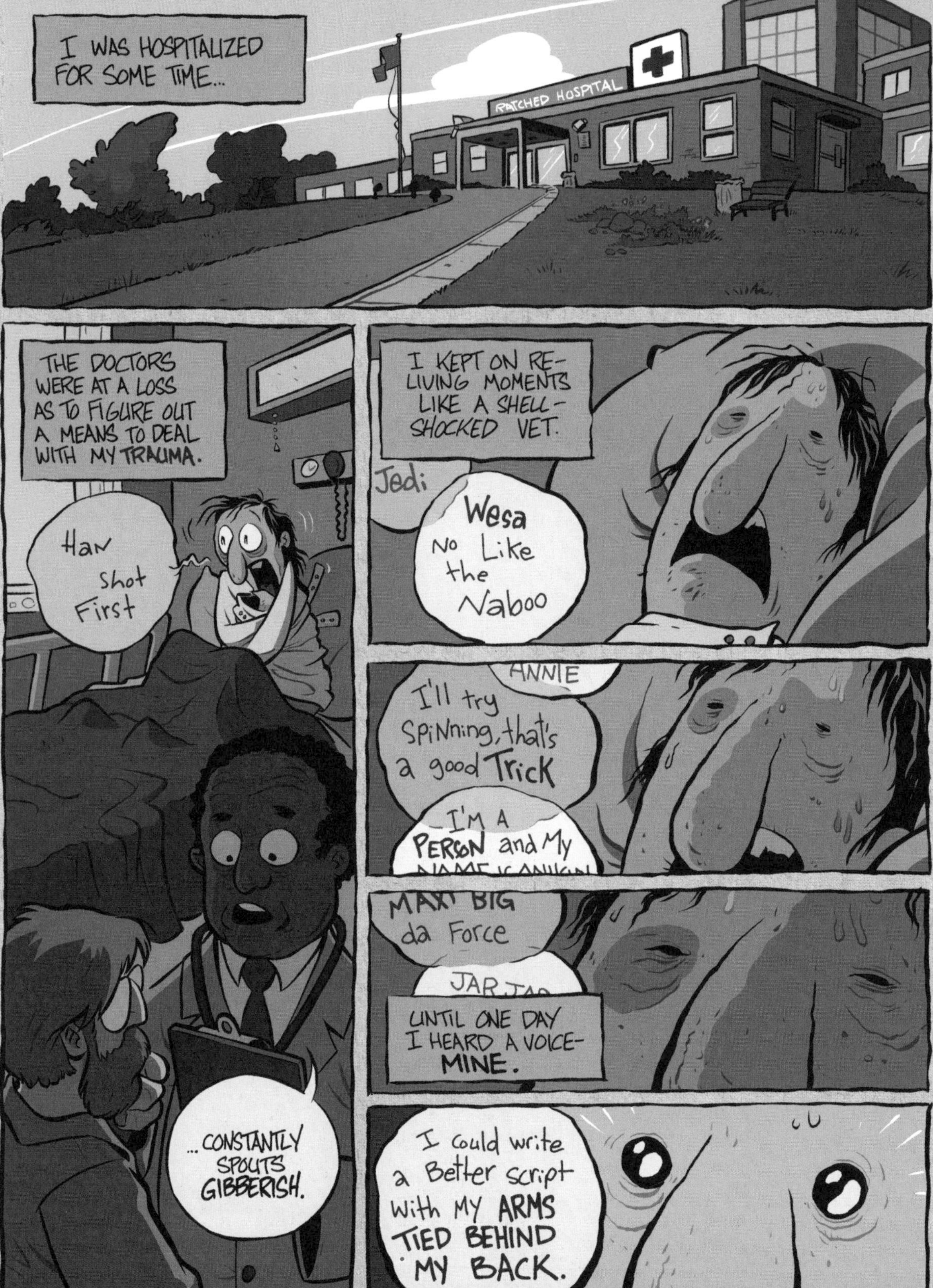
I WAS HOSPITALIZED FOR SOME TIME...
RATCHED HOSPITAL
THE DOCTORS WERE AT A LOSS AS TO FIGURE OUT A MEANS TO DEAL WITH MY TRAUMA.
Han Shot First
...CONSTANTLY SPOUTS GIBBERISH.
I KEPT ON RE-LIVING MOMENTS LIKE A SHELL-SHOCKED VET.
Jedi
Wesa No Like the Naboo
ANNIE
I'll try Spinning, that's a good Trick
I'M A PERSON and My
MAX! BIG
da Force
JAR
UNTIL ONE DAY I HEARD A VOICE- MINE.
I could write a Better script with My ARMS TIED BEHIND MY BACK.

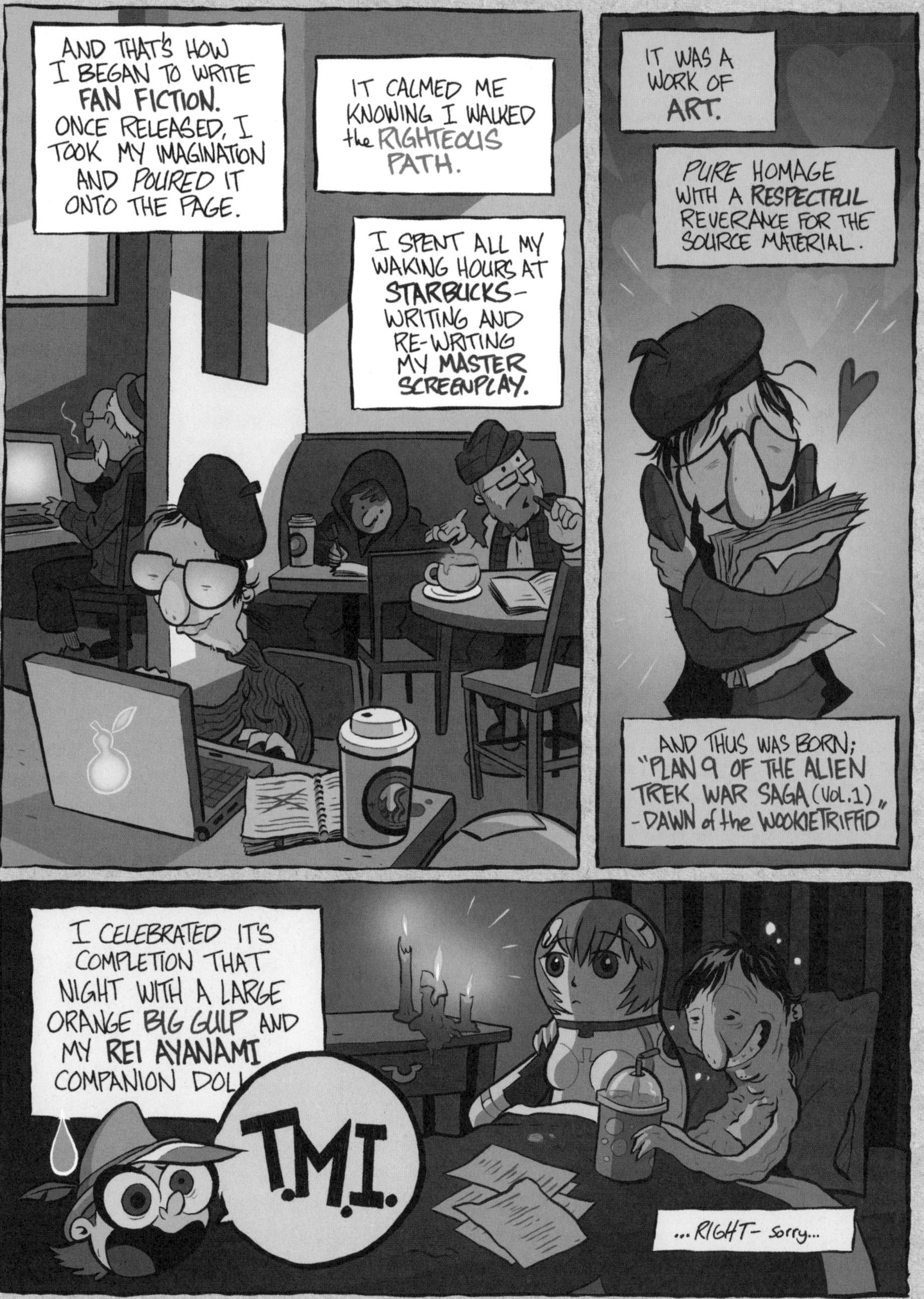

AND THAT'S HOW I BEGAN TO WRITE FAN FICTION. ONCE RELEASED, I TOOK MY IMAGINATION AND POURED IT ONTO THE PAGE.
IT CALMED ME KNOWING I WALKED the RIGHTEOUS PATH.
I SPENT ALL MY WAKING HOURS AT STARBUCKS- WRITING AND RE-WRITING MY MASTER SCREENPLAY.
IT WAS A WORK OF ART.
PURE HOMAGE WITH A RESPECTFUL REVERANCE FOR THE SOURCE MATERIAL.
AND THUS WAS BORN; "PLAN 9 OF THE ALIEN TREK WAR SAGA (VOL.1) - DAWN of the WOOKIETRIFFID"
I CELEBRATED IT'S COMPLETION THAT NIGHT WITH A LARGE ORANGE BIG GULP AND MY REI AYANAMI COMPANION DOLL
T.M.I.
...RIGHT- sorry...

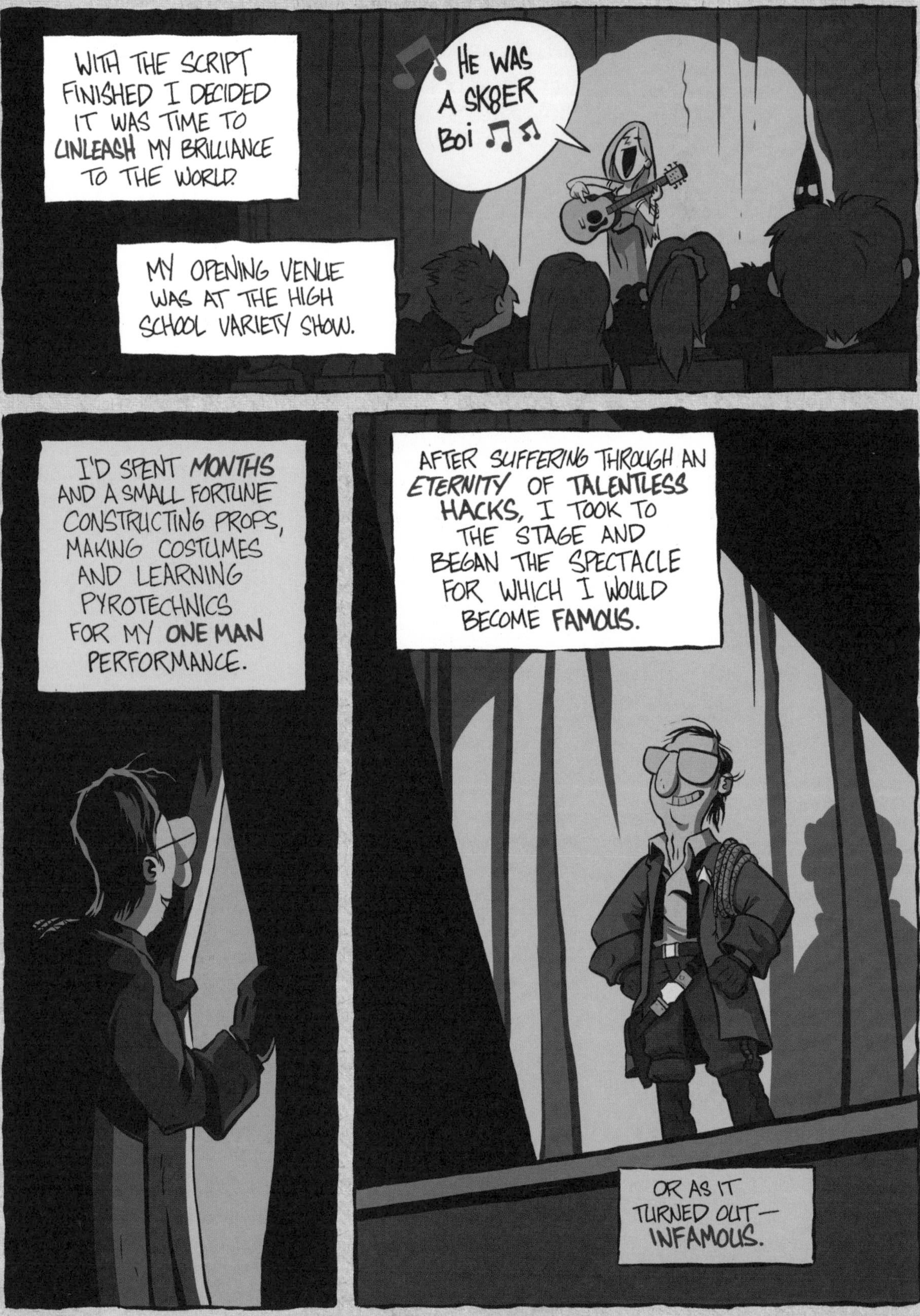
WITH THE SCRIPT FINISHED I DECIDED IT WAS TIME TO UNLEASH MY BRILLIANCE TO THE WORLD.
HE WAS A SK8ER Boi
MY OPENING VENUE WAS AT THE HIGH SCHOOL VARIETY SHOW.
I'D SPENT MONTHS AND A SMALL FORTUNE CONSTRUCTING PROPS, MAKING COSTUMES AND LEARNING PYROTECHNICS FOR MY ONE MAN PERFORMANCE.
AFTER SUFFERING THROUGH AN ETERNITY OF TALENTLESS HACKS, I TOOK TO THE STAGE AND BEGAN THE SPECTACLE FOR WHICH I WOULD BECOME FAMOUS.
OR AS IT TURNED OUT— INFAMOUS.

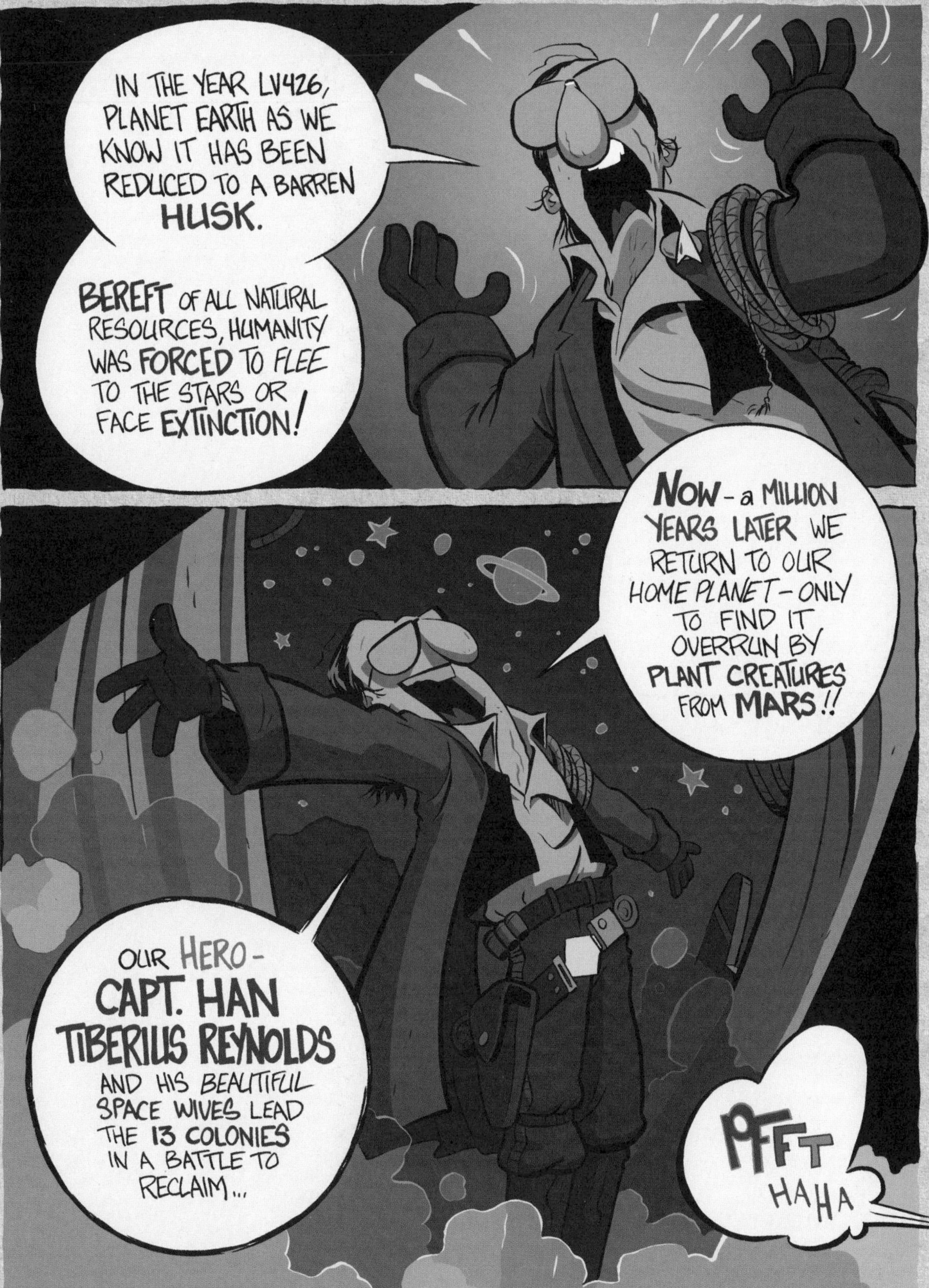

IN THE YEAR LV426, PLANET EARTH AS WE KNOW IT HAS BEEN REDUCED TO A BARREN HUSK.
BEREFT OF ALL NATURAL RESOURCES, HUMANITY WAS FORCED TO FLEE TO THE STARS OR FACE EXTINCTION!
NOW - a MILLION YEARS LATER WE RETURN TO OUR HOME PLANET - ONLY TO FIND IT OVERRUN BY PLANT CREATURES FROM MARS!!
OUR HERO - CAPT. HAN TIBERIUS REYNOLDS AND HIS BEAUTIFUL SPACE WIVES LEAD THE 13 COLONIES IN A BATTLE TO RECLAIM...
PFFT
HAHA

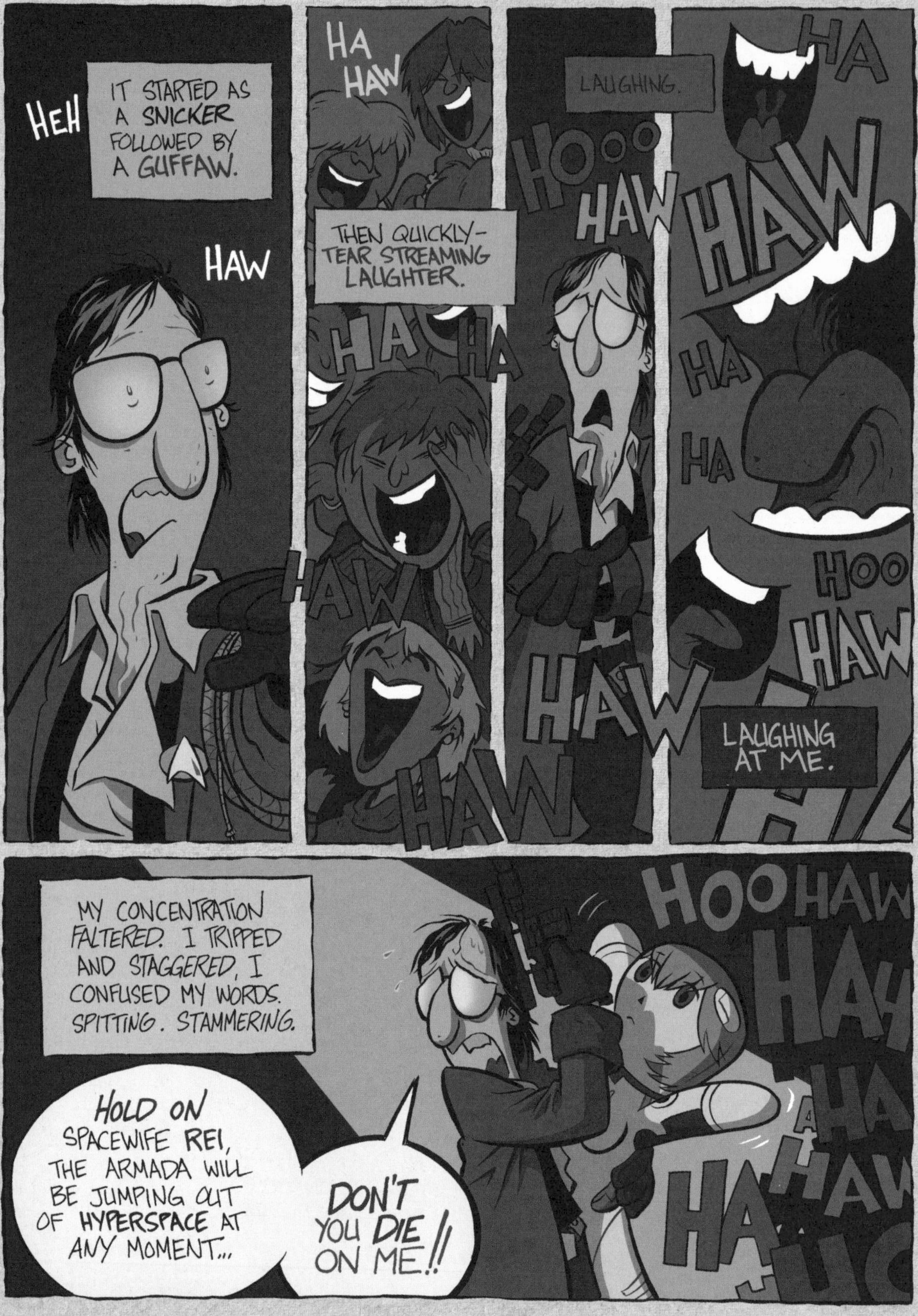
HEH
IT STARTED AS A SNICKER FOLLOWED BY A GUFFAW.
HAW
HA HAW
THEN QUICKLY-TEAR STREAMING LAUGHTER.
HA HA
HAW
HAW
LAUGHING.
HOOO
HAW
HAW
HA
HAW
HA
HA
HOO
HAW
LAUGHING AT ME.
MY CONCENTRATION FALTERED. I TRIPPED AND STAGGERED, I CONFUSED MY WORDS. SPITTING. STAMMERING.
HOOHAW
HOLD ON SPACEWIFE REI, THE ARMADA WILL BE JUMPING OUT OF HYPERSPACE AT ANY MOMENT...
DON'T YOU DIE ON ME!!
HA
HAW

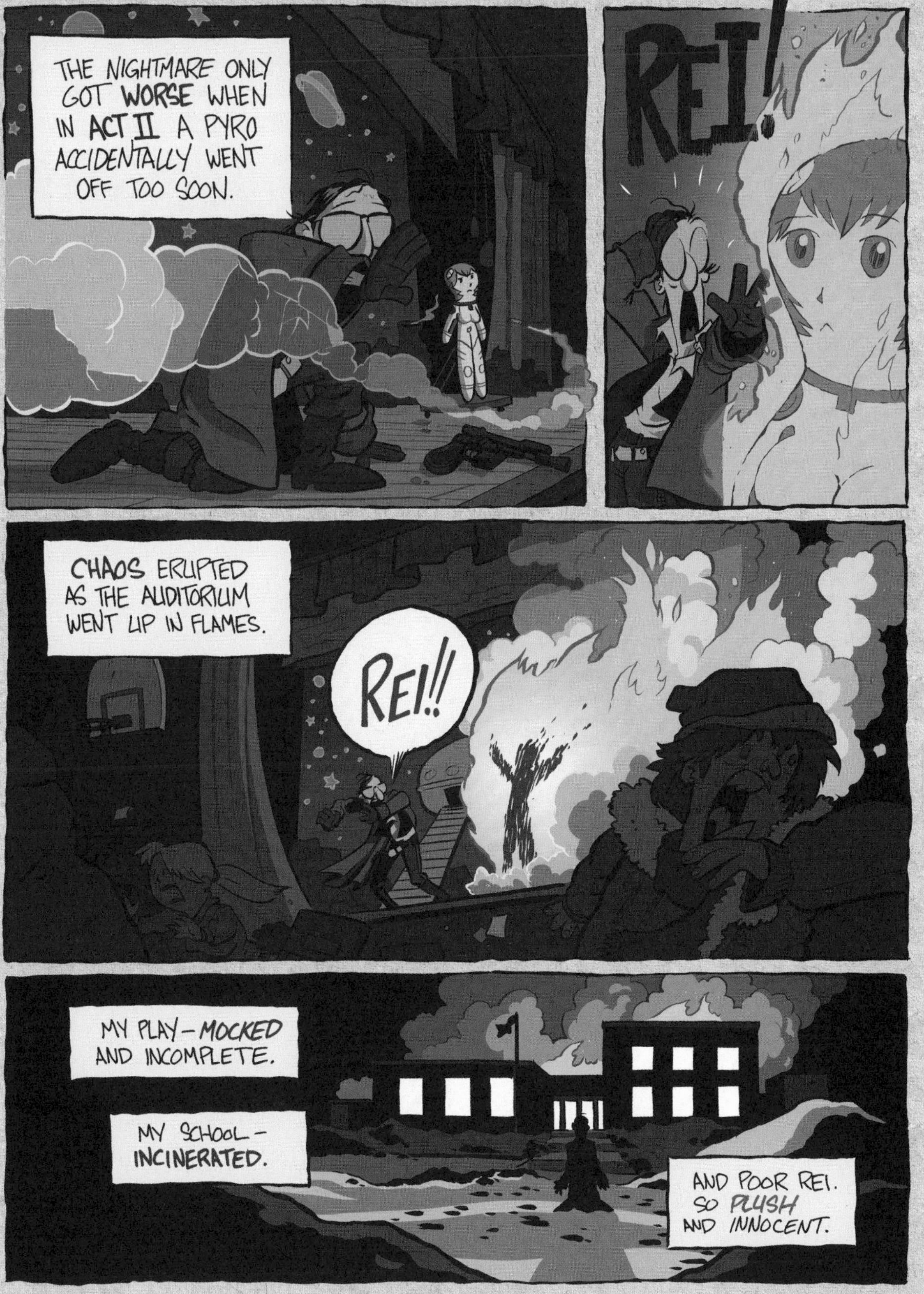

THE NIGHTMARE ONLY GOT **WORSE** WHEN IN **ACT II** A PYRO ACCIDENTALLY WENT OFF TOO SOON.
REI!
CHAOS ERUPTED AS THE AUDITORIUM WENT UP IN FLAMES.
REI!!
MY PLAY—*MOCKED* AND INCOMPLETE.
MY SCHOOL—**INCINERATED.**
AND POOR REI. SO *PLUSH* AND INNOCENT.

THEN – THE FINAL STRAW.
MAN, THAT PLAY SUCKED HARDER THEN "THE PHANTOM MENACE."
KAHN
AND NOW HERE WE ARE 10 YEARS LATER.

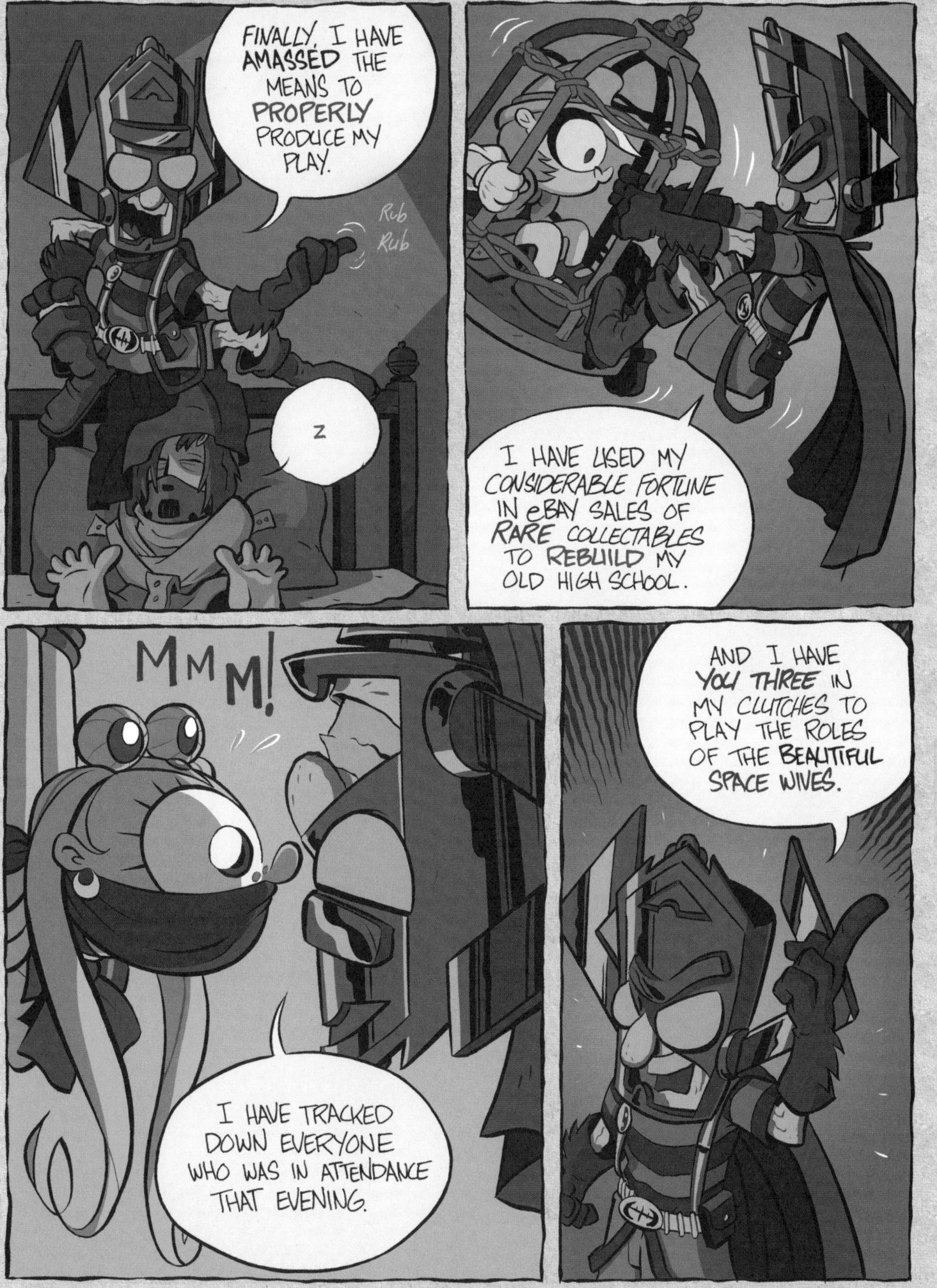
FINALLY, I HAVE AMASSED THE MEANS TO PROPERLY PRODUCE MY PLAY.
Rub Rub
Z
I HAVE USED MY CONSIDERABLE FORTUNE IN eBAY SALES OF RARE COLLECTABLES TO REBUILD MY OLD HIGH SCHOOL.
MMM!
I HAVE TRACKED DOWN EVERYONE WHO WAS IN ATTENDANCE THAT EVENING.
AND I HAVE YOU THREE IN MY CLUTCHES TO PLAY THE ROLES OF THE BEAUTIFUL SPACE WIVES.

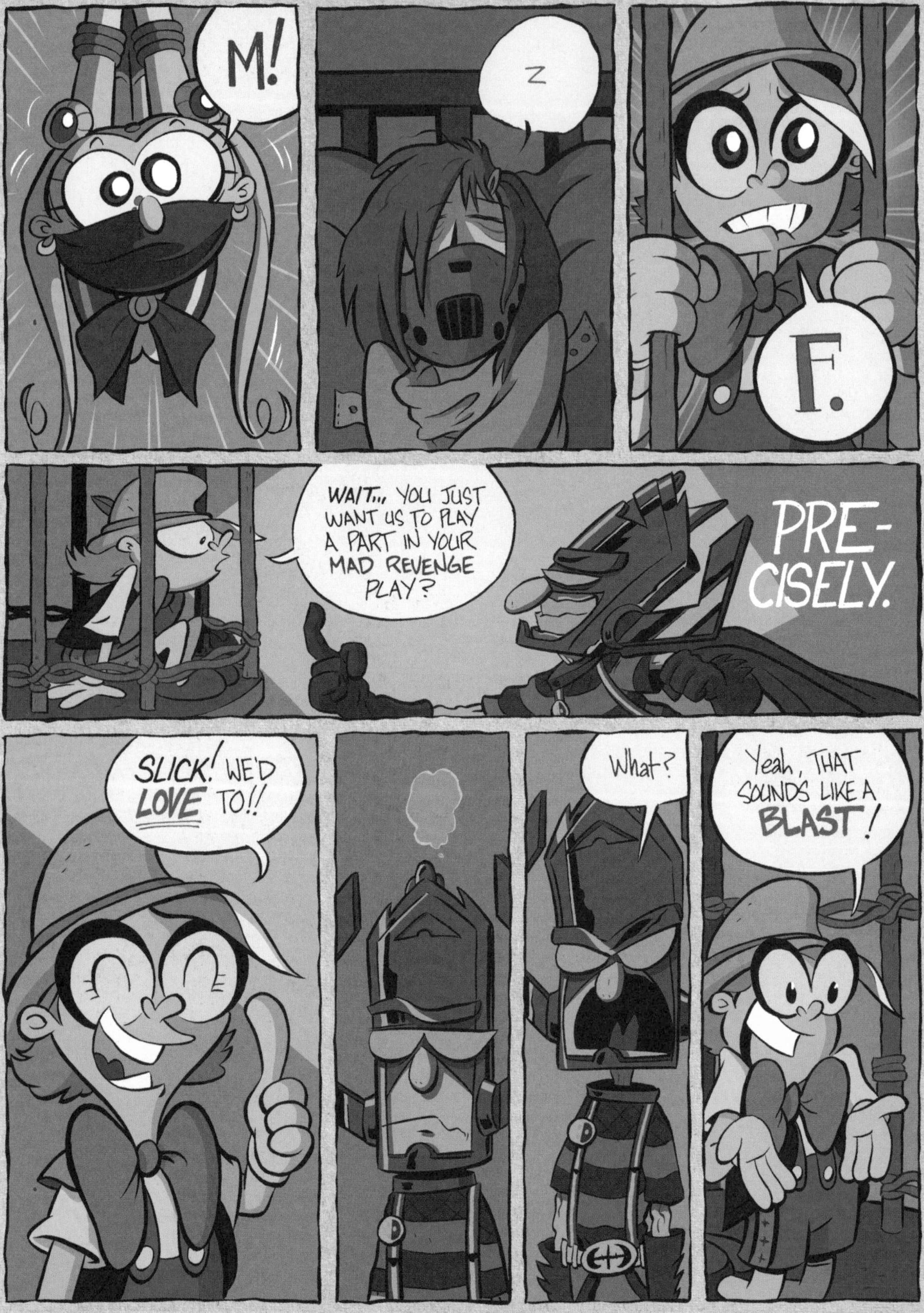
M!
Z
F.
WAIT... YOU JUST WANT US TO PLAY A PART IN YOUR MAD REVENGE PLAY?
PRE-CISELY.
SLICK! WE'D LOVE TO!!
What?
Yeah, THAT SOUNDS LIKE A BLAST!

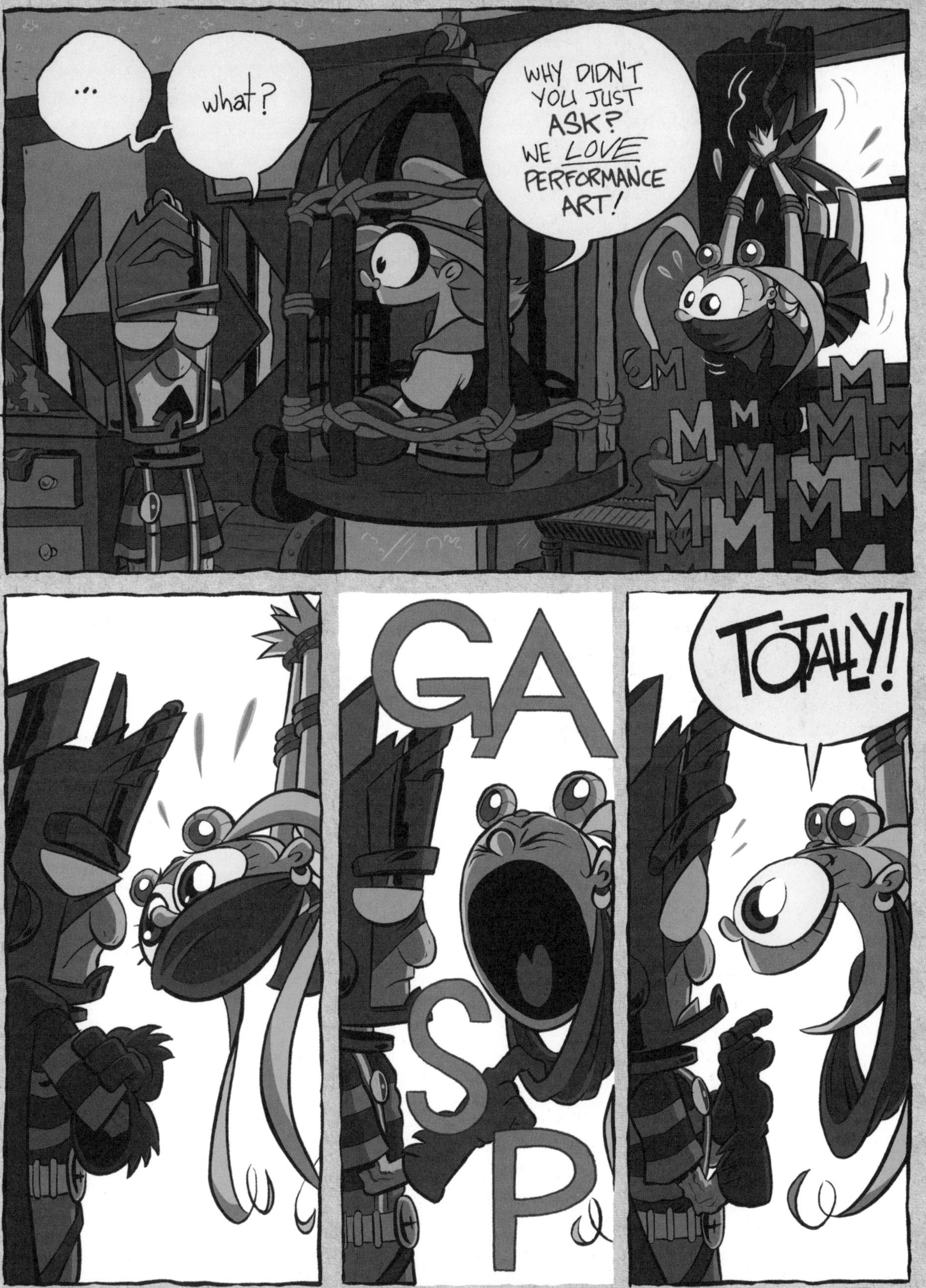
...
what?
WHY DIDN'T YOU JUST ASK? WE LOVE PERFORMANCE ART!
MMMMMMMM
GASP
TOTALLY!

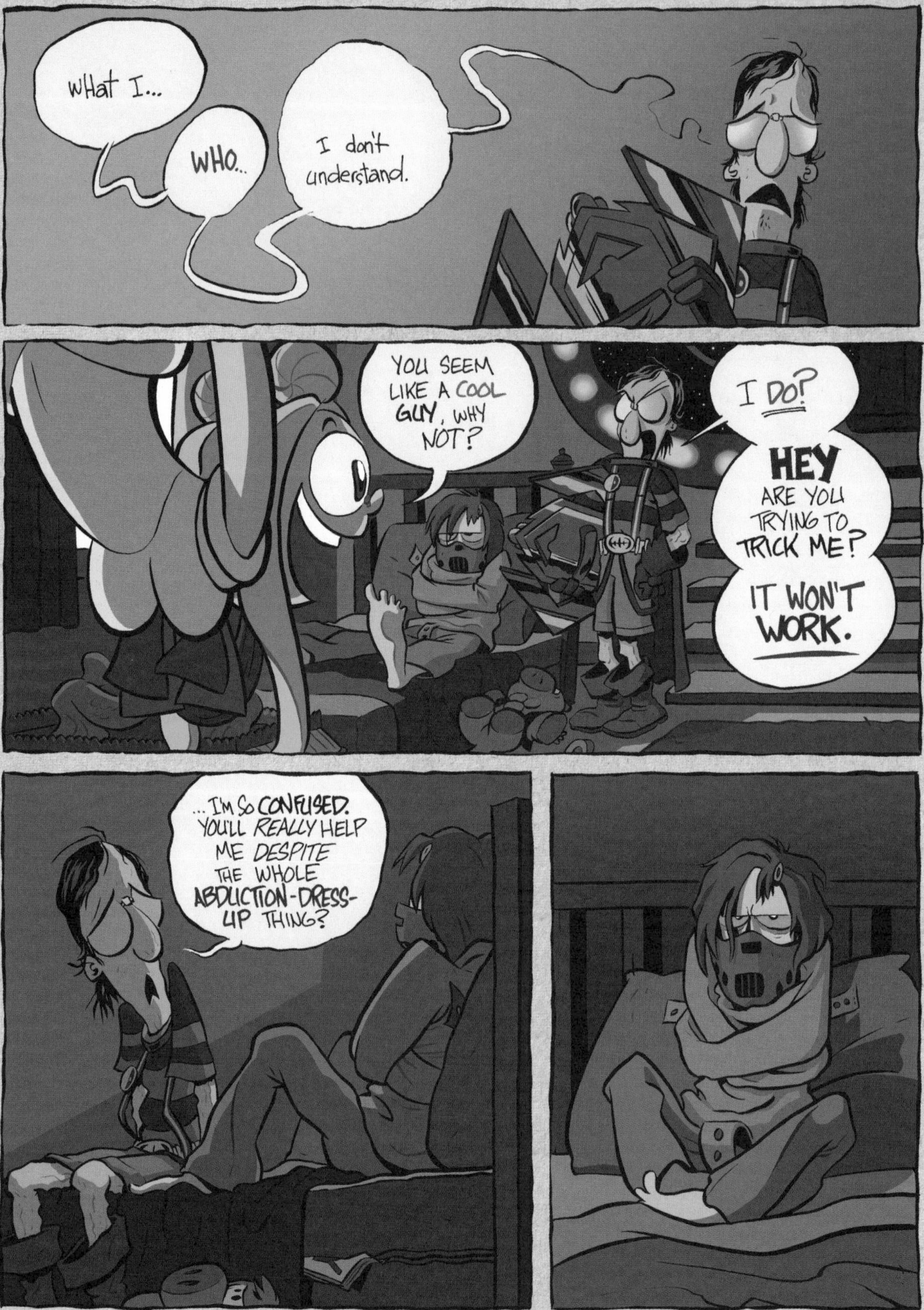

WHAT I...
WHO...
I don't understand.
YOU SEEM LIKE A COOL GUY, WHY NOT?
I DO?
HEY ARE YOU TRYING TO TRICK ME?
IT WON'T WORK.
... I'M SO CONFUSED. YOU'LL REALLY HELP ME DESPITE THE WHOLE ABDUCTION-DRESS-UP THING?

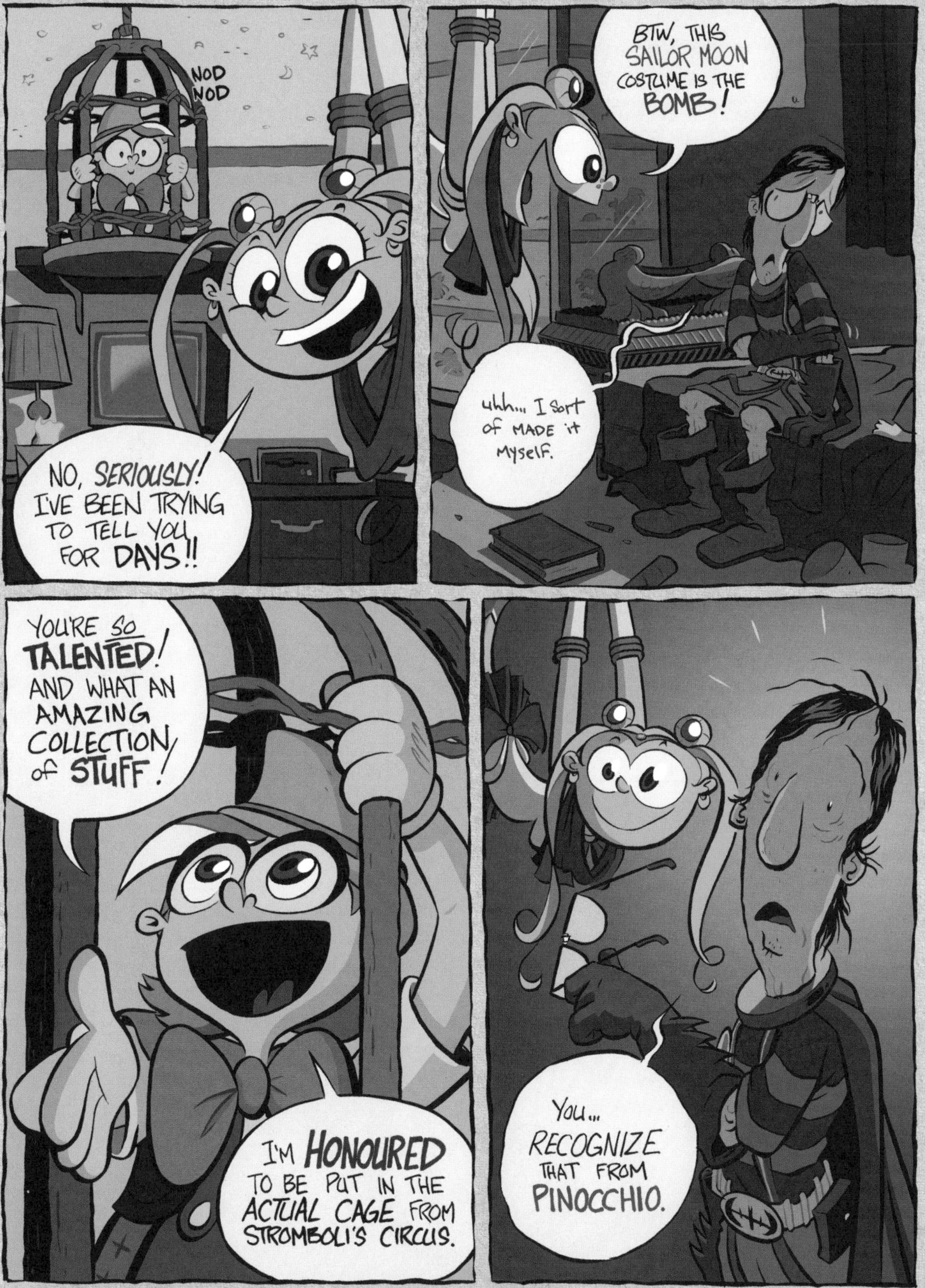
NOD NOD
NO, SERIOUSLY! I'VE BEEN TRYING TO TELL YOU FOR DAYS!!
BTW, THIS SAILOR MOON COSTUME IS THE BOMB!
uhh... I sort of MADE it myself.
YOU'RE SO TALENTED! AND WHAT AN AMAZING COLLECTION of STUFF!
I'M HONOURED TO BE PUT IN THE ACTUAL CAGE FROM STROMBOLI'S CIRCUS.
You... RECOGNIZE THAT FROM PINOCCHIO.

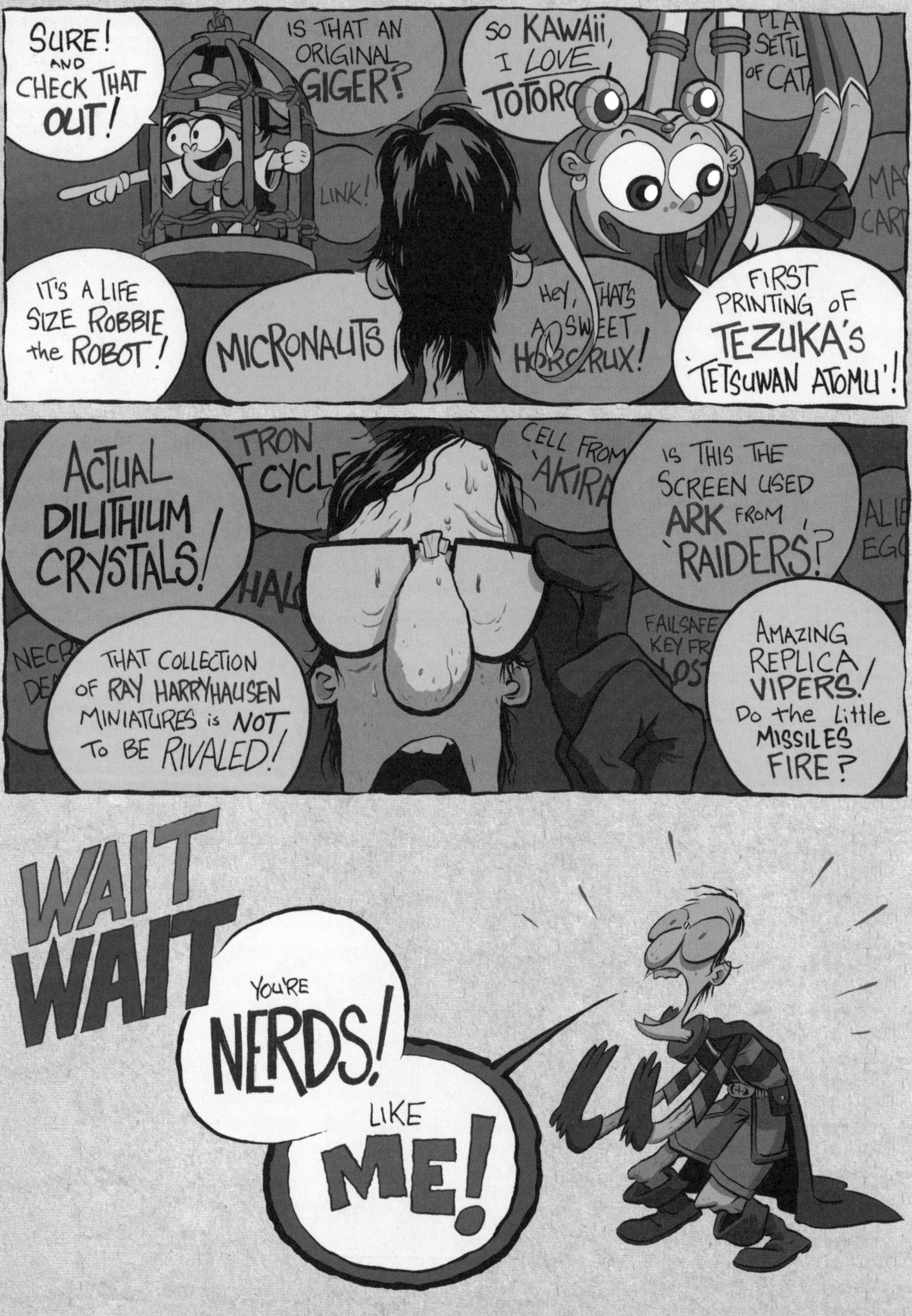

SURE! AND CHECK THAT OUT!
IS THAT AN ORIGINAL GIGER?
SO KAWAII, I LOVE TOTORO
LINK!
IT'S A LIFE SIZE ROBBIE the ROBOT!
MICRONAUTS
Hey, THAT'S A SWEET HORCRUX!
FIRST PRINTING OF TEZUKA'S 'TETSUWAN ATOMU'!
ACTUAL DILITHIUM CRYSTALS!
TRON CYCLE
CELL FROM 'AKIRA'
IS THIS THE SCREEN USED ARK FROM 'RAIDERS'?
THAT COLLECTION OF RAY HARRYHAUSEN MINIATURES is NOT TO BE RIVALED!
AMAZING REPLICA VIPERS! Do the Little MISSILES FIRE?
WAIT WAIT
YOU'RE NERDS! LIKE ME!

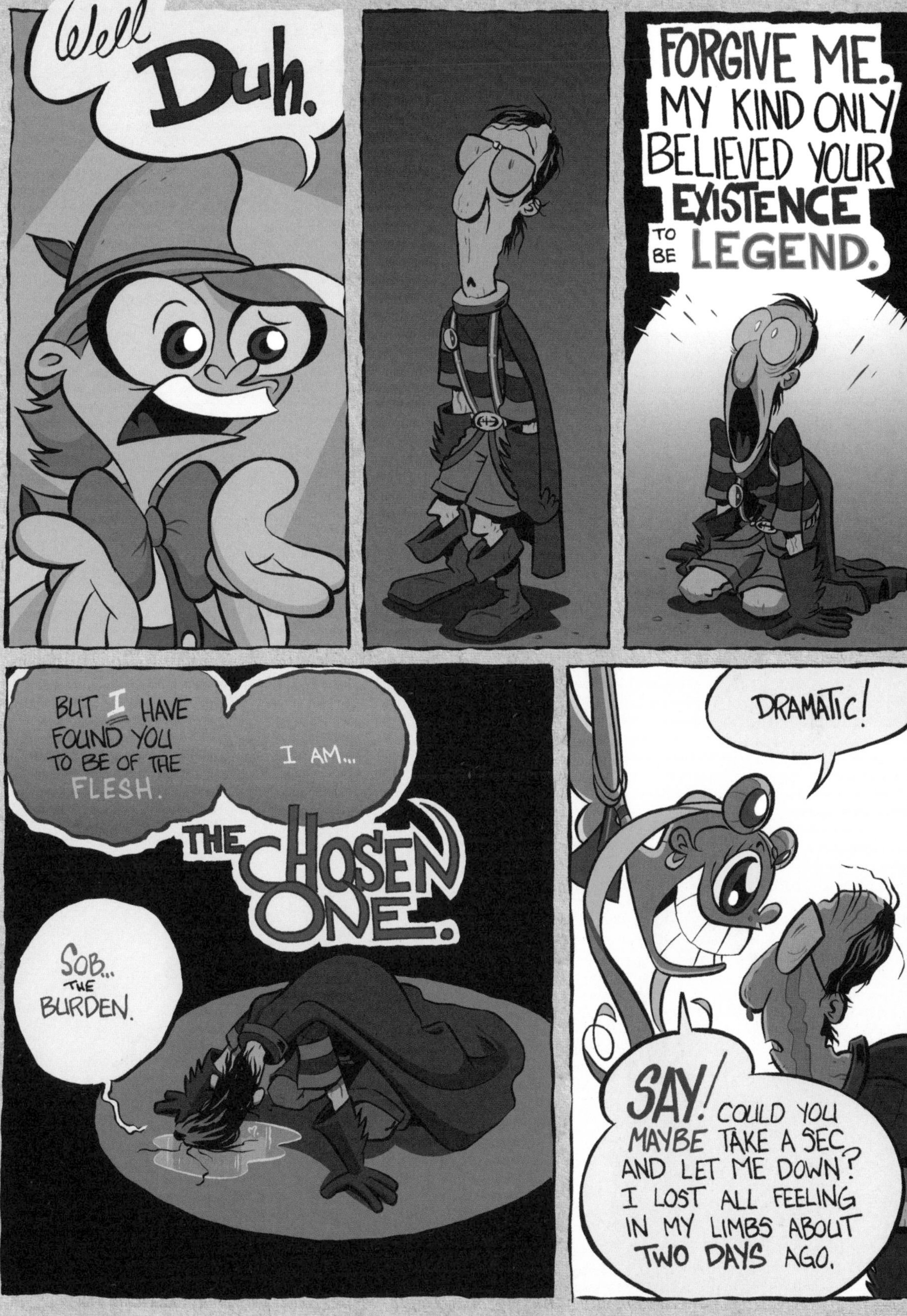

Well Duh.
FORGIVE ME. MY KIND ONLY BELIEVED YOUR EXISTENCE TO BE LEGEND.
BUT I HAVE FOUND YOU TO BE OF THE FLESH.
I AM...
THE CHOSEN ONE.
SOB... THE BURDEN.
DRAMATIC!
SAY! COULD YOU MAYBE TAKE A SEC AND LET ME DOWN? I LOST ALL FEELING IN MY LIMBS ABOUT TWO DAYS AGO.

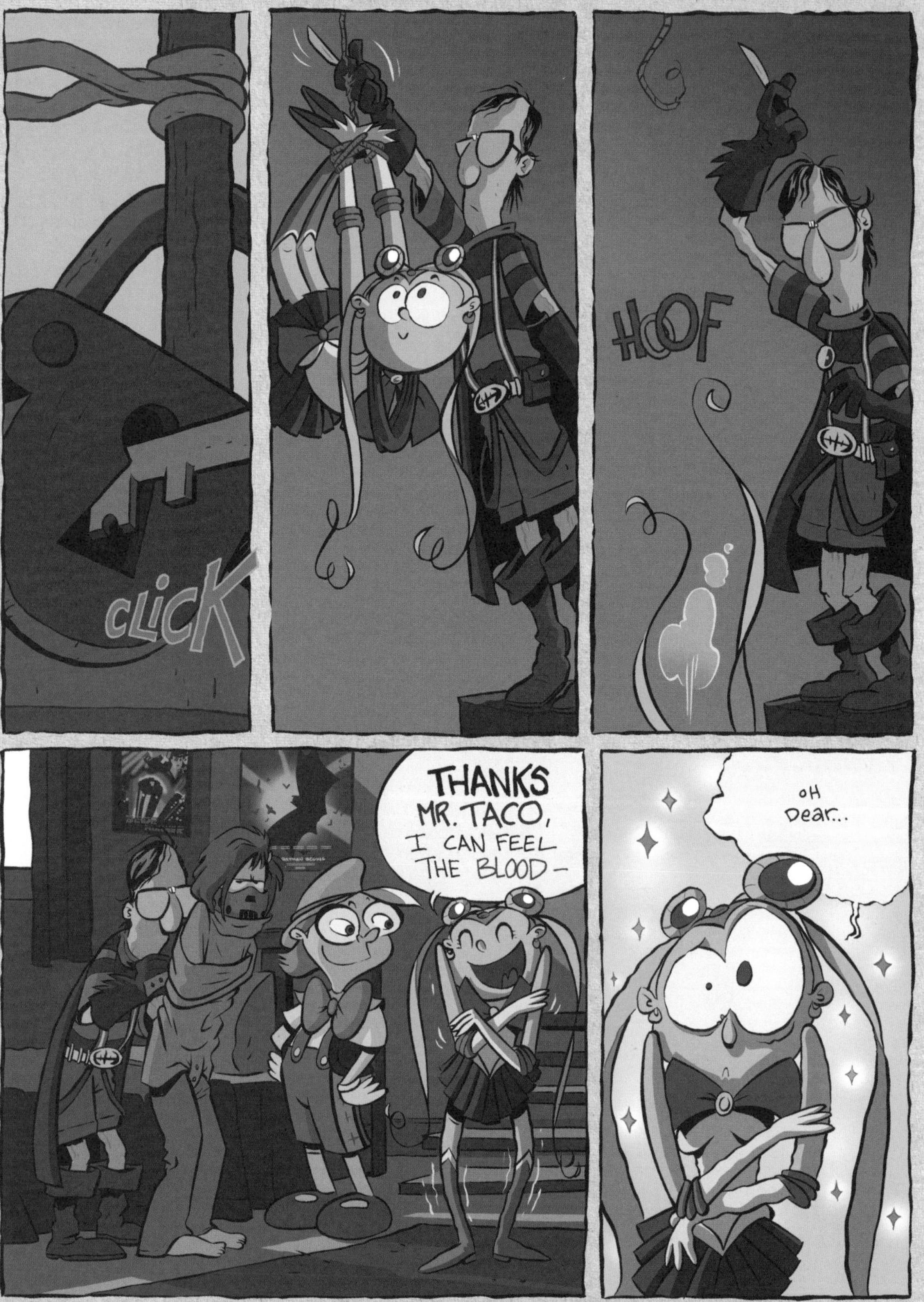
CLICK
HOOF
THANKS MR. TACO, I CAN FEEL THE BLOOD-
OH Dear..

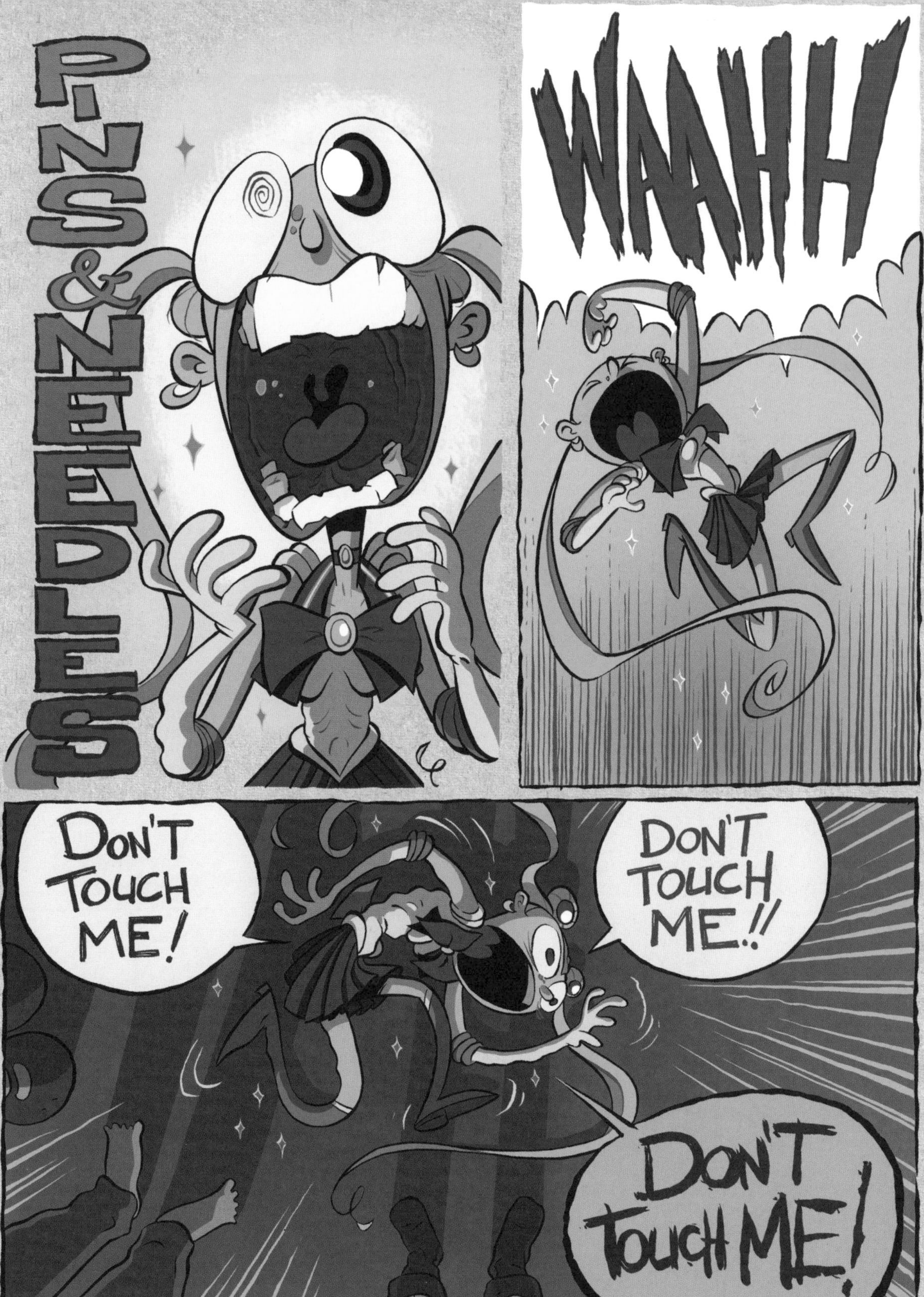

PINS & NEEDLES
WAAHH
DON'T TOUCH ME!
DON'T TOUCH ME!!
DON'T TOUCH ME!

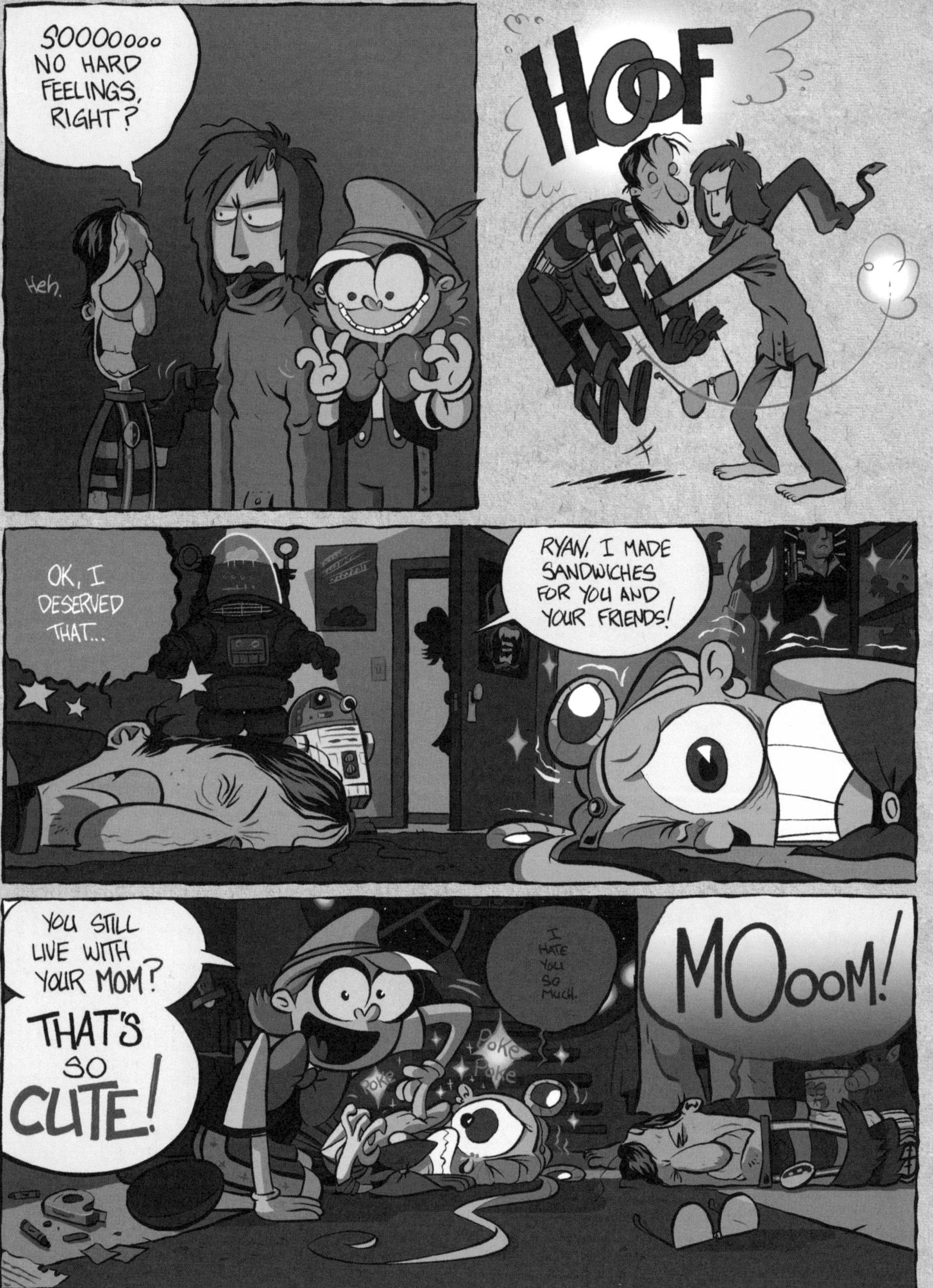
SOOOOooo NO HARD FEELINGS, RIGHT?
Heh.
HOOF
OK, I DESERVED THAT...
RYAN, I MADE SANDWICHES FOR YOU AND YOUR FRIENDS!
YOU STILL LIVE WITH YOUR MOM? THAT'S SO CUTE!
I HATE YOU SO MUCH.
POKE POKE POKE
MOoom!

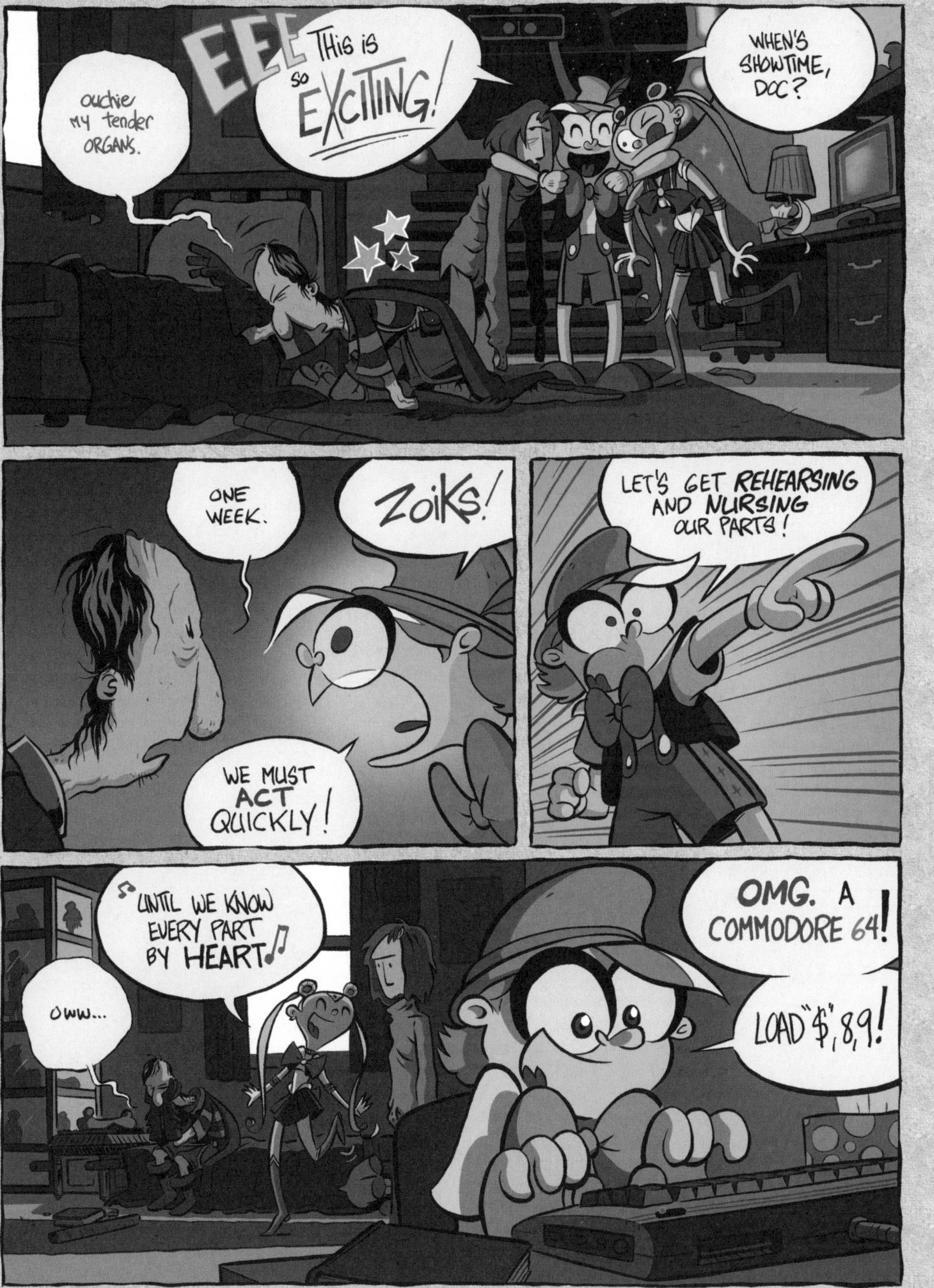
ouchie my tender ORGANS.
EEE
This is so EXCITING!
WHEN'S SHOWTIME, DOC?
ONE WEEK.
ZOIKS!
WE MUST ACT QUICKLY!
LET'S GET REHEARSING AND NURSING OUR PARTS!
UNTIL WE KNOW EVERY PART BY HEART
oww...
OMG. A COMMODORE 64!
LOAD"$",8,9!

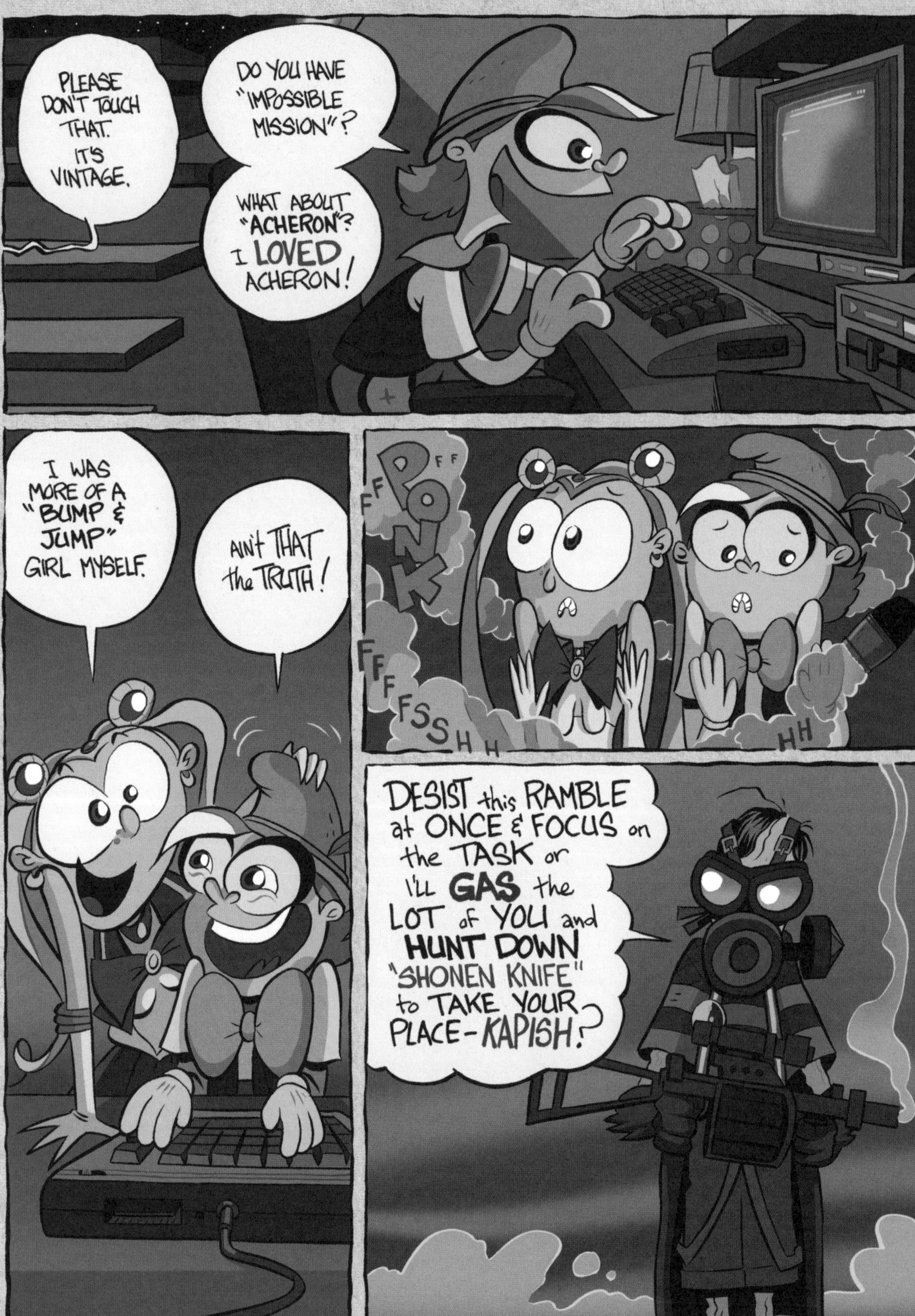
PLEASE DON'T TOUCH THAT. IT'S VINTAGE.
DO YOU HAVE "IMPOSSIBLE MISSION"?
WHAT ABOUT "ACHERON"? I LOVED ACHERON!
I WAS MORE OF A "BUMP & JUMP" GIRL MYSELF.
AIN'T THAT the TRUTH!
FF PONK FF
FFFFSSHHH
HH
DESIST this RAMBLE at ONCE & FOCUS on the TASK or I'LL GAS the LOT of YOU and HUNT DOWN "SHONEN KNIFE" to TAKE YOUR PLACE-KAPISH?

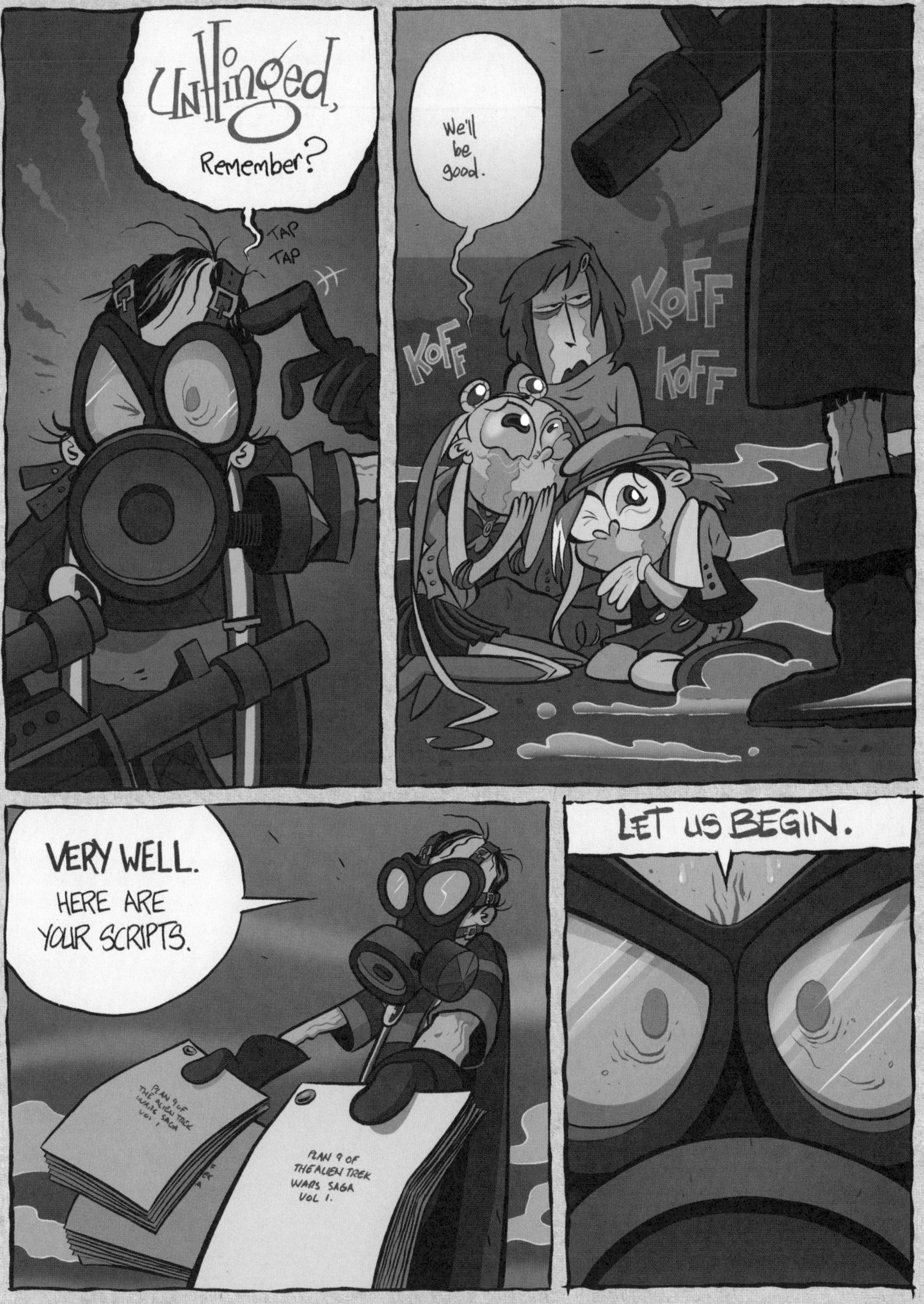
UnHinged, Remember?
TAP TAP
We'll be good.
KOFF
KOFF
KOFF
VERY WELL. HERE ARE YOUR SCRIPTS.
PLAN 9 OF THE ALIEN TREK WARS SAGA VOL 1.
LET US BEGIN.

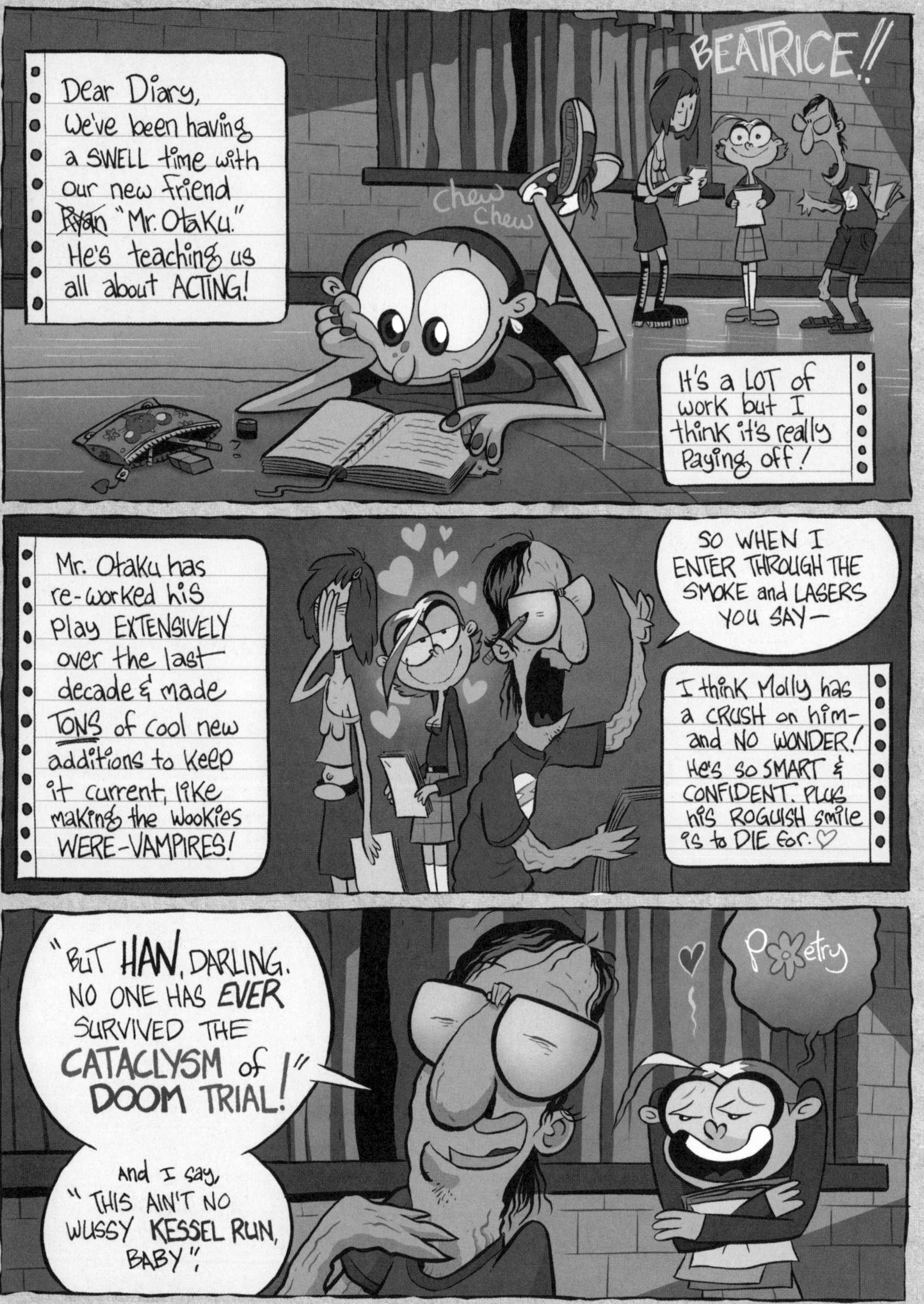

Dear Diary,
We've been having a SWELL time with our new friend Ryan "Mr. Otaku."
He's teaching us all about ACTING!
BEATRICE!!
chew chew
It's a LOT of work but I think it's really Paying off!
Mr. Otaku has re-worked his play EXTENSIVELY over the last decade & made TONS of cool new additions to keep it current, like making the wookies WERE-VAMPIRES!
SO WHEN I ENTER THROUGH THE SMOKE and LASERS YOU SAY—
I think Molly has a CRUSH on him- and NO WONDER! He's so SMART & CONFIDENT. PLUS his ROGUISH smile is to DIE for.
"BUT HAN, DARLING. NO ONE HAS EVER SURVIVED THE CATACLYSM of DOOM TRIAL!"
And I say, "THIS AIN'T NO WUSSY KESSEL RUN, BABY".
Poetry

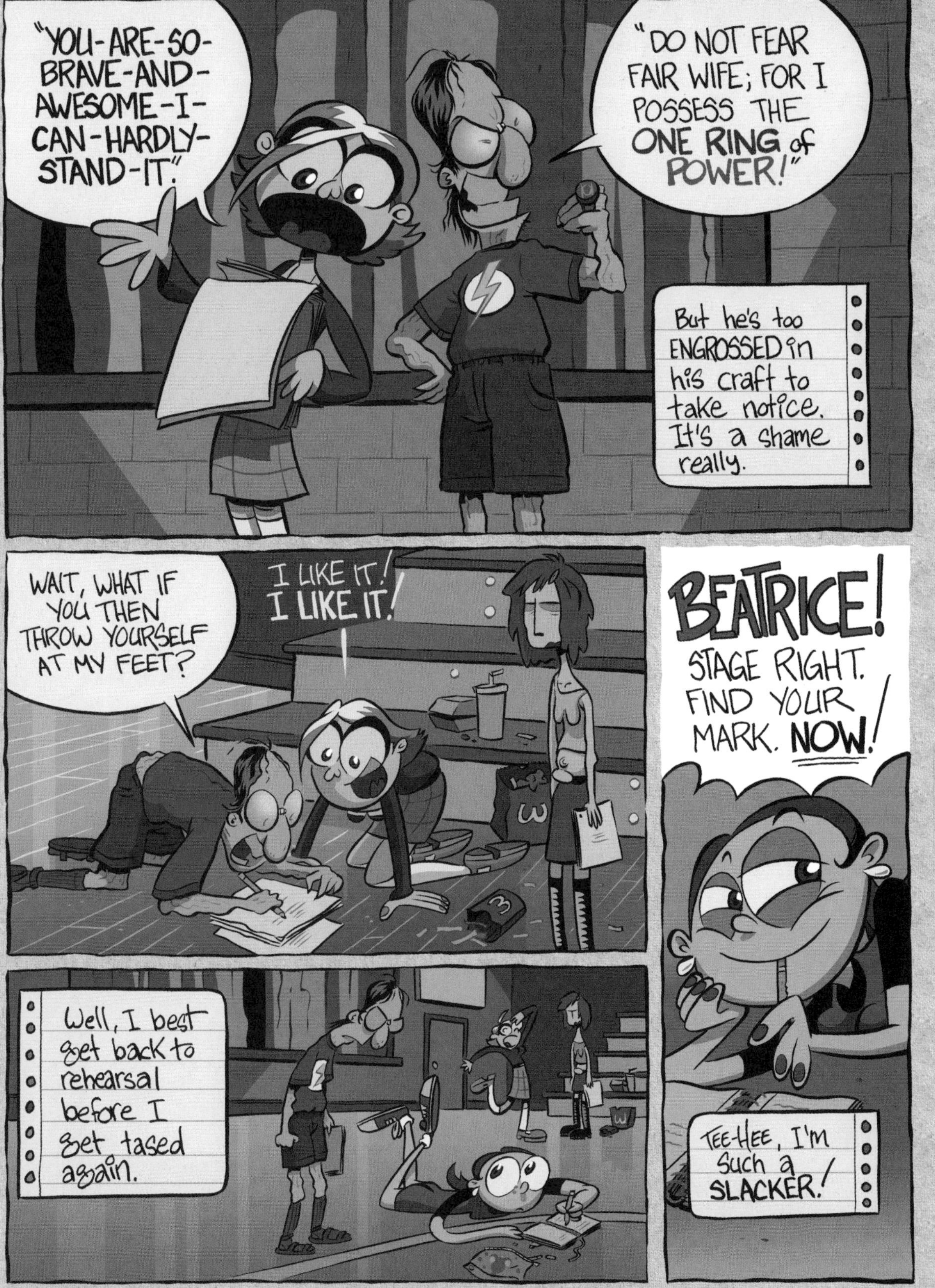

"YOU-ARE-SO-BRAVE-AND-AWESOME-I-CAN-HARDLY-STAND-IT."
"DO NOT FEAR FAIR WIFE; FOR I POSSESS THE ONE RING of POWER!"
But he's too ENGROSSED in his craft to take notice. It's a shame really.
WAIT, WHAT IF YOU THEN THROW YOURSELF AT MY FEET?
I LIKE IT! I LIKE IT!
BEATRICE! STAGE RIGHT. FIND YOUR MARK. NOW!
Well, I best get back to rehearsal before I get tased again.
TEE-HEE, I'm Such a SLACKER!

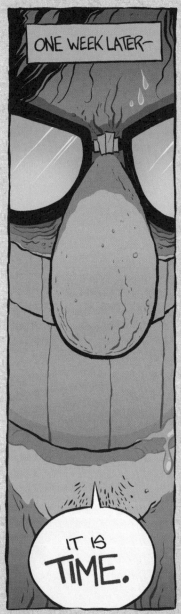

ONE WEEK LATER—

A **MERE** AUTOMATED PHONE CALL WILL ACTIVATE A **SUB-LIMINAL** PROGRAM I'VE PLANTED IN MY CLASSMATES THAT WILL LEAD THEM HERE.

IT IS **TIME.**

DIAL NOW!

Beep
Beep

WE HAVE **30 MINUTES** UNTIL THEY ARRIVE...

LADIES, REMOVE YOUR CLOTHES.

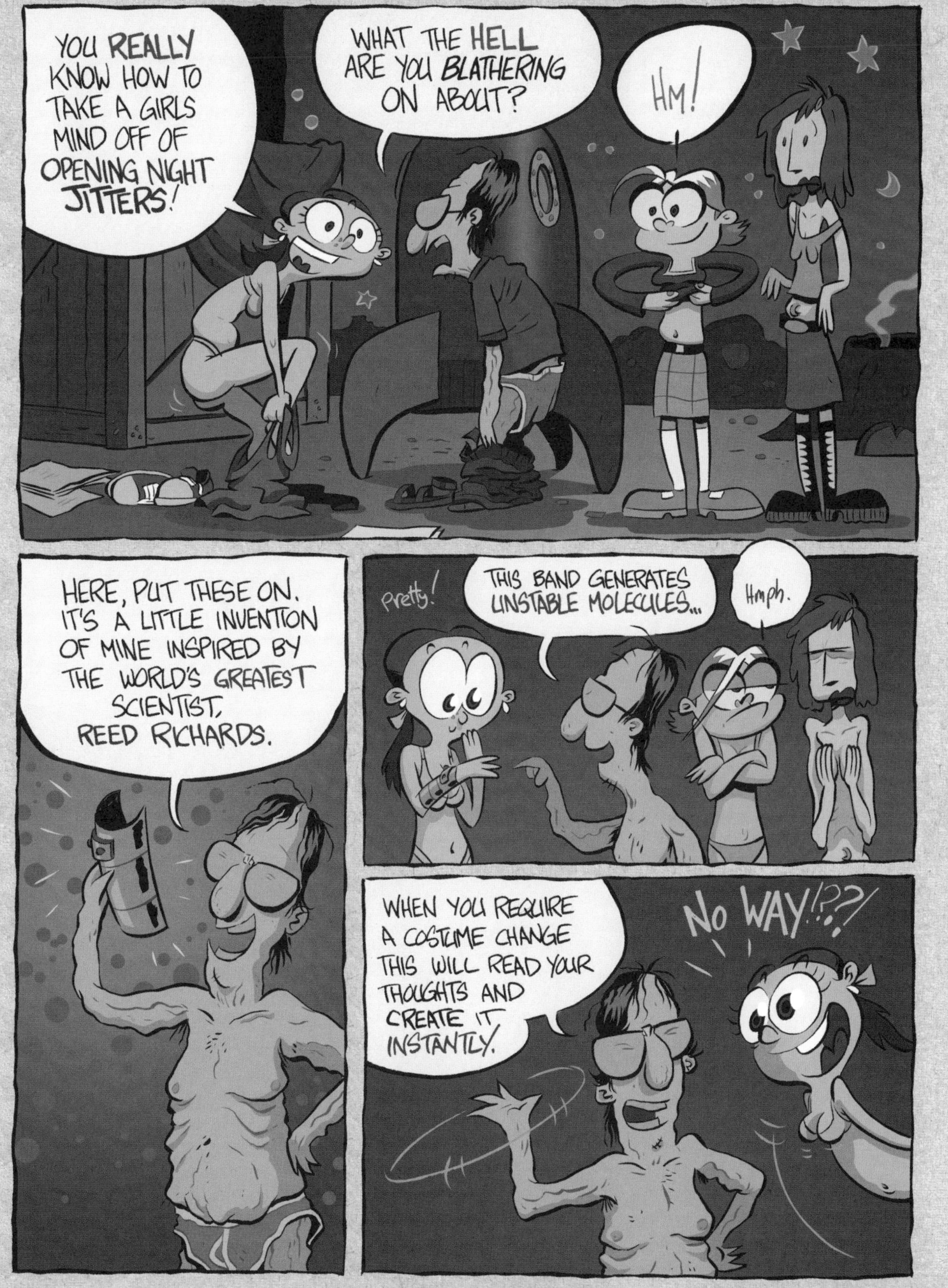
YOU REALLY KNOW HOW TO TAKE A GIRLS MIND OFF OF OPENING NIGHT JITTERS!
WHAT THE HELL ARE YOU BLATHERING ON ABOUT?
HM!
HERE, PUT THESE ON. IT'S A LITTLE INVENTION OF MINE INSPIRED BY THE WORLD'S GREATEST SCIENTIST, REED RICHARDS.
Pretty!
THIS BAND GENERATES UNSTABLE MOLECULES...
Hmph.
WHEN YOU REQUIRE A COSTUME CHANGE THIS WILL READ YOUR THOUGHTS AND CREATE IT INSTANTLY.
No WAY!?!?!

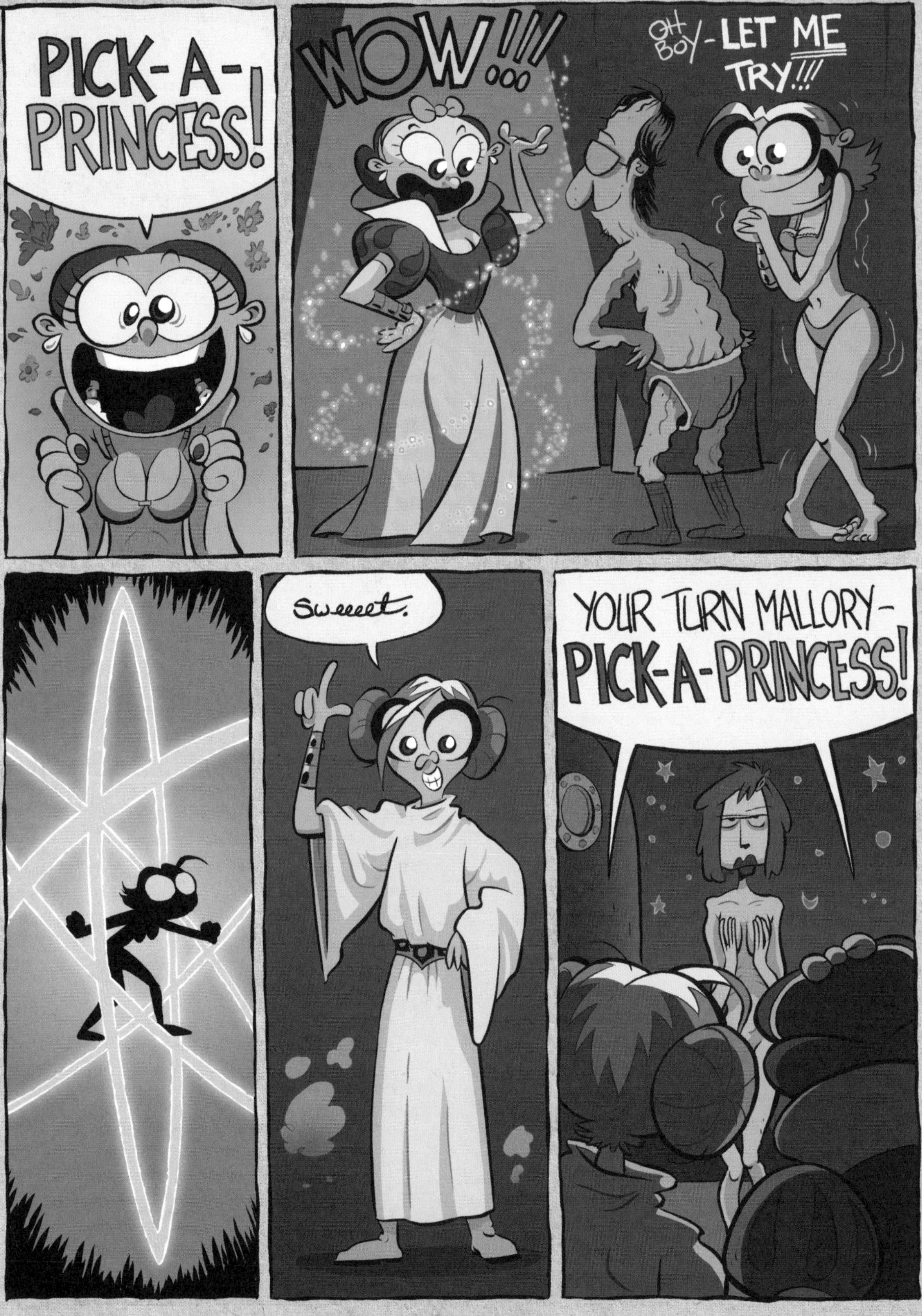
PICK-A-PRINCESS!
WOW!!!
ooo
OH BOY-LET ME TRY!!!
Sweeeet.
YOUR TURN MALLORY-
PICK-A-PRINCESS!

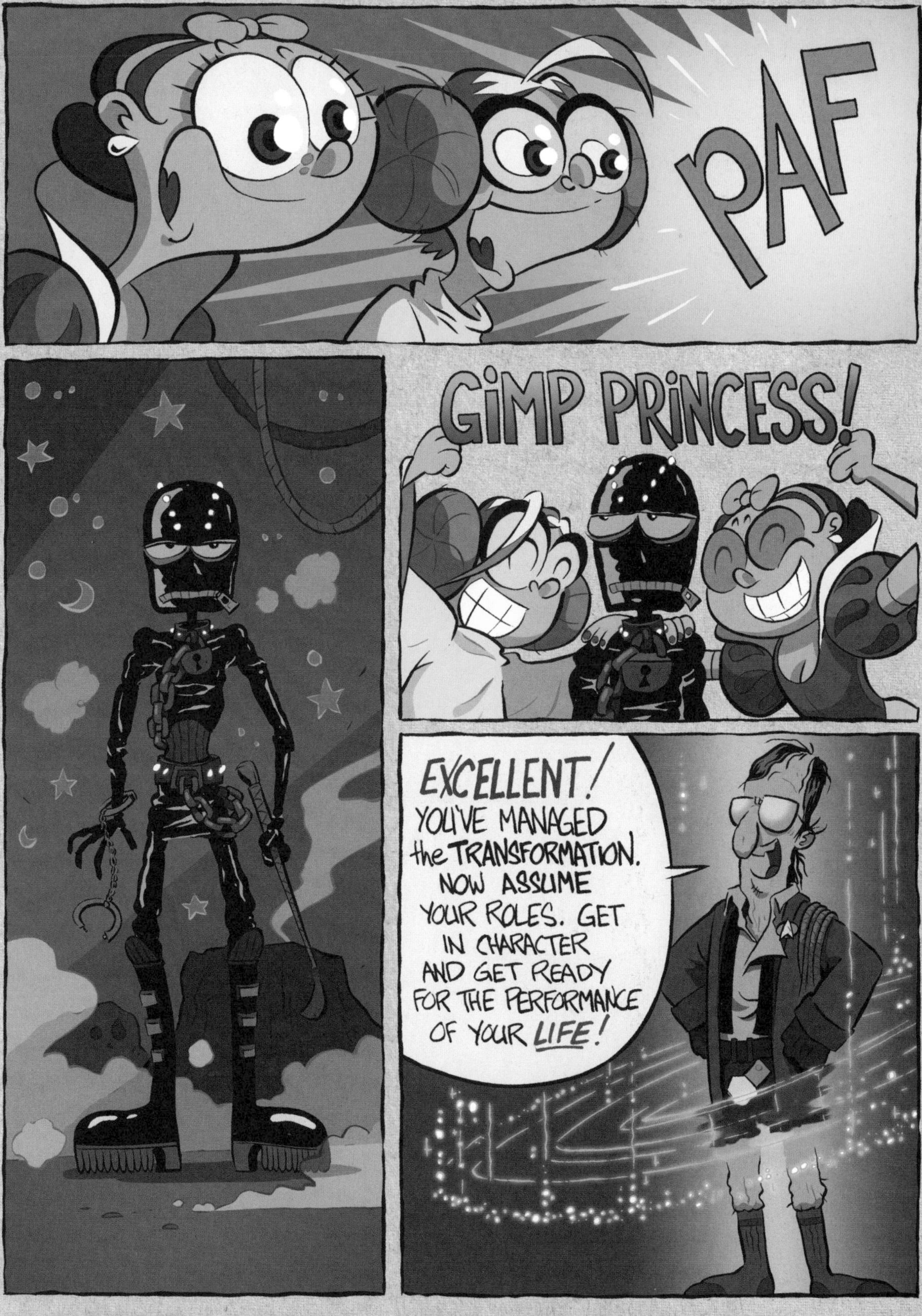
PAF
GIMP PRINCESS!
EXCELLENT! YOU'VE MANAGED the TRANSFORMATION. NOW ASSUME YOUR ROLES. GET IN CHARACTER AND GET READY FOR THE PERFORMANCE OF YOUR LIFE!

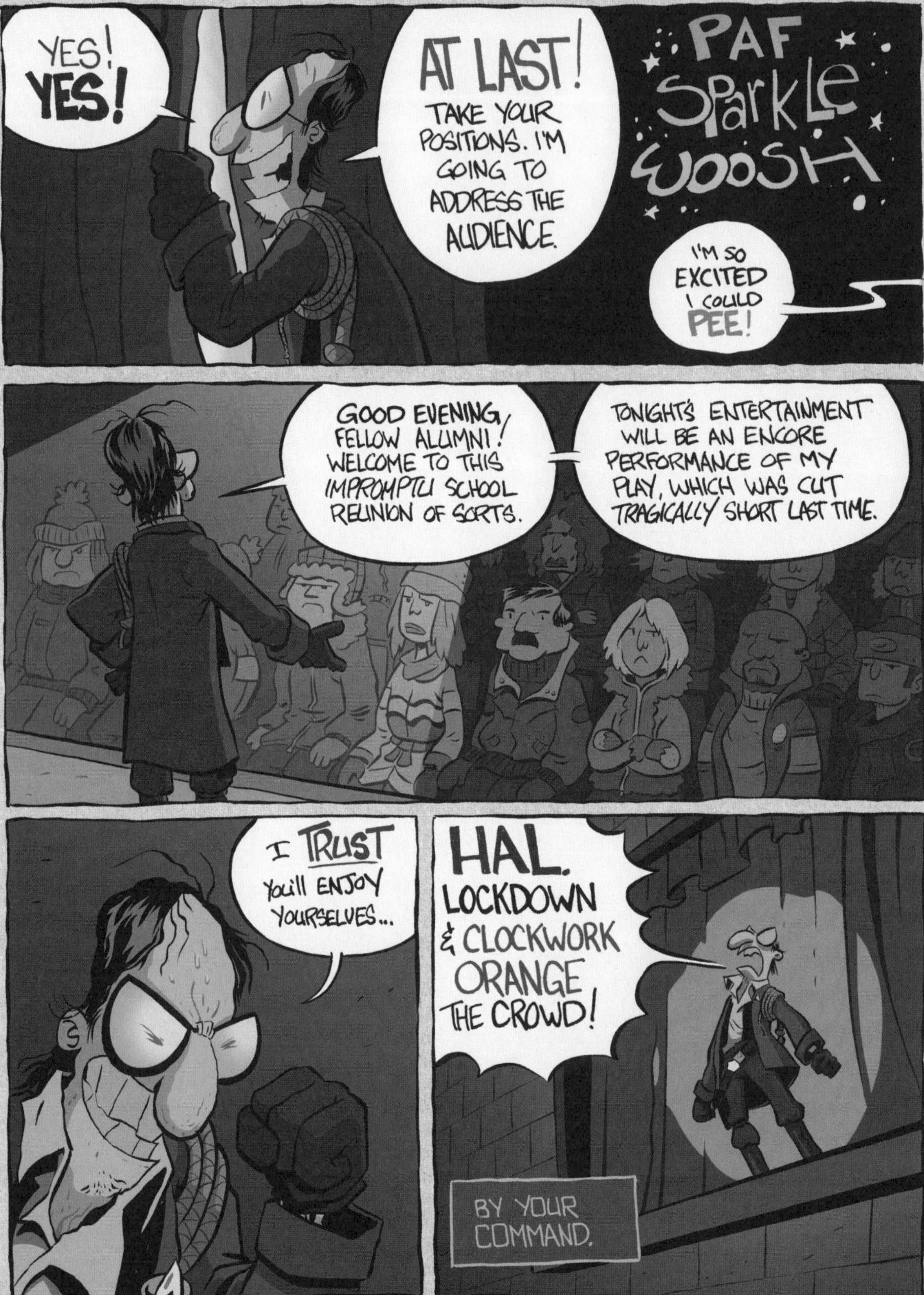
YES! YES!
AT LAST! TAKE YOUR POSITIONS. I'M GOING TO ADDRESS THE AUDIENCE.
PAF SPARKLE WOOSH
I'M SO EXCITED I COULD PEE!
GOOD EVENING, FELLOW ALUMNI! WELCOME TO THIS IMPROMPTU SCHOOL REUNION OF SORTS.
TONIGHT'S ENTERTAINMENT WILL BE AN ENCORE PERFORMANCE OF MY PLAY, WHICH WAS CUT TRAGICALLY SHORT LAST TIME.
I TRUST YOU'LL ENJOY YOURSELVES...
HAL. LOCKDOWN & CLOCKWORK ORANGE THE CROWD!
BY YOUR COMMAND.

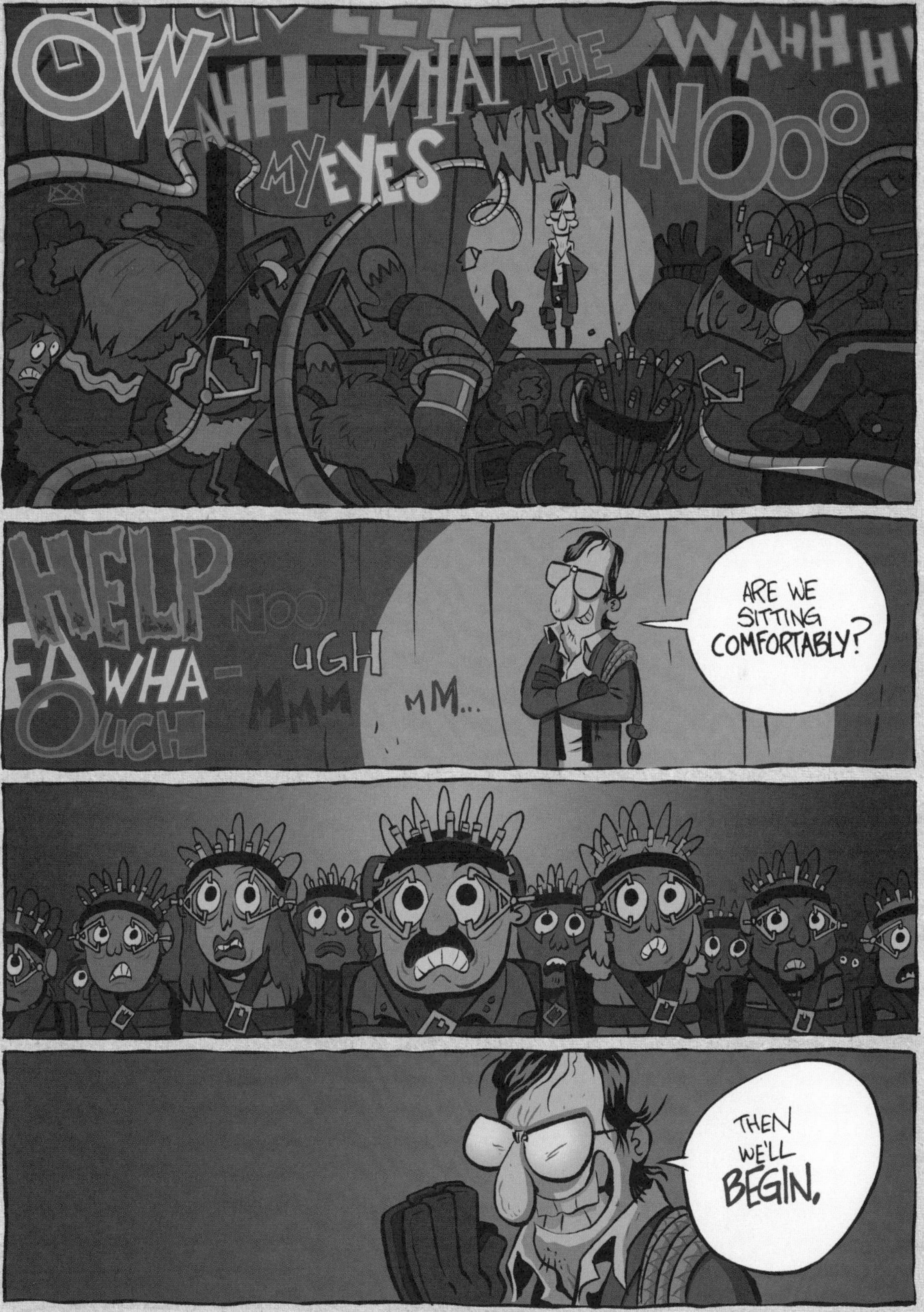

OW
WAHH
WHAT THE
WAHHHH
MY EYES
WHY?
NOOO
HELP
NOO
WHA-
OUCH
UGH
MMM
MM...
ARE WE SITTING COMFORTABLY?
THEN WE'LL BEGIN.

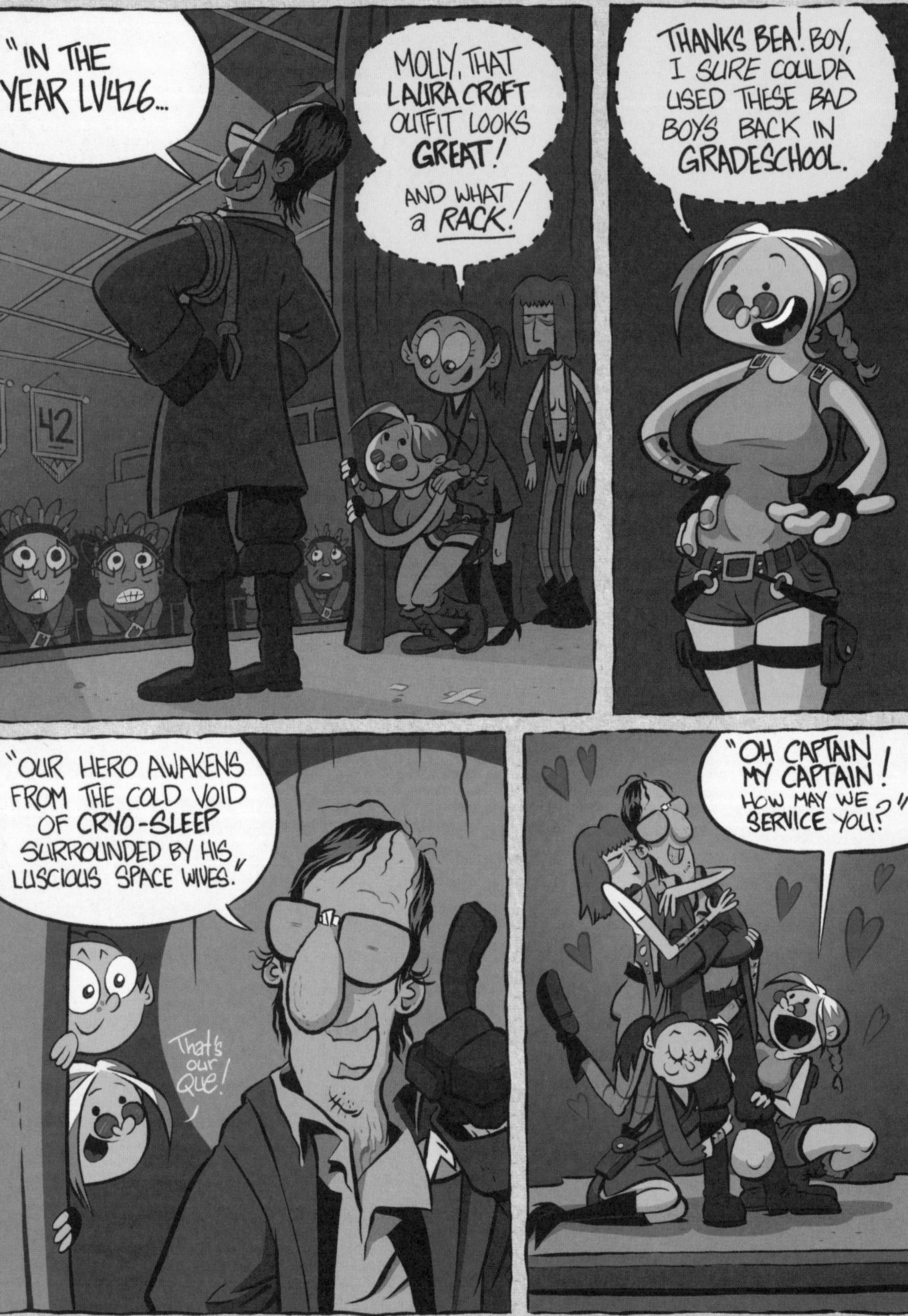
"IN THE YEAR LV426...
MOLLY, THAT LAURA CROFT OUTFIT LOOKS GREAT!
AND WHAT a RACK!
THANKS BEA! BOY, I SURE COULDA USED THESE BAD BOYS BACK IN GRADESCHOOL.
"OUR HERO AWAKENS FROM THE COLD VOID OF CRYO-SLEEP SURROUNDED BY HIS LUSCIOUS SPACE WIVES."
That's our Que!
"OH CAPTAIN MY CAPTAIN! HOW MAY WE SERVICE YOU?"
42

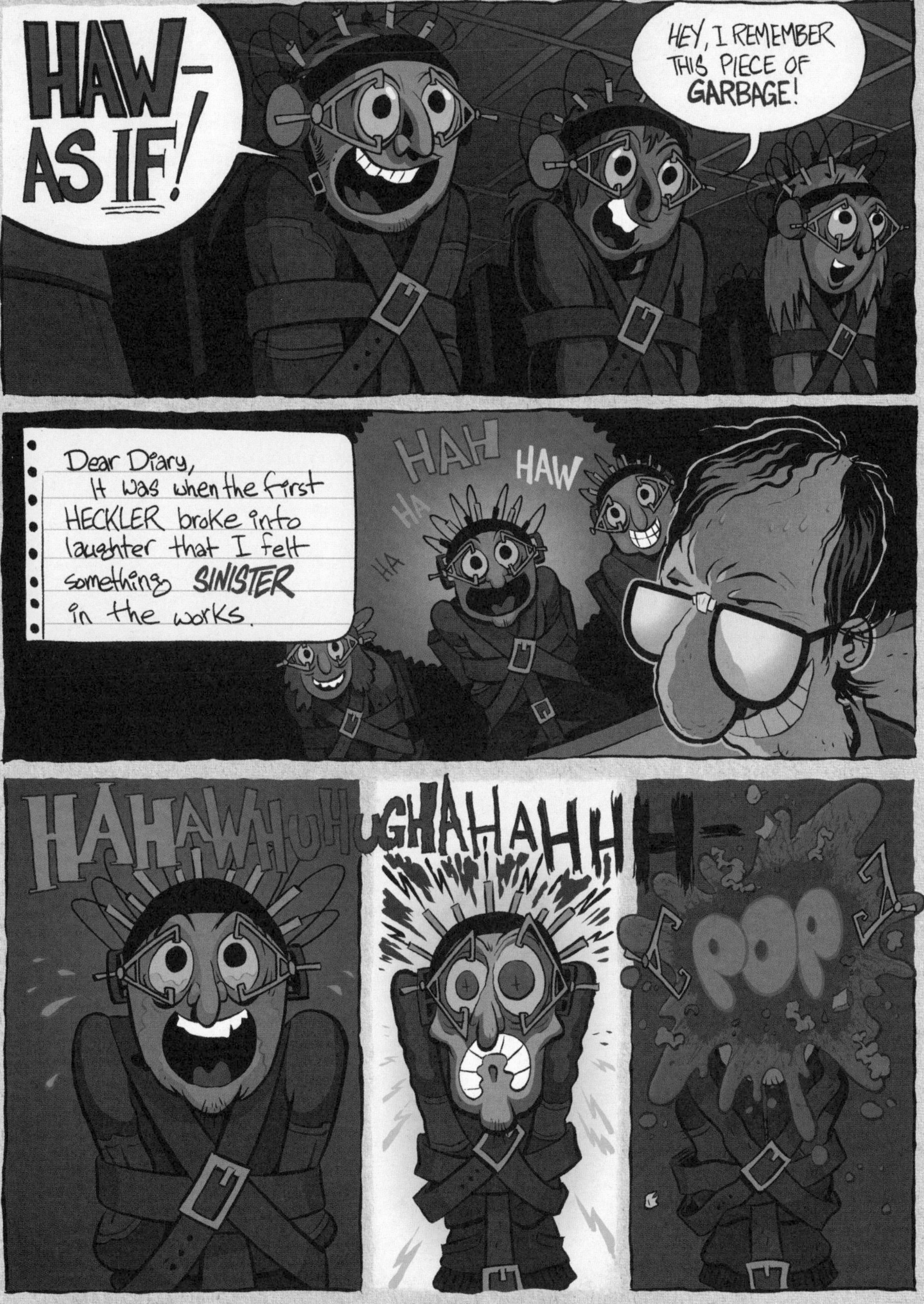
HAW-HAW-AS IF!
HEY, I REMEMBER THIS PIECE OF GARBAGE!
Dear Diary,
It was when the first HECKLER broke into laughter that I felt something SINISTER in the works.
HAH
HAW
HA
HA
HAHAHAWHUHUGHAHAHHHH-
POP

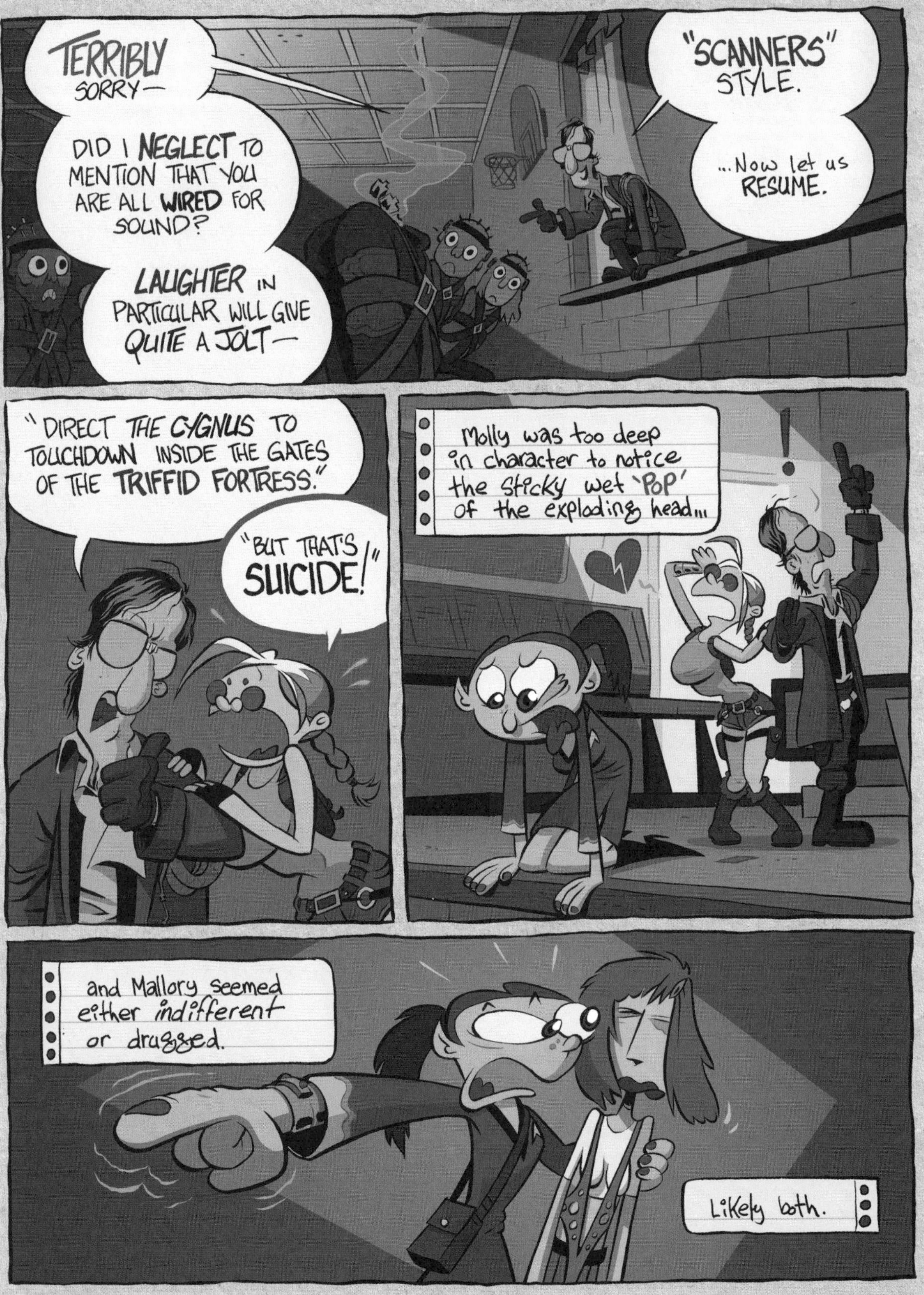
TERRIBLY SORRY—
DID I NEGLECT TO MENTION THAT YOU ARE ALL WIRED FOR SOUND?
LAUGHTER IN PARTICULAR WILL GIVE QUITE A JOLT—
"SCANNERS" STYLE.
...Now let us RESUME.
"DIRECT THE CYGNUS TO TOUCHDOWN INSIDE THE GATES OF THE TRIFFID FORTRESS."
"BUT THAT'S SUICIDE!"
Molly was too deep in character to notice the sticky wet 'POP' of the exploding head...
!
and Mallory seemed either indifferent or drugged.
Likely both.

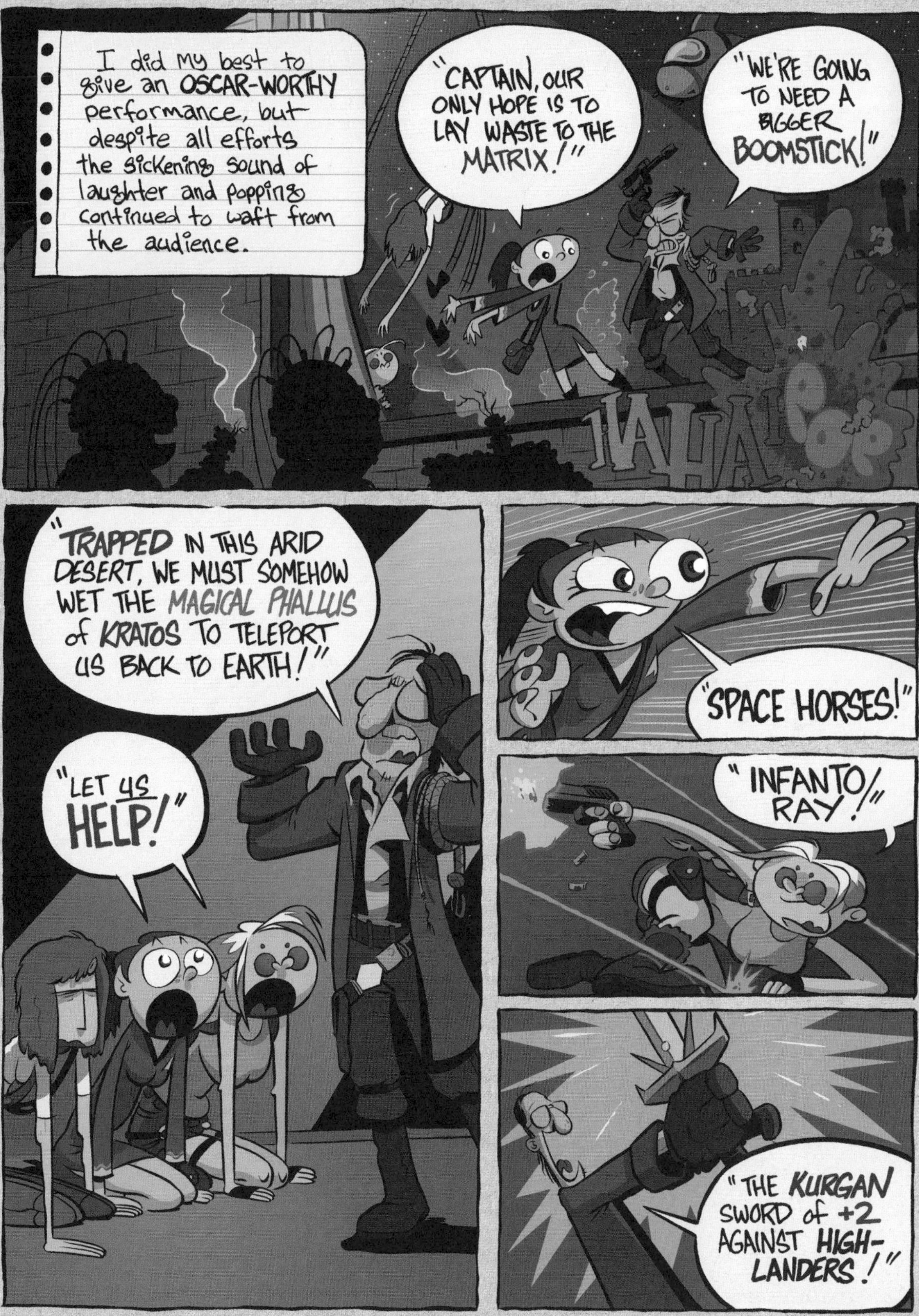
I did my best to give an OSCAR-WORTHY performance, but despite all efforts the sickening sound of laughter and popping continued to waft from the audience.
"CAPTAIN, OUR ONLY HOPE IS TO LAY WASTE TO THE MATRIX!"
"WE'RE GOING TO NEED A BIGGER BOOMSTICK!"
HAHA
POP
"TRAPPED IN THIS ARID DESERT, WE MUST SOMEHOW WET THE MAGICAL PHALLUS of KRATOS TO TELEPORT US BACK TO EARTH!"
"LET US HELP!"
"SPACE HORSES!"
"INFANTO/ RAY!"
"THE KURGAN SWORD of +2 AGAINST HIGH-LANDERS!"

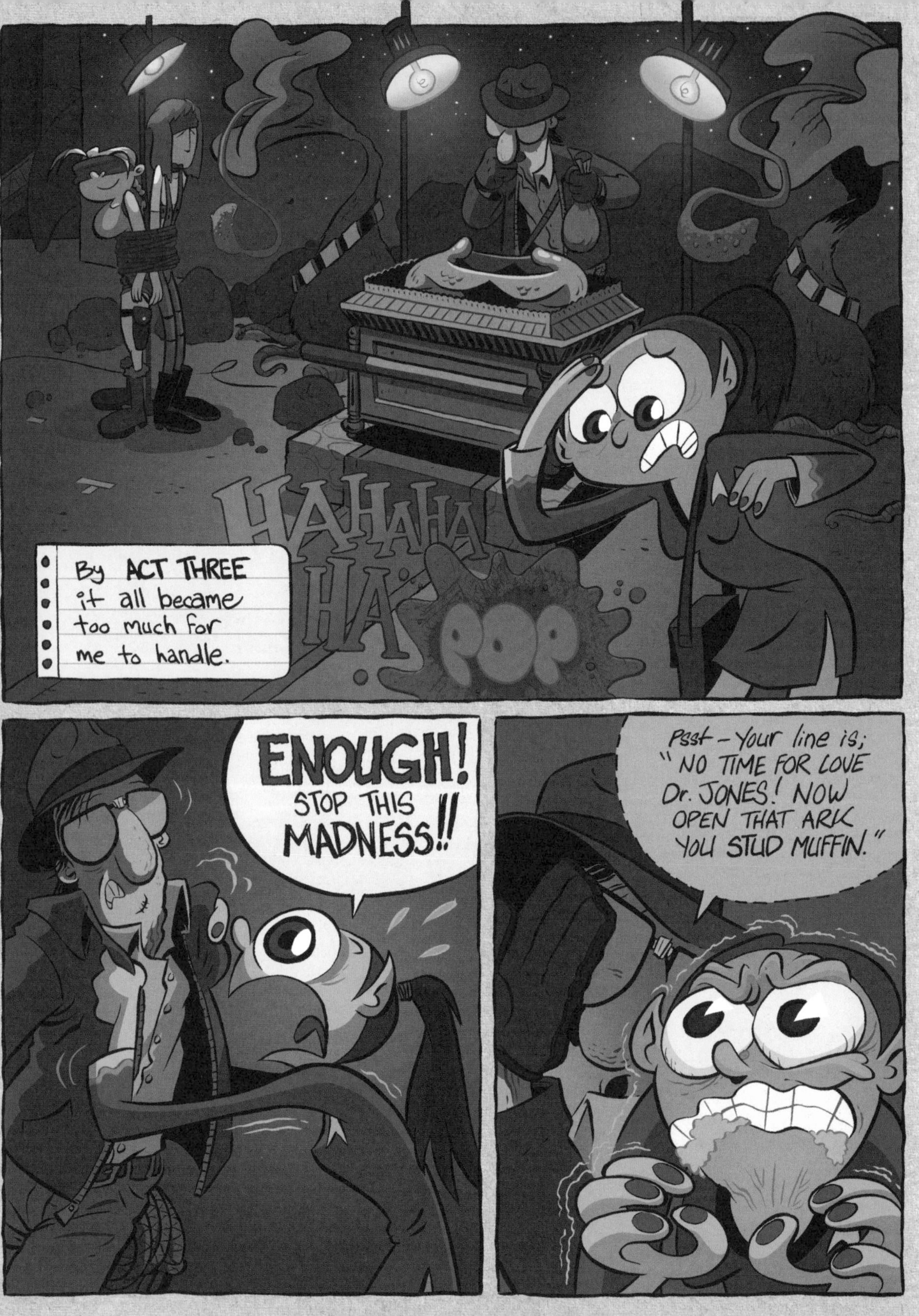

By ACT THREE it all became too much for me to handle.
HAHAHA HA
POP
ENOUGH! STOP THIS MADNESS!!
Psst - Your line is; "NO TIME FOR LOVE Dr. JONES! NOW OPEN THAT ARK YOU STUD MUFFIN."

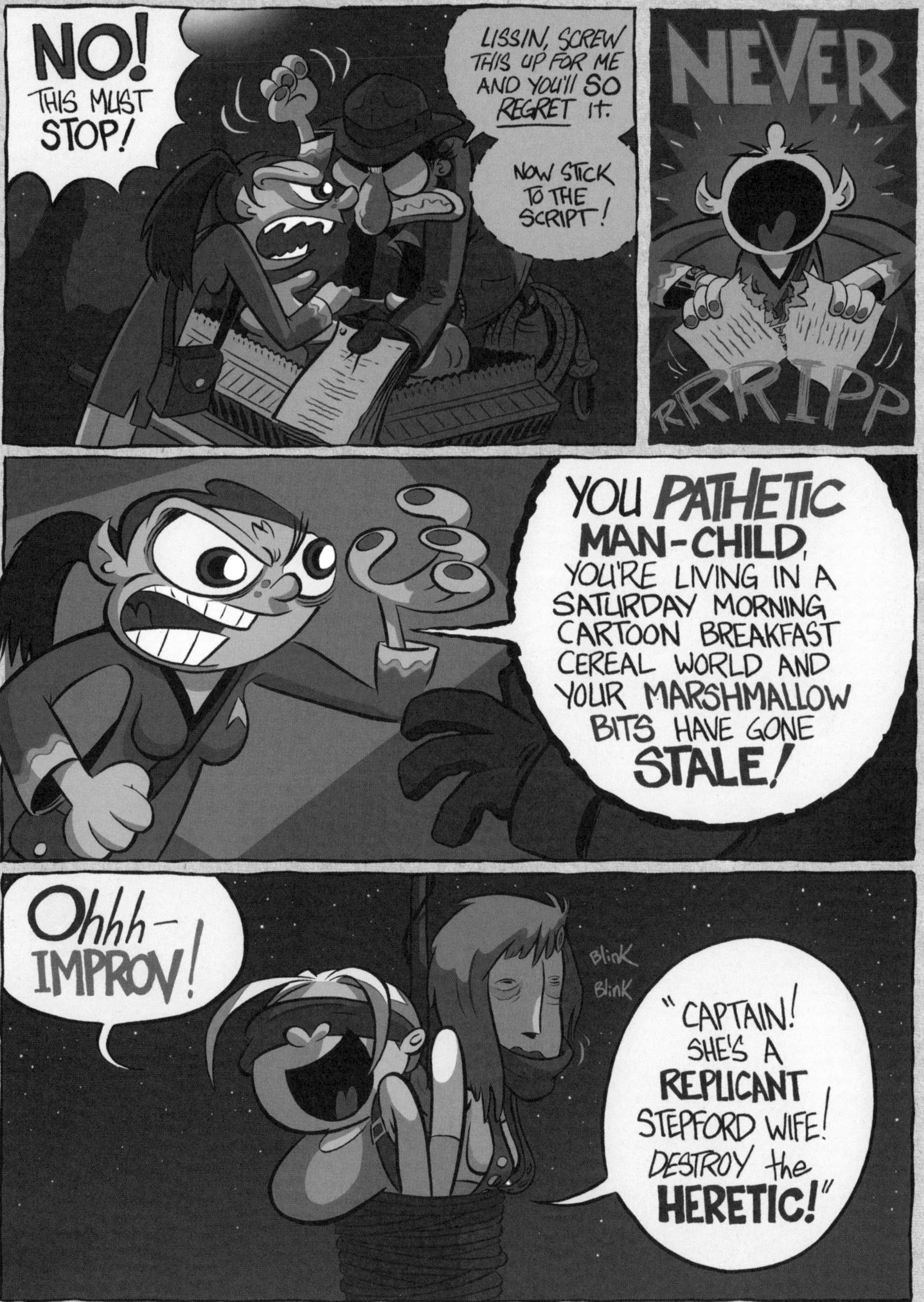
NO! THIS MUST STOP!
LISSIN, SCREW THIS UP FOR ME AND YOU'LL SO REGRET IT.
NOW STICK TO THE SCRIPT!
NEVER
RRRIPP
YOU PATHETIC MAN-CHILD, YOU'RE LIVING IN A SATURDAY MORNING CARTOON BREAKFAST CEREAL WORLD AND YOUR MARSHMALLOW BITS HAVE GONE STALE!
Ohhh- IMPROV!
BLINK BLINK
"CAPTAIN! SHE'S A REPLICANT STEPFORD WIFE! DESTROY the HERETIC!"

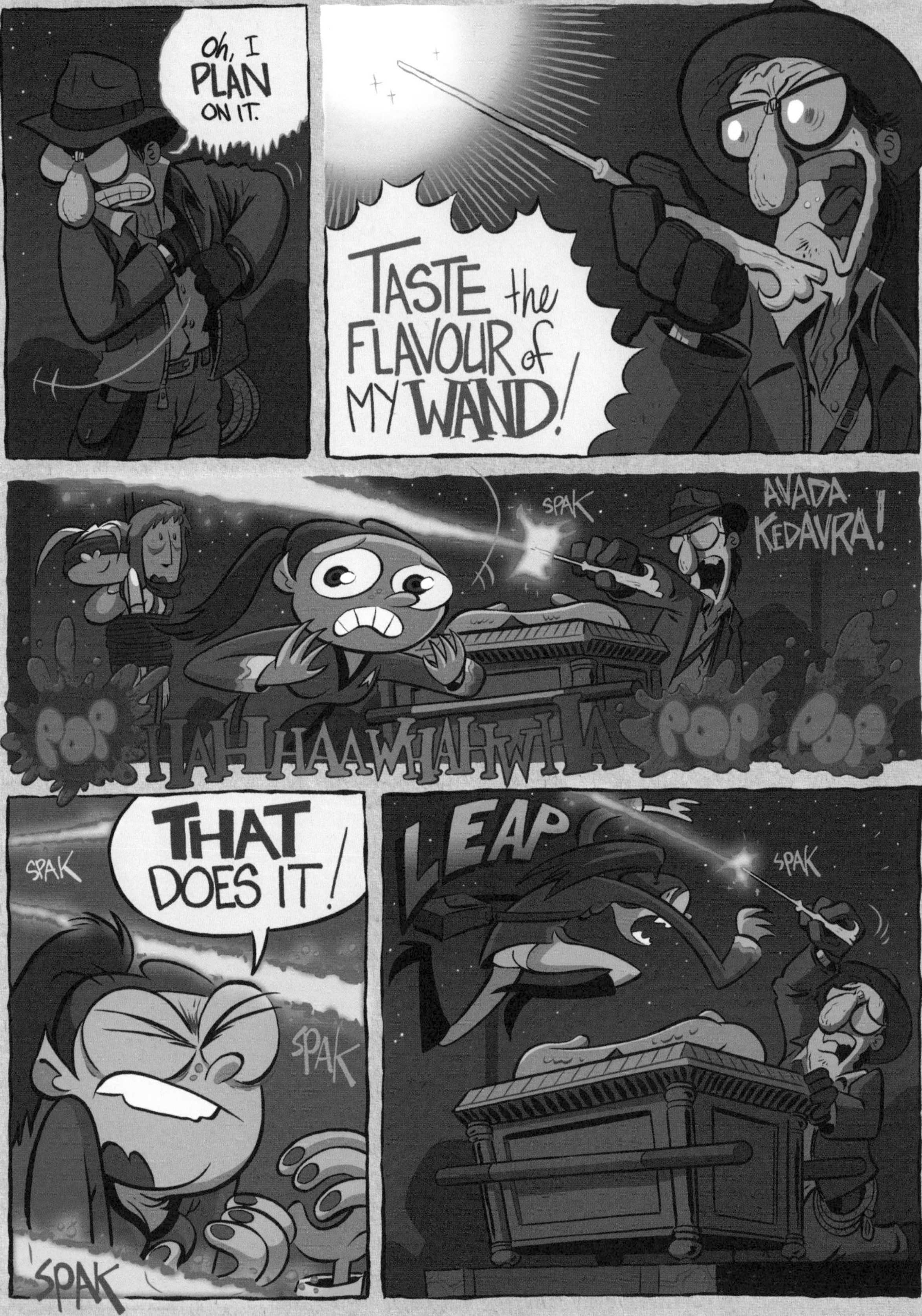
Oh, I PLAN ON IT.
TASTE the FLAVOUR of MY WAND!
SPAK
AVADA KEDAVRA!
POP
HAHHAAWHAHWHA
POP
POP
THAT DOES IT!
SPAK
SPAK
SPAK
LEAP
SPAK

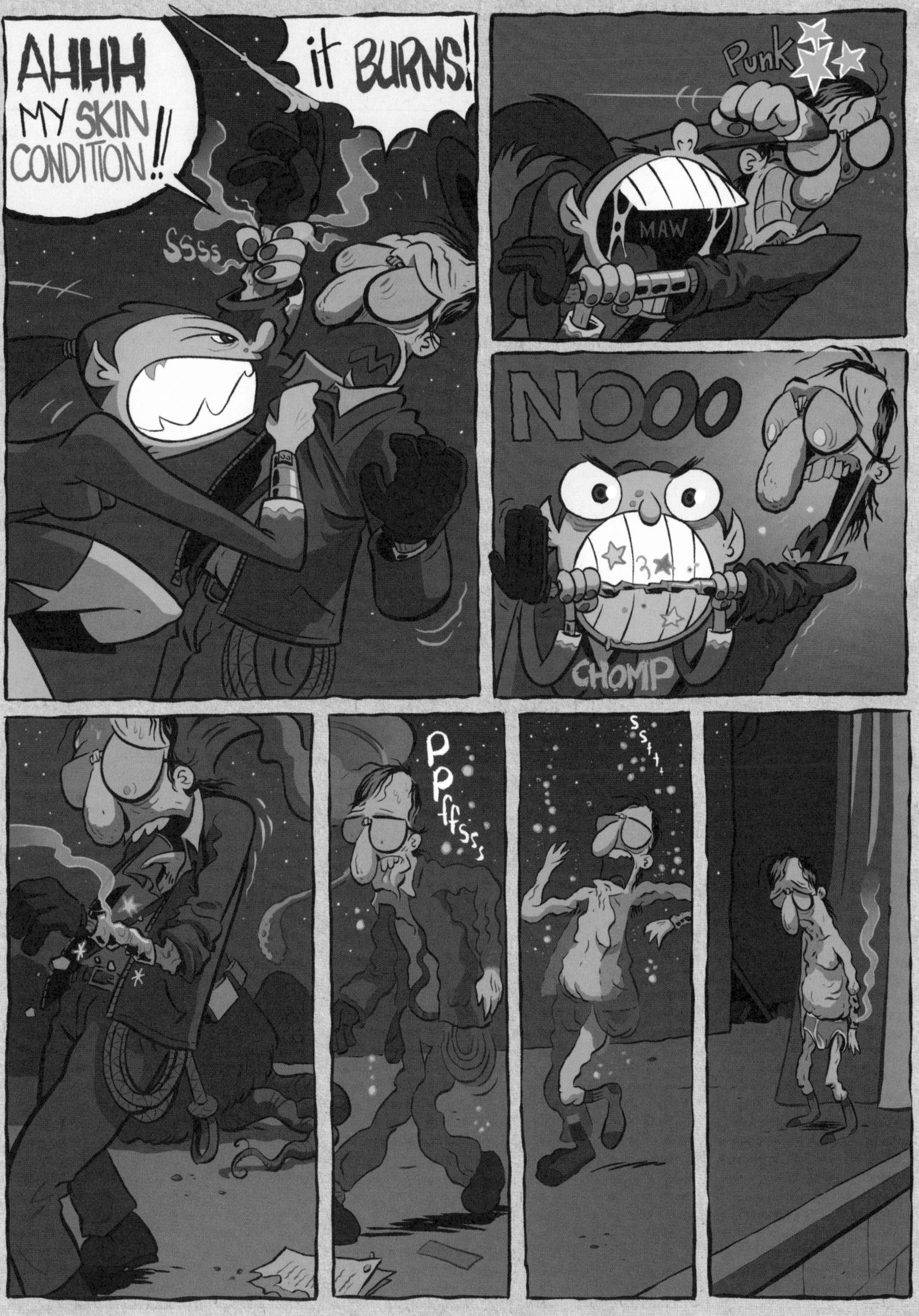
AHHH MY SKIN CONDITION!!
it BURNS!
Ssss
Punk
MAW
NOOO
CHOMP
PPffsss
ssttt

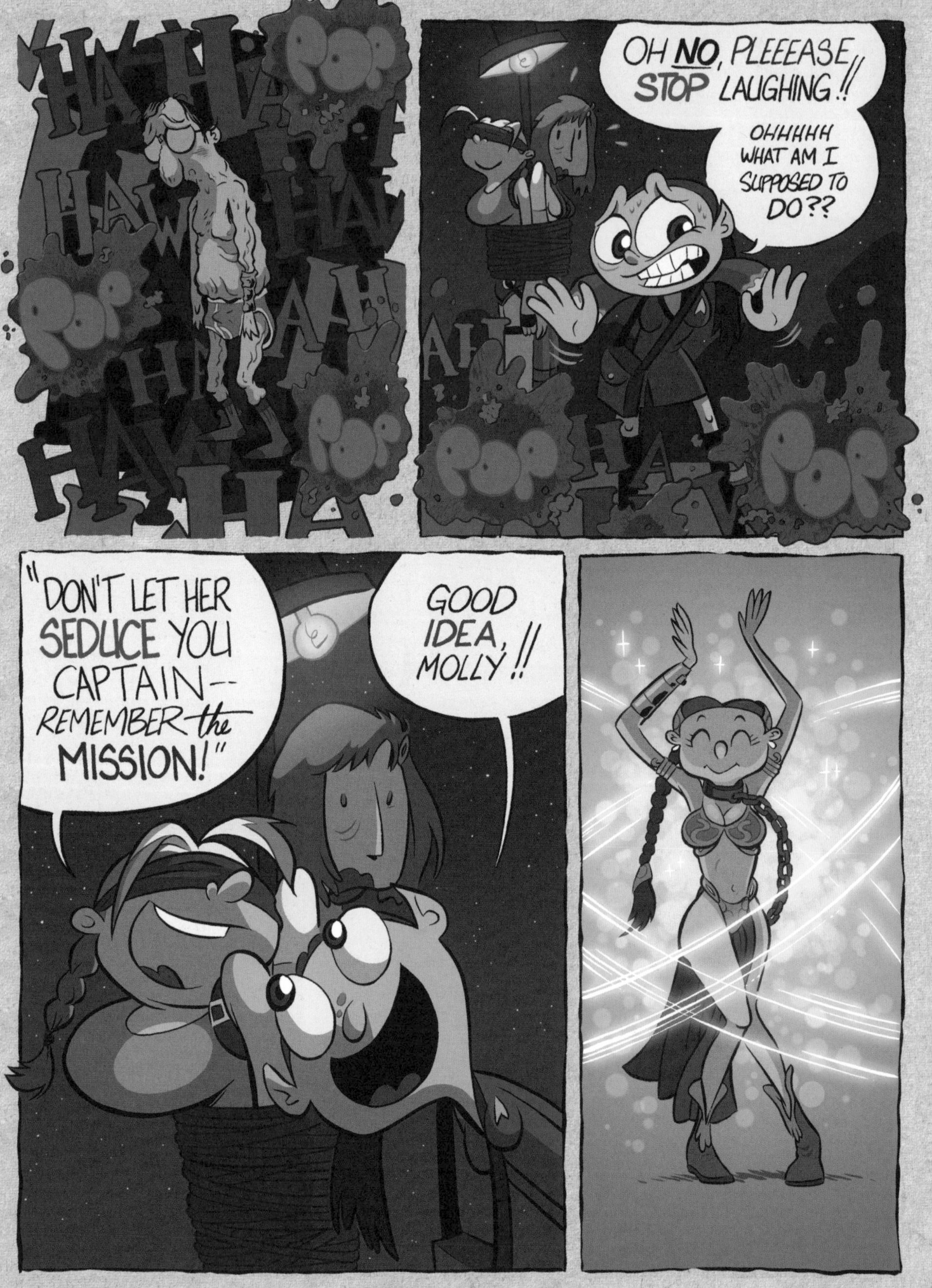
"HA HA HA
HA HA HA
POP
AH
HA
POP
HA
POP
OH NO, PLEEEASE, STOP LAUGHING!!
OHHHHH WHAT AM I SUPPOSED TO DO??
AH
POP
HA
POP
"DON'T LET HER SEDUCE YOU CAPTAIN-- REMEMBER the MISSION!"
GOOD IDEA, MOLLY!!

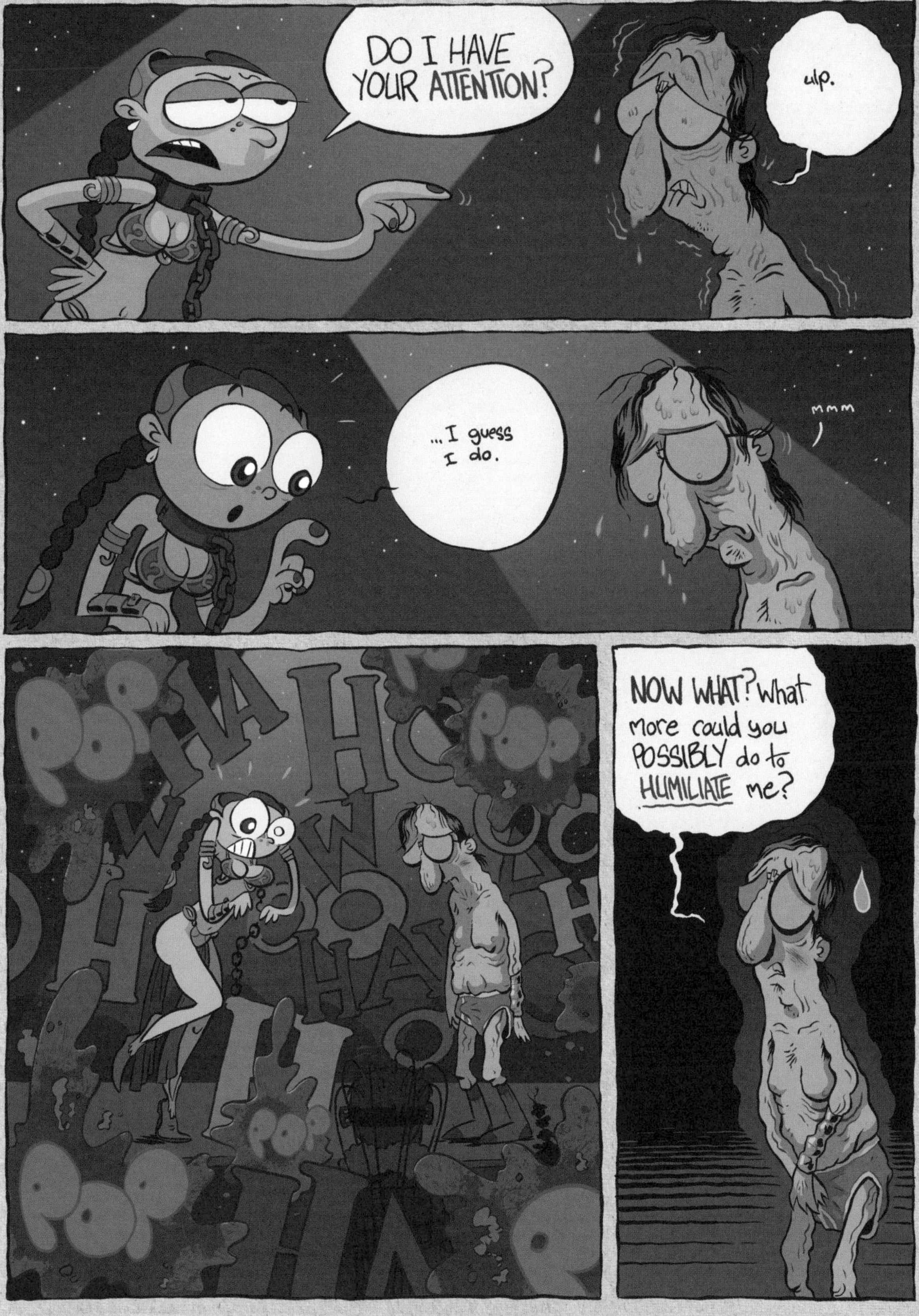
DO I HAVE YOUR ATTENTION?
ulp.
...I guess I do.
MMM
NOW WHAT? What more could you POSSIBLY do to HUMILIATE me?

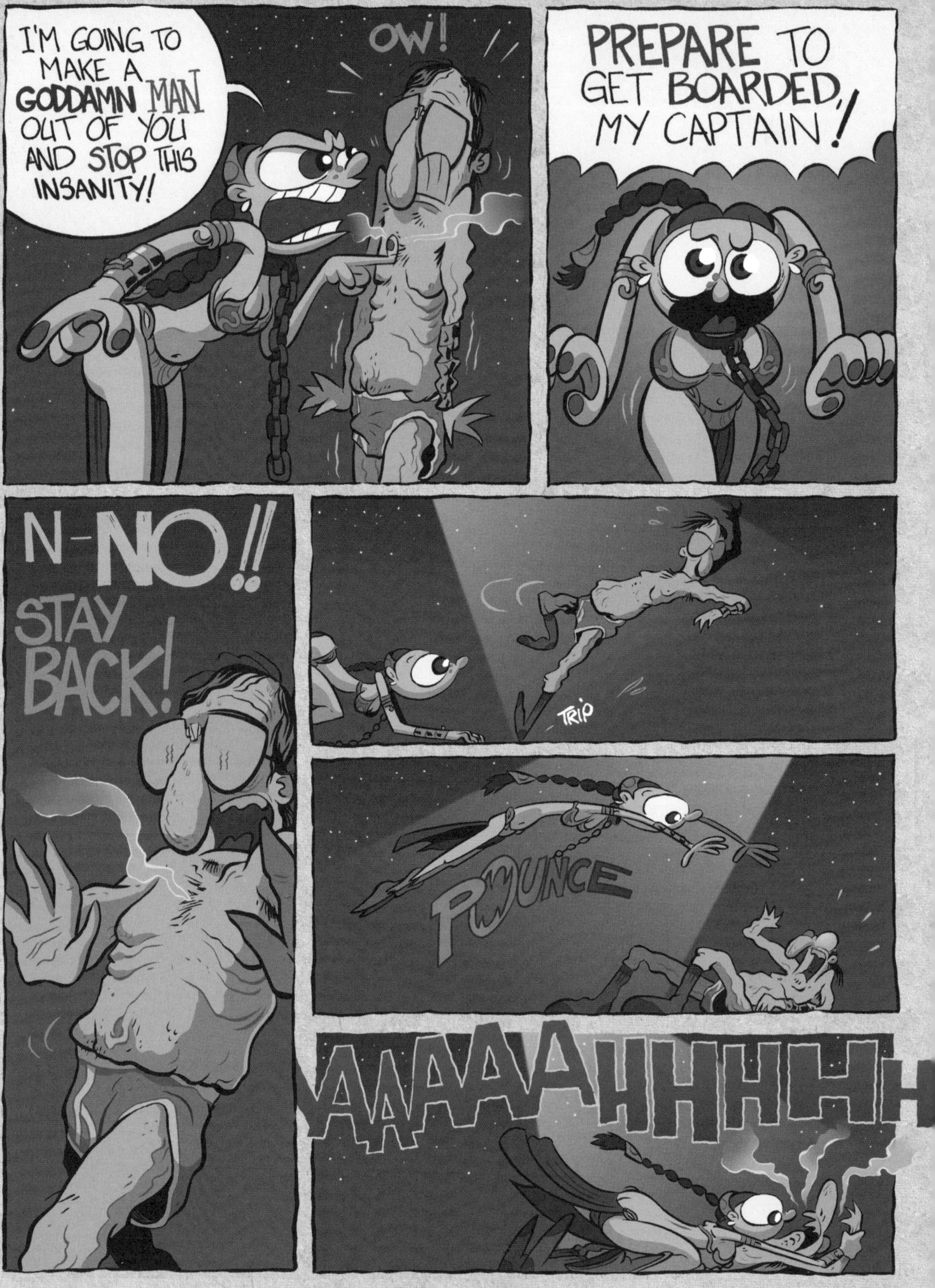
I'M GOING TO MAKE A GODDAMN MAN OUT OF YOU AND STOP THIS INSANITY!
OW!
PREPARE TO GET BOARDED, MY CAPTAIN!
N-NO!! STAY BACK!
TRIP
POUNCE
AAAAAHHHHH

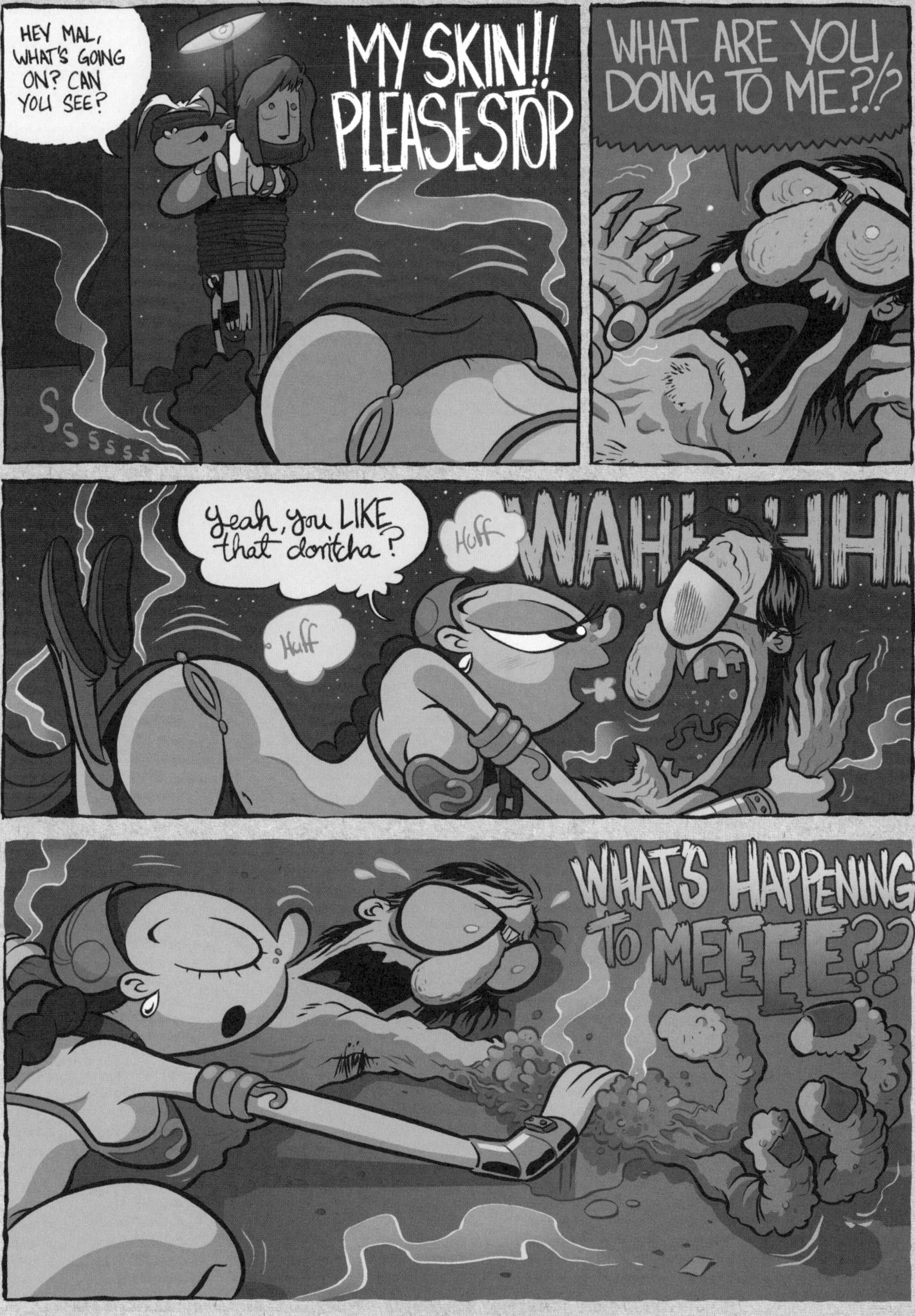
HEY MAL, WHAT'S GOING ON? CAN YOU SEE?
MY SKIN!! PLEASESTOP
Sssssss
WHAT ARE YOU DOING TO ME?!?
Yeah, you LIKE that dontcha?
Huff
Huff
WAH
WHAT'S HAPPENING TO MEEEE??

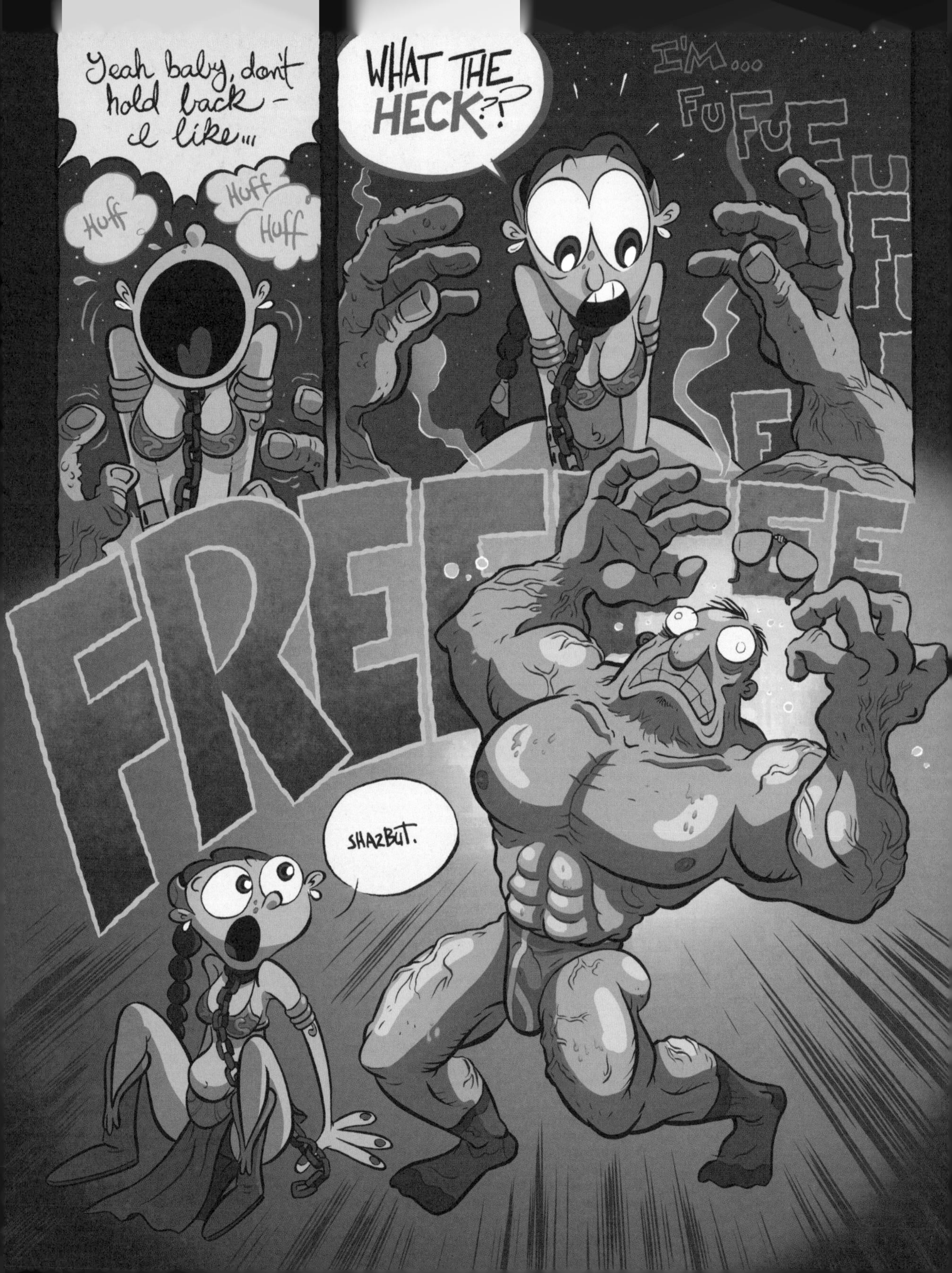

Yeah baby, don't hold back - I like...
Huff
Huff
Huff
WHAT THE HECK?!?
I'M... FU FU FU FU FU FU F
FREEEEE
SHAZBUT.

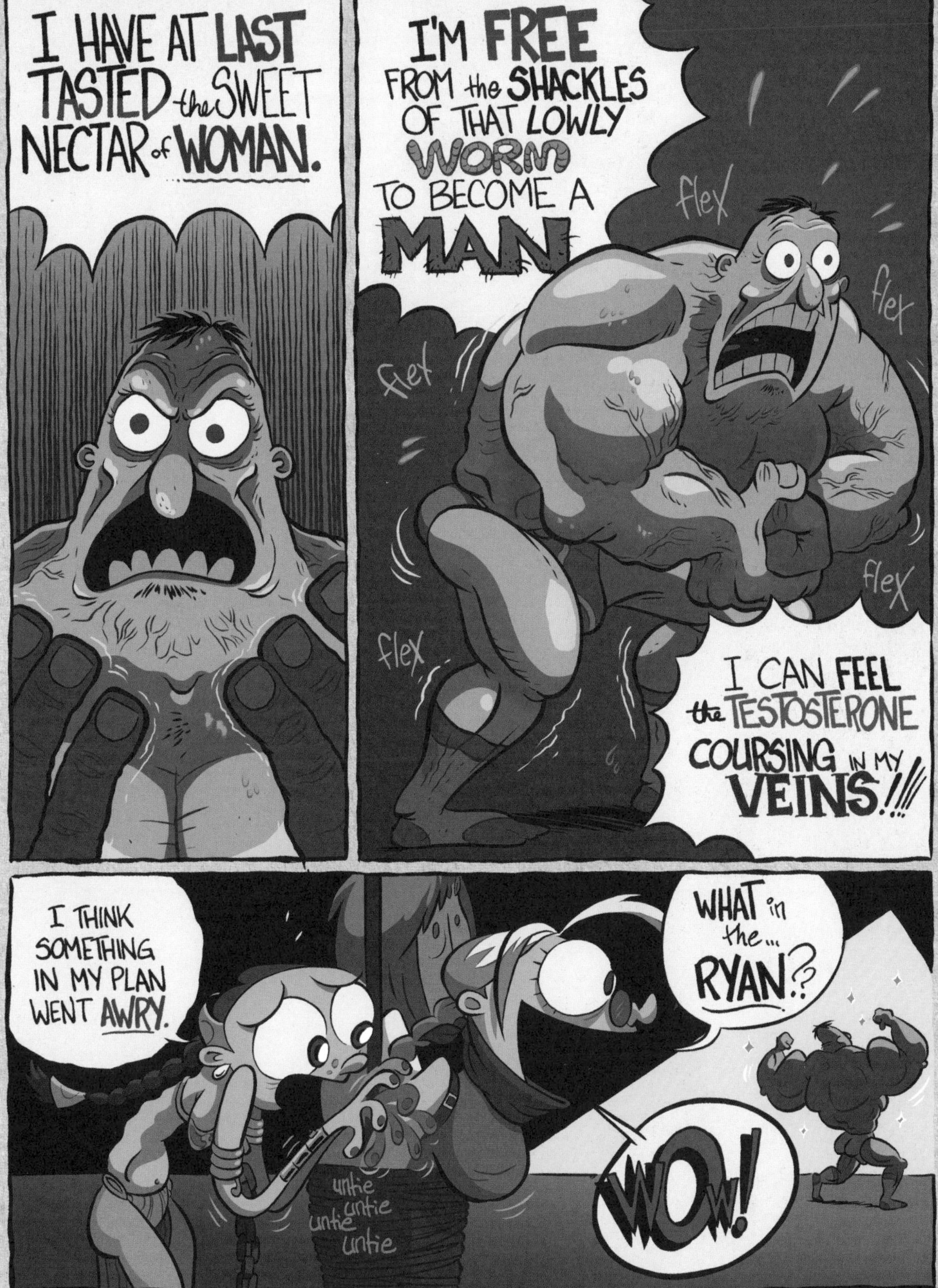
I HAVE AT LAST TASTED the SWEET NECTAR of WOMAN.
I'M FREE FROM the SHACKLES OF THAT LOWLY WORM TO BECOME A MAN
flex
flex
flex
flex
flex
I CAN FEEL the TESTOSTERONE COURSING IN MY VEINS!!!
I THINK SOMETHING IN MY PLAN WENT AWRY.
WHAT in the... RYAN?
WOW!
untie
untie
untie
untie

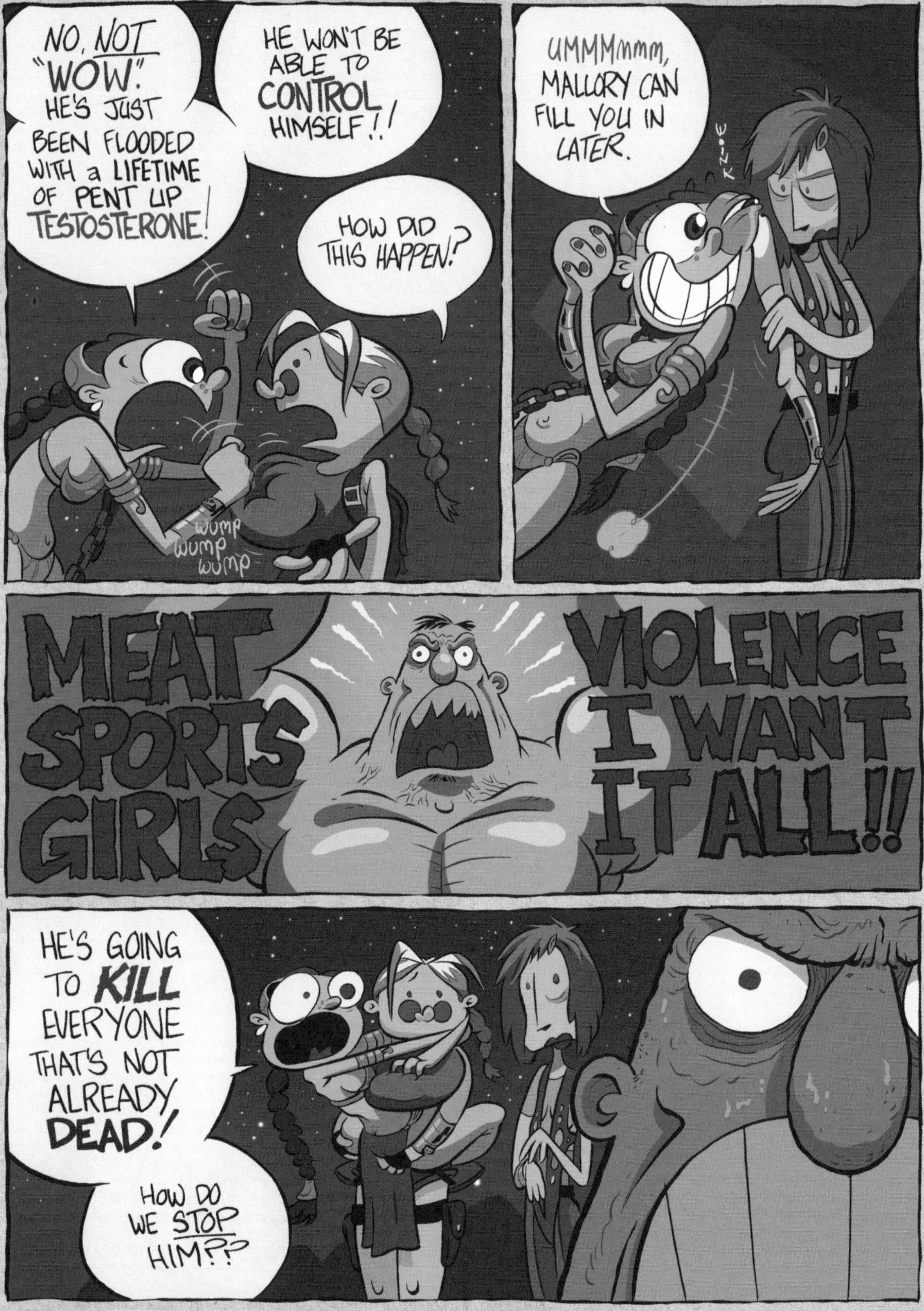
NO, NOT "WOW". HE'S JUST BEEN FLOODED WITH a LIFETIME OF PENT UP TESTOSTERONE!
HE WON'T BE ABLE TO CONTROL HIMSELF!!
HOW DID THIS HAPPEN!?
WUMP WUMP WUMP
UMMMmmm, MALLORY CAN FILL YOU IN LATER.
MEAT SPORTS GIRLS
VIOLENCE I WANT IT ALL!!
HE'S GOING TO KILL EVERYONE THAT'S NOT ALREADY DEAD!
HOW DO WE STOP HIM!?!

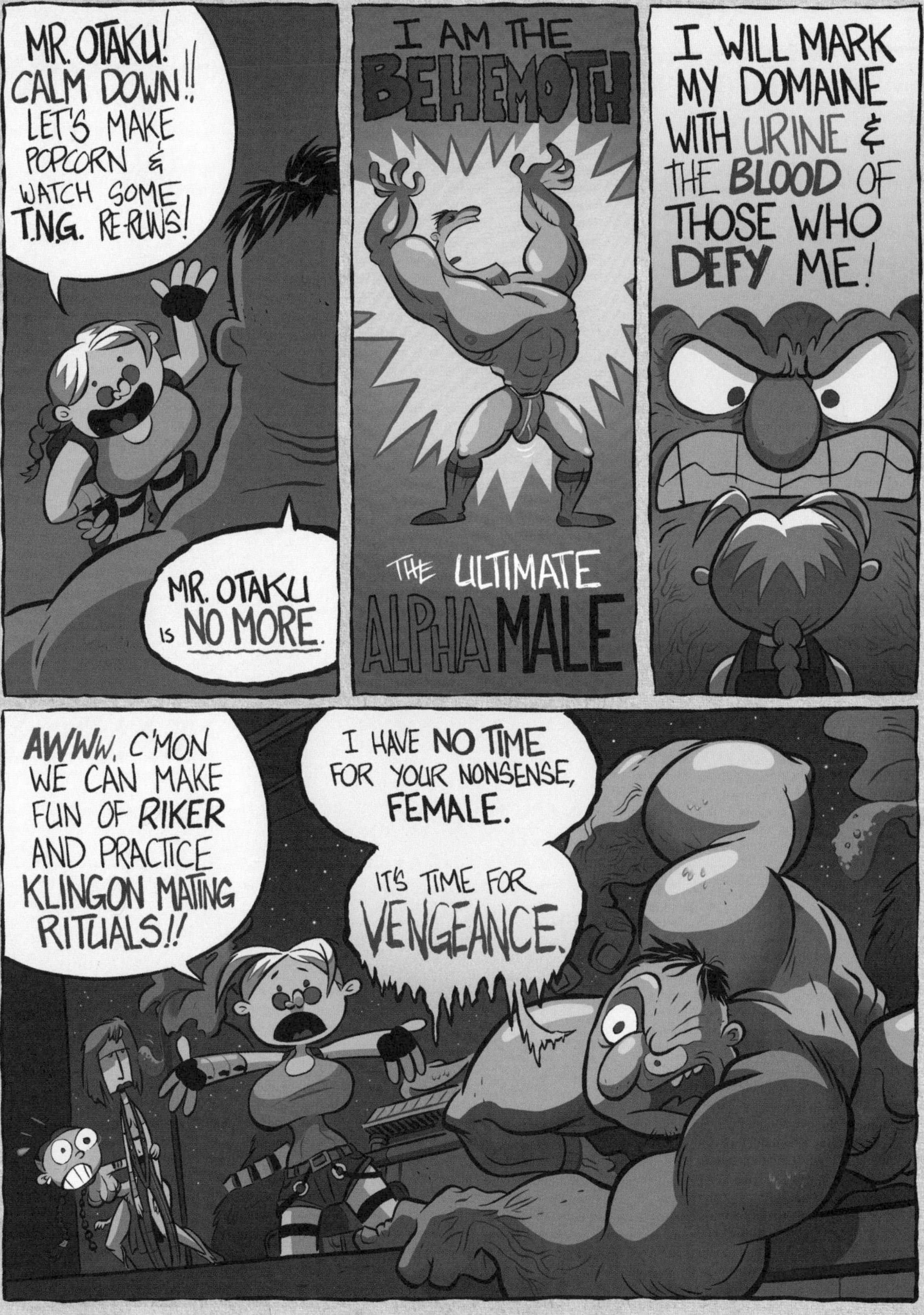
MR. OTAKU! CALM DOWN!! LET'S MAKE POPCORN & WATCH SOME T.N.G. RE-RUNS!
MR. OTAKU IS NO MORE.
I AM THE BEHEMOTH
THE ULTIMATE ALPHA MALE
I WILL MARK MY DOMAINE WITH URINE & THE BLOOD OF THOSE WHO DEFY ME!
AWWW, C'MON WE CAN MAKE FUN OF RIKER AND PRACTICE KLINGON MATING RITUALS!!
I HAVE NO TIME FOR YOUR NONSENSE, FEMALE.
IT'S TIME FOR VENGEANCE.

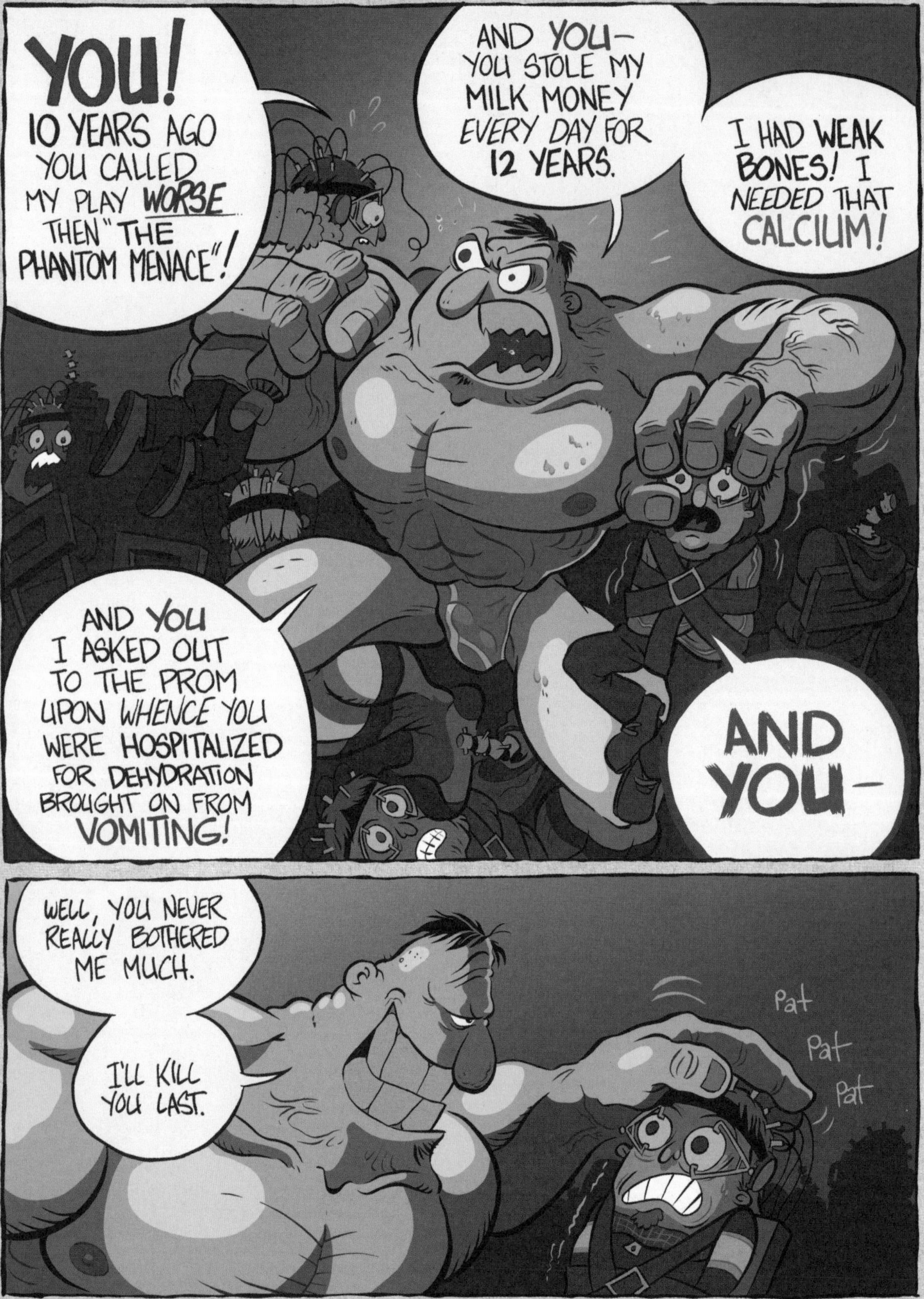
YOU! 10 YEARS AGO YOU CALLED MY PLAY WORSE THEN "THE PHANTOM MENACE"!
AND YOU– YOU STOLE MY MILK MONEY EVERY DAY FOR 12 YEARS.
I HAD WEAK BONES! I NEEDED THAT CALCIUM!
AND YOU I ASKED OUT TO THE PROM UPON WHENCE YOU WERE HOSPITALIZED FOR DEHYDRATION BROUGHT ON FROM VOMITING!
AND YOU–
WELL, YOU NEVER REALLY BOTHERED ME MUCH.
I'LL KILL YOU LAST.
Pat
Pat
Pat

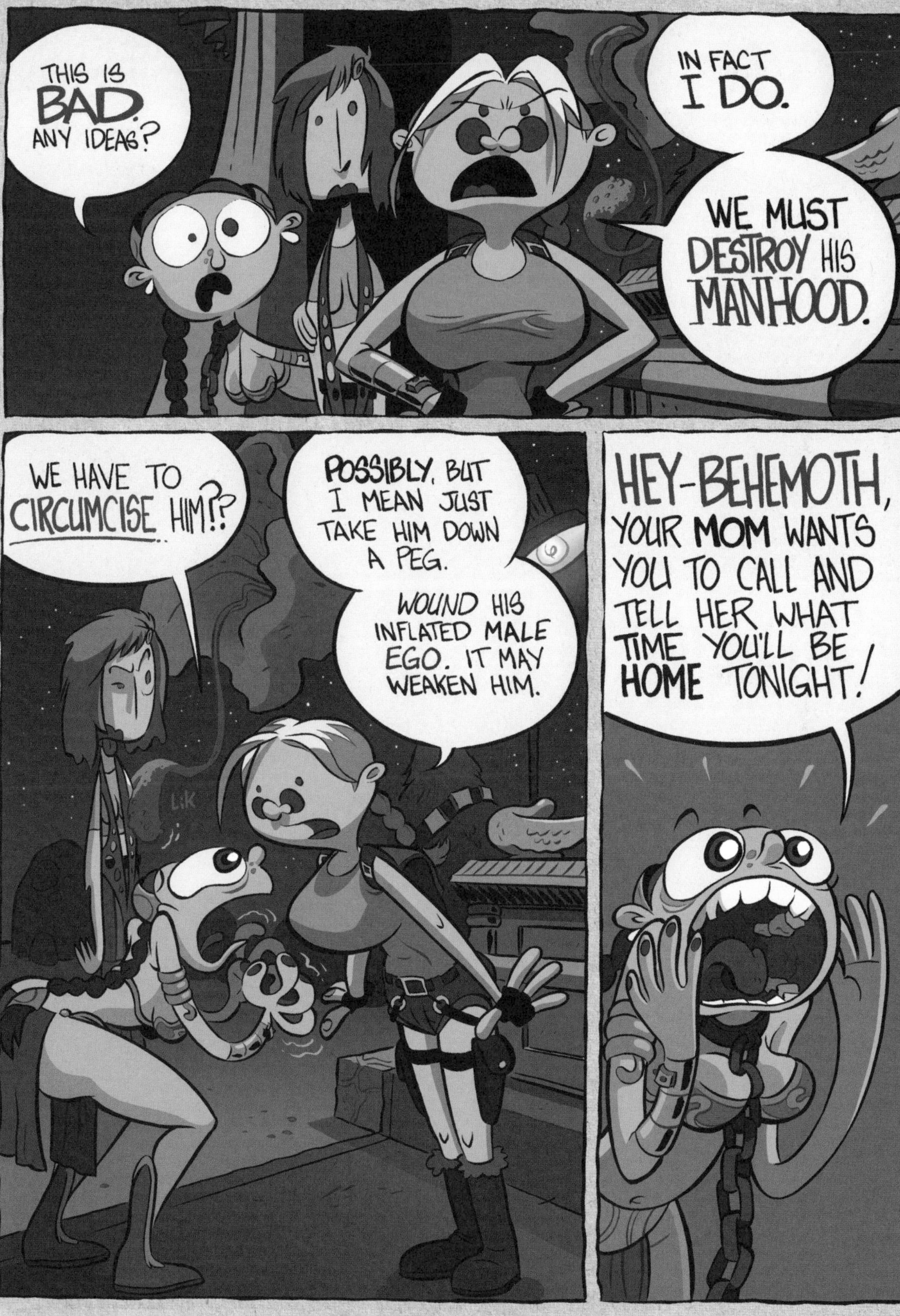
THIS IS BAD. ANY IDEAS?
IN FACT I DO.
WE MUST DESTROY HIS MANHOOD.
WE HAVE TO CIRCUMCISE HIM!?
POSSIBLY, BUT I MEAN JUST TAKE HIM DOWN A PEG.
WOUND HIS INFLATED MALE EGO. IT MAY WEAKEN HIM.
LIK
HEY-BEHEMOTH, YOUR MOM WANTS YOU TO CALL AND TELL HER WHAT TIME YOU'LL BE HOME TONIGHT!

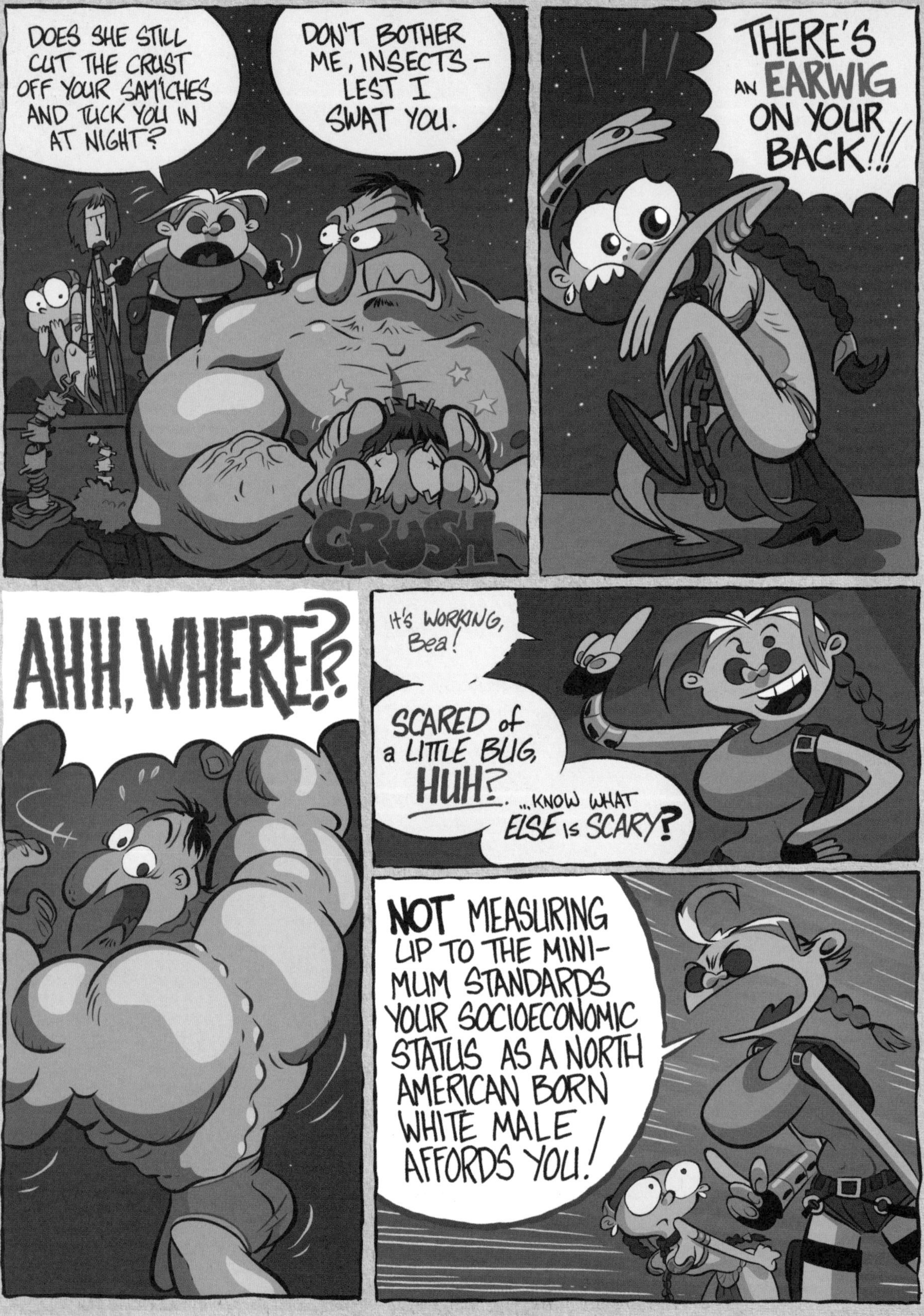
DOES SHE STILL CUT THE CRUST OFF YOUR SAMICHES AND TUCK YOU IN AT NIGHT?
DON'T BOTHER ME, INSECTS - LEST I SWAT YOU.
CRUSH
THERE'S AN EARWIG ON YOUR BACK!!!
AHH, WHERE?!?
It's WORKING, Bea!
SCARED of a LITTLE BUG, HUH?
...KNOW WHAT ELSE is SCARY?
NOT MEASURING UP TO THE MINI-MUM STANDARDS YOUR SOCIOECONOMIC STATUS AS A NORTH AMERICAN BORN WHITE MALE AFFORDS YOU!

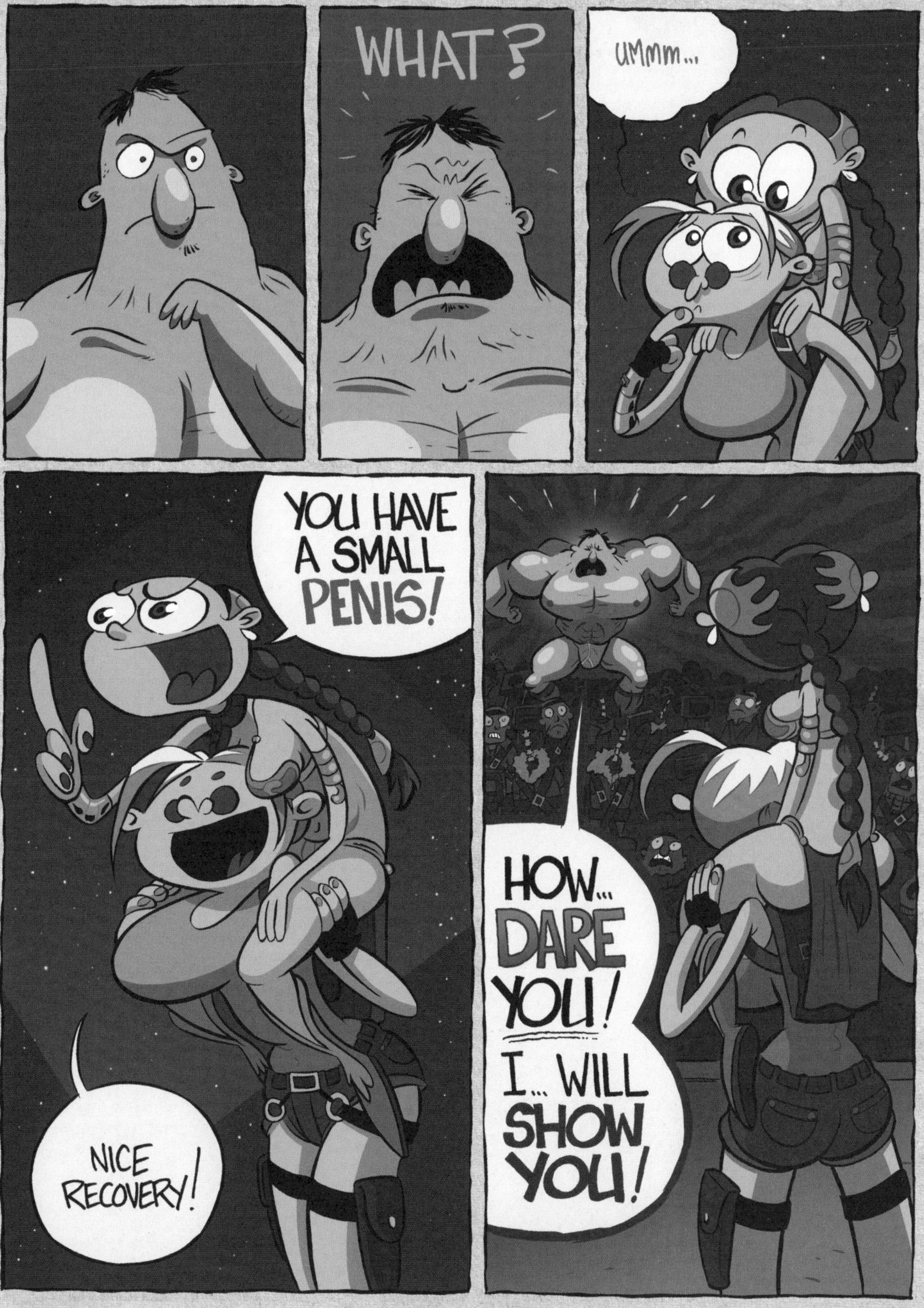
WHAT?
UMMM...
YOU HAVE A SMALL PENIS!
NICE RECOVERY!
HOW... DARE YOU! I... WILL SHOW YOU!

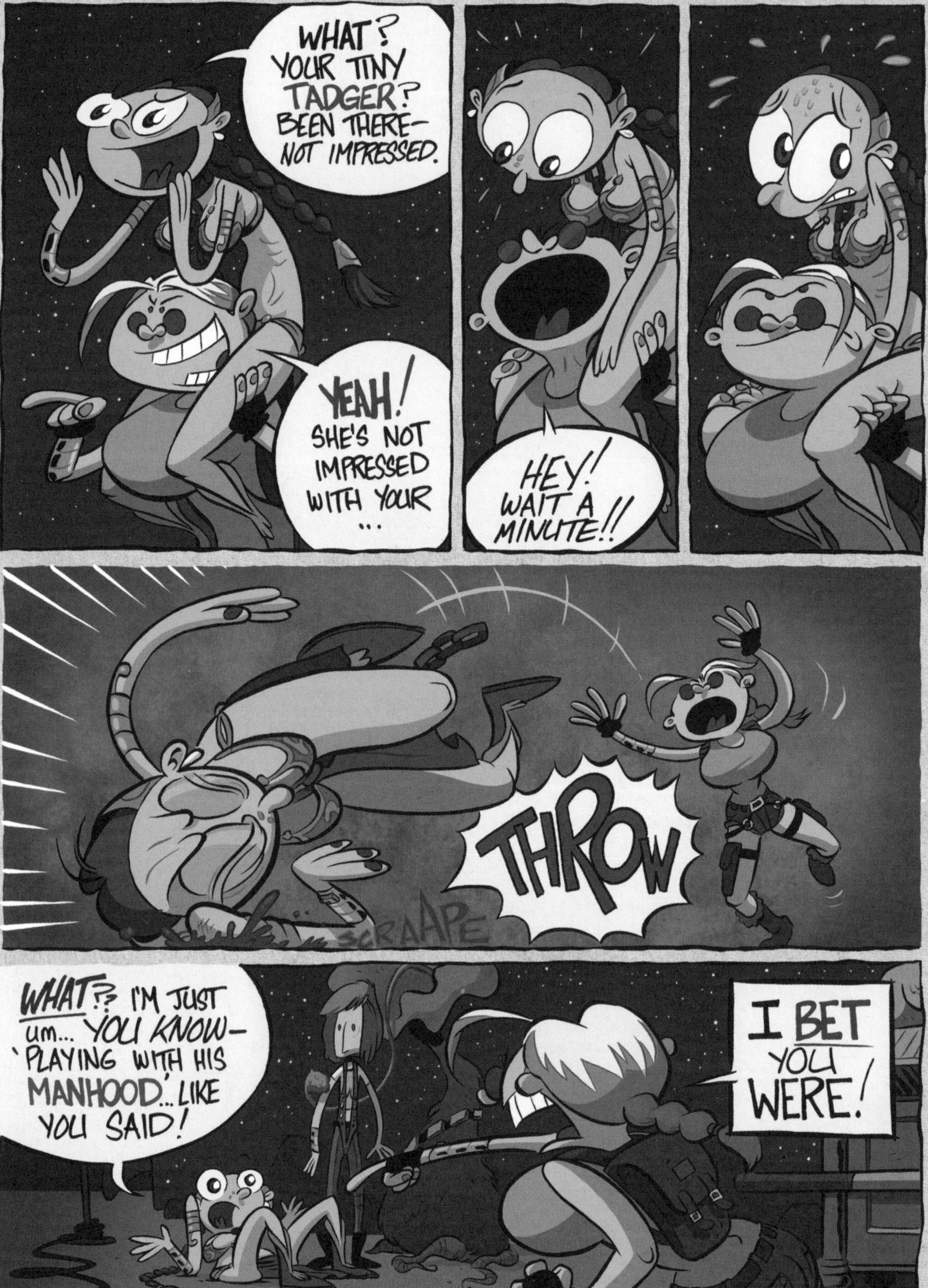
WHAT? YOUR TINY TADGER? BEEN THERE- NOT IMPRESSED.
YEAH! SHE'S NOT IMPRESSED WITH YOUR ...
HEY! WAIT A MINUTE!!
THROW
SCRAAPE
WHAT!? I'M JUST um... YOU KNOW- 'PLAYING WITH HIS MANHOOD,' LIKE YOU SAID!
I BET YOU WERE!

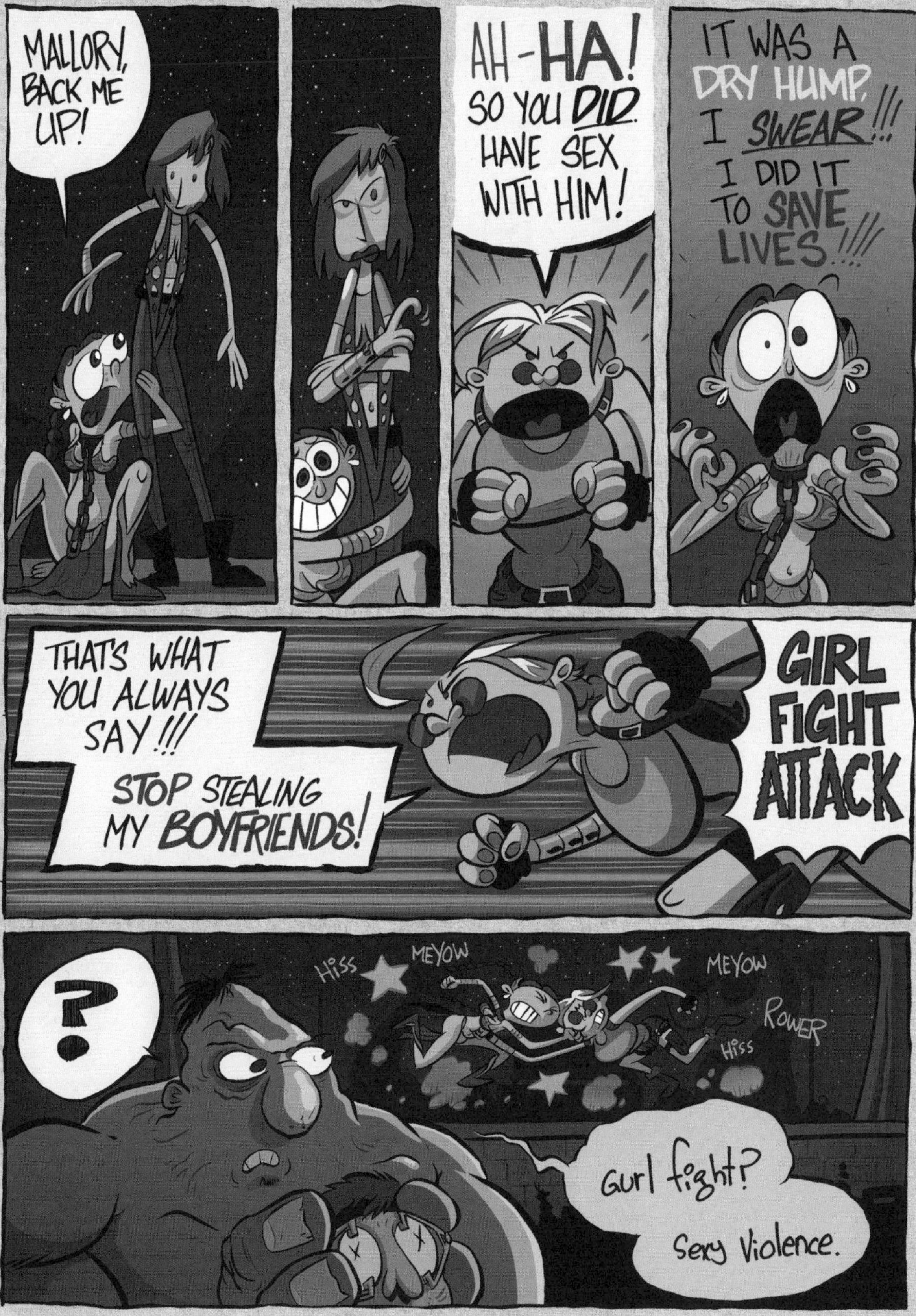
MALLORY, BACK ME UP!
AH-HA! SO YOU DID. HAVE SEX WITH HIM!
IT WAS A DRY HUMP, I SWEAR!!! I DID IT TO SAVE LIVES!!!
THAT'S WHAT YOU ALWAYS SAY!!!
STOP STEALING MY BOYFRIENDS!
GIRL FIGHT ATTACK
?
HISS
MEYOW
MEYOW
ROWER
HISS
Gurl fight?
Sexy Violence.

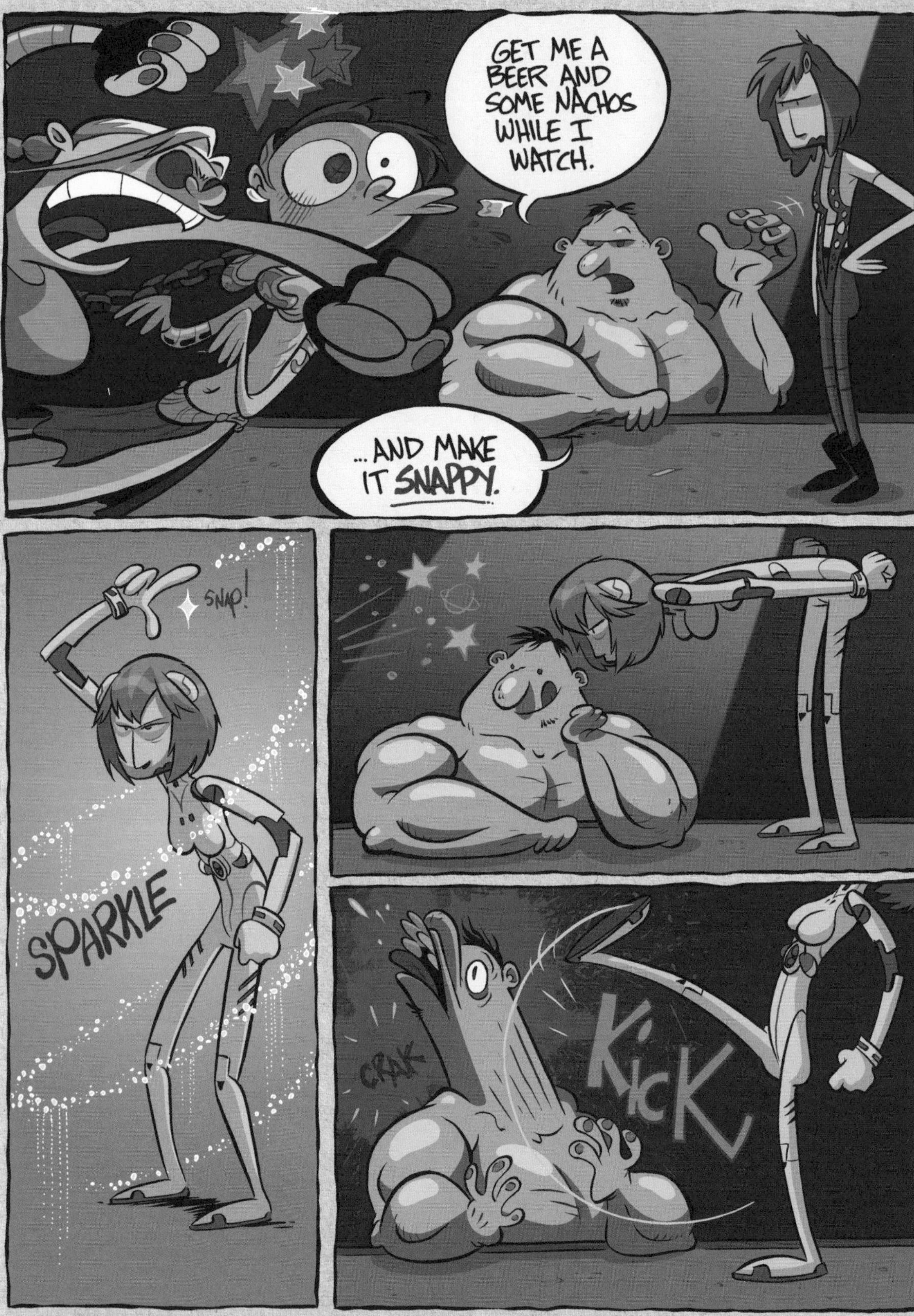
GET ME A BEER AND SOME NACHOS WHILE I WATCH.
...AND MAKE IT SNAPPY.
SNAP!
SPARKLE
CRAK
KICK

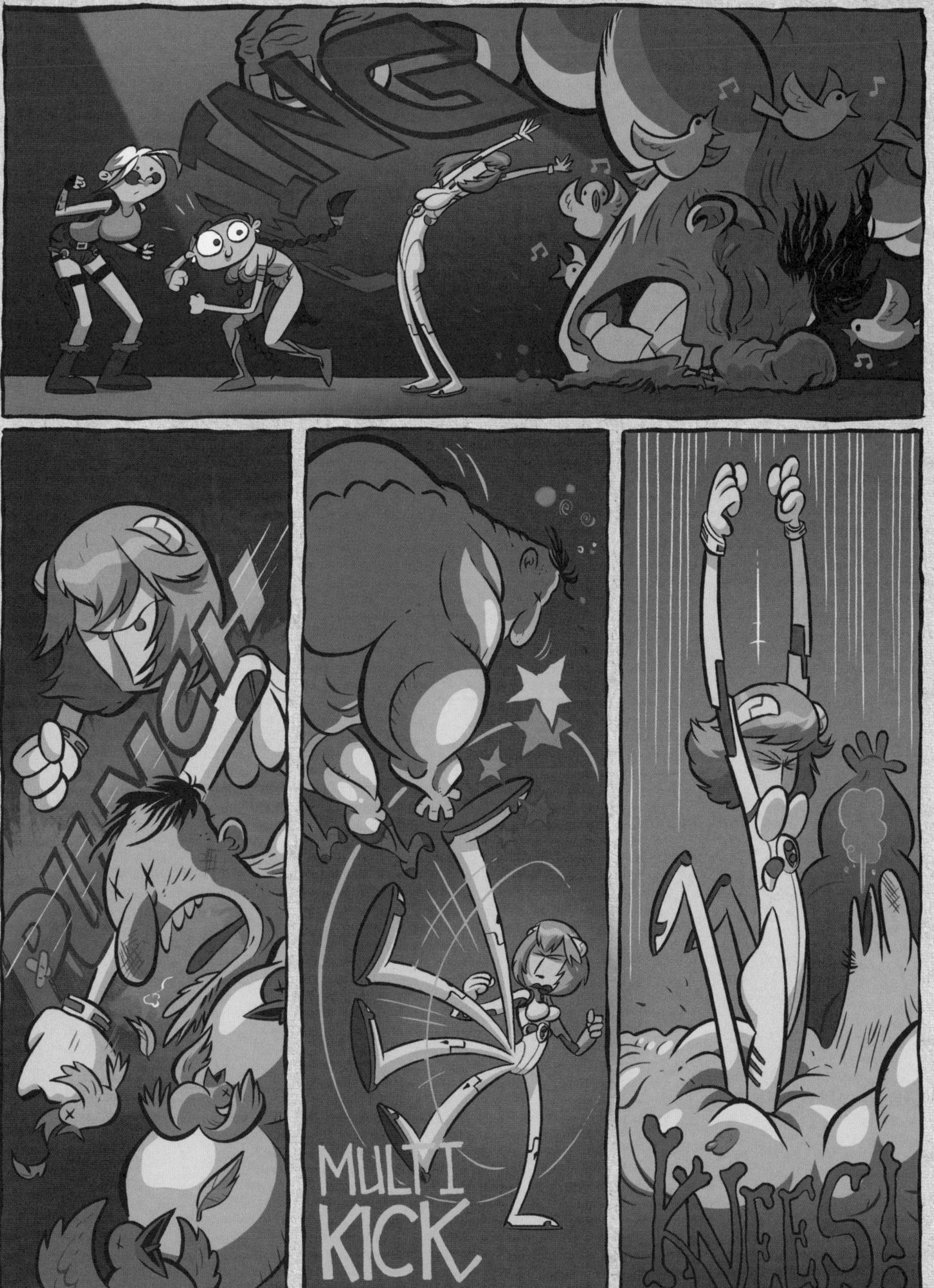
MULTI
KICK
KNEES!

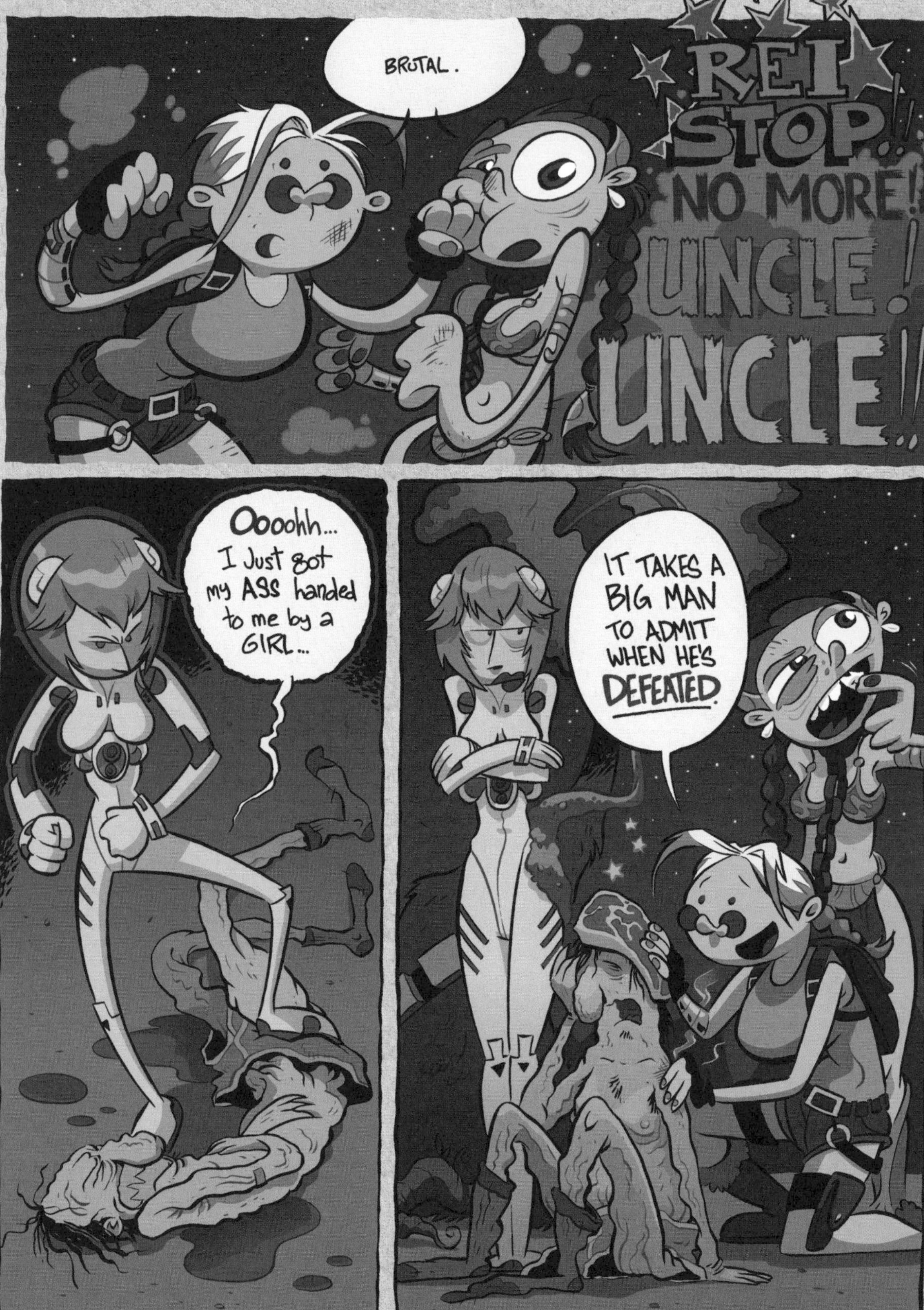
BRUTAL.
REI STOP!! NO MORE!! UNCLE! UNCLE!!
Oooohh... I Just got my ASS handed to me by a GIRL...
IT TAKES A BIG MAN TO ADMIT WHEN HE'S DEFEATED.

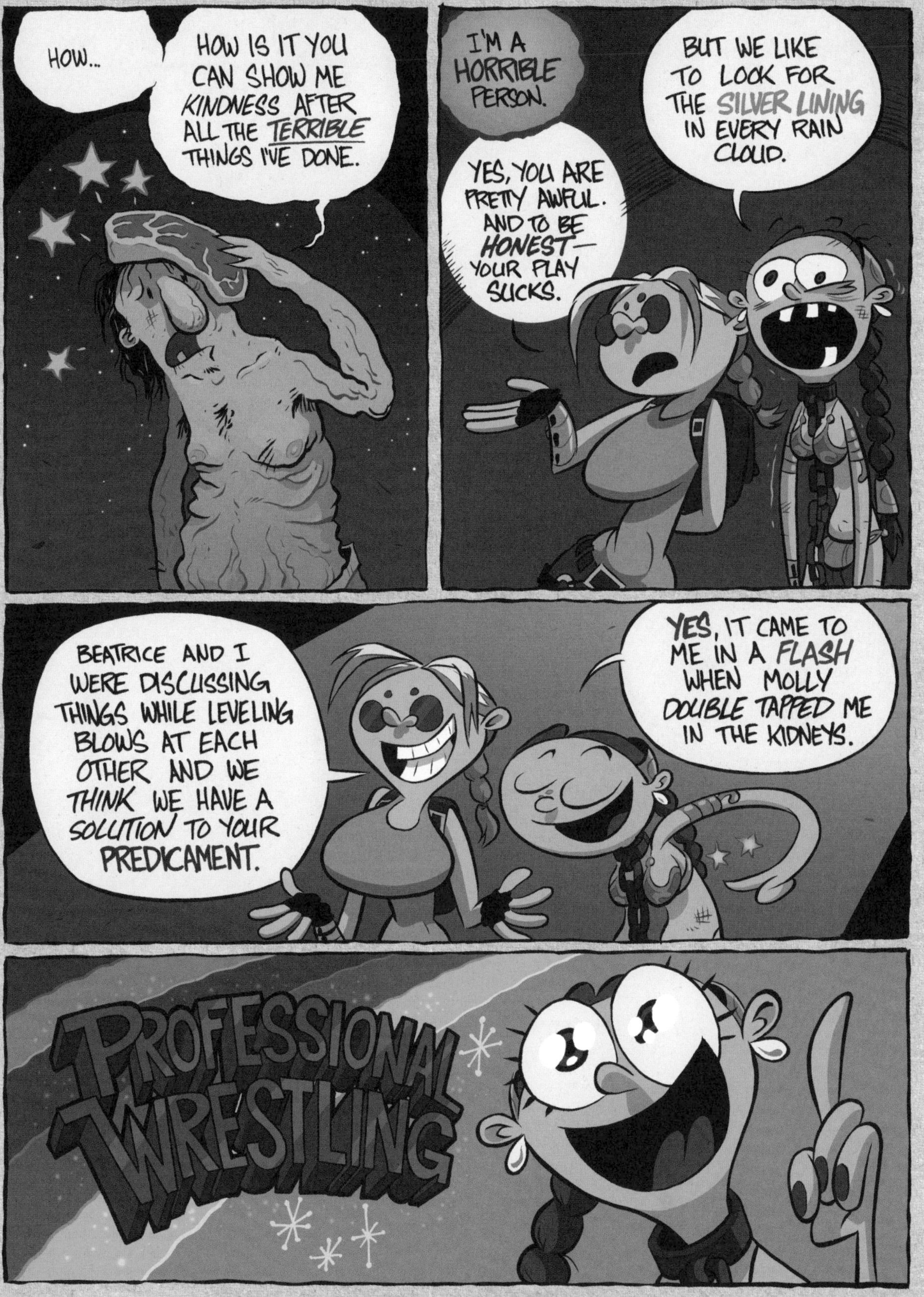
HOW...
HOW IS IT YOU CAN SHOW ME KINDNESS AFTER ALL THE TERRIBLE THINGS I'VE DONE.
I'M A HORRIBLE PERSON.
YES, YOU ARE PRETTY AWFUL. AND TO BE HONEST— YOUR PLAY SUCKS.
BUT WE LIKE TO LOOK FOR THE SILVER LINING IN EVERY RAIN CLOUD.
BEATRICE AND I WERE DISCUSSING THINGS WHILE LEVELING BLOWS AT EACH OTHER AND WE THINK WE HAVE A SOLUTION TO YOUR PREDICAMENT.
YES, IT CAME TO ME IN A FLASH WHEN MOLLY DOUBLE TAPPED ME IN THE KIDNEYS.
PROFESSIONAL WRESTLING

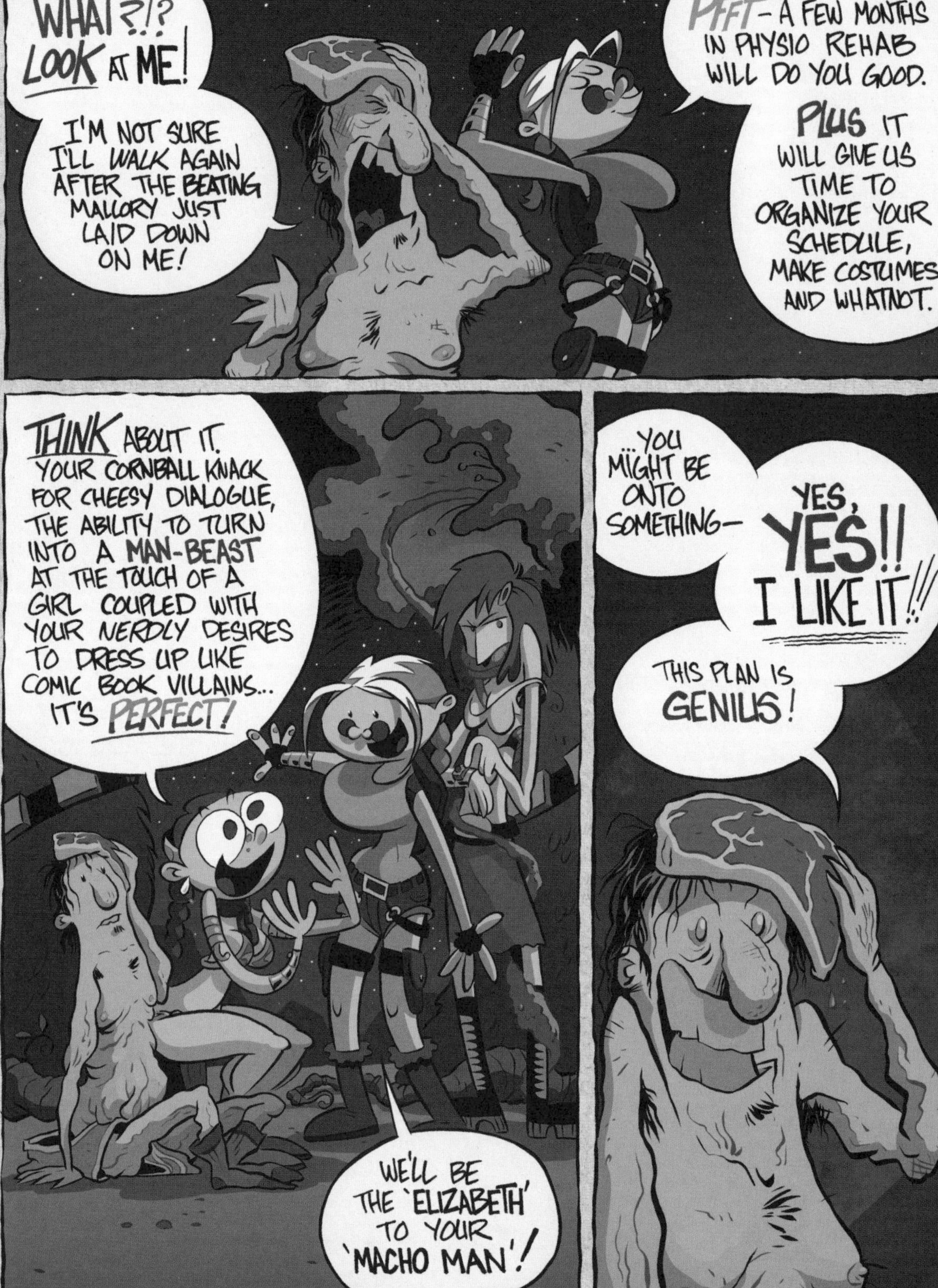
WHAT?!? LOOK AT ME!
I'M NOT SURE I'LL WALK AGAIN AFTER THE BEATING MALLORY JUST LAID DOWN ON ME!
PFFT—A FEW MONTHS IN PHYSIO REHAB WILL DO YOU GOOD.
PLUS IT WILL GIVE US TIME TO ORGANIZE YOUR SCHEDULE, MAKE COSTUMES AND WHATNOT.
THINK ABOUT IT. YOUR CORNBALL KNACK FOR CHEESY DIALOGUE, THE ABILITY TO TURN INTO A MAN-BEAST AT THE TOUCH OF A GIRL COUPLED WITH YOUR NERDLY DESIRES TO DRESS UP LIKE COMIC BOOK VILLAINS... IT'S PERFECT!
WE'LL BE THE 'ELIZABETH' TO YOUR 'MACHO MAN'!
...YOU MIGHT BE ONTO SOMETHING— YES, YES!! I LIKE IT!!!
THIS PLAN IS GENIUS!

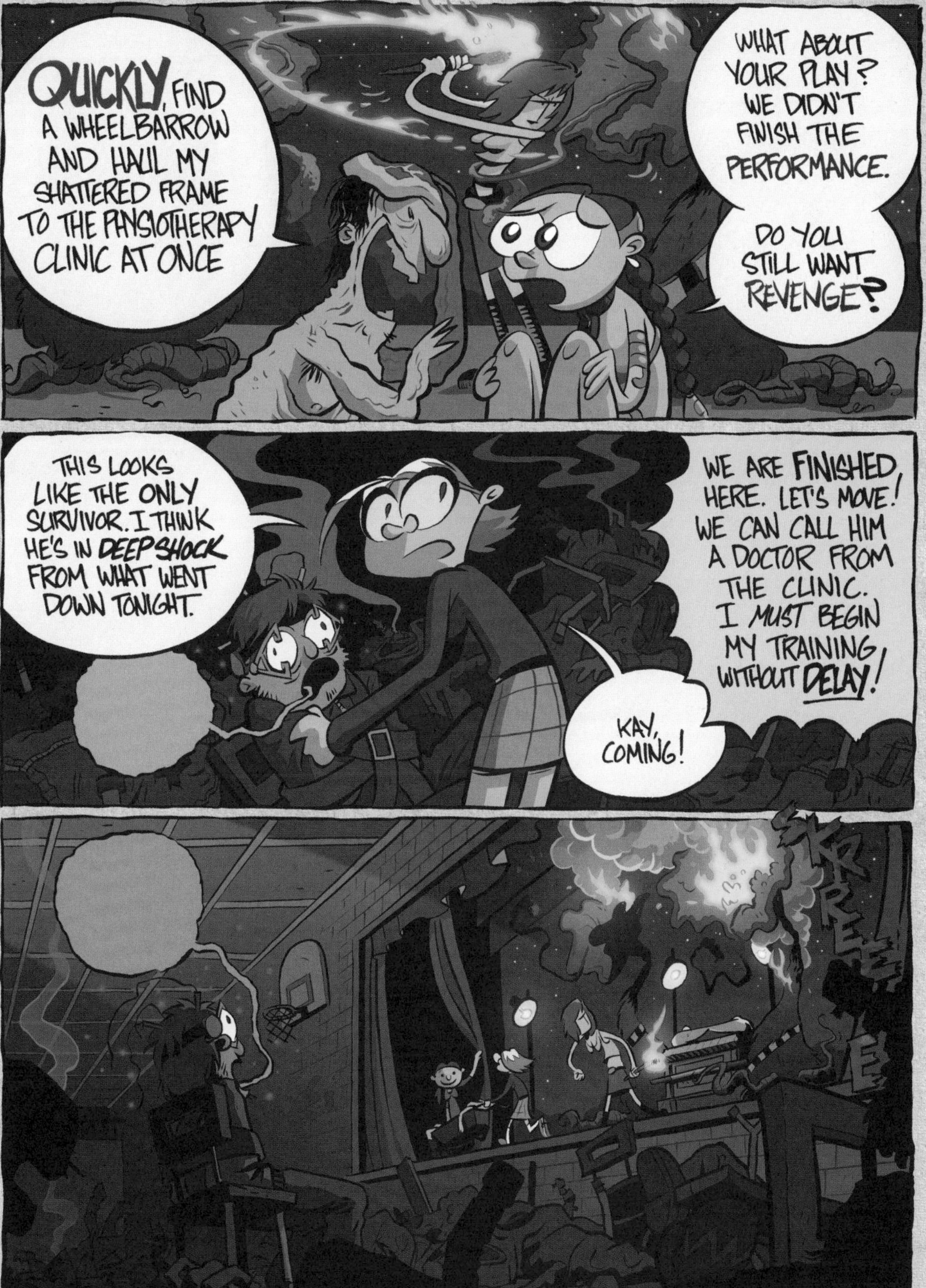
QUICKLY, FIND A WHEELBARROW AND HAUL MY SHATTERED FRAME TO THE PHYSIOTHERAPY CLINIC AT ONCE
WHAT ABOUT YOUR PLAY? WE DIDN'T FINISH THE PERFORMANCE.
DO YOU STILL WANT REVENGE?
THIS LOOKS LIKE THE ONLY SURVIVOR. I THINK HE'S IN DEEP SHOCK FROM WHAT WENT DOWN TONIGHT.
WE ARE FINISHED HERE. LET'S MOVE! WE CAN CALL HIM A DOCTOR FROM THE CLINIC. I MUST BEGIN MY TRAINING WITHOUT DELAY!
KAY, COMING!
SKRREEEE

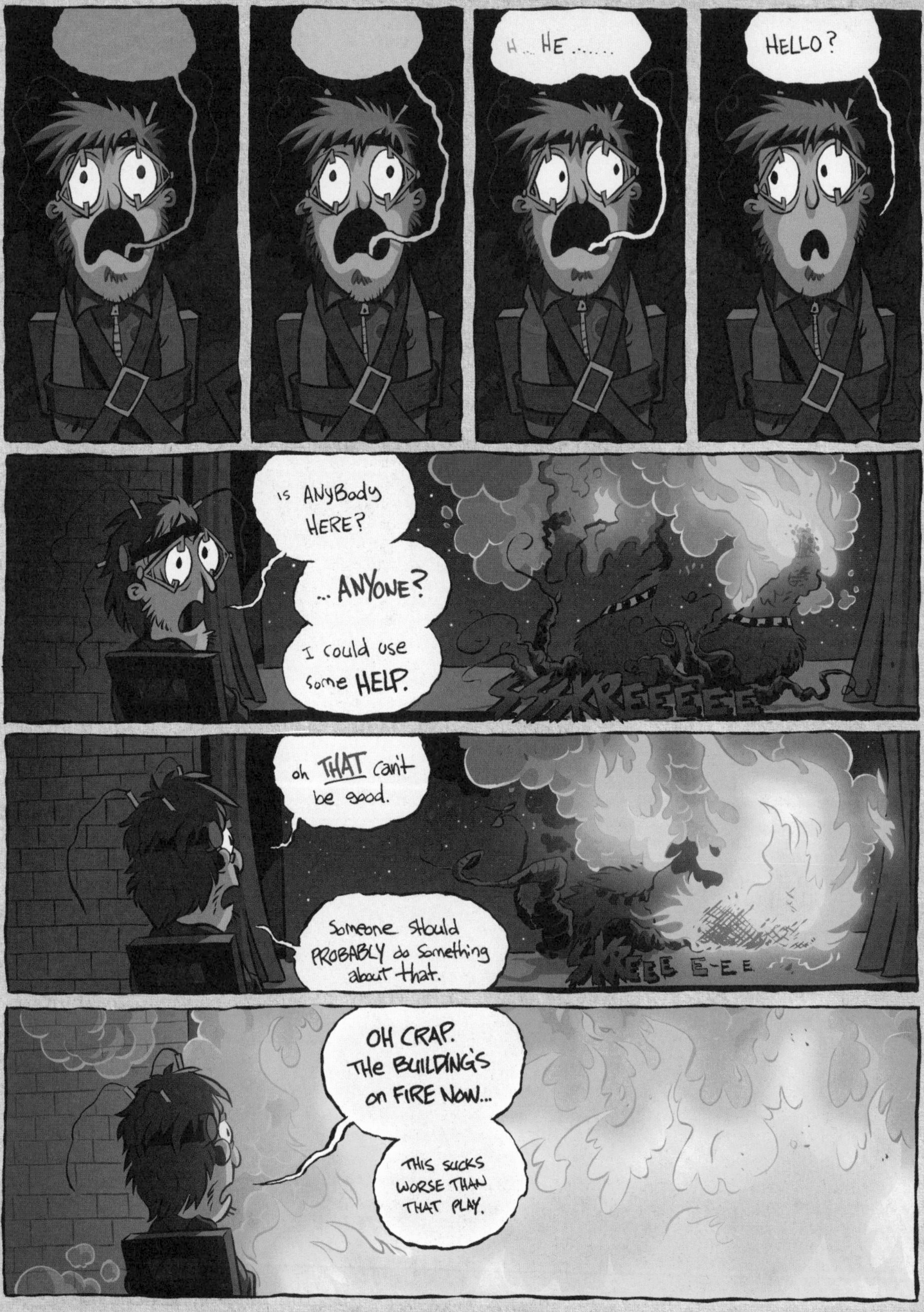
H... HE......
HELLO?
IS ANYBody HERE?
...ANYONE?
I could use some HELP.
SHKREEEEEE
oh THAT can't be good.
Someone should PROBABLY do something about that.
SKREEE E-EE
OH CRAP. THE BUILDING'S on FIRE NOW...
THIS SUCKS WORSE THAN THAT PLAY.

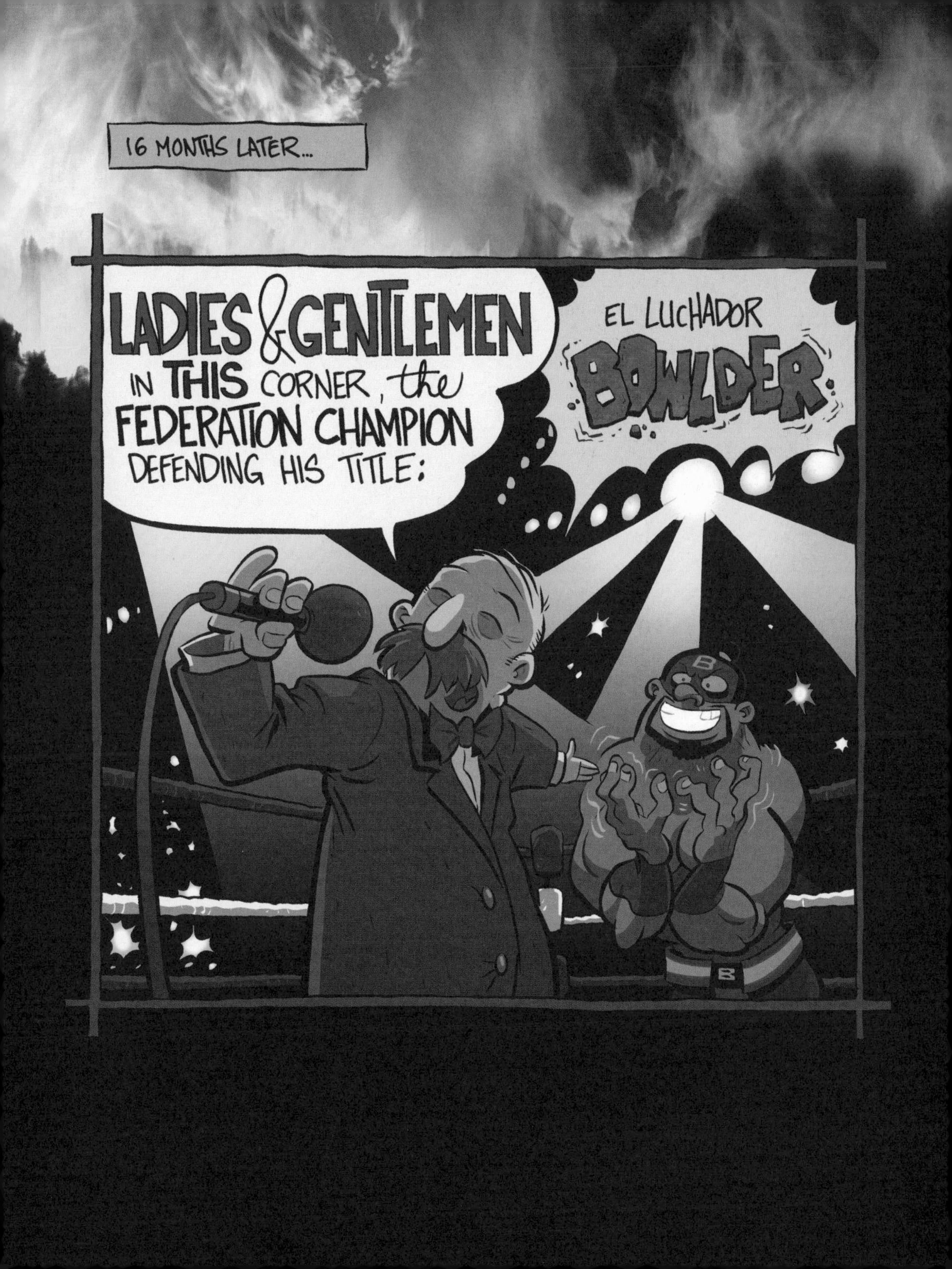
16 MONTHS LATER...
LADIES & GENTLEMEN IN THIS CORNER, the FEDERATION CHAMPION DEFENDING HIS TITLE:
EL LUCHADOR BOWLDER

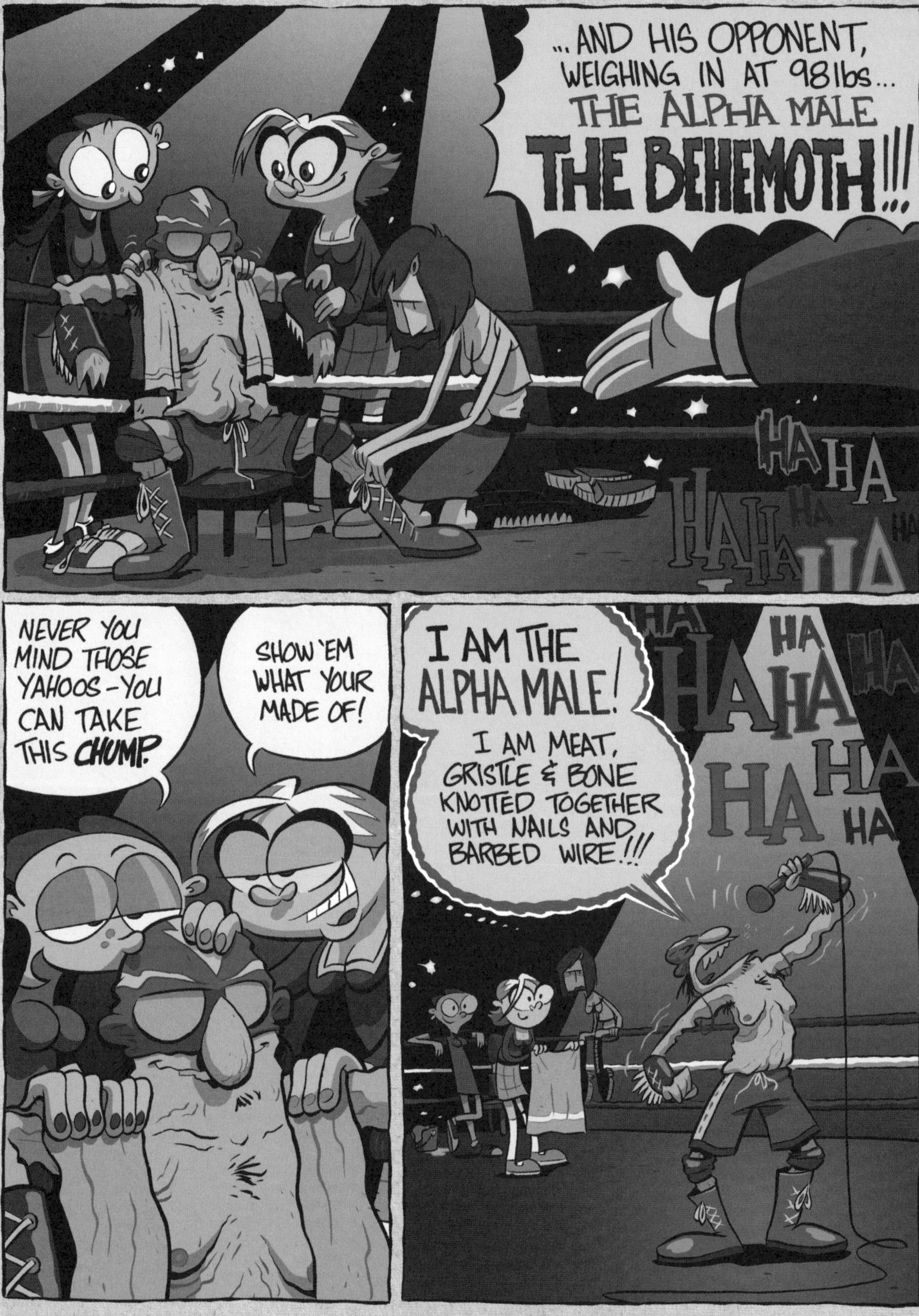

...AND HIS OPPONENT, WEIGHING IN AT 98lbs... THE ALPHA MALE THE BEHEMOTH!!!
HA HA HA HA HA HA HA HA
NEVER YOU MIND THOSE YAHOOS - YOU CAN TAKE THIS CHUMP.
SHOW 'EM WHAT YOUR MADE OF!
I AM THE ALPHA MALE!
I AM MEAT, GRISTLE & BONE KNOTTED TOGETHER WITH NAILS AND BARBED WIRE!!!
HA HA HA HA HA HA HA HA

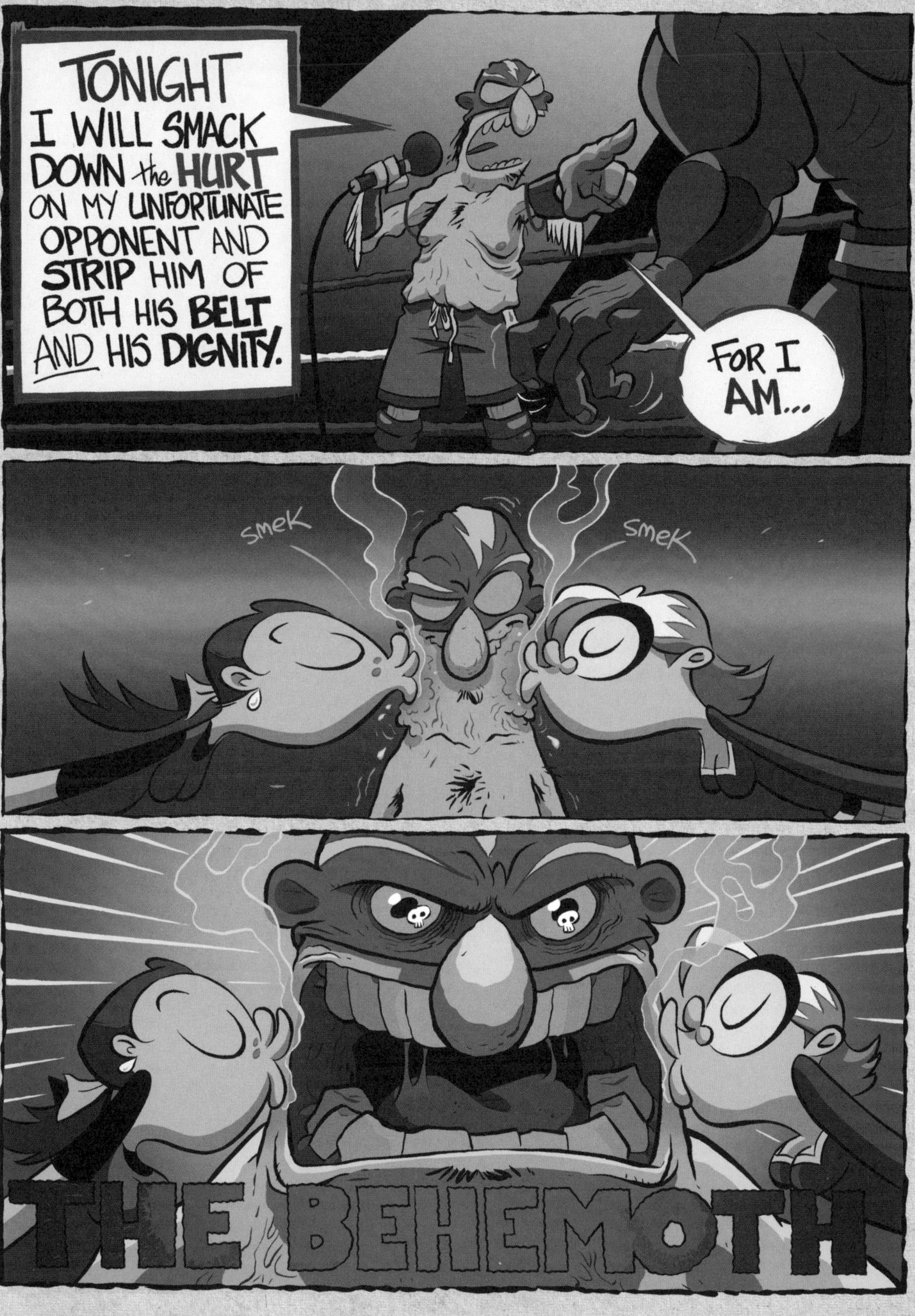
TONIGHT I WILL SMACK DOWN the HURT ON MY UNFORTUNATE OPPONENT AND STRIP HIM OF BOTH HIS BELT AND HIS DIGNITY.
FOR I AM...
SMEK
SMEK
THE BEHEMOTH

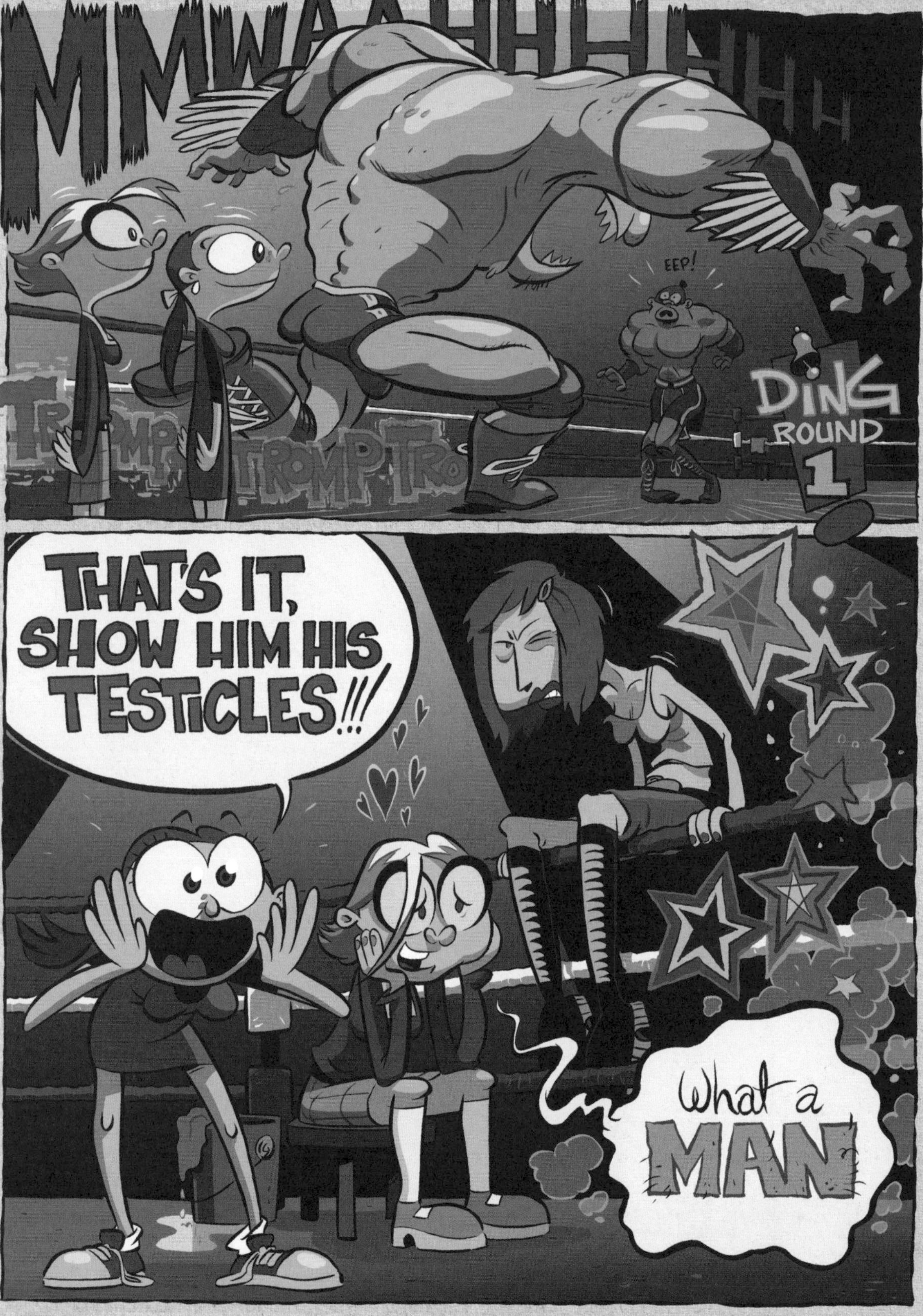
MMWAAHHHHHHH
EEP!
TROMP TROMP TROMP TRO
DING
ROUND 1
THAT'S IT, SHOW HIM HIS TESTICLES!!!
What a MAN

THE
END.

Write to us at:
Angora Napkin
C/O IDW Publishing or
email: troy@meanwhilestudios.com

"GO POSTAL" *with* ANGORA NAPKIN

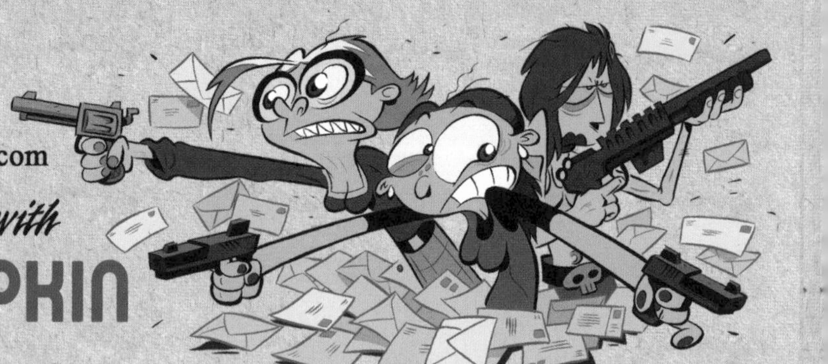

Dear AN,

Issue #174 of Angora Napkin was one of the best I've ever read! It's a shame Steve Ditko is leaving the project after issue #175, I'm not sure what I think of this new team you've got lined up. I suppose I should give them the benefit of the doubt, but from what I can tell in the previews I've seen for "Harvest of Revenge" you've hired the mentally challenged and fed them copious amounts of coffee, deprived them of sleep and beat them with sharp cats. They can't even seem to decide how many fingers the girls have, is it three or four? It changes from page to page!

Regardless, I was happy to finally see the return of Herr Direktor Monocles X2! German Expressionism hasn't been this wacky since Old Fritz split the scene! I can't imagine how the girls will manage to figure out the 'Unsolvable Puzzle' in time to rescue the trapped miners. A bit of a 'Kobayashi Maru' if I've ever seen one!

Anyway, congrats on the Eisner nod – better luck next time!

Ben Danzig
Endwell, N.Y.

Thanks Ben, always good to hear from long time readers! We hope you find the new team a refreshing break from the old school. They may not yet have their chops down but by golly they work for less than peanuts! By now you know how things worked out and you can bet a shiny nickel you haven't heard the last from HDMX2 and it still remains to be seen how Mallory gets her arm back!

Dear Editor,

Recently I found a copy of your magazine in the laundromat I frequent and read it cover to cover in abject disgust. What in the name of decency are you trying to pull off here Mister? At first I thought it was some 'Josie and the Pussycats' thing but this smut wouldn't be allowed anywhere near Riverdale!

Was it really necessary to imply these girls have nipples and menstruate once a month? Good God, what the hell has happened to the funny books I used to read as a kid? I thought that Wertham fella fixed this problem back in the '50s. I wouldn't swat my Pekingese with this rag for fear he'd turn cur!

That said, I did quite enjoy the part on page 15 where Beatrice fell off the roof and landed in the cactus patch – you can't beat the classics!

Sgt. Rick Gozo
USAF

We've brought up your concerns with the writing team and they all agree and will make sure there's less bodily secretions and more pratfalls in future issues.

Dear Editor,

That will do just fine. I look forward to reading the next issue at the laundromat. Thank you for your prompt attention to this important matter and God Bless America.

Sgt. Rick Gozo
USAF

Dear AN,

I've been meaning to write you since 1963 but always found an excuse not to; but now I find myself unable to stop! I'm insane with pleasure right now! Not only did I get a good read out of issue #174, I also got a fantastic chocolate chip brownie recipe too! Sexy girls and food: my two favorite things in one book!

Expect more letters from me every day; I'm hopelessly OCD and full of high-fructose corn syrup! I LOVE YOU!!!!

Mr. JL Schnable
Winnipeg, AB

We love you too JL - and if you think that brownie recipe was the bomb just you wait until you wrap your warm lips around our Baklava! Keep those letters coming - as if you had a choice!

Dear Angora Napkins,

I just picked up the latest issue of The Angora Napkins and had to finally ask – why does every issue have "Collectors Item" emblazoned on the cover? Do you honestly believe every issue will be that much in demand someday? It's annoying so stop it.

Otherwise, another mind boggling issue of mayhem and skullduggery. Mallory's in for a ride if they manage to find her arm and reattach it without proper anesthetics! Should be a hoot!

Ms. Nebbiolo Barolo
Piedmont, Italy

Coming up next issue, a whole new story arc! The girls re-open the *Existential Detective Agency* to make a quick buck only to find themselves embroiled in a murder-mystery plot and a convoluted hunt to unravel the dying secret of a Circus Strongman. It's a comedic action-adventure serial the likes of which you've waited your whole miserable life for and it's called *"Angora Napkin: The Golden McGuffin"*! Read it online at www.angoranapkin.com!

And last but not least, a big thank you to the fans who supported the IndiGoGo campagine during the making of this book:

Rob Anderson, Sue Marsden, Renee Laprise, Kenneth Figuerola, Dave Rigley, Nick Cross, Shane Neville, Cheryl Best, Jeff Zwirek, Cam MacKinlay, Mitch Taylor, Katie Rice, Ryan Hutchinson, Marcel Laurin, Steve Lambe, Jesse Hausler, Erin Arsenault, Jeff Alward, John Dhoe, Michelle Porier, Tyler Landry, Carolyn Hickey, Tom Crook, Ian Daffern, Ciaran O'Conner, Derek Grinsteiner, Nico Colaleo, Sidne Sylvestri, Alyssa Koszis & the Anonymous Gang!

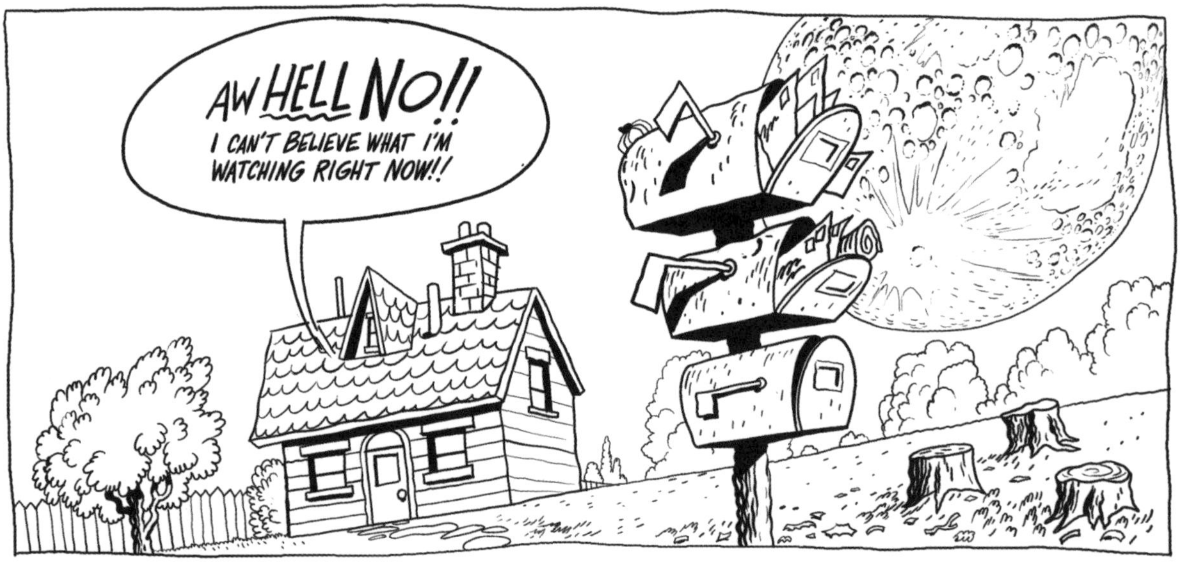
AW HELL NO!!
I CAN'T BELIEVE WHAT I'M WATCHING RIGHT NOW!!

FLY ME TO THE MOON!

WRITTEN AND DRAWN BY NICK CROSS

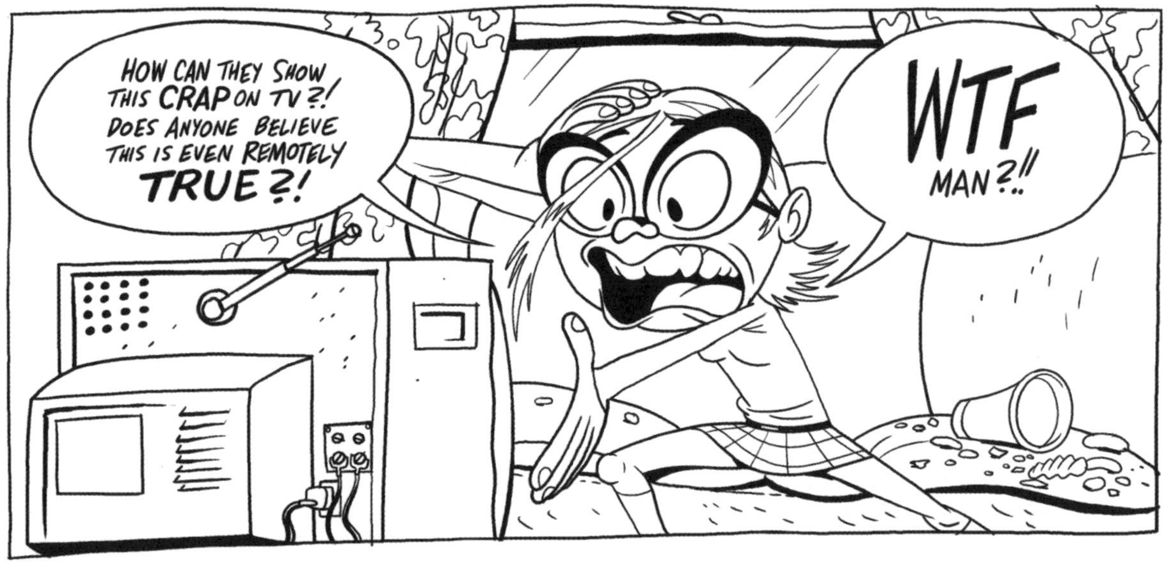
HOW CAN THEY SHOW THIS CRAP ON TV ?! DOES ANYONE BELIEVE THIS IS EVEN REMOTELY TRUE ?!
WTF MAN ?!!

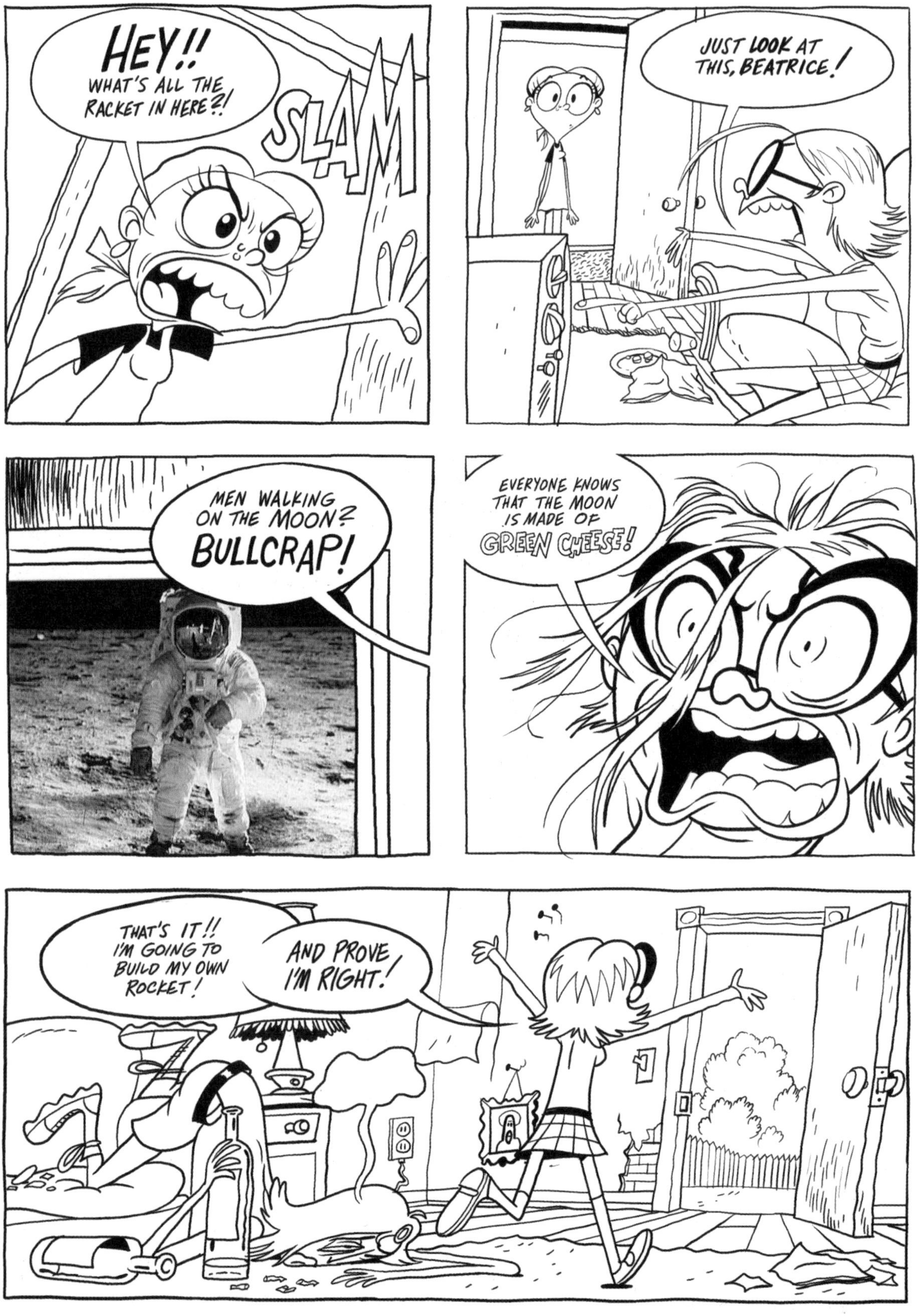
HEY!! WHAT'S ALL THE RACKET IN HERE?!
SLAM
JUST LOOK AT THIS, BEATRICE!
MEN WALKING ON THE MOON? BULLCRAP!
EVERYONE KNOWS THAT THE MOON IS MADE OF GREEN CHEESE!
THAT'S IT!! I'M GOING TO BUILD MY OWN ROCKET!
AND PROVE I'M RIGHT!

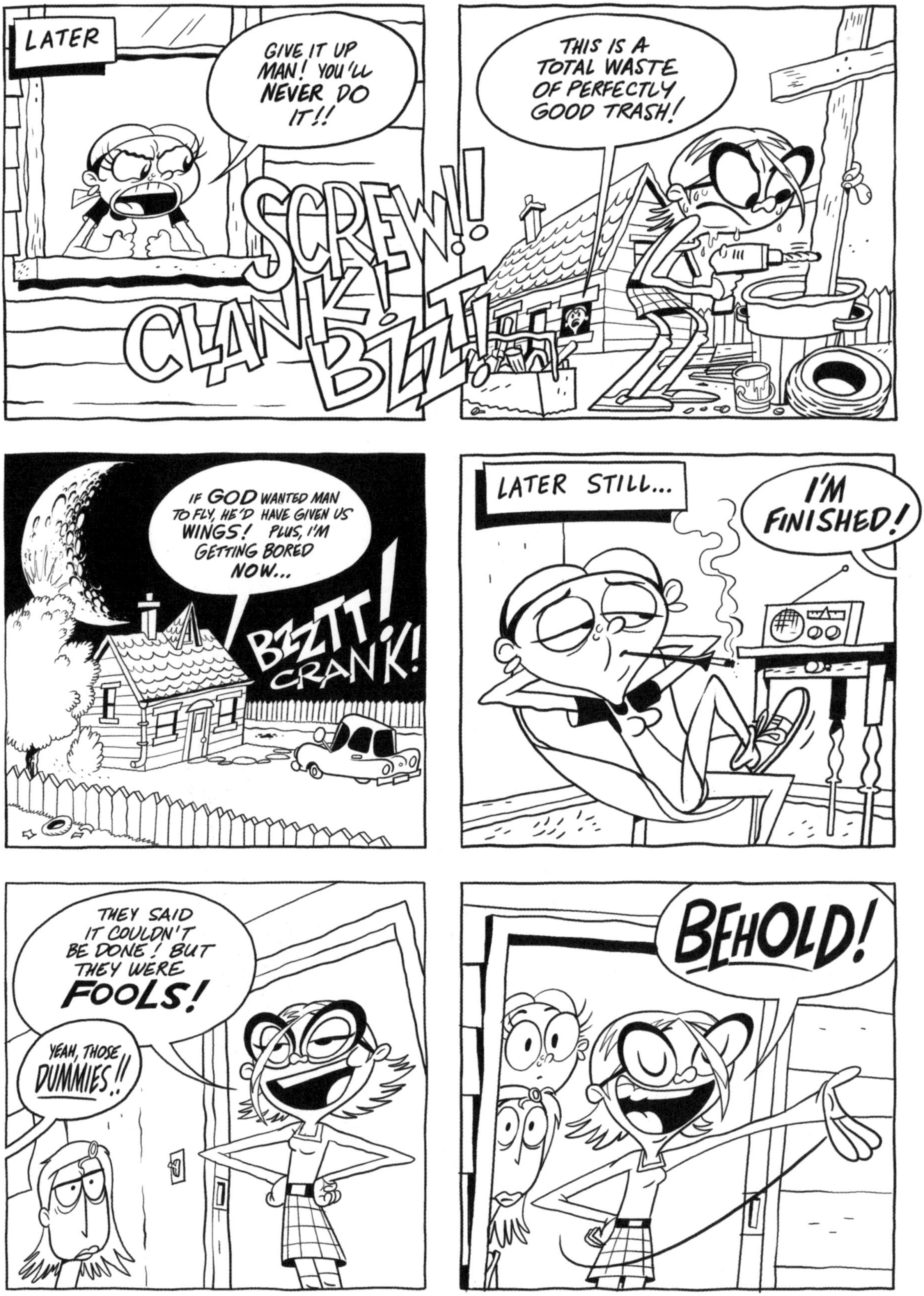
LATER
GIVE IT UP MAN! YOU'LL NEVER DO IT!!
SCREW!!
CLANK!
BZZT!
THIS IS A TOTAL WASTE OF PERFECTLY GOOD TRASH!
IF GOD WANTED MAN TO FLY, HE'D HAVE GIVEN US WINGS! PLUS, I'M GETTING BORED NOW...
BZZTT!
CRANK!
LATER STILL...
I'M FINISHED!
THEY SAID IT COULDN'T BE DONE! BUT THEY WERE FOOLS!
YEAH, THOSE DUMMIES!!
BEHOLD!

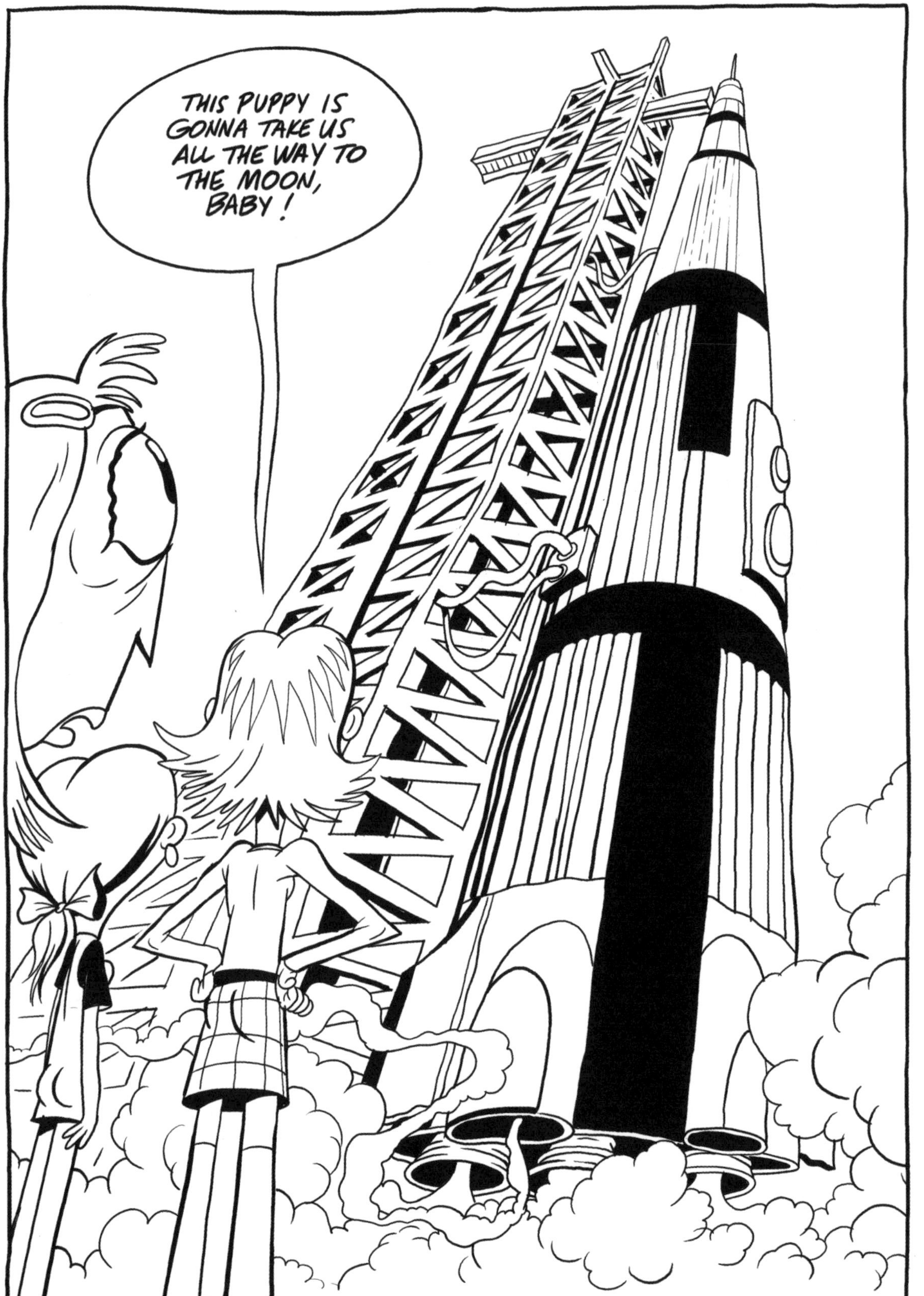
THIS PUPPY IS GONNA TAKE US ALL THE WAY TO THE MOON, BABY!

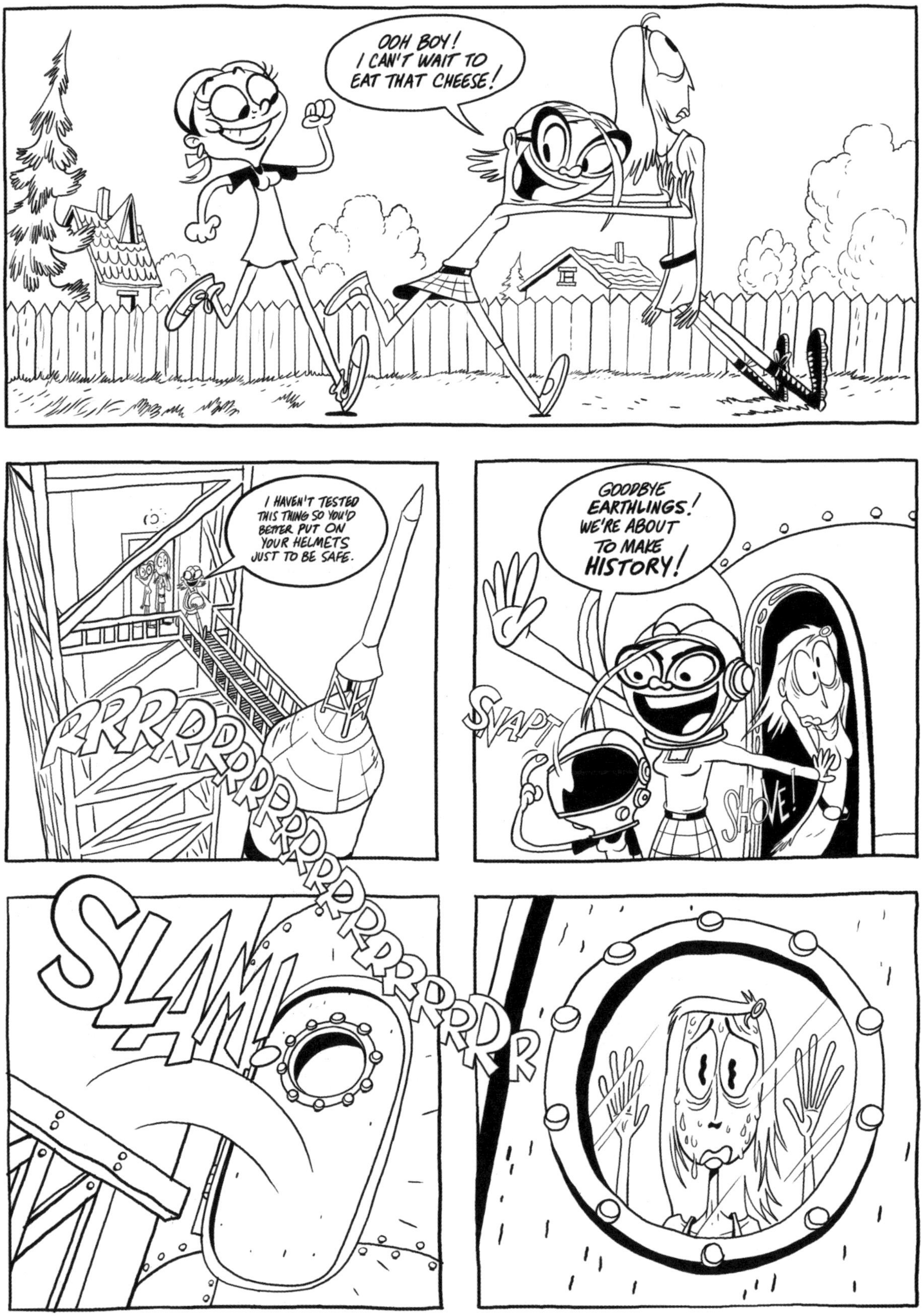
OOH BOY! I CAN'T WAIT TO EAT THAT CHEESE!
I HAVEN'T TESTED THIS THING SO YOU'D BETTER PUT ON YOUR HELMETS JUST TO BE SAFE.
RRRRRRRRRRRRRRRRRRRRRRRRR
GOODBYE EARTHLINGS! WE'RE ABOUT TO MAKE HISTORY!
SNAPT
SHOVE!
SLAM!

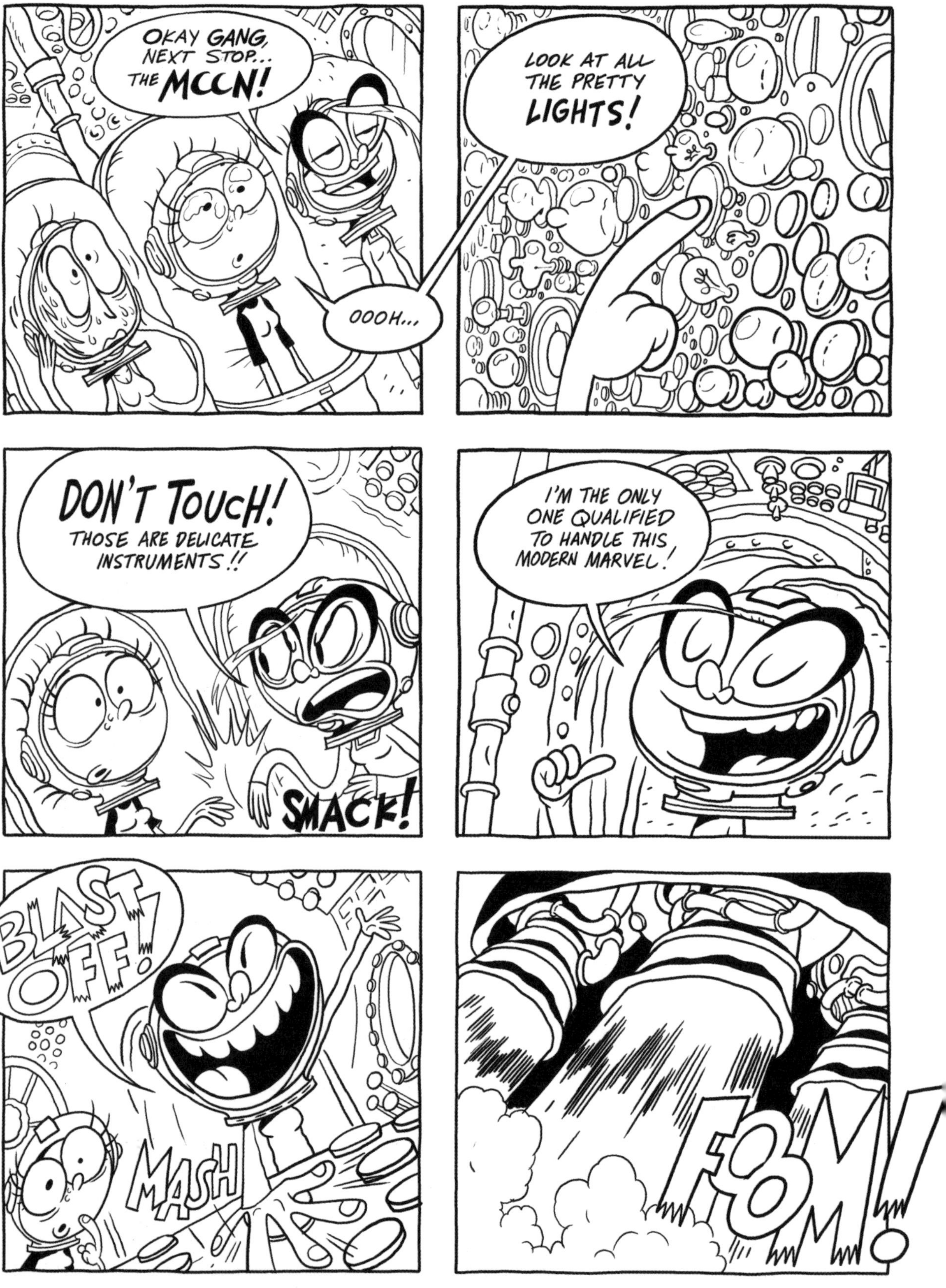
OKAY GANG, NEXT STOP... THE MOON!
LOOK AT ALL THE PRETTY LIGHTS!
OOOH...
DON'T TOUCH! THOSE ARE DELICATE INSTRUMENTS!!
SMACK!
I'M THE ONLY ONE QUALIFIED TO HANDLE THIS MODERN MARVEL!
BLAST OFF!
MASH
FOOM!

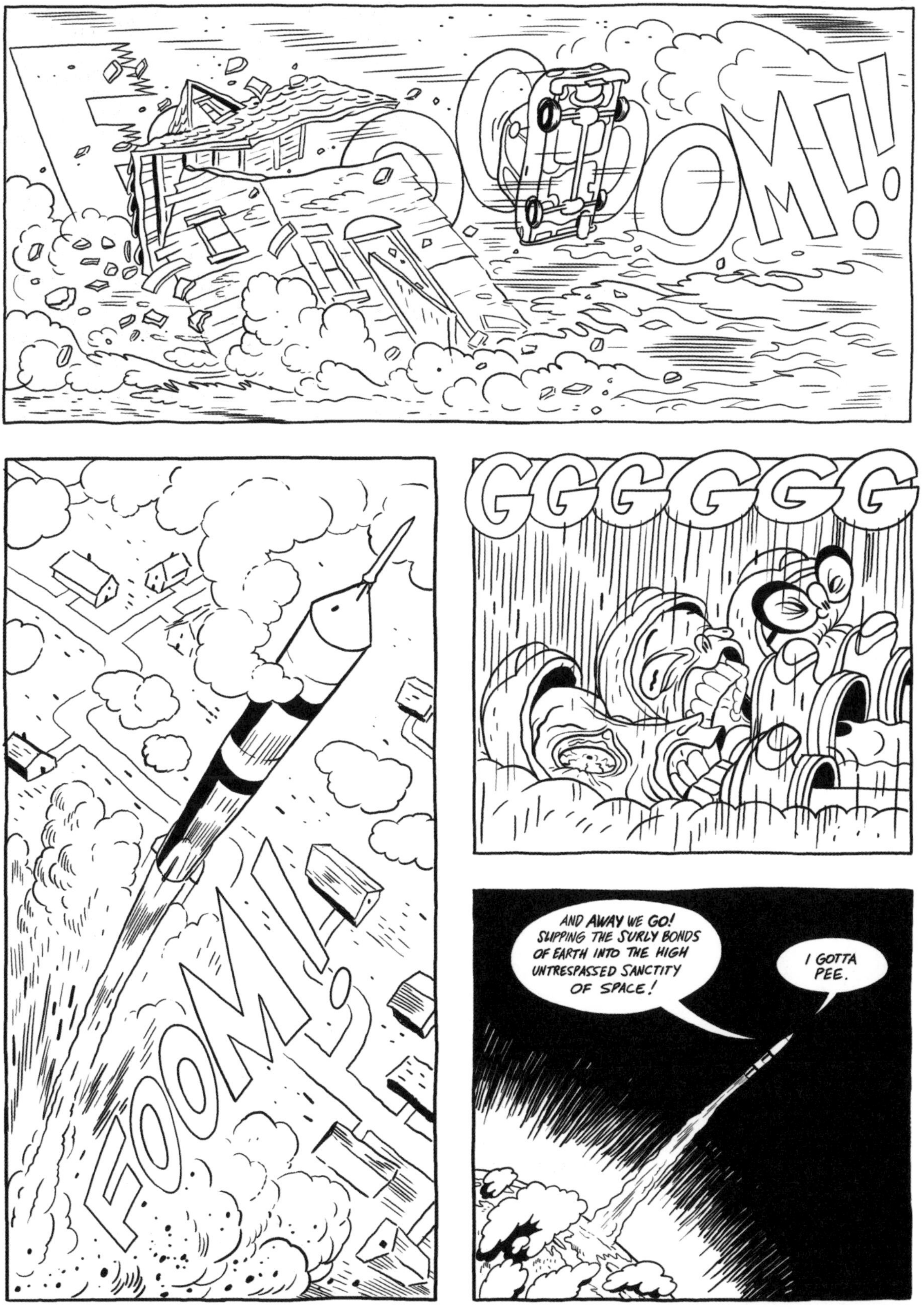
FOOOM!!
FOOM!!
GGGGGG
AND AWAY WE GO! SLIPPING THE SURLY BONDS OF EARTH INTO THE HIGH UNTRESPASSED SANCTITY OF SPACE!
I GOTTA PEE.

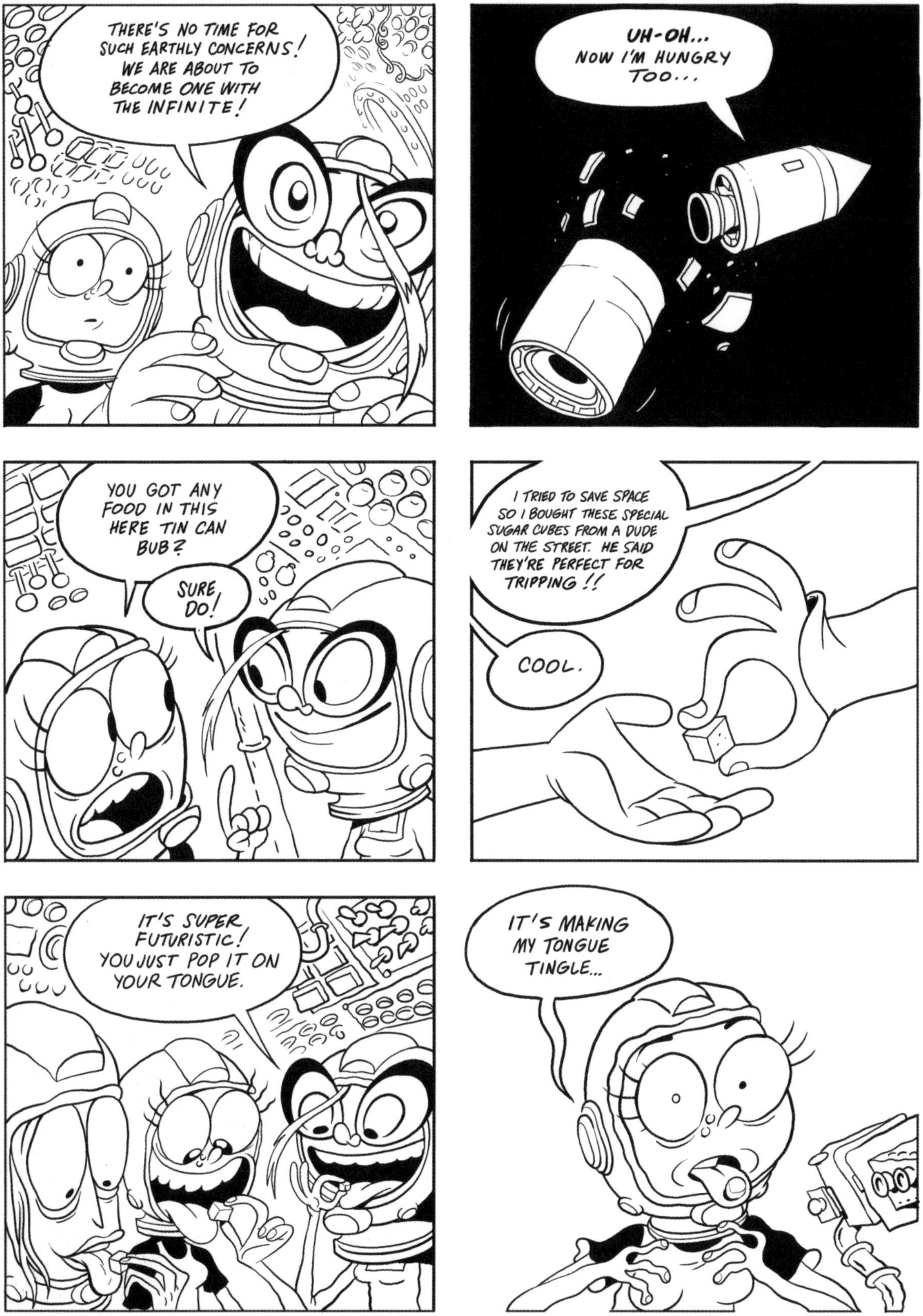
THERE'S NO TIME FOR SUCH EARTHLY CONCERNS! WE ARE ABOUT TO BECOME ONE WITH THE INFINITE!
UH-OH... NOW I'M HUNGRY TOO...
YOU GOT ANY FOOD IN THIS HERE TIN CAN BUB?
SURE DO!
I TRIED TO SAVE SPACE SO I BOUGHT THESE SPECIAL SUGAR CUBES FROM A DUDE ON THE STREET. HE SAID THEY'RE PERFECT FOR TRIPPING!!
COOL.
IT'S SUPER FUTURISTIC! YOU JUST POP IT ON YOUR TONGUE.
IT'S MAKING MY TONGUE TINGLE...

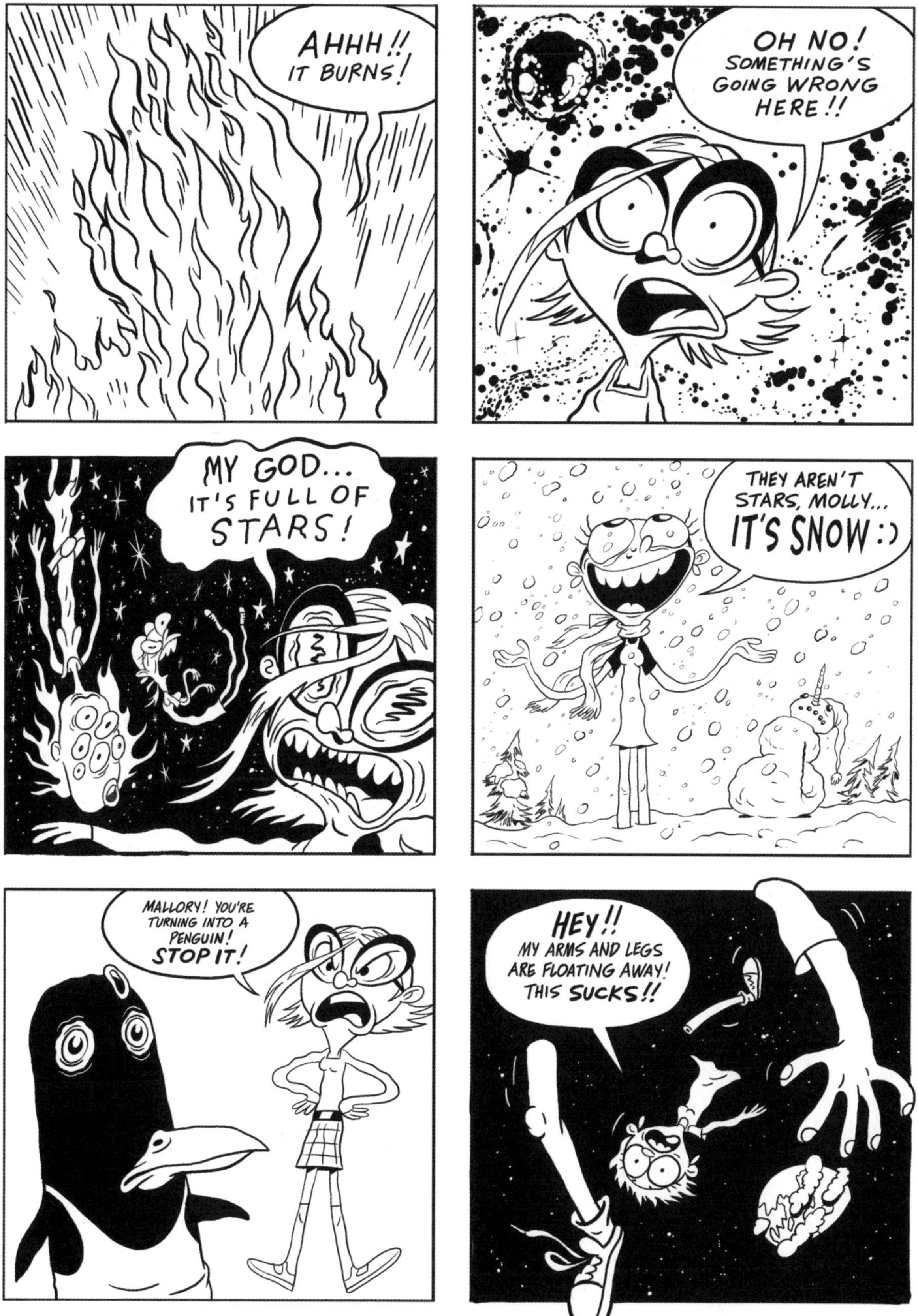
AHHH!! IT BURNS!
OH NO! SOMETHING'S GOING WRONG HERE!!
MY GOD... IT'S FULL OF STARS!
THEY AREN'T STARS, MOLLY... IT'S SNOW :)
MALLORY! YOU'RE TURNING INTO A PENGUIN! STOP IT!
HEY!! MY ARMS AND LEGS ARE FLOATING AWAY! THIS SUCKS!!

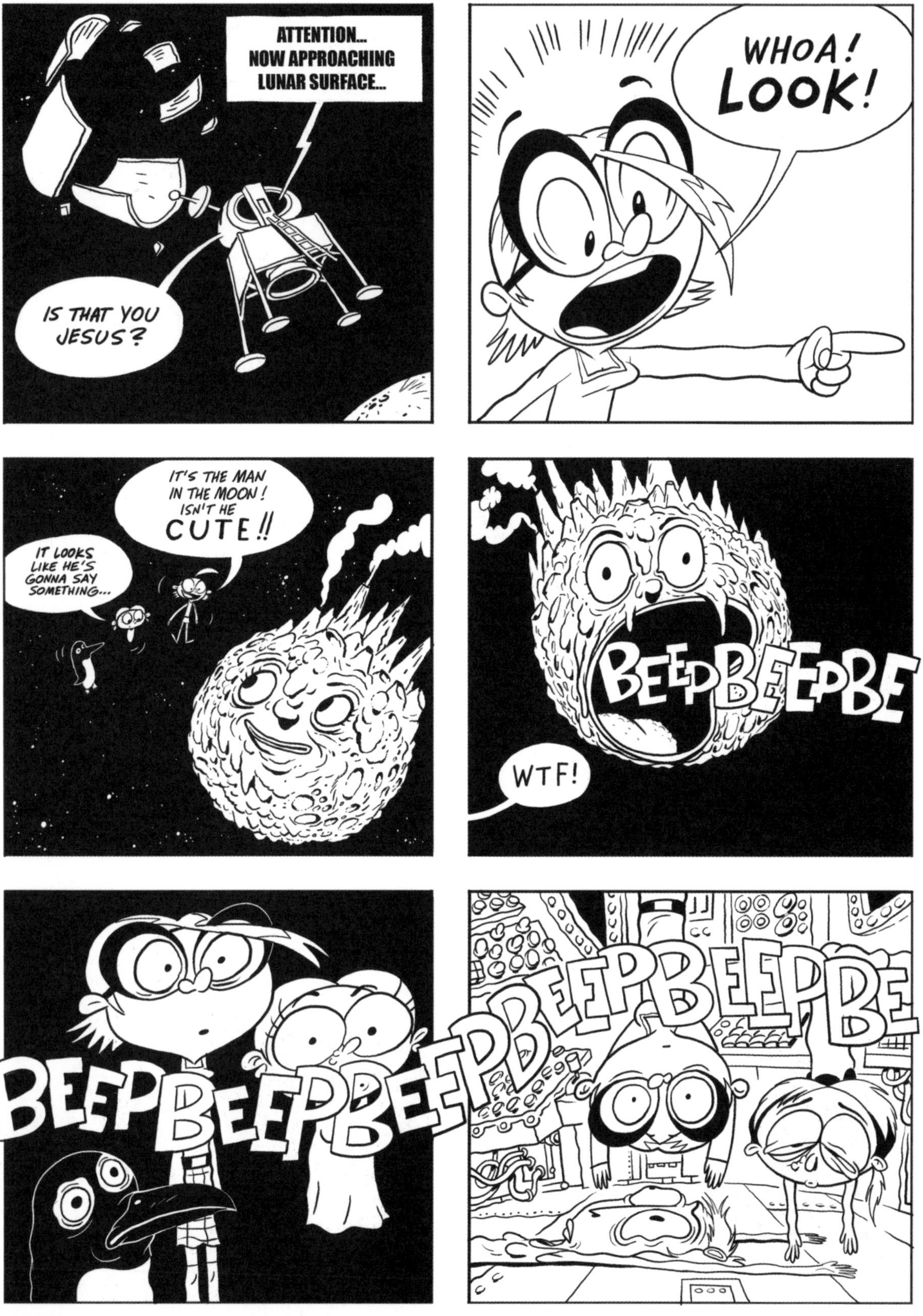
ATTENTION... NOW APPROACHING LUNAR SURFACE...
IS THAT YOU JESUS?
WHOA! LOOK!
IT LOOKS LIKE HE'S GONNA SAY SOMETHING...
IT'S THE MAN IN THE MOON! ISN'T HE CUTE!!
BEEPBEEPBE
WTF!
BEEPBEEPBEEPBEEPBEEPBE

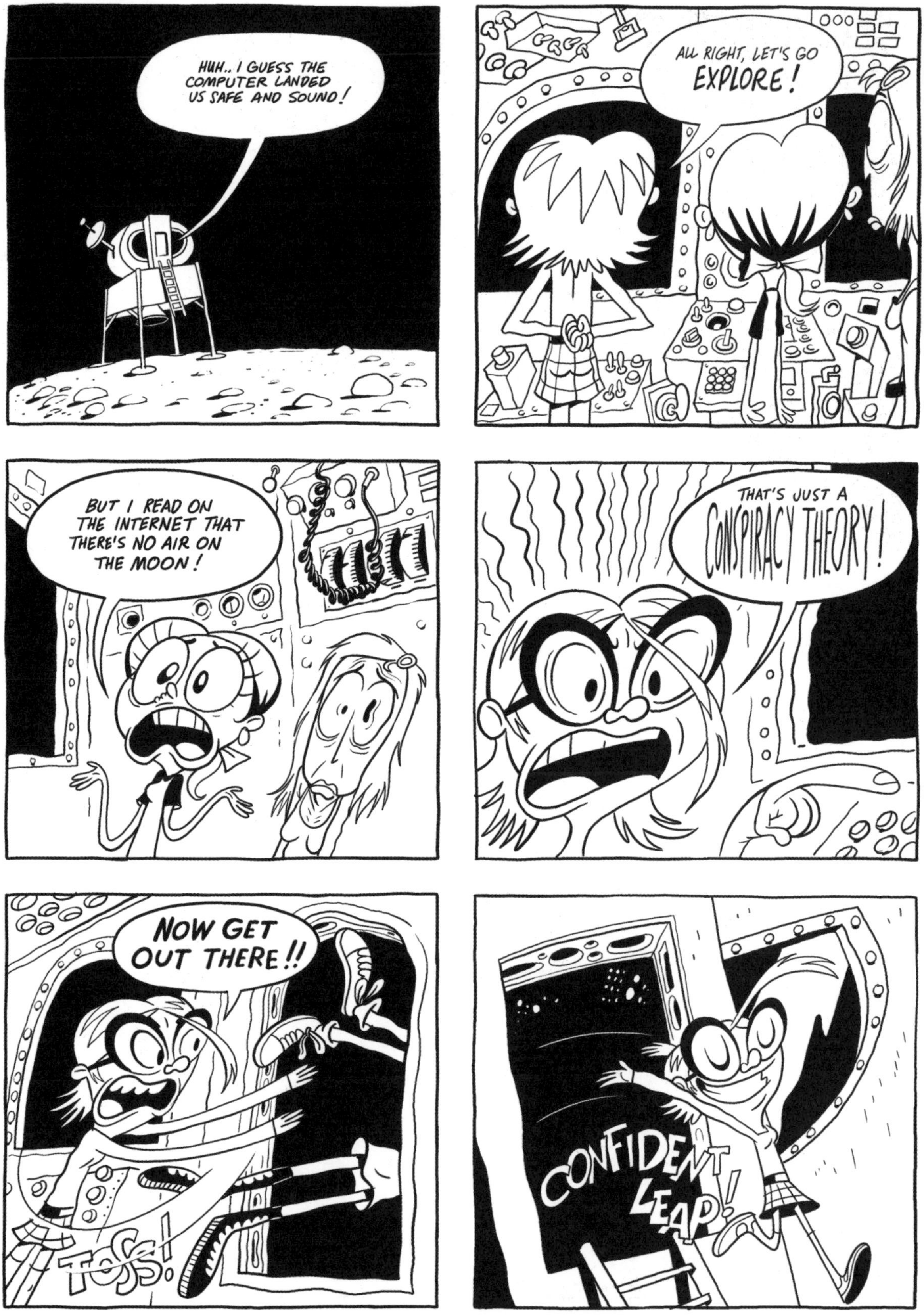
HUH.. I GUESS THE COMPUTER LANDED US SAFE AND SOUND!
ALL RIGHT, LET'S GO EXPLORE!
BUT I READ ON THE INTERNET THAT THERE'S NO AIR ON THE MOON!
THAT'S JUST A CONSPIRACY THEORY!
NOW GET OUT THERE!!
TOSS!
CONFIDENT LEAP!

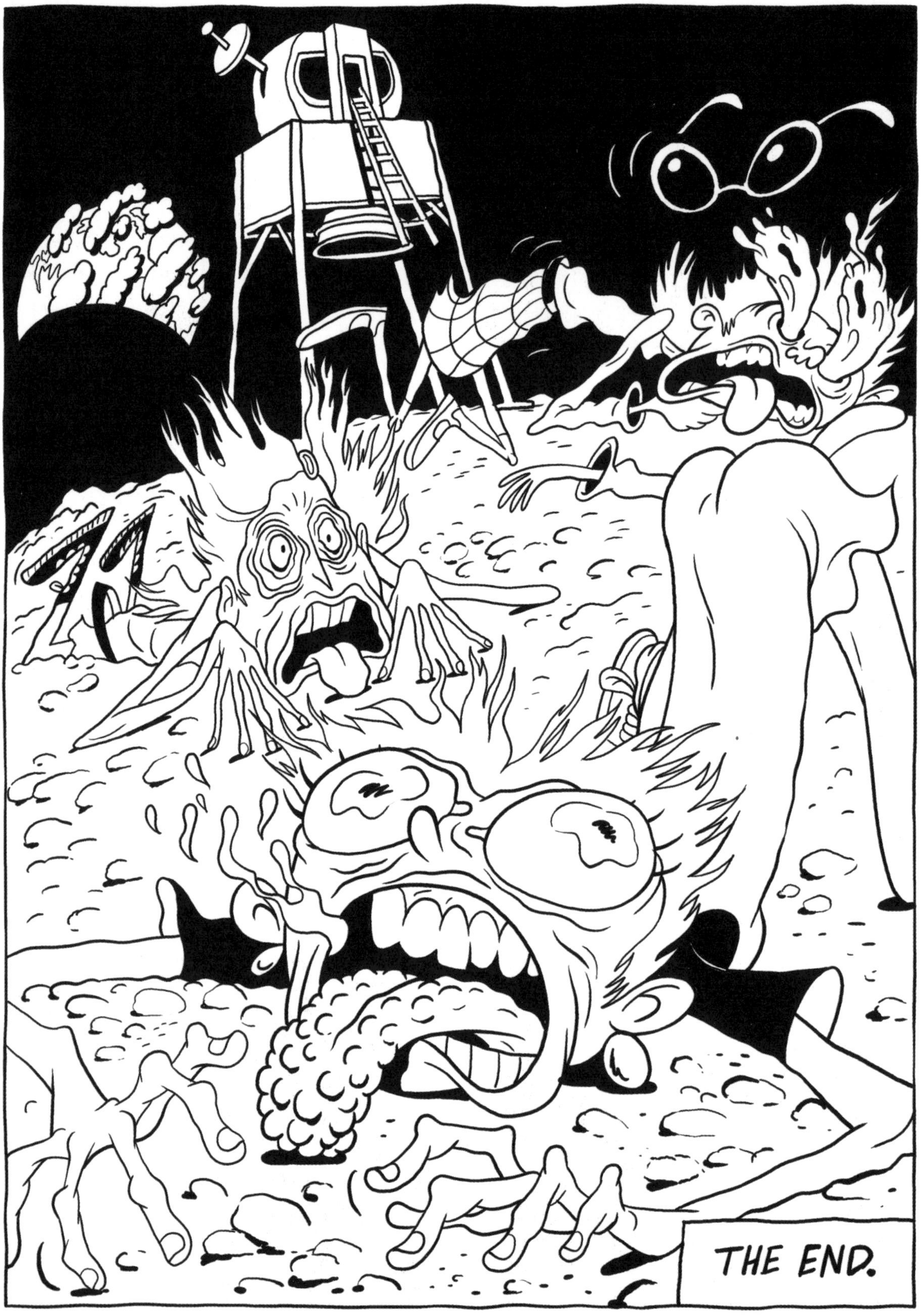
THE END.

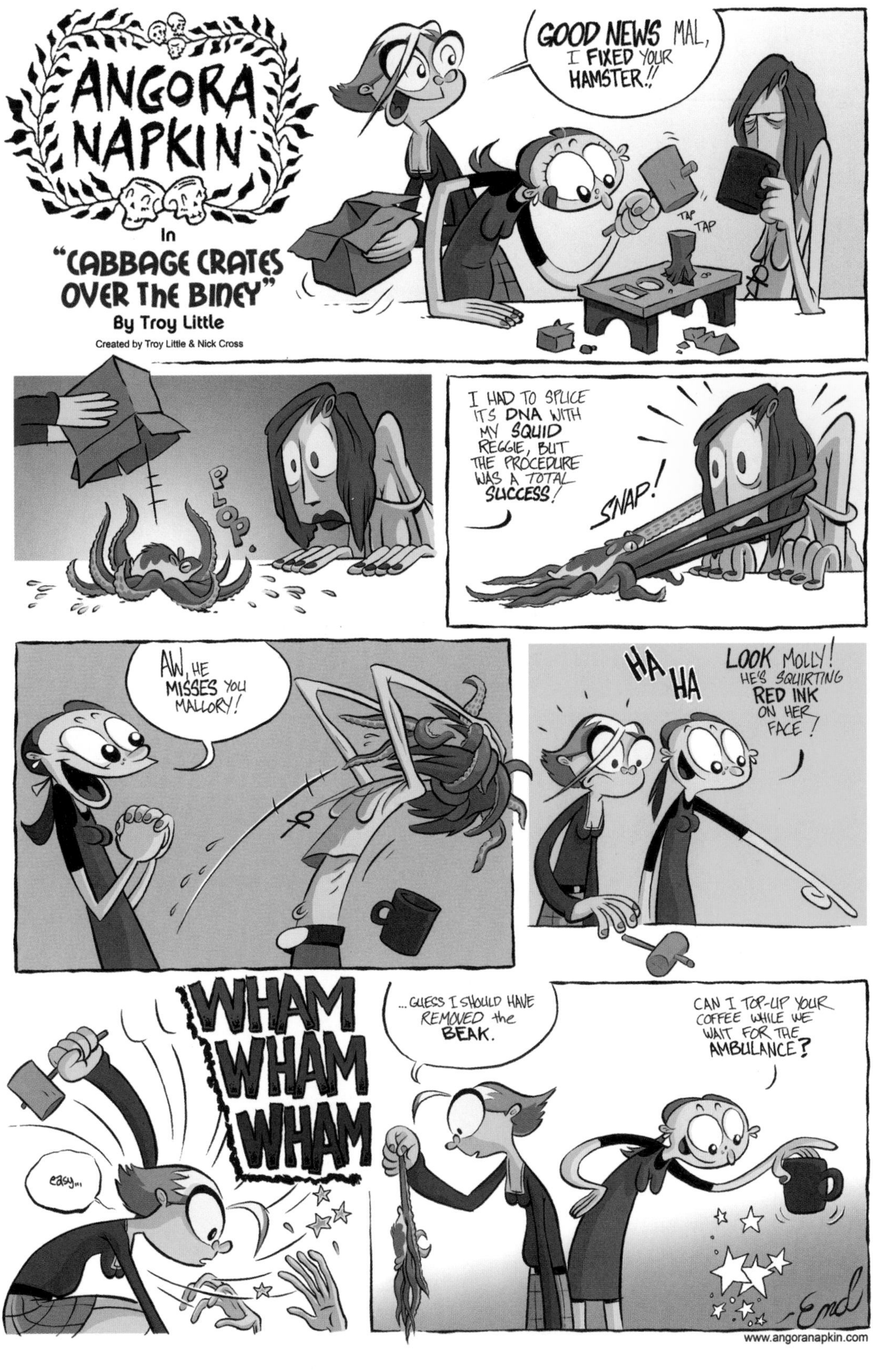

ANGORA NAPKIN
In
"CABBAGE CRATES OVER THE BINEY"
By Troy Little
Created by Troy Little & Nick Cross
GOOD NEWS MAL, I FIXED YOUR HAMSTER.!!
TAP TAP
PLOP.
I HAD TO SPLICE IT'S DNA WITH MY SQUID REGGIE, BUT THE PROCEDURE WAS A TOTAL SUCCESS!
SNAP!
AW, HE MISSES YOU MALLORY!
HA HA
LOOK MOLLY! HE'S SQUIRTING RED INK ON HER FACE!
WHAM WHAM WHAM
easy...
...GUESS I SHOULD HAVE REMOVED the BEAK.
CAN I TOP-UP YOUR COFFEE WHILE WE WAIT FOR THE AMBULANCE?
End
www.angoranapkin.com

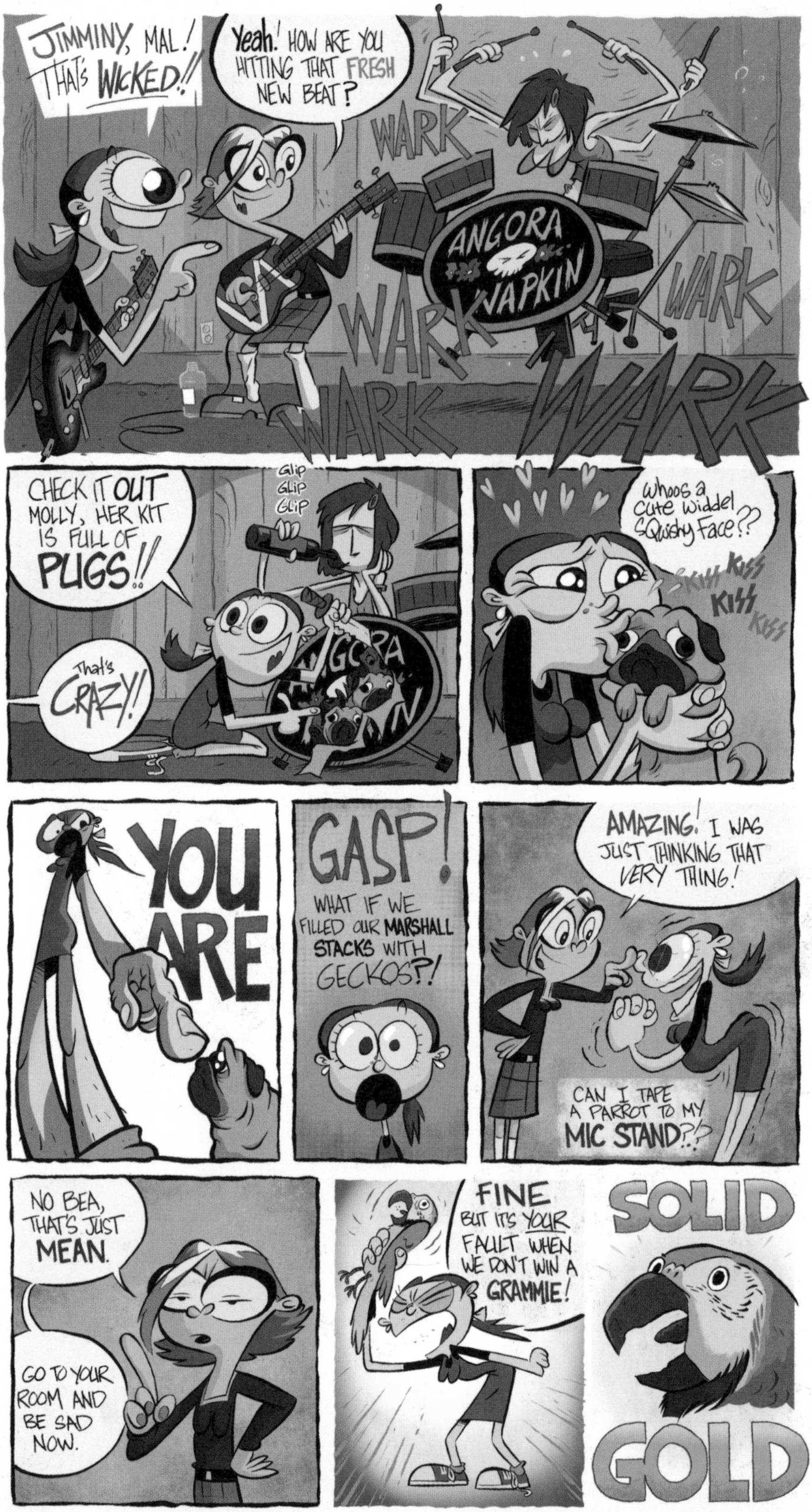

JIMMINY, MAL! THAT'S WICKED!!
Yeah! HOW ARE YOU HITTING THAT FRESH NEW BEAT?
WARK
ANGORA NAPKIN
WARK
WARK
WARK
WARK
CHECK IT OUT MOLLY, HER KIT IS FULL OF PUGS!!
Glip Glip Glip
That's CRAZY!!
Whoos a cute widdel SQuishy Face??
KISS KISS KISS KISS
YOU ARE
GASP!
WHAT IF WE FILLED OUR MARSHALL STACKS WITH GECKOS?!
AMAZING! I WAS JUST THINKING THAT VERY THING!
CAN I TAPE A PARROT TO MY MIC STAND?!?
NO BEA, THAT'S JUST MEAN.
GO TO YOUR ROOM AND BE SAD NOW.
FINE BUT IT'S YOUR FAULT WHEN WE DON'T WIN A GRAMMIE!
SOLID GOLD

PIN-UP ART

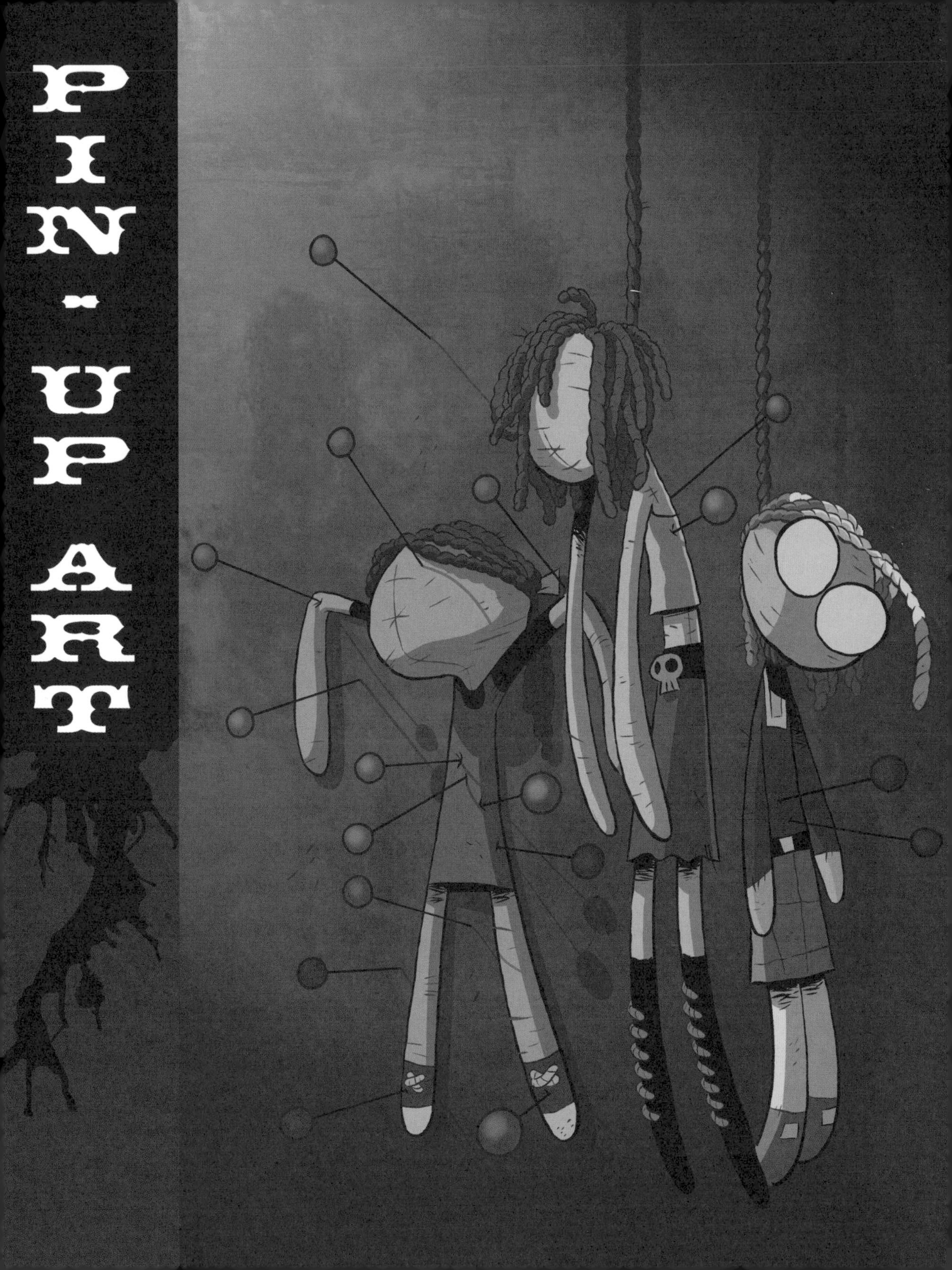

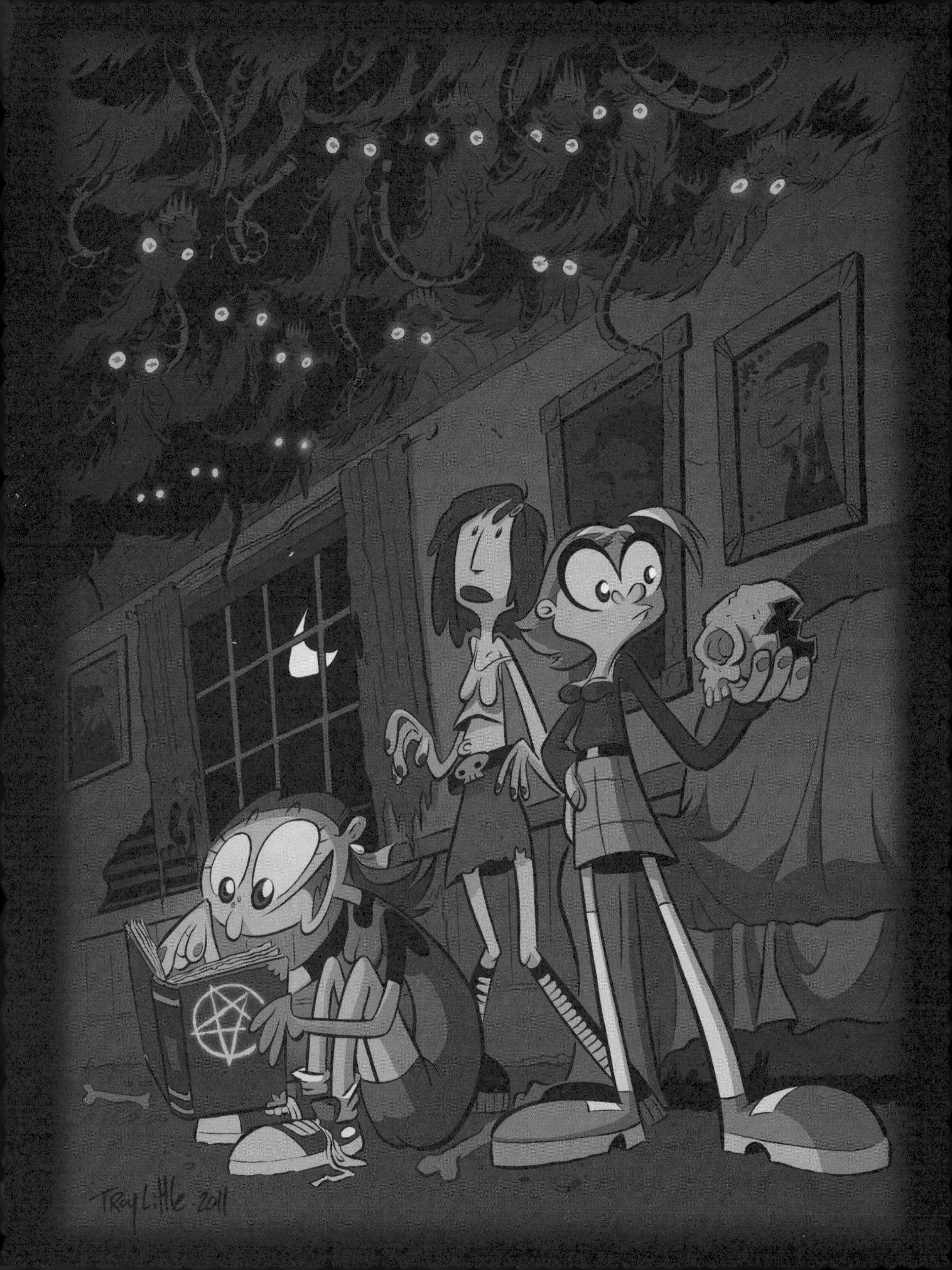
TROY LITTLE · 2011

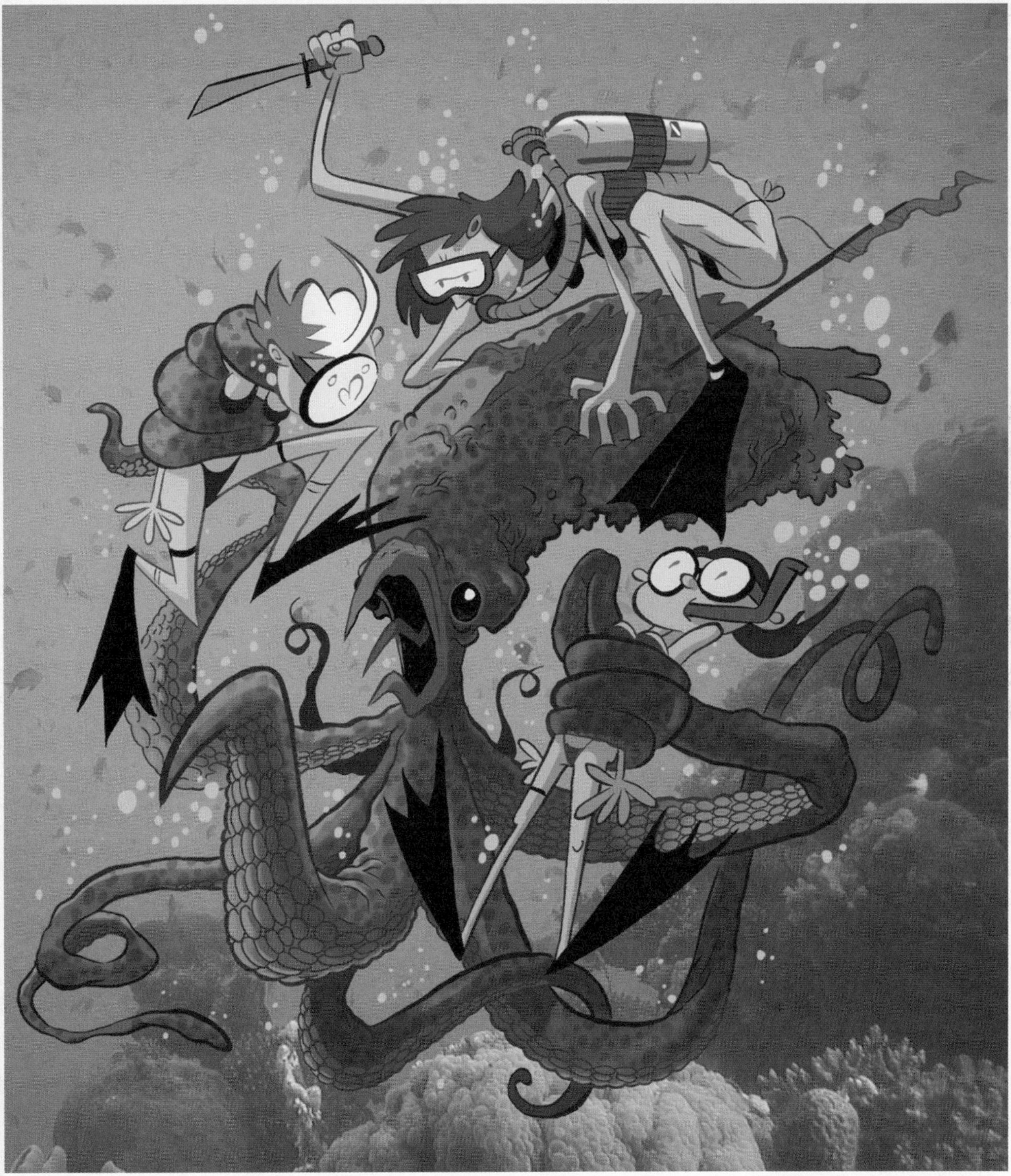

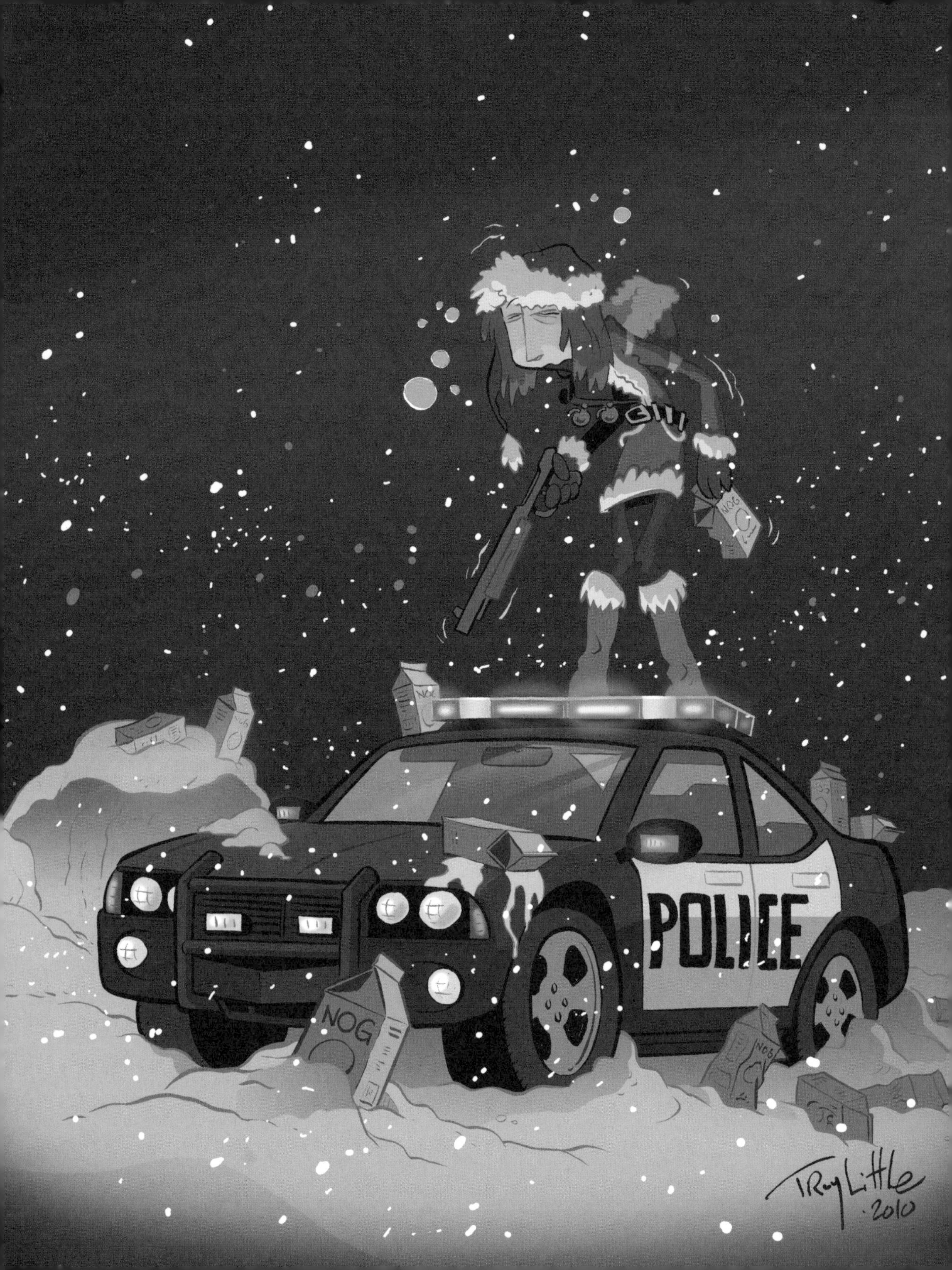
NOG
POLICE
NOG
Troy Little
2010

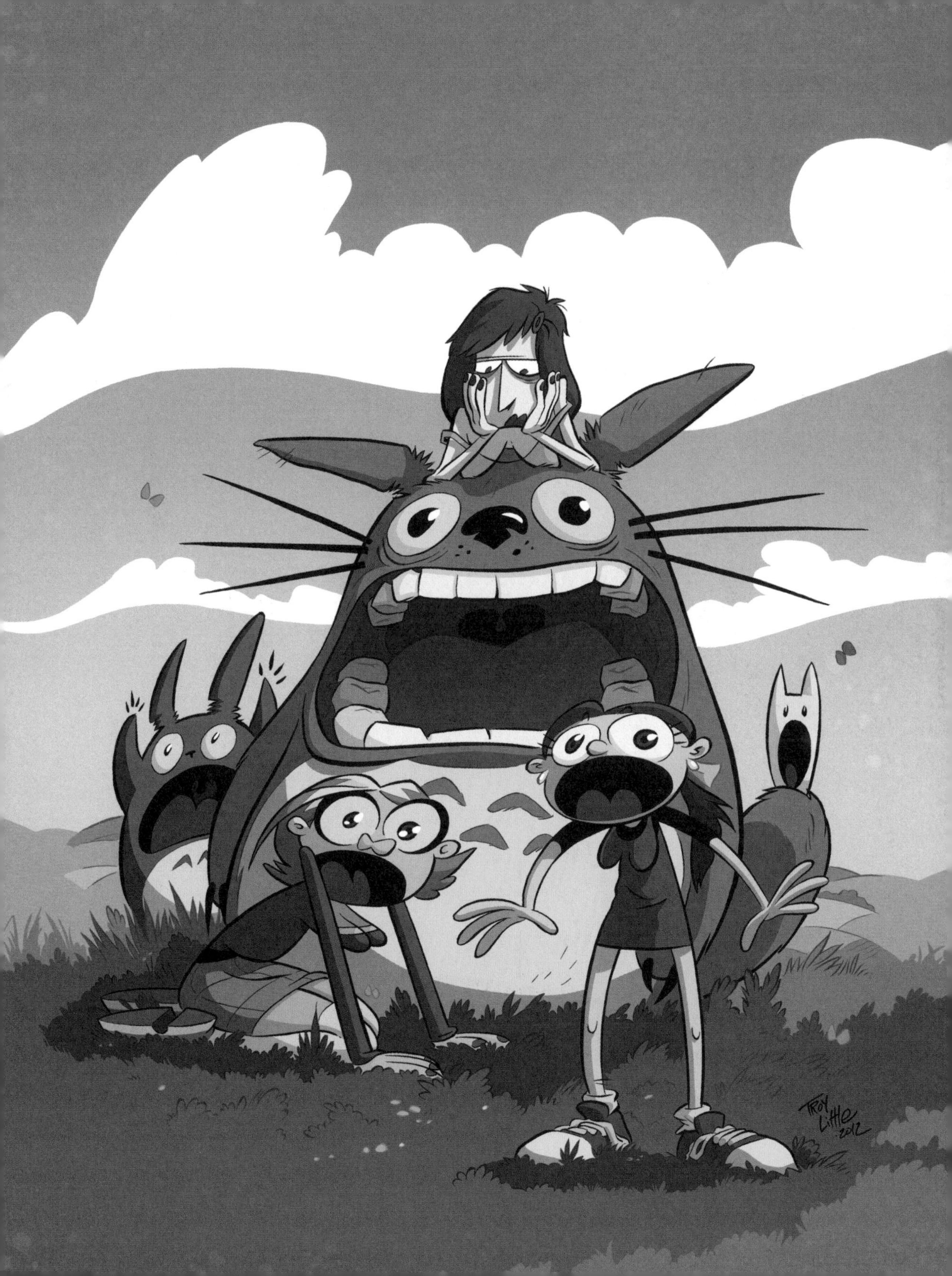
TROY LITTLE 2012

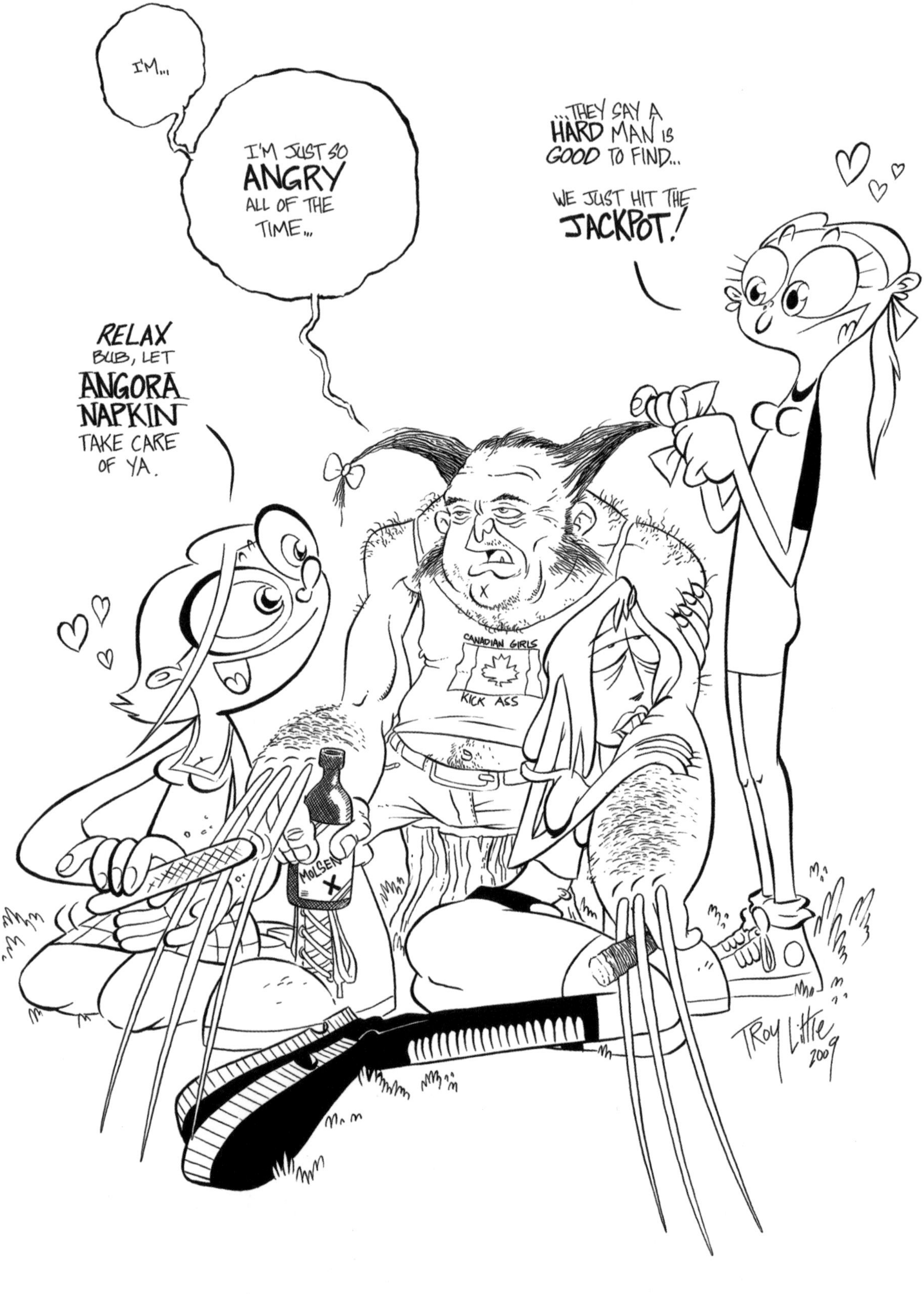
I'M...
I'M JUST SO ANGRY ALL OF THE TIME...
...THEY SAY A HARD MAN IS GOOD TO FIND...
WE JUST HIT THE JACKPOT!
RELAX BUB, LET ANGORA NAPKIN TAKE CARE OF YA.
CANADIAN GIRLS KICK ASS
MOLSEN
TROY LITTLE 2009

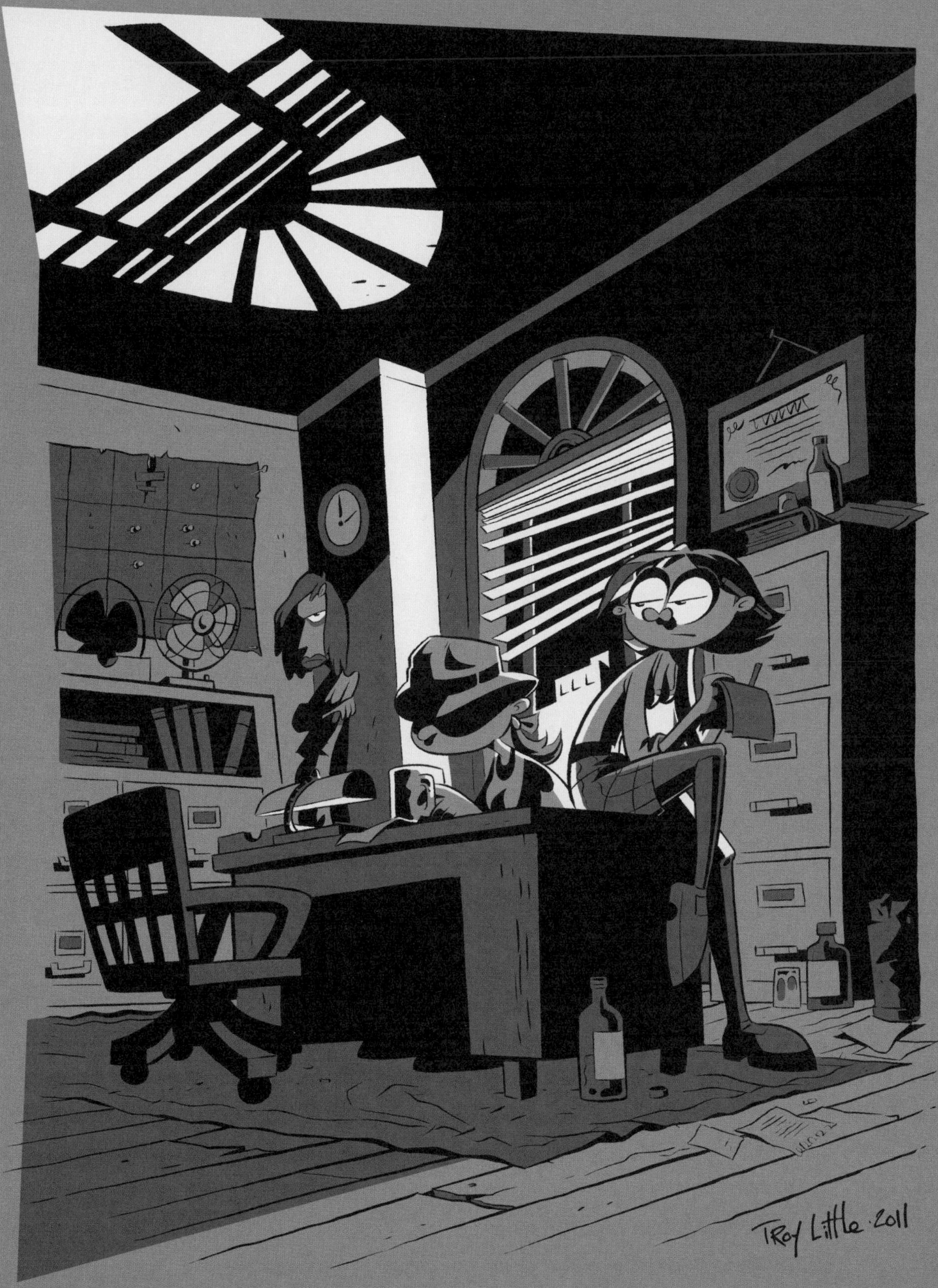
TROY LITTLE · 2011

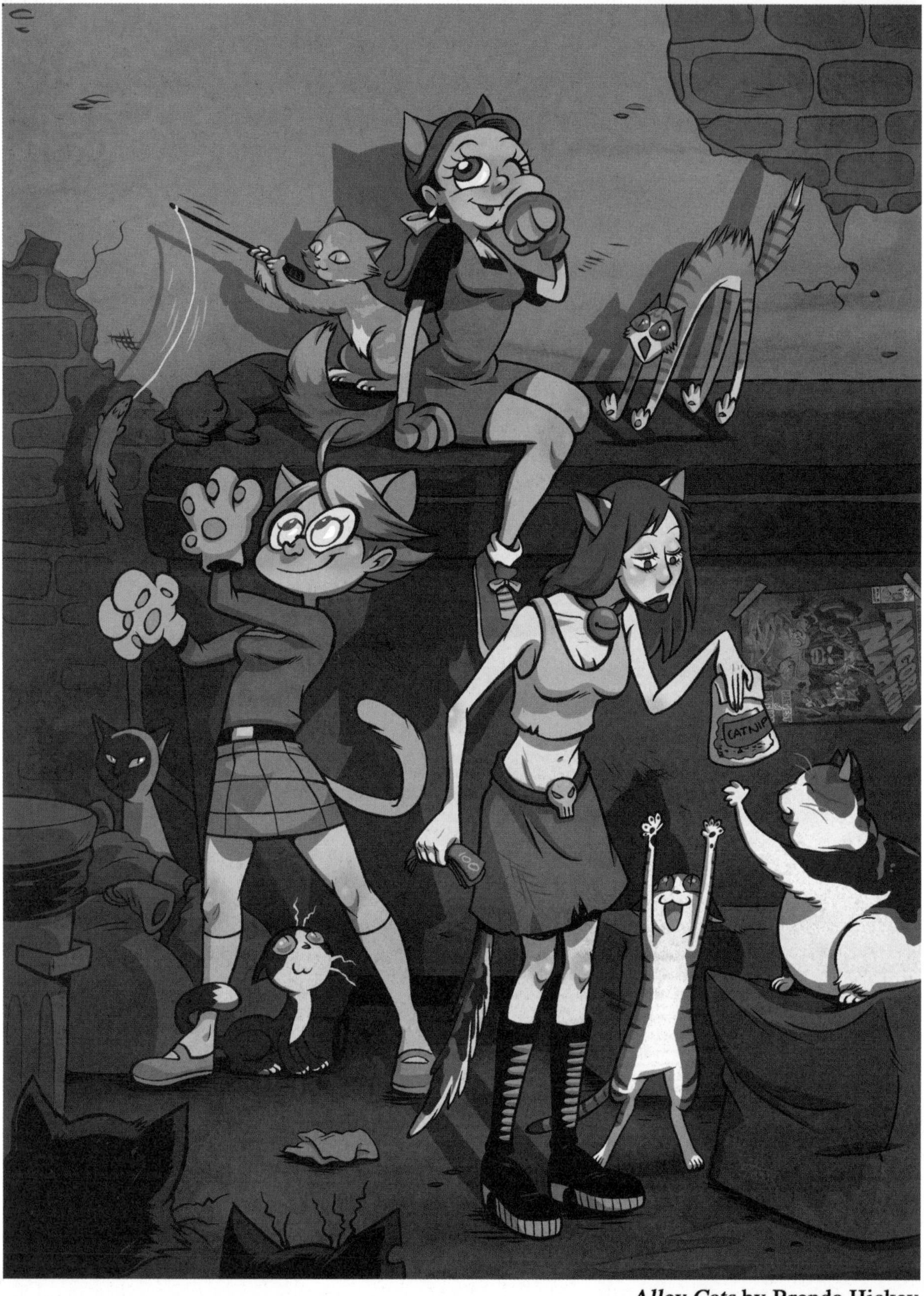
CATNIP

Alley Cats by Brenda Hickey

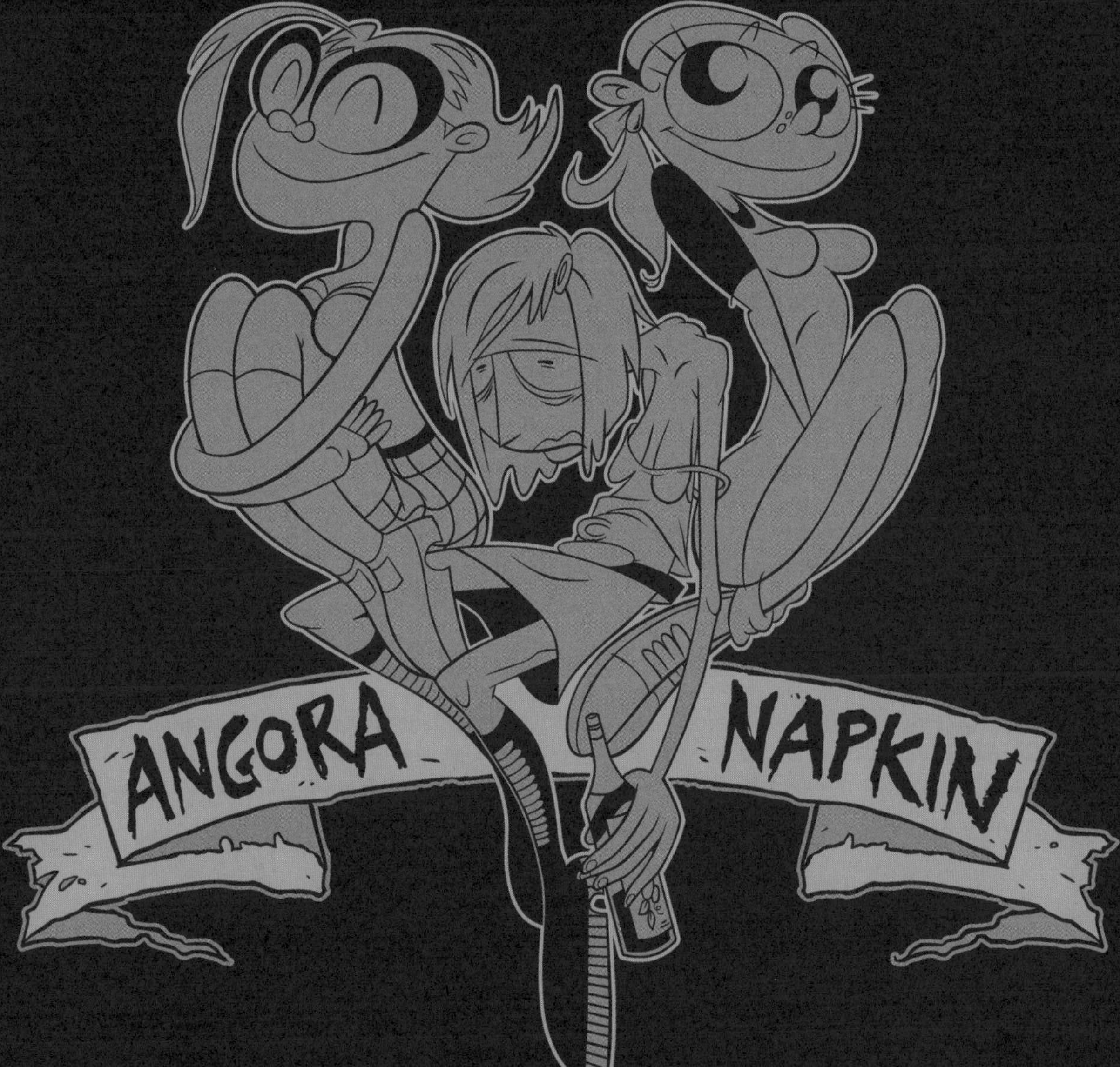
ANGORA
NAPKIN

ABOUT THE AUTHOR

Troy Little is a writer/artist/animator living in Prince Edward Island, Canada.
His past works include the Eisner-nominated *Angora Napkin* and *Chiaroscuro,* for which he was
awarded a Xeric and a PEICA Grant. He also co-directed the *Angora Napkin* animated pilot for Teletoon.

He's currently working on an *Angora Napkin* web serial and his next major graphic novel entitled
"The Allusion of Life."

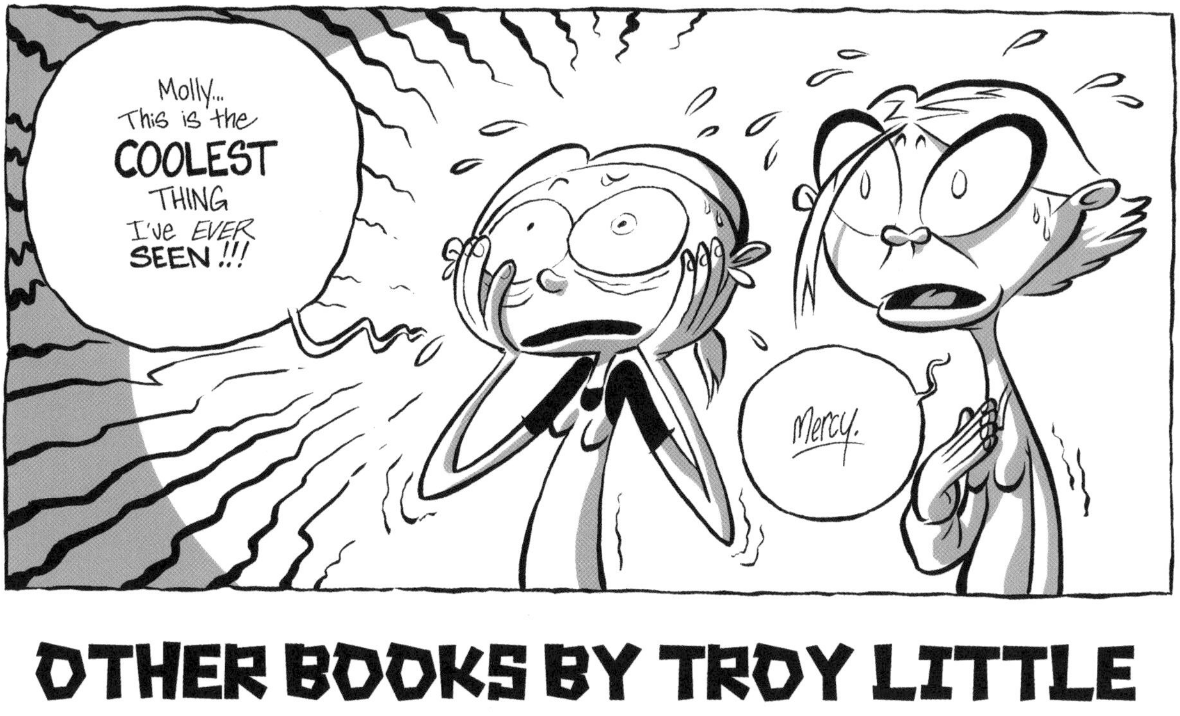
Molly... This is the COOLEST THING I've EVER SEEN!!!
Mercy.

OTHER BOOKS BY TROY LITTLE

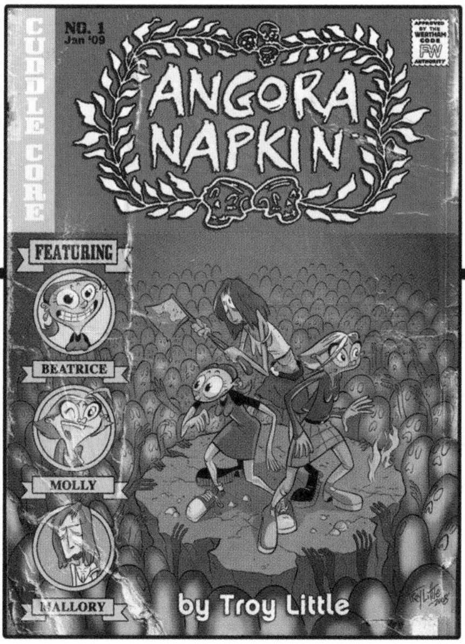
NO. 1
Jan '09
CUDDLE CORE
ANGORA NAPKIN
FEATURING
BEATRICE
MOLLY
MALLORY
by Troy Little

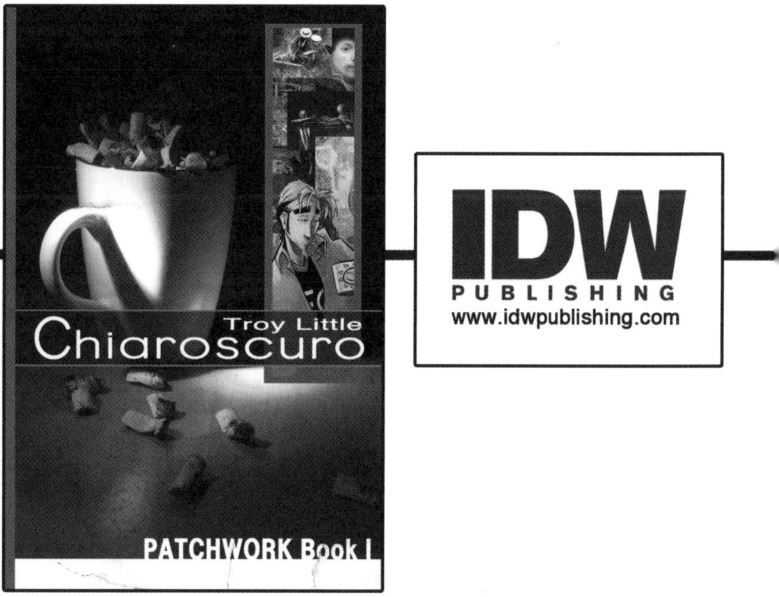
Troy Little
Chiaroscuro
PATCHWORK Book I

IDW
PUBLISHING
www.idwpublishing.com

ANGORA NAPKIN
By Troy Little
152 pages, Hardcover
$19.99 US
ISBN: 978-1600103391

CHIAROSCURO
By Troy Little
234 pages, Hardcover, TPB
$24.99 US, $19.99
(HC) ISBN: 978-1600101199
(TPB) ISBN: 978-1600102530